The Far Family

WILMA DYKEMAN

The Far Family

Holt, Rinehart and Winston · New York   Chicago   San Francisco

Library of Congress Catalog Card Number: 65-10131
ISBN: 0-9613859-4-4
New Edition: 1988

Grateful acknowledgment is made to the following Publishers and Agents for permission to quote from their publications:

Music Publishers Holding Corp., New York, N. Y. and Jerry Vogel Music Co., Inc., New York, N. Y., for lyrics from "Shine on Harvest Moon," copyright 1908 by Remick Music Corporation.

Shapiro, Bernstein & Co., Inc., New York, N. Y. and Jerry Vogel Music Co., Inc., New York, N. Y. for lyrics from "My Melancholy Baby," copyright 1911 by Ernest M. Burnett. Copyright 1912 and 1914 by Joe Morris Music Co. Copyright Renewed and assigned to Shapiro, Bernstein & Co., Inc. Copyright Renewed 1939 by Chas. E. Norton and Assigned to Jerry Vogel Music Co., Inc. All Rights Reserved.

A. P. Watt & Son, London, England for permission to quote briefly from "Gunga Din," by Rudyard Kipling.

Printed in the United States of America

"They're still my family, my folks,
no matter how far they've wandered."

—*Mountain saying*

The Far Family

CHAPTER 1
Today

A L W A Y S in autumn she thought of the farm. No, she did not think of it; she felt it again. The bitter smell of damp fallen leaves, the sight of purple farewell-summer blooming in a random field, the cry of a blue jay high in the noon sky—any of these or a dozen other sensations could bring the farm into the present; breathe the land to life again; dim the smell of gasoline, the sound of motors, the gleam of chrome and glass.

Even in Paris once, not long ago, walking along the Boulevard Hausmann, she had stirred a rustle of leaves under her feet and suddenly she heard Papa in the September corn rows of the Sandy Field: "You girls step lively now. Lay by all the fodder we can against a hard winter."

That same Paris afternoon there had been a letter from Kin (How the concierge, in her ageless, shapeless, faded sweater that was the color and texture of dried walnut hulls, had studied her countenance as she read! "Good news for Madame? Bad news, no?") which told her that Mama had broken a hip. She left Europe the next week, came home to look after Mama.

Now it was autumn again and this year the remembering and

the past lurked even closer to the surface than usual: Clay was home. Clay was home, displaced ("A machine, a lousy machine! That's what took my work, Ivy—took my place—mine!"), and divorced ("She wouldn't come back with me. Kathleen chose a clicking little typewriter and a cold pay check over me, Ivy! I hope to God she just tries to sleep with an adding machine once, or to say, 'I love you' in shorthand"). Clay, her brother, was home all right, full of bourbon whisky and homesickness for a time that never was.

She had never really left the farm, she supposed. Oh, in many ways she had gone farther from it than any of them—either Frone or Phoebe, Clay or Kin—but the feel of earth, of woods, of weather in the hills, was part of her and would always be part, as indivisibly as skin, as air she breathed. This morning, digging in her flower beds, she welcomed the raw smell of damp earth. She remembered that odor from the spring when Papa was clearing new ground for pasture and ripped open half the farm with dynamite. "We've got to look up, Martha," he had said to Mama, who stood by small and doubtful and troubled. "With these young ones coming on, there's nothing for us but to look up and get things done by main strength and awkwardness and be gaily when we can."

She smiled. Papa's optimism was contagious even across the years and after death. It gave her peculiar joy to work in the flowers this morning.

Joy is rare, she thought. This kind of joy to hold and taste like a ripe wild berry melting on the tongue.

Ivy Thurston Cortland rocked back on her heels beside the flower bed in the morning coolness and allowed herself this moment of total awareness. The dirt under her fingernails, the running of the creek in front of her house, the glow of early light drenched through copper-colored leaves, the fat white slug curled there in the moist darkness where her probing had just unearthed it—everything was part of her consciousness for the moment. Nothing large or small, lovely or repulsive, was alien to her. And she had special cause for joy this morning. On Saturday, three days from now, Phil would be coming home.

Crouched there in the patch of yard surrounded by wooded mountains, Ivy Cortland was a strong, simple and complex woman.

She was not pretty. Her eyes were wide and brown and shiny as new chestnuts; the auburn high lights of her crisp wavy hair were now grey; her figure was still slim and firm and agile. But growing up on the farm had not allowed for prettiness. Her face was lined with crow's-feet that came from looking into strong sunlight. The wrinkles around her mouth and eyes came from ready laughter and openness to weather. Her hands had enlarged and toughened with every chore she undertook. "Ivy's a master little worker," her father had said, beginning with the first cow she milked when she was seven.

Ivy Thurston's gift was more unique than prettiness. It was a capacity for joy. Where this came from—from Papa, Tom Thurston; or Mama, Martha McQueen; or stray gene or mischievous godmother—she could not have guessed. But after she became Ivy Cortland the capacity had matured, for "Cort," Henry Hudson Cortland, who came from another place and across a barrier of years, also possessed this rare gift of simple joy—delicate as cobwebs and tough as cowhide, healing as balm and searing as a white-hot coal on nakedness.

Now, however, she experienced her intensities alone, having discovered that the one gift many people cannot forgive in another person is this quality of surrender to life, this luminous *joie de vivre*. Had they, she wondered, she and Cort, handed this gift, this capacity, down to their child, to Phil?

The flower garden claimed her attention again. She bent over the bed of lily bulbs and carefully lifted them out of the ground. White tendrils of roots and new growth sprouted from each bulb. With gentle muscular hands she laid them in a basket to store for planting again next season. Beside the basket she caught sight of a thriving plantain weed. She grasped its leaves, but at the first tug they broke off, leaving the main stem tight in the ground. With her trowel she dug down into the tenacious roots and wrenched them from the ground. Thick, tough, far-reaching, they were prepared to feed that plant through drought or flood.

Roots: how strange and wonderful, Ivy thought, the means by which a placement was made permanent and nourishment was provided. Reaching down into darkness for strength to work up toward the light. Anchoring by a hundred filaments to thrust up into

rain and sun and storm. Underneath the ground all around her this
hidden web of woven tendrils and searching taproots—unseen,
silent, moving to hold, sustain, bring life and strength and growth.
During planting season on the farm Mama had always said, "Be
getting the seeds deep enough, children. Remember, it may come a
dry time before harvest."

Ivy pulled a stray morning-glory vine out of the bed and considered its shallow broken tentacles. How quickly indeed the sur-
face-rooted things died in a hard season. It seemed to Ivy that this
was a hard season everywhere for roots. The predatory jaws and
wheels of great iron cats and shovels and 'dozers wrenched, gouged,
removed, repacked the earth. Concrete laced and layered it with a
man-made crust. Less and less was there earthly room. Fewer and
fewer were the personal encounters with weather or that delicate
balance of all living things which was needed for a stoutness of roots.
And what plant or creature could survive the want of them? She
rubbed the back of her wrist across her forehead.

It was then, there, on a midmorning in October, as she worked in
her late flower bed and heard the creek splashing and blue jays calling and considered the need and strength of roots, that the telephone rang.

She heard its insistent tattoo through an open window in the
house at her back. She frowned, laid down the trowel and stood up.
The good moment was gone. She brushed off her flannel wrap-
around skirt. Sunlight fell full on her face and arms and legs, warm
as the summer past, with a foretaste of chill to come. She shivered at
its sudden touch, at its warmth and its chill. The bell summoned her
again. She hurried inside.

"Ivy?" The voice was weak, miserable, uncertain.

"Yes . . ."

"Ivy, is that you?" Clearer, more confident.

How many times before had she heard that familiar voice and
awaited the ashamed, the aggressive tone, not wanting to speak to
her at all, but forced to by need, warning her of sudden trouble.

"Yes, Clay, this is Ivy. What's wrong?"

In the pause, the moment's lapse for breath and courage before
he went on, Ivy had a strange fleeting vision of the morning-glory

vine she had pulled up and dangled in her hand only a few minutes earlier.

The impression lasted the length of a breath, then her brother's voice came again, loud and defiant in its uncertainty.

"Some fellows want to give me free lodging for the night. Oh, hell, Ivy, I'm down here at the courthouse. Can you come and keep me out of jail?"

"Jail? What happened? What have you done, Clay?"

"I'm—well, I'm not sure. Look, you can't let Mama know anything about this. Oh, it's a mess, one pure damned mess. Hawk Williams was killed last night."

Ivy felt the blood rush from her knees and head and churn in her stomach. Her legs trembled. She sat down. "What does that have to do with you?"

"They say I did it."

"Who? Who says so, Clay?"

"Some of the fellows on the hunt."

"*Did* you do it, Clay?"

There was another pause. She could hear his heavy breathing, almost smell the stale whisky breath, see the cloudy frightened glaze of his dark eyes.

"I don't know," he answered at last. "That's the hell of it, Ivy. I don't know whether I killed him or not."

"Did you have a gun with you, Clay?"

"Of course I had a gun. It was supposed to be a hunt——"

"I can guess how much hunting went on," Ivy said. There was a pause. Then she asked, "How could you possibly not know whether you killed a man——"

"Now hold on, sister of mine; just hold the line." Confidence was returning to his voice. She could imagine his stance changing there before the phone in the dingy courthouse, now that he had unburdened his bad news, that he no longer bore it alone, that there would be someone to help him. From defeat and chagrin he would be shifting to the cover-up of overconfidence, combativeness. She had known him such a long time now. "Dear sister, there are those who would argue with you about that—whether or not shooting Hawk Williams was shooting a man——"

"Clay!" Her voice was sharp. "Stop that kind of talk right now. This is no time to be cute. Do you understand, Clay?"

She could feel him wilt. "Oh, Lord! Yes, Ivy. I understand. Can you come right on down and get me out of here?"

"All right, Clay."

"I tried to call Hugh Moore, but the secretary said he hadn't come in the office yet. Please, Ivy——"

"I don't know whether Hugh's the best lawyer for you or not. If Hawk weren't—well, you know it, Clay, as well as I do—his being Negro might make a difference."

"If you're trying to say he got killed because he was Negro, you're way off beam, Ivy. Whether I did it or not, Hawk's dead because he was an s.o.b."

"Hush, Clay. Don't say another word or do a thing till I can get there." Ivy sighed and tried to make her voice firm. "I'll be right down." She was ready to hang up when she heard him say, "Ivy—thanks."

She sat at her desk and looked at the silent phone. Black, inanimate instrument. Absently she ran her finger along one edge and wiped off a skim of dust. How undemanding it would be to be an instrument. Carrying messages but free of their grief; conveying news and aloof from its impact. The only penalty would be, of course, the forfeit of life.

Her hand shook slightly. What should she do first? Kin wouldn't be at home this time of day. He'd already be at his cabin up in the woods or at work on some garden. She would have liked to have Kin go with her to rescue their brother. Clay simply could not go to jail. She wondered if this trouble could affect Phil's career. Everything that happened now between a white person and a black person became more than an encounter of individuals—it became a confrontation of groups, of two races, two histories. It received attention, especially political attention. And Phil was a senator of the United States. He might even be an able senator. But he was certainly vulnerable.

Her hand rested on the telephone. Eventually she would call Frone up in Connecticut and Phoebe down in South Carolina. She would see what a lawyer said and if this were bad enough, her sisters would have to come and help see them through. It was time they came to see Mama anyway. But first she would have to keep Clay out of jail. The sound of the words in her mind was sickening. Jail. Hawk Williams. How could Clay have been mixed up with such ugliness? This would have killed Papa, she thought. I'm glad he's not here to know about it. How, how could Clay have wasted it all?

All at once she could see Clay as a boy when they lived on Thickety Creek: brown-skinned in summer, barefooted, not large but tough as saw briers, and always eager to try anything once; his hair thick and curly even then, his eyes bright and quick as minnows, flashing with the light of instant anger or love or a burst of humor, each distinctly his own and he fully committed to it until he moved on to something else. He had brought wit and flavor and upheaval to their days even when he was a child. She remembered one night in particular.

They all sat out on the porch under the stars. It was deep summer and fireflies dotted the lawn with light. Mama sat on the long porch in a rocker, humming "Rock of Ages" in time to the gentle motion of the chair, with the light from the lamps in the house pouring through the windows behind her. Papa lounged with the hired hands out under the trees where they took the cool air after a long burning day of sweat and grime. And the children—Frone, Ivy, Phoebe, Clay, and Kin only a toddler—sat on the wide steps between porch and lawn and told tales, made wishes on the stars. As they sat there, Clay began to toss his silver dollar in the air, the silver dollar Uncle Burn had brought each of them last year from the West. Clay tossed and caught the big round coin in a sort of rhythm and the other children watched his deceptive carelessness with a sleepy fascination.

The silver dollars were their most valuable possessions. Frone's and Phoebe's and Ivy's lay tucked in corners of their trunks in the upstairs bedroom. But Clay had insisted on carrying his with him, enjoying the feel of its heaviness in his pocket.

"What are you doing, Clay?" Mama asked, rocking gently on the porch.

"Catching my old dollar," Clay answered gaily, spinning it up again and watching it plummet like a dead bird into his out-stretched palm.

"I wouldn't be throwing Uncle Burn's present around like that," Mama said. "You might lose it. Be careful."

And Ivy was incredulous at the thought of such treasure being lost, at even the possibility Clay was flirting with now.

"Put it up, Clay," Frone said impatiently, with older-sister authority, authority born of her favoritism toward him. "Stop showing off."

"I won't lose it! Why, I could find this old silver dollar anywhere."

Then suddenly, without an instant's thought or warning, he tossed it, with a twist of his wrist, a quick flick of his fingers. Ivy could see the gesture now, as clearly as the October sun streaming through her windows. The coin arced out beyond the men, far beyond the circle of light from the windows on the porch, out into the edge of the yard where snowball bushes and red rambler roses grew, out into the darkness.

They were all silent a moment, then Phoebe piped up, "Where did it go, Clay?"

"I'll find it," Clay said casually to all of them. He sauntered to the edge of the darkness and began to look down at the grass there.

"I told you to be careful," Mama called from the porch.

Frone went to help Clay find the dollar-piece.

"Where did you put yours, Kin?" Ivy asked.

Kin, sitting on the bottom step, still so little he looked like a curly-haired cherub in some church painting, but always his own master. "I buried it," he answered gravely.

"Buried it? Where?" she asked.

"In the ground. Out at the orchard. I figure things in the ground are safe. I know where it is. It's not lost."

Phoebe and Ivy laughed.

Their father called to Clay, "Did you lose something, son?"

"His silver dollar," Frone answered from the edge of the yard.

Papa whistled. One of the hired men, old man Gunter, went to join Clay's search for the coin. Ivy and Phoebe and Kin ran to help, too.

Clay had lost his swagger now. Down on his knees he clawed at the grass, thrust his hands in the dark places under the rosebushes. A thorn brought blood to his finger. His little brown eyes were wide with alarm.

"I was afraid he'd lose it," Mama called to Papa. Papa shook his head soberly.

They didn't find Clay's dollar that night. After a while they all went to bed. Clay was up at first daylight the next morning, looking. He didn't find what he was seeking that day either, or the next, or ever. It was as if that silver coin had been tossed into nothingness. How could he have just sat there and thrown it away? After that, Ivy often wondered at the differences between brothers and sisters, made of the same flesh and blood, yet as unlike as oil and water.

And now, after she had gone down to the courthouse and upstairs to the jail where she had never been before, after Clay was free on bond, after he had come home, what then? What rowdiness, what stirring of troubled waters, had led to Hawk Williams' death?

She tried to look at Clay's predicament coolly, tried to understand what might have happened, but she simply could not believe that Clay had killed anyone, not even Hawk of the mean yellow eyes and the brutal fists. Hawk with his locust walking stick that could draw quick blood from any helpless beast at the stockyards where he worked; from a man, too, for that matter, she had heard. Clay had raged at the Hawks of the world since he was a child—once throwing Thickety school into an uproar (in the midst of Uncle Fayte's class in the third-year speller) because a boy in the back of the room was slowly cutting a live tortoise out of its shell and Clay took a flying leap from the top of his desk like a boomer squirrel out of a poplar tree, knocking boy, tortoise, knife, desk, slate against the wall. Maybe over the years the rage had grown too large. And if it had, what nightmare lay in store for Clay? What of the scalding humiliation for her own Phil, for Frone and Phoebe? And here she was at the end before there had been a beginning, but who was she to make up endings? Endings made themselves; they took shaping, but their final form no one could foresee. She looked at the dirt still clinging to her fingers. Her hands no longer shook. She stood up.

Thus the family drew together again—out of trouble, need, a crisis of survival.

Frone, tall and spare, alternated from fury to pity and exaggerated each. "I wish to God we could get Clay straightened out." She spoke on the line from Connecticut, but she might have been in the next room, her voice was so clear. (Ivy could see the shining brass knocker on her front door, the precise manicured lawn behind a white picket fence, matching all the other lawns fronting on the village green.) "He's an albatross around our necks and I for one am getting tired of the load. I'm too old to put up with this the rest of my life." Ivy knew Frone was only saying words, and she did not bother to answer them. But then her older sister's tone altered subtly. "How does he seem, Ivy? How was he when you brought him home? Oh, I know before you say it: like a whipped pup. That grin on his face as if he didn't know whether to laugh or cry. Yes, I'll come, Ivy—the first bus I can get. Poor Clay."

She came on Friday—tall, blue-eyed, angry and affectionate, speaking with the abruptness of her husband Jud's Connecticut accent and some of the leftover drawl of her own Southern mountains.

When Ivy told Kin, he was puzzled and disturbed. "Hawk Williams—and Clay? Why, good gracious, it's like a bad dream. I'd have helped you out, Ivy, gone with you to the jail, if I'd known——"

"I know you would, Kin. Clay didn't call until after you'd gone to work. I didn't know where to reach you."

"I've been searching out wild flowers for the Austin's garden," Kin said. He leaned forward in his chair, holding his old hat between his knees, looking at her appealingly. "Last week I went way up to the head of Thickety Creek, Ivy, and under the Devil's Brow there I found . . ."

She didn't really want to hear about his projects now. Being alone, no wife, no children, made him always eager to talk to her, especially about his plants. He and Clay might have been born on different planets, so widely were they separated.

Phoebe, on the phone from South Carolina, was shocked. "Oh, Ivy, a colored fracas! I wouldn't have Rutledge and his family know about this for anything. You don't think it'll be serious, do you, Ivy?"

"It's already serious, Phoebe."

"Yes, yes, of course it is. What ails Clay anyway? He always would run around with riffraff. Is Mama all right? I'll fly up Saturday afternoon. You can count on me, Ivy, Saturday afternoon."

And on Saturday morning Ivy went to the airport to meet Phil. She had looked forward to this home-coming with such pride after the mission that had taken him halfway around the world, and now she knew that the news she had to tell him might sink her son's whole career in treacherous quicksand. She had tried to reach him by wire, warning only of some difficulty, delaying the details till he was home.

Ivy drove out to the airport slowly. Since Frone was there to stay with Mama, she had left the house early. The mountains stood out sharply against the autumn sky, rich with color. In the distance to her left were the Great Smokies, but even they were bold and distinct this morning, free of their characteristic haze. As her own inner mind and feeling was thrown into turmoil, the physical world around her seemed to become clearer, more well-defined. Yes, the world would spin on. The dust flies, but the earth remains, someone had written, forgetting to add that the dust in its brief human flurry could suffer keenly.

Clay had suffered as she arranged the bond for his release. "He's a good feller," the sheriff had said to Ivy as they left. "I'm sorry he's mixed up in something like this, Mrs. Cortland." With stubbled beard, bloodshot sleepless eyes, bedraggled hunting clothes, Clay had left the courthouse as if he were taking leave of a resort hotel, calling good-by to the drunks behind bars, snapping a mock salute to the deputies until they grinned. It was they who seemed chagrined by the situation, not Clay. Yet Ivy glimpsed the wound behind the bravado of his countenance. When they were in the car, he said to her, "I wish Kathleen were here."

"The divorce was final three months ago, Clay," Ivy said.

He nodded slowly. "You can't warm over cold potatoes."

In Hugh Moore's office, a little later, Clay had been so quiet, so conciliatory that Ivy felt pity wash over her like a sharp briny wave. And how pompous, how dissipated and smug Hugh Moore, their second cousin and their lawyer, had seemed as he gathered "the facts" from Clay.

"You say Hawk was standing near the campfire, broiling the steaks, when you heard a shot?"

Clay nodded. "He slumped down like a rag doll with all the stuffing emptied out."

"And you had that twenty-two in your hands at the time?" Hugh Moore's beady eyes gleamed in his smooth fat face, permanently pink from years of hot towel packs.

Clay shook his head. "I couldn't say for sure. I'd had it, shooting at a little old target we put up . . ." He pounded his right fist into the palm of his left hand. "I was drunk. But surely I couldn't a-killed Hawk. Especially without taking some kind of aim."

"Take it easy, fellow," Moore said smoothly. "We'll get this all fixed up. Nothing for us to fret about."

"Nothing to . . ." Clay looked at him incredulously. "The hell you say. Maybe nothing for 'us' to fret about, but a God's plenty for me."

"Take him on home, Ivy," Hugh Moore said. "Get some breakfast into him. Put him into some fresh clothes. If he had just come to see me before going to Sheriff Doggett, we wouldn't have had anything a-tall to worry about."

Clay had flushed at mention of his appearance. He ran his hand over his prickly chin. "But I thought——"

"Something like this, you'd better let a lawyer do your thinking." Moore stood up. "Well, we'll do what we can now. Don't worry, Ivy. We're lucky it was Hawk Williams."

Clay had started to speak, then, confused and cowed and with a throbbing head, he plunged out of the office and downstairs to the sidewalk.

Yes, she thought as she drove along, they were all suffering in this flurry of dust.

There was plenty of parking space at the new airport. When the modernistic building had been dedicated last spring, Governor

Wentworth had commended leaders of the mountain region for "building for the future." Unfortunately, the flood of new industry they had counted on to bring the cement and bricks and payrolls for that building boom had been only a trickle. And the exodus of mountain people looking for better jobs, a brighter chance in life than cultivating rocky acres on a tilted hill farm, crowded the bus stations, not the airport.

"In this region we have to run just to stand still," Phil had said at that same dedication ceremony.

Ivy thought of the mission from which Phil was just returning. Her pride in him was the central fact of her life. She had anticipated this moment of meeting him—and now it had become an ordeal. She switched off the engine of the car and dropped the keys into her purse. Strange, she thought, how pride and shame interlocked in one family. There were those who gave—satisfaction and honor; there were those who took—patience and tolerance and more understanding than you could muster sometimes.

Inside the terminal Ivy checked her watch with the gleaming brass clock on the wide expanse of wall above the flight schedules. Fifteen minutes to wait.

A man—tall, angular, with a countryman's long stride—was crossing the room toward her. He seemed vaguely familiar. "Now who'd ever a-thought we'd meet up here in a airport waiting to see little old Ivy Thurston's son come back from across the waters?" he said to her.

She smiled. "Leck. Leck Gunter." They shook hands.

"It's me, all right, Ivy. Old and ugly but able to pull, pull up to the table three times a day. I'm right proud to see you. Like I say, it's something to ponder, that boy of yours being a full senator of the United States."

"It does seem strange in a way, Leck." Ivy was curiously pleased that old Leck Gunter was so happy to see her. Leck was from away back, both in time and place. "A master hand with cattle," Papa had always said of him. She could see other people in the airport noticing as they talked together.

"It's been a time and a half since I laid eyes on any of Tom Thurston's young'uns," Leck went on, holding his sweat-stained felt hat awkwardly with both hands in front of him. The hide of his hands was tough and scarred as that of the steers he'd once driven. Surrounded by the vivid turquoise and orange cushions of the starkly modern waiting room, his clothes appeared faded and formless. The overalls were as pale a blue, verging on white in the worn patches of knees and pockets, as his watery, watchful, hopeful eyes. "Your folks all right, Ivy?" he asked.

"I guess so, thank you, Leck."

She unbuttoned the jacket of her tweed suit. October sunlight poured through the glass expanses overlooking the airport and the room was too warm. "Clay's home from up North. Maybe you know about . . ." She paused, testing him.

Leck Gunter shifted from one foot to the other. He flushed in embarrassment for her, but his eyes were at the same time eager for himself, for his curiosity, that mountain curiosity Ivy knew so well. "I heard a little something . . ." he began.

He had heard about Clay and Hawk Williams' death, no doubt of that. She could picture him tilted against the wall in a straight-backed chair at some little forks-of-the-road store, just as other more recent friends of hers would be assembled at the country club, and each talking about "the trouble," as she and Frone and Phoebe and Kin—yes, the whole family—talked and talked, until their misery was layered over with words.

"Don't fret, Ivy," the old man said. "I reckon nobody in Nantahala County but knows that the Thurstons are the finest sort——"

"Thank you, Leck."

Ivy did not want to talk about it. How Papa would have crackled with laughter, hearing a character reference from Leck Gunter!

"You expecting someone here at the airport, Leck?" she asked. "Or are you getting ready to try wings?"

"Why, I reckon I come out to catch sight of Senator Phil——" He broke off, and the shy country grin creased his bearded face once more. "What was the name of that feller you married, Ivy?"

"Cortland. Hudson Cortland."

"So your boy would be Senator Philip Cortland. It's got a good enough ring to it, even if he is little old Ivy's tad."

Ivy laughed. "Wait till you see him, Leck. That tad stands six feet two."

"Whoopee!"

Three ladies and a man near the exit turned discreetly to stare.

"Come on, Leck, let's go down to the coffee shop. I want to buy you a cup of coffee."

He stepped back and shook his head. "No, reckon not, Ivy." The hat twisted in his hands. With grave courtesy he said, "Much obliged for the offer though. Nobody I'd sooner a-seen today than you. Everything moving so fast these days, nothing staying the same, seems like a feller sets special store by old friends." He shook his head slowly, as if to brush away a bothersome swarm of wasps without being stung. "Bombs and these-here miss-iles and all the other such—well, it just don't seem like the same old world any more, Ivy. Not the one me and your daddy enjoyed."

"No, Leck," she said. "I guess it will never be the same again, the way we knew it out on Thickety Creek. The changes are too big. 'A new dimension of death,' I believe Phil called it in one of his speeches not long ago."

"That's a mighty hard knowledge to live with," Leck Gunter said. "Old-fashioned dying, one at a time, that's tough enough for most of us to face up to. My mind just can't lay hold of anything much bigger."

She looked at him in genuine surprise. Who would have thought this old man, knowing only oxen and mules and hard drudgery next to the earth all his days, would be so intimately aware of the backlash of Hiroshima and Nagasaki, Sputnik and survival? Ivy realized then that she had frozen him in her memory as he had been half a century ago when she knew him: slow, steady, attentive to every word her father read or spoke on politics or the state of the nation or the world, without knowledgeable convictions of his own, ignorant but hungry to learn. But he, too, had gone on living, changing. She imagined him listening to the radio, perhaps watching television now, learning of crises in Africa as quickly as troubles in an adjoining country. He knew of fallout and the threatening clouds.

"Yes, Leck, we're old folks in a new world."

He grinned slightly. "Reckon, as Tom Thurston used to say, we

stirred up a strange beestand before we knew the price of honey.
Well, there's a feller out here I've got to see . . ."

She recognized the ultimate excuse. How many times had she
heard it over the years—Papa, brothers, uncles, sawmill hands—
that nameless waiting "feller" beckoning them, rescuing them from
any work or encounter they wished to avoid.

He turned toward the door leading to the parking lot and the
highway into town. "I'm proud I run into you."

"Thank you, Leck. You come see us sometime."

He didn't get the hat on till he was beyond the door.

She pulled off her suit jacket and went to one of the long seats
overlooking the landing field. A voice on the loudspeaker announced
that flight number seven for Washington and New York was now
loading. Ivy could see passengers, men with brief cases, women with
make-up bags, climbing aboard a plane directly in front of the airport. She sat down. The sky filled two thirds of the window.
A bright blue October sky above the massive jagged mountains.
She wondered if the Devil's Brow was visible from here. That's
where the farm had been—Great Grandpa Jesse Moore's farm that
her mother and father had bought so many years ago—in sight of
the majesty of the Devil's Brow. Now it seemed to her that that time
had been in another world, a century ago, until old Leck Gunter had
spoken to her a few minutes past and brought it all back. All morning it took Papa to get into town then. ("Smell the good coal
smoke!" Phoebe always called out when she was along, preferring
the smell of the city to the familiar odor of blue smoke from wood
burning in cookstoves and fireplaces in the valley.) Now Phil would
be coming from across the waters, as Leck said, and he would take
only a few hours.

Ivy heard the roar of the powerful motors. The plane came in
high over the mountains, then banked, dropped, circled, as she
watched it.

Like a hawk, she thought, or a dove.

She waited until the plane had made an easy landing and taxied
up the runway to a standstill before she put on her jacket and gathered up her purse and gloves from the foam rubber cushions. She
stood waiting for her son while he checked out the cowhide bag and

brief case. Phil was bareheaded and his crisp brown hair had the first early flecks of grey at the temples. His skin was a golden tan, but as he came closer she could see new lines in his face, a strain that belied that leisure tan. He looked extremely urbane and worldly in his dark brown business suit, carefully tailored because he was conscious of his height and the breadth of his shoulders.

He spoke to everyone, the stewardess who walked in from the plane with him, the baggage clerk, a ticket agent nearby, and Ivy was interested in the way he spoke, with a combination of open cordiality and hidden haste under a patina of professional ease. His smile was still tentative, shy, familiar, but she knew at once that this was a different Phil coming home. She and the rest of the family would have to remember that this was Senator Philip Cortland. She noted a new confidence overlaying the awkwardness that had been, when he was a boy and even as a man, his special handicap and special grace. She wondered if this were a veneer from without or growth from within.

He turned, caught sight of his mother and strode toward her. He bent to kiss her cheek. "How are you?"

"Hello, Phil. I'm fine. And I can tell just by looking at you that you're very much all right. Could I carry the brief case for you? Would that help?"

"No, no thanks. I'll handle them both." He put his hands on her shoulders and studied her face briefly. "Well, if everyone at home looks as well as you . . ." He smiled. "It's good to see a familiar face."

"A friendly face at least." She patted his hand. She was wondering how people could hide their feelings so capably, even from those who knew them best. Didn't her worry over Clay show through a fraction, even to Phil? "The car's in the parking lot . . ." She led the way toward the door.

Phil looked around, nodded at someone across the room. A man near the door came up and spoke to him. "How's our senator today?" His big square face was creased with a total smile and his heavy-lidded eyes under thick grey brows gazed directly at Phil.

"Mr. Austin." Phil set down his brief case and they shook hands. "Fine, thanks, just fine."

Miles Austin, president of Universal Paper Company, extended a cordial hand to Ivy. "Nice to see you again, Mrs. Cortland."

"I'm glad to see you, Mr. Austin."

"And Sherry, how is she?" Phil asked.

Miles Austin gave a deep easy laugh. "To quote from the young lady herself, she's making a few ripples. Spent the summer in Europe with some friends."

"I'm glad." Phil spoke easily, but Ivy saw the rigid set of the muscles in his jaws.

"You know, Mrs. Cortland," Austin went on affably, "I used to think our young people might develop a real interest in each other . . ." He left the sentence dangling. It was not characteristic of Miles Austin to leave anything dangling.

"It's always hard to tell about young people," Ivy said. "I gave up trying long ago."

"You're so right, Mrs. Cortland. Well"—Austin resumed his briskness—"home for long, Senator?"

"I think not," Phil said. "Just here between planes, you might call it."

"The pressures of high office!" Austin shook hands with both of them again. "Stop by and see us before you leave, Senator. We'll try a little peartenin' juice, toss around an idea or two about this new industrial park the county is thinking of developing."

"It depends on how much time——"

"Oh, you can always juggle in a minute or two here or there," Miles Austin said, smiling at both of them as he left.

When they were outside, walking toward the car, Ivy said to Phil, "You did have a successful trip?"

He nodded. "It's real success remains to be proved, I guess: in our report and the action it arouses, or fails to arouse. But I learned a lot." They had come to the car. "Don't you want me to drive?"

"Be my guest this time. We'll put you to work soon enough." She wanted something to occupy her as she told him of Clay.

He folded his long legs into the front-seat space. When they had pulled out into the highway, he relaxed against the seat. "Well, I got your wire. There's some trouble?"

"Clay . . ." Ivy hesitated.

Phil gave a mock groan. "It would be. Maybe I should have followed my hunch and bypassed home, gone straight to Washington." When she did not answer, he asked, "Well, what did he do this time? Wreck a car? Or somebody's bar?"

"I wouldn't have wired you about a wrecked car, Phil."

"All right. Tell me."

And she told him as well as she could. He sat quite still during her brief recital. "What's the background?" he asked at last, looking straight ahead. "I didn't even know Clay and Kathleen were divorced."

"I wrote you about it. You've been so busy—anyway, last month Clay came back here."

"Looking for work?"

She frowned, concentrating on her driving and her effort to be both accurate and clear. "He said machines were cutting down on men needed in his construction work. I suspect he was homesick. I can understand Clay up there in the city suddenly feeling the presence of October."

Phil nodded, but his attention was clearly not on what she was saying about Clay's moods.

She sighed. "He lost his job. He's been on one big party ever since he came home."

"Soaking up the sauce?" Phil was listening now.

"Like a desert after a drought, to use his own words." Ivy turned off of the expressway. They would take the longer but quieter way home.

"This happened while he was drinking, of course."

"He kept wanting to go hunting. For weeks he talked about getting some men together and going on a good old-fashioned hunt. Those are the times he remembers from childhood: being in the woods, a man's world, clean and simple. He wanted to find it again."

"Poor dupe."

"A motley crew he found to go with him: McHones, Putnams, Hawk Williams. You remember Hawk, famous around here for cooking on hunts, fish fries, providing for hungry men. And thirsty ones."

"I remember we kids at school used to scare each other with tales of what would happen if Hawk Williams fixed anyone with those yellow, bloodshot eyes."

"That's the group Clay rounded up for his big hunt last Tuesday night."

"Mighty hunters out for buffalo in the canebrakes, after bear and bobcat and wild boar on the mountains!" Phil laughed.

But Ivy did not smile. "They began to drink and nobody seems to know exactly what happened then, only Hawk fell over dead without speaking a word."

"Did they check the shot that killed Hawk? And Clay's gun?"

"The sheriff told Clay he'd let him know how the tests came out." The big knuckles on Ivy's hands were white from the force of her grip on the steering wheel. Neither of them spoke for a moment. Noise of other cars around them did not seem to break the silence in which they were enveloped.

"Well, Phil?" she asked finally.

"It's a time bomb with the pin pulled," he said quietly. "I'm a Southern senator."

"But you can't be blamed——"

"It's not a question of blame. It's involvement. After all, I'm just coming back from visits with Negro leaders on the other side of the world. And Hawk Williams is"—he caught himself—"was Negro."

"Oh, Phil!" Her eyes looked straight ahead, filled with sudden tears.

"Don't panic, Mother. We'll do our best to handle it all the right way."

"The newspaper had only one brief story so far. No names except Hawk's."

"That's a break."

"But Clay's hearing is set for Monday morning. Then everything will come out."

"In that case, we'll have to whip things into shape before Monday morning," he said.

His confidence gave her a great sense of relief. How she needed him! How she wanted someone's strength to bolster her own occasionally, now that Cort's strength was no longer beside her. "You can stay till Monday?" she asked almost happily.

"I'll have to. This has to be settled one way or another." He rubbed his eyes with the thumb and middle finger of his left hand. "After all, Negroes are voting in this state, you know, voting in numbers."

Suddenly the burden of being home again was heavy. When he had run into Miles Austin there at the airport, he had felt the first misgivings. Now his feet seemed to be firmly planted on quicksand. He didn't ever want to see Sherry Austin again. And why was it that every family seemed to have some fool like Clay to throw a hitch into the machinery? If Clay Thurston were determined to destroy himself, why couldn't he just crawl off somewhere and do it quietly, without any mess, without dragging his sisters and brothers and all the rest of them along in misery and humiliation—and for Phil perhaps even defeat?

He took a deep breath, sat up straighter and tried to grin at her. "And I thought we had troubles abroad!"

"I *do* want to hear about your trip," Ivy said. "It's just that I've been sick with worry." She paused. "How many went along?"

"There were three of us on the committee. Both of the others were senior senators."

He could imagine those two shrewd gentlemen reading about his uncle's trial for murder down here in the hills. And the daughter of one of them . . . What if Ann Howard read the story in the news magazines? He visualized how it might be written: "Certain white Southerners seem to feel that senatorial immunity can be stretched to include even a senator's uncle, and murder, if that murder has as its victim a Negro and if the murderer is member of a prominent white family. It remains to be seen whether Philip Cortland, freshman member of that exclusive club called the Senate, filling out the unexpired term of . . ." Phil could see Ann reading it, her expressive face reflecting shock and anger stirred by the story.

"You were looking at some of the so-called backward countries?" Ivy asked.

He shifted on the seat, put memory of Ann out of his mind. "We were trying to evaluate our aid—especially agricultural aid—to some of them. (Ann had come down with her father to see them off on the plane. When she kissed him good-by, had it been casual—"Have a good time, Phil"—or had it borne special meaning—"Come home very soon"?)

Ivy sighed. The wrinkles around her mouth and eyes made her face homely and handsome at the same time. "It's so much easier to worry about Mankind than about individual men, one, two, three."

Phil did not reply. Was she upbraiding him, warning him, challenging him? He let it ride.

They had passed the city limits and were heading into the country. "Well," he said presently, "I guess I'd better have a talk with the lawyer."

"Hugh Moore."

"The devil you say!"

"I know he's not the best in town. But he's our cousin and Clay thought——"

"Clay will have to think," Phil said shortly. "And he'll have to come up with better ideas than that. Believe me, we all will."

She turned the car off the county road onto the drive that crossed a bridge over the stream and led into her yard. Maples and poplars were alive with color along the stream and in the steep boulder-filled yard. Farther up the road and within sight of Ivy's stood the big white square house called the home place, where Kin lived all alone when he was not in his cabin farther up in the mountains.

"Just don't judge us too harshly, Phil," she said, trying to make it light as she stopped in the driveway.

"Oh, sure." He distrusted this vague talk of intangibles, this avoidance of getting down to facts and solutions. One thing he was learning in Washington: practicality, how to get things done.

"A family can be a pretty cumbersome load," his mother said.

"Oh, it has its advantages, too," he countered easily, in his best senatorial voice, but Ivy heard the retreat behind that newly acquired patina of reassuring reasonableness.

He climbed out of the car and looked around the familiar landscape. There was a time when he had known every nook and bypath on this pleasant place—a solitary time—before Sherry Austin had shown him how desirable and susceptible to conquest the world of other people could be.

"Remember the place in the creek down there where you built a flutter wheel once?" Ivy asked, catching the reminiscent look on his face.

He nodded. "On the headwaters of the faraway ocean, as we used to say." He wondered what Ivy might have said if she had known what he was really remembering—about Sherry.

Frone opened the door for them. Her long tense face, framed by greying hair drawn into a tight knot at the back of her head, reflected a mixture of girlish eagerness and suspicious coldness. She had always favored Phil above any other immediate relatives, except Clay. Phil threw an arm around her shoulder and kissed her cheek.

"Aunt Frone. It's good to see you here. And how are Uncle Jud and the boys?"

"All my men are fine, Phil. And no need to ask you. As old Aunt Tildy used to say, you're looking every way but wrong."

He set his brief case and bag inside the coat closet in the little hall.

"A newspaperman called a few minutes ago," Frone went on. Ivy, hanging up the jacket to her suit, paused. "He said they'd had word you were to be in town and he wanted to ask you a few questions."

"What did you tell him, Aunt Frone?"

"I told him I'd just had a long trip from Connecticut and I hadn't learned all the family schedules yet, but if and when you came I'd relay the message."

"Good girl. How about coming to Washington as my official buffer?"

"Do you think he wants to question you about the killing?" Ivy asked.

Phil shrugged, but Ivy knew when he was worried, and he was worried now. "Might be. Or this reporter might just be an eager beaver who had heard about my trip, wants to learn about that. Don't let it bother you."

"Clay's in the living room," Frone said.

The room was just as Phil had always known it—wide windows, the rich glow of walnut and well-aged cherry furniture, books: light, warm, neat—not neat only but orderly, orderly in a deep quiet way, and livable. A home. What a shame, it seemed to him, that there was no man now to share this home.

Ivy went over to the delft-tiled fireplace and chunked up the small log fire blazing there. "I like a little open fire this time of year," she was saying. "It keeps off the chill."

"Far as I can tell, Ivy, you've always liked an open fire any time except maybe July fourth," Frone replied.

Phil, standing in the door, looked down the length of the room at Clay, who turned away from the big window where he had been standing, hands behind him, watching grey squirrels in a hickory tree on the hillside. He grinned tentatively, self-consciously, defiantly.

Clay was a full half-foot shorter than his nephew, but the hard muscular power of his body dominated the room. He wore a chamois shirt and his shoes were polished till, as he said, "a damned gnat would break its heel trying to walk there." Under the wide-brimmed dove-grey hat pushed on the back of his head, his dark hair was short and thick. Another patch curled up from his chest through the open collar. But it was his skin that Phil noticed first, skin not unlike the shirt he wore, or the shoes he kept so carefully polished: tough, tan leather. That skin was the hallmark of a special club of men Phil had known: hard-living senators and lesser politicians, hard-driving business and professional executives, wary old leaders in foreign countries. There was a difference, however, in the texture of Clay's skin. It was burnt by sun and wind, as well as an inner fire, the outdoor work of many seasons and many places as well as indoor indulgencies. Deep lines furrowed his forehead. "Senator Cortland, I presume?" he said.

Phil held out his hand, crossing the room. "Mr. Thurston, if I'm not mistaken?"

They laughed, shook hands, each trying to be casual. "How's the Duke of Nantahala?" Phil asked.

"Well, Senator, let's put it this way"—Clay laid a heavy hand on his nephew's shoulder—"as old Uncle Lazarus Shook always said, 'We've just let a litter of kittens out of the bag that was meant for drowning in the creek.'"

"Did you give Mama her medicine this morning, Frone?" Ivy asked.

"No, I wasn't sure about it. I'll do that now, Ivy."

"You'll have to go up and say hello to Mama, too," Ivy said to Phil. "She knows you're coming today."

"Watch old Ivy scurry her chick away from my evil influence." Clay grinned savagely.

"No, Clay," Ivy said, "you're too sensitive. Phil should go up and speak to Mama."

"Yes, sir; right now, right this minute, up you go, Senator Cortland, to exchange words of wisdom with your dear old grandmother, Martha McQueen Thurston, God bless every dear inquisitive hair on her white head and have mercy on every wicked lock of her boy's head for being such a hell of a son to her." As Clay talked, he escorted Phil to the steps in the front hall.

"I'll give her your message," Phil said.

"The devil you will!"

Frone came out into the hall. "I'll go up with you," she said, and started up the stairs ahead of Phil. "Why don't you just go on in the living room and pipe down, Clay?"

Clay started to reply, shrugged, and rejoined Ivy. As they remained in the living room, they could hear Frone and Phil upstairs shouting to make themselves heard.

"Yes, Mama, he's right here. He just now arrived and he came right up to see you."

"You look fine, Grandma Thurston, just fine."

Clay had returned to the window and stood looking outside into the deep woods again. Ivy rearranged a bowl of chrysanthemums on the mantel, picking off dead leaves, looking at the harmony of yellow and bronze flowers in the lustrous old brass bowl.

"Frone always has to start running things," Clay said.

Ivy did not answer.

"When that newspaperman called, you'd have thought the sky caved in. I swear she's going to rampage around here and one of these days she'll find herself talking to the head shrinkers." The banter in his voice was suddenly overlaid with misery. "If I don't beat her to it," he added.

"Come on, Clay," Ivy said, "now that Phil's here we'll have to——"

"Phil? How does Phil change anything? Why, Phil's nothing but a little bare-faced boy to me. He may be a senator of the United States to everybody else in these forty-eight—fifty—states, but to me he's just a bare-faced, overgrown boy and if he says a damned word to me, I'll——" He choked suddenly and turned and walked across the room, then walked back. "You know what that feisty lawyer said to me this morning, that Hugh Moore? He said, 'They may want to give us a test or two, Clay.' I stopped him right there. 'Us?' I said. 'I don't see how *us* can take a test. If you mean me, say so, man.' 'Well, then,' he went on, 'they may want to give *you* a test, Clay. Don't be surprised if we should set up an appointment with a psychiatrist.'"

"A psychiatrist?" Ivy dropped one of the chrysanthemums, picked it up quickly. She wasn't sure whether she was more alarmed or amused at this news.

"'Psychiatrist, hell!' I told that pimple of a lawyer," and Clay slammed a clenched fist into his open palm. "'You bring one of those long-hair fellows around here and he'll be needing two pairs of glasses for his work! I can tell him things they haven't invented words for yet.' That's what I told that fine cousin of ours. 'There's very few men and no boys can boast the life I've lived!' That's just what I said."

"All right, Clay, I know what you said, but what did he say?"

"Oh, I hadn't finished talking to him yet. 'If you or anybody else thinks I'm squirrelly just because I may have killed a damn poor excuse of a man named Hawk Williams, you're the one better be examined. That trouble came out of a bottle. A bottle and old Hawk's meanness. And that's the God's truth.'"

There was no sound for a moment but the crackling of wood on the fire. It was a quiet, intimate sound following Clay's wrath.

Ivy said presently, "Phil thinks it will help your case that no one but the McHone boy says you were actually the——" She hesitated.

"The killer?" he supplied for her. "Maybe it does help the case, Ivy. I don't know." The anger had passed like a summer storm.

Now he seemed almost weary. "Oh, hell, yes, of course it helps the case. But I hated old Hawk, Ivy. I hated his guts. I can't hedge around and pretend I didn't. Every inch of that shiny black hide of his, every ounce of those two hundred sledge-hammer pounds he carried around, every gleam from those eyes set in whites as yellow as old beef tallow—all of it was mean. Mean as snake venom. I hated everything he stood for. And that doesn't help a thing."

Ivy shuddered. Clay's recreation of Hawk Williams was so vivid that although she had never seen him more than three or four times in her life, she felt he was standing right here in the room with them. And she was gnawed by a secret fear, so well buried she did not acknowledge it even to herself: Was any part of their fear and hate intensified because this was a Negro? As a family they had never been reared with any overt or stated prejudices—Grandfather Mark McQueen had fought with the Union in the Civil War— and they were Mountain South, not Deep South, and yet . . . She found it difficult to know herself. How much harder to know others —poor Clay, caught like a wounded rhino in a morass deeper and more treacherous than he knew.

"I didn't know Hawk Williams," she said. "Only when I saw him, or what I heard."

Outside, a gust of wind brought a heavy flurry of leaves off the poplars and other smaller trees on the hill. Clay and Ivy heard Frone and Phil reassuring Mama upstairs that someone would be back up with her in a few minutes. Then their footsteps came closer.

"Poor old Mama seems pretty alert today," Frone said as they came into the room.

"Why, she's sharp," Phil agreed quickly, not admitting how shocked he had been to see his grandmother's pinched face and thin shoulders under the edge of the white sheet and electric blanket.

"She's keen as a bird dog," Clay said.

The family's self-protective devices, the pattern of their assurances and reassurances, was familiar. Phil felt himself swept back, as though Washington and those foreign countries he had just visited did not exist, as though all his adulthood was null and void.

Here he was still son, grandson, nephew; each with its own little role. He could play the part, say the words, but it was as though he had suddenly cut himself off from the outer world, the new roles of leadership and decision he had been assuming out where they kept the score. He was tired and puzzled and irritated. Just now he had neither time nor inclination for lengthy and laborious self-analysis. He felt his vexation fix on his mother. Somehow on the drive home she had set the tone for this cut-rate philosophizing, this bull session self-examination. Well, it was interesting enough, if you had time, to sit around and talk about yourself, how it was, how it could be, how it might have been. But . . .

"We'll have lunch in a few minutes," she was saying.

"You still carrying a good old mountain appetite, Senator?" Clay asked.

"I manage," Phil answered.

"Once when I was growing up, that age when I couldn't ever get filled up," Clay said, "I remember Mama telling Grandpa Thurston that I ought to be fat, I ate so much, and he just looked at me and answered, 'Er—ah'—you remember how he stuttered, Ivy? —'er—ah—that chap eats so much it makes him p-poor just to carry it around!' " Clay slapped his thigh and his laughter filled the room. It was full, loud, healthy laughter, not a snigger which fed on embarrassments of others or timidity of self, not a raucous yell which belied uncertainty and the need of reassurance, but laughter born of the knowledge of incongruity and a sense of the ridiculous and an awareness of the smallness of self. Clay's laughter, Ivy thought, is like Papa's used to be.

"Maybe it's carrying my appetite around that keeps me fit," Phil smiled.

"Fit?" Clay looked at him, repeating the word slowly. Then he turned to his sisters. " 'Fit,' he says. Hell, Senator, you don't have to be proper with us. You can come off it. We're all going to vote for you."

"Now, Clay——"

" 'Oh, that keeps me fit,' " Clay minced the words. "Fawncy that!" His mood had changed, the laughter abruptly gone. "Say," he demanded, "you want to know a little story I heard in town about your appointment, Senator?"

"Clay!" Frone warned.

"Well, I think Phil ought to know about it," Clay pursued. "He's a big boy now. I heard that old Governor Wentworth said every politician was entitled to one big damn-fool gamble in his life and he hadn't filled his quota yet. He said he was going to take his damn-fool chance by appointing a rawhide mountain boy like you to fill out the rest of that dead senator's term."

Frone looked away, embarrassed. Ivy flushed. "That's a mighty nice way to greet your——" Frone began, but Phil only laughed. "Oh, I don't think it's a story, Clay," he said. "Way I heard it the first time, that's just what Governor Wentworth told the delegation that went to him asking for an 'older, wiser, more experienced man.'" His tone put the last words in quotes.

There was a pause. Then the tough, tanned masculine skin of Clay's face crumpled like tissue paper as he grinned. "Well, Phil, you're all right." He looked at his nephew for the first time with real friendliness. "I like a man who can laugh at himself."

"Like you!" Frone said.

The irony of the little words cut like a razor. The grin, the friendliness left Clay's troubled face. "Like me," he said. "Trust old Frone, she'll tell you every time. Maybe your best friends won't tell you, but Frone here, the truth doesn't bother her; she'll let you have it, right where you live."

"Hush up, Clay. I didn't mean to start something." Frone flushed. "Just seems like you're so handy with criticizing others . . ." Ivy could tell that the quick-tongued sister regretted the words she'd thrown between them.

"Dear big sister," Clay said very quietly, mockingly pedantic, "the art of criticism among friends is being sure that what you insinuate is only half true. That way you leave the poor devil a refuge. The whole truth and nothing but the truth so-help-me-God— that's for courtrooms."

There was a little silence.

"Good Lord, what a mess!" Clay paced across the room and then turned back to Phil. "Speaking of courtrooms, Ivy's told you all about my little difficulty?"

"That's right," Phil said.

"And what's your opinion on the situation, as one bastard to another?"

"Well"—Phil hesitated, more for his mother and aunt than for Clay—"in the first place, neither you nor anyone else seems to be sure you did anything."

Clay sat down and put his face between his hands in a gesture of weariness, impatience and despair. "They say I killed a man."

"Yes. A Negro," Phil responded.

"A Negro all right. And I guess you're thinking, Senator, that if some of the papers and organizations across the country get hold of this——"

A stick of wood on Ivy's fire broke in two and one of the pieces rolled out on the hearth. She went over and lifted it with the tongs back onto the fire.

"I'm suggesting," Phil said, "that because Hawk was a Negro there may be more emotion than good sense surrounding everybody's reaction."

"Yes." Clay nodded. "I can see that. I'm no fool."

"What do you think about bringing in another lawyer to help Hugh?" Phil was standing in front of the fireplace now, one elbow leaning on the mantel. He was decisive and his words were quick and clear.

"Hell, Phil, I don't know. I'm no fan of that soft slob's, but everything happened so quick down at that jail; they were bugging me about bond and lawyers and Hugh was our kin——"

"Sure, Clay, I understand. Actually he may be your best man. I doubt if there's anyone in Nantahala County knows his way around that courthouse like Hugh does."

"I don't give a damn whether he knows the courthouse." Clay slapped a balled fist into the arm of his chair. "Did he know Hawk? Does he know me? Can he understand one stinking bit of how it was the other night out there on that hunt? And if he understands, can he get it across to the judge—or a jury, if it comes to the worst?"

"Of course, those are basic," Phil said. "But there are lots of factors that enter into every case. And it wouldn't hurt for Hugh to have some of those x-factors in his pocket when he stands up to argue for you."

"I don't want a lot of finagling——"

"You do want to get the case over? You do want to stay out of prison?"

Clay looked at him out of bravado and misery. "Yes. Why, hell, yes."

"Then you'd better settle for finagling or influence or anything you can get."

Her son's and brother's differences suddenly troubled Ivy. Somehow it seemed to her that each one was saying what she might have expected of the other. And she felt helpless before the whole situation. "Can't we settle about Hugh Moore after lunch?" she asked. "The casserole will be ready in ten minutes. Phil, why don't you go on to your room and catch your breath, wash up——"

"Maybe Phil and I better catch our breath together," Clay said. Ivy looked at him sharply. Did that mean he had a bottle, that he wanted to give Phil a drink and then take one himself and begin again on one of his long bouts? He avoided her gaze.

"Just don't catch too long a breath," she began, as the doorbell rang. "It's Kin," she called back as she opened the door to their other brother. "Come on in, Kin. Just in time for lunch."

He stepped heavily, carefully into her well-groomed living room. "Law," he said slowly and looked around and grinned, "I reckon that's plumb good timing on my part." He wore heavy, mud-splattered boots and overalls and his work shirt was a faded plaid. When he pulled off his shapeless hat, Phil was surprised to see that he had become quite bald just above the forehead. And although his face was unlined and his eyes were a clear light brown, this receding hair line made him appear to be the oldest instead of the youngest Thurston. There was a day's stubble of beard on his round, placid face. His arms and legs and torso, like those of his older brother, Clay, were powerful with muscle. But Kin, lacking the other's quickness of motion, seemed too strong, ill at ease, in this pleasant room that was nonetheless bounded by four walls. He was as sturdy, ponderous and long-enduring as a locust post.

"Hello there, Uncle Kin," Phil said.

"Now say, Phil, it's good to see you." Kin shook hands carefully, his big fingers catching an easy grip as he smiled around at all of them, trying to sense their mood, be one of them. "He's mighty fine-looking since he got to be Senator Cortland, isn't he?"

"Oh, just my usual appearance, as Clay here would say," Phil tried to hold on to the fragile joviality of the moment.

"Sit down, Kin," Ivy said. "I'm just getting lunch on the table——"

"I can't." He remained standing in the center of the room. "I've got to get on home. Just thought I'd stop by and see if Phil had come, and then say hello to Mama."

"Good old Kin." Clay slapped him on one massive shoulder. "Always the faithful son, holding the fort for the prodigal. Well, I guess it's a poor family can't afford one bastard. Say, were we going to wash up, Phil?"

"Well, yes . . ."

"You go on, Phil," Kin said. "I'll be seeing you a little later on." When Clay and Phil were out of the room, he looked around at his sisters. "Anything new?" he asked. "You heard anything about Clay's trouble?"

Frone shook her head. Ivy said, "Not a thing."

"Now I heard something in town today . . ."

They looked at him. They did not move as they waited for him to go on in his own good time. "Well, Kin?" Frone finally said.

"This fellow I know came by where I was building this little pool and waterfall out on the Austin estate. It's in their wooded section there and I've brought all manner of wild plants to set out. One or two I've never tried transplanting before, so it's sort of an experiment, too. It's going to be a fine place when I finish. The Austins have let me have a free hand, landscape, plant any way I want to. I wish you-all would come out and see it when——"

Frone glanced at Ivy impatiently. "And what about the fellow?" she demanded.

"Oh, yes. Yes. Well, he came by and we got to talking and he said somebody around the courthouse told him they had some new evidence."

"New evidence?"

"Yes, in Hawk Williams' killing." Kin's voice was remarkably soft for such a large man.

"But what is it?" Ivy asked.

"Is it for or against Clay?" Frone asked.

"This fellow didn't know what the evidence is. Just said the feller told him it 'fastened the hooks on old Clay Thurston.'"

Frone and Ivy looked at each other.

"Didn't the man tell you anything else?" Ivy pleaded.

Kin shook his head. "That was all he knew."

"What in heaven's name could the evidence be?" Ivy asked.

"We haven't heard a peep out of that Hugh Moore about it," Frone said angrily. "What kind of a Thickety Creek jackleg is he anyway?"

Ivy hurried into the kitchen. She stood alone, clutching the edge of the sink, regaining her composure. The aroma of her casserole, baking slowly, filled the room. She wondered if she could cushion the blow of Kin's news with an excellent lunch?

She moved about the kitchen, her face tense and concerned. How happy she had been working in this room when Cort was still alive and Phil was a child, when life had seemed, for several years successively, settled and steady and permanent. That was the only really quiet time, satisfying in every way, that she could remember, and the memory of it was green in her mind.

But now she had all her family—and she had no one. She had never grown reconciled to that immaculate single bed she faced every night. She had had passion to bring to marriage and for a short, sweet while she had shared it with a man she loved completely. It had been hard to divert and deny and destroy that passion during the long nights since Cort's death. At this moment, however, it was almost as if Cort had never existed. Her family was coming together again and the echoes of all that held them together and apart reverberated in the secret caverns of her mind and memory. They were bound together by reason of the closest kinship there is; they were separated by margins of temperament and experience as wide as a continent. Whatever was to come—trivial or tragic, revealing or revolting—part of it was here now, had always been here.

She paused beside the sink, looking out the window, and she was sorry for her son. Phil couldn't know the subtlety of their relationships, for he didn't know, in that ancient knowledge of blood and bonds, where they had come from. She knew that Phil was irritated by Clay's trouble and would like to be rid of any involvement in it. She also knew that no matter what developed, she was part of the predicament and the solution, because whatever had happened on the mountains last Tuesday night had begun a long time ago—yesterday—and would not be finally settled until some time to come—tomorrow. She remembered the first time she had ever heard of a world outside . . .

CHAPTER 2

Yesterday

"**N** AG-A-SAKI. Nagasaki!" The word seemed to roll like a shiny marble across the floor where Frone and Ivy were playing until it reached the shadows in corners beyond the pools of lamplight. "Lord, you've gone a long way across the waters," Papa said.

Uncle Burn and Uncle Gib McQueen laughed and said, "That's a fact, Tom."

"Been so far you've brought back names I couldn't turn over with a cant hook."

They laughed again and their laughter came back to the shadows, too, and made the girls warmer and lighter than the lamplight.

The grownups sat scattered around the room—Papa and Mama beside the little round table. In the center of the table stood an amber glass oil lamp, flickering a tall yellow flame against the darkness. It outlined Papa's face clearly for he was close to the light. His face was square, with high cheekbones and a good firm jaw, distinct yet not hard or brutal. His shock of curly brown hair and heavy dark eyebrows were in contrast to his bright blue eyes, the prettiest eyes Ivy had ever seen. His nose was straight and prominent, not quite aquiline. It was a thoroughly masculine face, as Mama's was feminine.

Mama's sewing lay in her lap and on the edge of the table beside her. Every once in a while she reached into the colorful nests of cloth and drew out a sock or shirt or petticoat and after examining the piece carefully, turning it over in her hands, probing with her fingers, frowning slightly as she stretched the garment until she found its weakness, she began to thread her needle again, wetting the thread with the tip of her tongue against her forefinger. Her skin was very white in the lamplight and her eyes very brown.

Aunt Tildy (their great-great-aunt Mama had told them she was, which made her more ancient than anything they knew, than trees or terrapins or the boulders where they played behind the house) sat beside the fireplace. Her white hair was covered by a dark brown shawl (dyed out of walnut hulls and woven during "that War," she had told Ivy once). It fell down over her shoulders and back and from its loose folds her face peered like a watchful bird's. During the day Aunt Tildy's tongue was quick and harsh, but her hands were slow and gentle. When any of them were sick, they trusted her to cure them and never doubted that she could. Sometimes she fretted at the space she took up in the little house, especially since the most recent baby, Phoebe, had been born. But Ivy suspected that Aunt Tildy only wanted Mama's reassurances of their need of her.

Now one rough gnarled hand held the long skirts of her dress back from her legs so that the thin rheumatic limbs were directly exposed to the heat on the hearth. "Eh law, it's a satisfaction to bake these old bones," she said each night when they settled her in the chair just after supper. Tonight, up later than usual because they had company, her head was drooping forward slowly, like a leaf falling; presently she would snatch it erect again, blink brightly and look at everyone slyly, hopefully. Once in a while she made a comment and then waited and gradually wilted again. Frone nudged Ivy and they watched her as the others (the ones in between, neither seven and eight nor eighty) talked along. Their voices were like a swell of water washing over the room out into the corners, easy and relaxed and monotonous, covering them all with certainty and love and a knowledge of who they were, a knowing warmer than blankets, softer than fleece.

Papa, Mama, Aunt Tildy were there every night. Tonight was better, however, made special by Uncle Burn and Uncle Gib. They took up the middle of the room—not by size only but by the fullness of their presence—Uncle Gib McQueen tilted back in his cane-bottom straight chair till it seemed the legs would surely slip or crack, but never giving or breaking under his sure riding of the wood and cane; and Uncle Burn McQueen, big and easy, with his broad friendly face set between ears that were large and fleshy. Ivy cherished these two uncles, brothers of Mama's, who wandered in and out of their lives like summer breezes. They had come to the logging camp up in the Great Smokies and the rough little Thurston house only this morning, but they were already calling half of Papa's workmen by their first names. Since supper they had been spinning strange tales of the Spanish-American War and distant places.

"Yessir, it was aboard the US transport *Grant* that we sailed for home by way of Nagasaki, Japan," Uncle Burn was saying. "We got passes and spent two days on the town."

He and Gib looked at each other and their grins were for the private secret memories between them.

"Martha, we rode in little high-wheeled carriages called jinrickshas, pulled by men. They go in a trot all day long."

"Guess you fellers learned to live pretty high off the hog over there," Tom Thurston said.

Martha bit an end of thread in two, then smiled.

"Eh law"—Aunt Tildy spoke suddenly from her rocker—"time you two get done telling it, the Cuban War and the Philippine Insurrection was just a plumb frolic. Where be those heathenish places anyway?"

"Well, now, it's a pretty far piece they've been, Aunt Tildy," Tom Thurston said solemnly, rocking forward in his chair as if for a long reply. "I'll tell you: you go down this road here past the sawmill till you come to the big road, then you turn left and follow that on for two or three miles till you come to the forks of Buckhorn . . ."

Ivy watched her father's eyes shine as blue as fox fire in the light. Uncle Burn and Gib looked merry, too. And Aunt Tildy did so despise Papa's teasing!

"You'd better be careful, Tom," Martha spoke up, "before you reach the bounds of your own geography."

He winked at Martha and laughed, booming it to the limits of the narrow room till the little girls smiled, too, not knowing why, not caring, only loving the sound of his merriment mixed with that of Uncle Burn's and Gib's.

"Eh law, Tom Thurston, you varmint——"

Martha placated the old woman. "You're in good company, Aunt Tildy, not being able to place the Philippines. The newspaper printed that President McKinley himself said that after Commodore Dewey defeated the Spanish fleet in Manila Bay, he couldn't have told within two thousand miles where the islands were till he searched them out on a globe."

"Leastways I'm not heading up the United States Government with my ignorance," Aunt Tildy snorted. "And I can't see our need to have much truck with all them out-of-the-way countries."

"I couldn't say, Aunt Tildy," Burn answered slowly. "But it's a mighty big world out there and that's a fact."

Tom Thurston moved his chair a shade closer and spoke eagerly. "It's a thing I dream on, seeing part of it sometime." Ivy, in the back of the room, could see Mama's face grow tense when Papa talked like this. "Go on, boys," Papa continued, "tell us more about this Nag-a-saki, for instance. Is it pretty much like the Philippines, there in Japan, or different?"

"Well, now," Burn said, "there's a big difference between the cities we'd known in the Philippines and this Nagasaki. The Japs are bright. They're quick as chipmunks."

"Remember the women with jet-black teeth?" Gib asked.

Burn nodded. "We asked a native about it and he said the black teeth were to identify the married women."

"Made it handy to have them labeled." Gib grinned.

Mama frowned and glanced back at the children.

"Reckon you boys were sorry, in one way, to leave all those adventures behind," Papa said.

Gib nodded. "You know, it's a funny thing. There was only one fist fight broke out our whole return trip. Going over we'd had two, three scraps a day on the boat."

"Maybe you fellers had had your bellyful of fighting," Aunt Tildy said.

"Maybe we had, Aunt Tildy, maybe we had," Burn answered.

The room was silent except for the clock ticking on the mantel.

"Anyway, it was better than the coal mines up in Kentucky," Gib finally said.

"That's right." Burn nodded.

"You remember," Gib said, his face brightening, "that day I had to report the great whisky rebellion to the captain?" Their laughter exploded in the little room.

"It was this way," Burn finally said to the others. "One day right after we got to the Philippines, a small party from our company was out on patrol. One of the men got hold of some whisky and after we returned to camp, the sergeant put him in the guardhouse under charges of drunk and disorderly. He sent Gibbon to report the case to the captain and Gib told him, 'Captain, one of our men is confined for capturing a bottle of whisky on patrol, sir.' The captain asked, 'How did he capture it?' And Gib answered, 'I figure he surrounded it, sir.'"

They laughed. Aunt Tildy smiled.

"Mama," Ivy asked from the shadows, "while baby Phoebe's asleep, could I sit in your lap?"

"Now I don't know why not," Martha said. She stitched her needle into the shirt she was mending and laid it on an edge of the table. She pulled off her thimble and slipped it into her apron pocket. Ivy climbed into her lap and laid a curly head on one shoulder. Martha beckoned her other girl to come, too, but Frone went to the edge of the hearth and sat there alone, knees hunched up under her chin.

"Ah, here's something you young'uns will like to hear about," Uncle Burn said. "How about a place where bananas and coconuts would cost nothing only to eat them?"

They were all lost for a moment in thought of the luxury of unlimited bananas: rare, delicious, yellow bananas, rich to the taste, smooth and strange as the tropic lands where they grew. And coconuts for the light tender cakes that were Papa's favorites.

"I'd eat bananas all day long," Ivy announced, "was I Uncle Burn and Gib and in that tropic land."

"Then you'd grow sick of them," her mother said.

"Be wishing you had a good tart Limbertwig apple," Aunt Tildy added.

"Always yearning after something else, it's human nature," Tom Thurston said.

"I reckon we don't know when we're well off," Martha went on, and Ivy could see how straight she looked at Papa. "What about the water over there in that rich place, Burn?"

"Water?" Uncle Burn repeated in disgust. "Why the only way you could tell you were drinking that lukewarm stuff was that it was a little bit wet."

"One thing about this jumping-off-place your sawmilling dragged us to, Tom Thurston," Aunt Tildy said, "it's got as good water as ever I tasted."

"Now that's a fact," Tom agreed, pleased.

"Only better water I know of anywhere," Martha said quietly, "is the spring on Grandpa Moore's farm."

Silence settled on the room. A pool of silence as real as the lamplight engulfed them. Ivy looked at her mother's face. Mama was biting her lower lip, holding her eyes close on Papa's face.

"You still wanting that farm, Martha?" Gib asked.

"The children need a better place to grow up in than a lumber camp," she said quietly, not looking at her brothers but at her husband. "A family needs roots and land of their own——"

Tom Thurston slapped his hand down on the table so hard that the glass chimney on the lamp rattled. "I'm trying to make up my mind to it," he said. "Can't you see that, Martha?"

"All I see," she went on steadily, "we lost money again on this timber deal. And there are others waiting to get their hands on Grandpa Moore's plantation——"

"Plantation! That hillside farm?"

"Three hundred acres in all and several of them are good bottom land——"

"All right, that creek-bottom farm then. No offense, fellers, to your grandpa's farm; it's a nice enough piece of land for these hills —but a plantation!" He threw back his head and his curly hair shook with the force of his laughter. Burn and Gib laughed, too.

"None of the rest of us want the place, Martha," Burn said. "Since Papa died and sister Jessie married and moved to Missouri, seems like Fayte's been content with his schoolteaching and living on the mountain in the old home place. And I don't look for Gib and me to give up our rambling for a while."

"There's Aunt Dolly Moore," Martha said. "She'd like to get her hands on Grandpa's place for Tim and his son, that little old Hugh——"

"Bickering over parcels of earth," Tom interrupted. "I won't be party to it. If we can get it freely and wholeheartedly . . ." He hesitated, seeing the trap toward which his words propelled him.

But his wife pounced and sprang the catch. "Will we? If we could get it without any trouble, Tom, would we take it?"

"Don't crowd me, Martha." He had always prided himself on being a man who kept his word down to the last jot, to the smallest intimation. "Maybe so. Just don't crowd me." He ran one hand through his hair.

Burn and Gib glanced at each other and stood up. Gib stretched his arms over his head and yawned. His arms made tall shadows against the wall. "Time for taps," he said.

Aunt Tildy was drowsing in the rocker, her head slumped forward on her chest. Frone's and Ivy's watchful eyes were bright as foxes'. Martha sat very still in her chair. Tom ran his hands through his hair again and strode to the fireplace where he kicked at the last stick of wood smoldering on the fire. It crumbled to hot coals.

"All right, Martha," he said finally, "we might go over and talk with your Uncle Robert and the others. We could see what they have to say about us having the old home place——"

"Why, that's fine, Tom." Martha stood up brightly, caught Ivy by the hand and motioned to Frone. "Come on, children. It's sleepy time."

After Frone and Ivy were in bed up in the loft, they heard Mama

helping Aunt Tildy into her bed in a corner of the kitchen. Uncle
Burn and Gib were sleeping on quilts out in the little kitchen store-
room. Mama had straightened it up that afternoon. The living room
was empty except for Papa and Mama. Ivy could tell even from the
loft that the lamp chimney was smoky after the long evening's talk.
Whenever Papa grew excited or enthusiastic he kept turning it up
and up. The girls heard the bed springs in the main room creak and
sag.

"You want me to put out the light, Tom?" Ivy heard Mama say
gently.

"You going to reward me, Martha?" Papa asked in a tight voice.

There was a pause. "Reward you?" Mama's voice had hardened
now, too.

"For coming around to what you want. I thought you might
be inviting me to a party."

"Our girls need a better chance . . ." Mama's voice quivered.

Neither spoke for a moment. Then Papa said quietly, "Well, I
reckon we could all use a better chance. You go on to sleep, Martha.
I'll sit here by the fire another minute."

Streaks of light filtered up into the loft, through cracks of the
rough flooring, from the room below. Ivy looked at the patterns the
light made. Words marched through her mind: Nag-a-saki . . .

Something new had come into their family tonight. Uncle Burn
and Gib had brought it back from the Spanish-American War. None
of them would ever again be as small or private or isolated as they
were yesterday. Ivy knew now that the road that began right outside their door led to places called Philippines and Manila Bay
and Nagasaki.

When she heard Frone breathing deeply, steadily, beside her,
she slipped out of the bed. Frone grew irritated if she were waked
in the night. Ivy had learned to turn over quietly, even in her sleep.
She went to the top of the stairway. She could see her father sitting
below her, drawn up before the fireplace and a heap of glowing
coals. Ivy watched him draw a plug of tobacco from his pocket and
slowly bite off a corner with his firm white teeth. She felt the deep
satisfaction of his chewing as he settled in a stoop before the fire,

his clasped hands hanging loosely before him as he gazed into the orange glow.

Ivy huddled on the steps, hearing the sounds of deep sleep all over the little house except where she and Papa sat. After a while she shivered and realized that she was cold. Then she tiptoed back to bed and Papa was left alone by the fire.

CHAPTER 3
Today

"**Y**ou want to run downtown with me, Senator?" Clay asked when they had finished lunch. He pushed the tall walnut chair back from Ivy's table and stood up. He slipped both thumbs under his tight alligator belt and hitched up his trousers. The muscles of his abdomen were hard and visible under the cloth.

"I wish you'd eaten more lunch, Clay," Ivy said.

"You don't have any business going to town, Clay," Frone said, "not right now."

"What do you mean, 'not right now'?" He stopped beside the table.

"I mean you ought to wait till after Monday at least before you start tearing around town. Wait till we get through the hearing Monday morning on your—your difficulty with Hawk Williams. Then you can start out on the town again."

"And how am I supposed to get through that hearing, dear Frone, if I don't have consultation with my lawyer?"

"Oh, I thought——"

"No, no, no, Frone. 'I thought' isn't admissable in this court. What do you *know*, sister?" With elaborate pantomime he pointed a heavy forefinger at her. "What do you know of your own knowledge, neither hearsay nor guesswork from your busy little brain, but knowledge of fact? What do you, in fact, know about my proposed journey into town within the hour?"

"I know you've started nipping——"

Clay's face flushed with both shame and irritation. He flung up his right hand in a mock oath. "Never. Never let it be said that I 'nipped.' I have not started nipping, Frone. I did take a drink before lunch, in which I was joined by your successful nephew, the Senator here. A good healthy man's gulp, not any nip. As the old lady said, a little spirits before mealtime for the appetite and a little afterward for the digestion."

"Phil, you shouldn't have encouraged him——"

"Now you're in for it, boy," Clay interrupted. "I've got three sisters, and just as soon as little Phoebe rolls in this afternoon from her big mansion down in South Carolina, you can watch the trio of them go into action together."

Ivy laughed. She poured hot coffee into Phil's cup and refilled her own. The reflections of their faces in the gleaming silver pot were long and distorted. "I'm afraid Clay doesn't appreciate our friendly counseling service," she said, trying to retrieve the good humor they had managed to maintain during lunch.

Clay ignored her. He was still looking at Frone. "Say, did I tell you about seeing Azalie Shook the other day? I ran into her in town, right after I first came home."

"No, you didn't tell us you'd seen Azalie," Frone said. "Why, I haven't seen her in years. I guess she's dried out as a prune by now, living out her life over on Thickety Creek."

"She looks old as the hills," Clay agreed.

"Poor Azalie," Ivy said. "She was always so goodhearted and so funny."

"And inquisitive," Frone added.

"Inquisitive?" Clay said. "Like a beagle in a rabbit patch. That's why I thought of her just now. I hadn't talked to her a minute the other day till she squared off and asked me if I'd stopped drinking. Stopped drinking, mind you, and us almost strangers after all these years. Wasn't that a hell of a greeting?"

"Just like Thickety Creek," Frone agreed with him. "Always had their noses in other people's business when we lived there."

"After Azalie asked me that," Clay went on, "I looked her right in the eye and I said, 'Yes ma'am, Azalie Shook Gunter, I've stopped drinking.' She half-dropped her mouth open. 'You have? How long since you stopped, Clay Thurston?' And I told her, 'Day after to-morrow it'll be three days, ma'am.'" He shook with laughter and slapped one knee as the others laughed, too.

"You'd better have stuck to it," Frone said.

"Well, how about it, Senator?" Clay turned briskly toward the door. "You lost anything in town you need to find?"

"Not right now." Phil took his last swallow of coffee. "Maybe a little later we can run over to Hugh Moore's——"

"Don't you have any idea what that new evidence Kin heard about could be, Clay?" Frone asked.

"Do you think I'd be standing here beating my gums to you about it if I already knew? No, Frone, I'm not hiding a damn thing."

"I didn't say you were."

"Well, if I can get that lazy Hugh Moore off his sitting apparatus and onto this case——"

"Papa always said his grandmother, Dolly, wouldn't work in a pie factory."

"Well, folks," Clay said, "I'll just cruise around town a little while, see if I can pick up any information. I'll meet Phoebe's plane, too. Three o'clock she's due?"

"Two fifty," Ivy said. "You'll be there on time?"

"Will you be all right?" Frone asked Clay.

He had started to adjust his hat, but his hand stopped in mid-air and he let it fall limply to his side. "Will I be all right? I will be all right, sister. I am not drunk. You said yourself I had only nipped. And I am a much-right fellow."

"You're what?" Ivy asked, recognizing a cue.

"You know what a much-right man is, don't you, Phil?"

"I'm afraid not, Clay."

"This old gal in town here was up on trial in court for cutting up her boy friend with a butcher knife. The judge asked her if they were married or what their arrangement was. 'Well, your honor,'

she said, 'he's my much-right man.' 'What do you mean by that?'
the judge asked. 'Well, your honor, he ain't married and he ain't
spoke for and I figure I got as much right to him as anybody.'"

With that they heard him leave the house in a peal of laughter
and slamming of doors. "Be careful," Frone called after him, inef-
fectually, routinely. "He's on his way up now," she said to the others. "All those big tales, that big humor. He'll have to crest and then
hit bottom again. I tell you, I don't know how much longer we're
all expected to take his carrying-on."

"As long as necessary, I guess," Ivy said. Then she went on, "Naomi's coming to fix our dinner tonight. I thought we'd have a regular old-fashioned family meal—the first time in years we've all been
home at the same time. And after Monday . . ." She and Frone
looked at each other, looked away quickly.

Phil stood up from the table. "I need to make a few last-minute
notes on my trip," he said, "catch up on messages Jerry sent along
from my office. I need to think a little about Clay's situation, too."
He smiled reassuringly at his mother and aunt.

"Welcome home," Ivy said. Irony was not her style and its edge
in her voice surprised him.

Phil felt sad and slightly guilty as he went back to the study-bed-
room Ivy had fixed for him. He looked around at the comfortable
room, warm with biege and brown in its tweedy carpeting, splashes
of yellow and a gleam of brass decoration here and there. On a shelf
above the desk Ivy had collected all the trophies he had ever won.
Phil had not seen some of them in years. He grinned in unconscious
embarrassment at the small personal display. Tennis: doubles,
county championship. Swimming: backstroke, first place for junior
campers. Manual of arms: best in class in military academy. Others,
assorted sizes and competitions. All of them minor monuments to
two realities—a shyness that had almost suffocated him and a loneliness that had tormented and fulfilled him when he was a boy, and
his escape from both. His father had brought him to close compan-
ionship with himself and with the stream and woods and hills of
this place. When his father died, Phil was fifteen. He felt that the
universe was turned topsy-turvy and he wanted to retreat to the
paths and knowledge they had shared together. But his mother (at

what cost to herself, he wondered now) would not let him retreat. She made sure that he had time alone, but she thrust him among his own, too. Camp, boarding school. Not any camp, not the most convenient or stylish school—but honorable places where he could find men to emulate as he had his father, where he would share friendship—or hostility—with other boys.

"I'm not sure we always chose best," his mother said, years later, "but when you're left with decisions, you have to make them as wisely as you can, and then hope they're right."

"You could have kept me here, sympathized with that bashfulness," he had told her, "and I might have developed into a great Critics' Award playwright. But outside that, I'd say you chose well! If you don't mind having a struggling lawyer in the family."

"You won't be struggling long," she reassured him. He could see that she was pleased by what he had said, but her easy assurance irritated him. This was just after Sherry Austin had momentarily stripped him of all self-assurance, and his misery was too fresh to be soothed, especially by another female.

Well, he didn't have time now for this reminiscing. He opened his bag and began to unpack. Any way he looked at it, it was obvious he would have to stay home longer than he had planned, longer than he could really afford. As he put shirts into a drawer he realized that he felt more at home now in the hotel apartment in Washington, involved in the swift flow of daily crises and the flux of national life, surrounded by his own books and pictures, than he could ever again feel here in this landlocked backwash of uneventful and relatively unimportant daily routine, even if it did happen to be where he was born.

The phone on the desk rang. It rang again, the sound broken abruptly as someone in another part of the house answered. Presently his mother came to the door. "Phil, it's that reporter again. I had to tell him you were here. He had checked on the passenger list of the plane."

"That's all right. We aren't hiding my whereabouts. I'll talk to him." He sat down at the desk and picked up the receiver.

Ivy marveled at how relaxed, friendly, even casual he sounded as he talked with the insistent young man on the other end of the line. There were a few bantering remarks and inquiries, then Phil said, "No. No. It was on my schedule all the time to stop by here on my way back to Washington." After a pause: "I tell you, fellow, why don't you come on out here tomorrow sometime and we can have a real interview? Right now I'm covered up with family greetings——"

"Tomorrow morning," Ivy whispered. "Tell him tomorrow morning."

"It can't do either one of us much good right now, can it?" Phil spoke into the phone. "No, fellow, I'm not ducking any questions, but at the moment I don't know anything to tell you about what's happened here. I've just set foot in the territory. Now, if you ask me about some of the countries I've just visited . . ."

He paused, winked reassuringly at Ivy. "All right. You come by late tomorrow morning. It's Sunday remember. That still O.K.? Well, you come on by . . . No, I couldn't possibly make it today, too many obligations, but I'll try to answer every question you can throw tomorrow." He pushed back the chair, began to stand up. "Don't mention it. . . . Right!"

He laid the phone in its cradle and straightened to his full height. "Well, that ought to sew up anything big in the way of a story for the Sunday editions," he said.

"I wondered why you were so determined not to see him today," Ivy said.

"We'll be home free till Monday and that paper won't have anything like Sunday circulation."

"Did he ask about the shooting?" she asked.

Phil finished emptying his suitcase. "He mentioned my voting record, asked if I thought a story like this could damage my image. How the devil was I supposed to answer that? 'Image,'" he repeated, shoving the suitcase into a closet.

"It's just simply not a racial thing," Ivy said. "Why, Clay's been up north for thirty-five years, worked with a regular melting pot of men in surveying, engineering, building. I'm sure they were all equally s.o.b.'s when he was mad at them."

Phil nodded.

"The whole thing is crazy and confused," she cried out in frustration that could no longer be contained. "No clean-cut knowledge of what happened, of who is guilty or not guilty, no clear idea of what we can do, of what's right."

"That's the story of our times." Phil smiled wryly. "Later this afternoon I'll try to find Hugh Moore and get squared away on just what Clay's legal situation is."

His mother turned to leave the room, automatically straightening a picture on the wall, a water color of children on a lonely beach at sunset. "I had looked forward to such a good visit with you," she said. "I wanted to catch up on the news—on Ann Howard . . ." She hesitated, but he did not offer any comment, so she went on. "Now it's turned into this." Her hands made a little gesture.

He shrugged. "Can't win them all."

"Well, I'll finish in the dining room. Frone had a headache and I sent her up to take a nap. Naomi should be along in a little while. I do hope we can all have a good evening together."

The house was quiet as she cleared the dining room, carefully folded the pink linen place mats, washed dishes. She left the gleaming crystal and china to drain and went slowly upstairs. Mama might have dropped off to sleep after lunch. If not, she would want her back massaged and she would want to sit by the window for a while.

It was quiet in the pale green and white room. Casement windows were flung open to the afternoon sun. "Mama?" she whispered to the closed eyes and relaxed face.

When you reached ninety, she thought, the body's shriveling and sinking and calcifying took over all other visible processes. Cheeks caved in, eyes receded into their sockets. And Mama's breasts, once white and firm and full enough to nurse and nourish hungry babies, hung like empty sacs onto her sagging stomach. It was a hard chore, heavier than any amount of labor, to look after someone you loved and see her grow old, drawing back into the small tent of her own skin which had been her infant world: self-centered, demanding, a stranger even to those who knew and loved her best.

"What is it, Ivy?" she asked, and opened her eyes.

"I thought for a minute that you were asleep."

"Just resting my eyes. I haven't slept any today." And she had said this morning that she slept only an hour or so during the night. Why was it that old people were so jealous of their wakefulness, insulted if someone suggested they had had a good nap, a full night's rest?

"Would you like to sit by the window for a few minutes?" Ivy shook out the tousled white bedspread and left it folded smoothly over the foot of the bed. She picked up several bits of leaves from one of the green scatter rugs.

"That's right, Ivy," Mama said from the bed, smiling faintly to herself, "you straighten up."

"Just once you'd think one of the others might pick up some of the trash that gets tramped in here," Ivy murmured. "I guess they think I'm made of stainless steel, won't rust out, won't wear out. Well, I get tired, too."

Mama did not hear. She was back in an earlier time when she played a central role in the life of her family. "That's what your papa used to say: 'Just wait till Ivy comes back.' (You'd be off at school or visiting or somewhere.) 'Ivy will get things neated up around here,' he'd say. I never could get him out of the habit of saying 'neated.' And sure enough, just as soon as you came home, after you'd been in the house maybe an hour or less—I'd wait some time just wondering how long it would be before you'd say, 'Mama, I believe I'll straighten up a little.'"

Yes, Ivy remembered. She remembered very well. The disorganized kitchen with its big old range and the warmer stacked full of dishes of leftover food, the wrinkled clothes stuffed into dresser drawers or hung askew in the clothespress, the rank confusion everywhere. And although they made little jokes about her whirlwind efforts, they had all welcomed her results in restoring order. They spoke of the clear lamp chimneys glistening from the soapy water in which she washed them, the tidy living room, the polished brass bedsteads, the rearrangement of the kitchen with pans hanging along one wall and dishes organized in the cupboards. She was glad they enjoyed letting her do it; she found deep satisfaction in bringing some pattern out of the careless accumulation of their disarray. Only there were times when she needed help, when the lack of method involved something with which even she could not cope.

"Sometimes in spring your papa used to come in of an evening and he'd say, 'Well, Martha, do we know where we're going to sleep tonight? I see Ivy's been spring cleaning.'"

"We all did spring cleaning, Mama."

"Yes, but you did spring changing. You were always eager to see if there might not be a better way to arrange the furniture, the house, the way we did things."

"Do you want to get up, Mama?" She shifted the subject. This was the drain in caring for someone who lived in the past: she took you there, too. Before you knew it, yesterday and today were all mixed in together.

"Why, yes, Ivy. I'm just lying here waiting for you to help me." The eyes were wide and wounded above the mouth that tried to pucker into a fleeting smile.

Seated in her flannel robe beside the window, she looked out at the brilliant leaves and sun. "I can feel my arthritis this afternoon. Sometimes it seems to me I've never known an easy moment since I lost that first baby——"

"Let's don't talk about that, Mama," Ivy protested. "It was such a long time ago."

Mama's lips quivered. "Things happen a long time ago, but they last till today." She was hurt when someone did not want to share the litany of her life's suffering. Sometimes Ivy wondered if the memory of pain and sorrow was all that could keep her peaceful and happy today.

"I know they carry over, Mama, but let's not remember just the doleful times." Ivy was smoothing out the sheets, fluffing up the pillows. She decided to put fresh cases on the pillows. In the hall the light fragrance of lavender and soap, which she stacked between sheets and towels, spilled from her linen closet. She took a pair of white percale cases back to the bedroom, held one end of a pillow under her chin while she slipped the pillowcase over the other end.

"What was that you were telling me the other day about Papa and the strawberries, Mama?" She racked her brain to think of humorous moments that would counterbalance the woes of the past.

"Way back when we lived in the Smokies, before we moved over to Thickety Creek?"

"Yes."

"Why, your papa took a load of lumber in town one day and he saw a basket of big red strawberries, the first of the season. He did like strawberries the best in the world. So he bought that basket, but he wasn't coming home till next day. Of course, he didn't want to be fooling around with them overnight. So your papa wrapped that basket in stout paper and tied it with heavy cord and he asked Leck Gunter's daddy—that was your papa's head teamster—to bring that package on back to me that night. But he told Gunter to handle it carefully, it was dynamite."

Ivy laughed loudly, so that Mama could hear her laughter.

"When your papa said 'dynamite,' old Gunter's eyes nearly popped out and he told Tom he'd take care. Way up in the night he came rolling into our yard. 'Mrs. Thurston,' he called out, 'here's a package your man sent out from town by me. Do you be cautious handling it, because this-here's dynamite!'

" 'What on earth, Gunter?' I said.

" 'Dynamite. Mr. Thurston told me. I plumb crawled around those curves and over that rocky stretch of road coming home.' And he handed it to me like eggs.

"I knew there was something wrong. Tom wouldn't be sending on any dynamite to have around the house. So I unwrapped that package right there before Gunter, and there was the prettiest basket of strawberries you ever set eyes on.

" 'I'll be damned——' Gunter began, and I had to remind him he couldn't swear in front of me and you children. 'I'm sorry, Mrs. Thurston,' he said, 'but when I think about the way I just eased that team along and how I sweated over every jog that wagon made —I tell you, that husband of yours has given me provocation to swear and cuss both!' "

Ivy laughed and Mama's eyes twinkled with old gaiety for a moment. "Your papa was afraid Gunter would eat up the berries before he got home," she murmured, "but he didn't pull his trick because of that. He just couldn't pass up the chance for a good joke."

Ivy could imagine Papa's rolling laughter when he saw Gunter the next day. It would have been a little like Clay's laughter downstairs at lunch, only freer, easier, happier. She surveyed the smooth cool bed with satisfaction.

"How your papa did relish good food!" Mama said. "Whether it was the first strawberries of the season, or a big pan of hot baked sweet potatoes with yellow butter melting into them, or a glass of fresh-churned buttermilk still cool from the springhouse."

Ivy nodded. "I remember how he'd send Frone and me back to the kitchen for hot biscuits after the bread plate had been passed once. He wanted biscuits so steaming the butter melted before it had even left the knife and touched them."

"And creamed corn and fried apples for breakfast, you remember that, don't you, Ivy?"

She remembered. They had to have the stove hot before they went out to pick the ears of corn in the garden. Then they cut off the grains, scraping the milk down the cobs in heavy strokes, and cooked it all with butter and salt until it was tender and luscious. With flaky biscuits, slices of ham or bacon, eggs fried in little islands of white and yellow, scalding coffee or cold milk, and glass dishes of preserves, jams, jellies—they ate heartily. And as Papa took that first bite of fresh nut-flavored corn and popped a whole buttered biscuit in his mouth, he always said, "No Astor or Vanderbilt has better eating than this. You young'uns just remember, the richest man living on Park Avenue in New York City can't eat what we've got set before us right here this morning. His corn's stale, his eggs have been shipped in from someplace, his milk's all treated some way—I tell you, we're lucky folks!" And before he had finished, Ivy and the other children were sorry for millionaires who had only money and could not enjoy the fruits of the earth at the peak of their season.

"It was always so good when we were on the farm," Mama was saying plaintively. "I couldn't understand why your papa was never content with the land."

"He liked the land, Mama, but in a different way," Ivy said.

"That place where you and Frone and Phoebe were born. Oh, it was rough and wild."

"I know, Mama."

"Oh, I'll never forget how it was when we got back to Thickety Creek on Grandpa's land. If only Tom could have . . ." Her voice trailed off and she sat huddled in her chair, staring down at her gnarled and knotted hands.

"Don't fret about it now, Mama."

"I want to go back to bed, Ivy," she said at last.

When she was back between the sheets and covered with the light blanket, Ivy said, "Mama, I saved a nice surprise to tell you."

"Oh?" Her eyes looked up fearfully out of the drawn, clay-colored face.

"Phoebe's coming this afternoon," Ivy said.

At the unexpected and pleasant news, a variety of expressions passed over Martha Thurston's face like cloud shadows over the mountains. Incredulity, then happiness, then a complete shattering of composure as tears rolled down her cheeks. "Phoebe . . ." She faltered. "Phoebe is coming? And Frone's already here, isn't she?"

Ivy nodded. "Phoebe was due at two fifty. Clay's gone to meet her."

"Phoebe." The old lady repeated the name almost wonderingly, with gratification. "And Frone. Why, all my children will be here together. It isn't Christmas or anything, is it?"

"No, Mama. We just thought it would be good to see each other again."

In the years since Phoebe had married Rutledge Harris and moved to South Carolina she'd had two children, Rutledge III and Lucy Kate, and since Frone had married Jud Mather and moved to her little Connecticut village to live in Jud's old family place and raise four boys, neither of the girls had come home often. There was no denying that Frone had gone from these Southern hills and made a place for herself in that tightly knit Northern community until at last, thought Ivy, Frone had become, in many ways, almost more New England than the Yankees themselves.

Just as Phoebe had become part of her low-country town, helping preserve its legends, leading its social life, fitting the pattern in her tall brick house behind the live oaks and their drapery of Spanish moss. Ivy wondered at the effort it must have cost them—Phoebe, the quick, small, industrious Phoebe who looked like Mama and had been, along with Kin, Mama's favorite; and Frone, tall, self-conscious, dreaming and ashamed of dreams, blue-eyed like Papa, whom she worshiped.

"I hope you'll all get along all right together," Mama said tentatively, looking at Ivy.

"Of course we will, Mama," she replied, and tried to laugh. "We're all grown now."

"But there used to be so many differences——"

"Why don't you take a nap now, Mama," Ivy interrupted, "and perhaps when you wake up, Phoebe will be here."

She knew that her mother wanted her to stay and talk more. Ivy could sew, dust, file her fingernails, anything so long as she was right there where Mama could see her, call upon her. But Ivy was suddenly weary. She went across the hall to stretch out on her bed for a few minutes.

"Anyone has to have a few minutes to himself every now and then," Cort used to say. And there was no denying that in some ways she dreaded the weekend. Not that there weren't pleasures in expecting Phoebe home and having Phil and Frone and being with her family, but she dreaded the frictions that had always seemed inevitable among them; they would be fearful and depressed and nervous over the shadow that Clay was under—or she thought they would be.

They were a vocal people, her folks. They loved to talk. Before movies, radio, television brought them an outside voice, they had handed down their past, their genealogy, their intricate and numerous legends, their loyalties and conflicts, by word of mouth. They knew they were alive when they talked, for they invested their remembrances and their opinions with such gall and bile and warmth and tenderness that they became not merely chroniclers but those living and creating the chronicle, too. They told stories and were descendants of taletellers. They recounted events with vivid clarity and were in the line of bards who had once roamed the highlands of Scotland and Ireland and England. They kept yesterday alive

and strode into tomorrow with zest because they had a love of
words, of talk and of the people who give words blood and breath
and high drama.

They were also mimics. They imitated each other, and relatives
near and distant, and friends they only barely remembered, and
their imitations were achievements of keen observation and skillful
caricature. They could seize the key word, the characteristic gesture, the habitual tic or stutter and enlarge it into a life-size portrait.
They remembered with all the tenacity of the Scotch, all the substance of the English and all the sentiment of the Irish, and when
they came together the past remembering was as important as the
present doing.

After a while she heard Naomi in the kitchen and she got up
and put on a fresh dress and went downstairs.

One person on whom she could always count, Ivy thought, was
this lean, wiry, little Negro woman who had spent the afternoon before making preparations for tonight. ("I can't come Saturday morning, Mrs. Cortland, I've got a meeting for my church. But I'll come
by Friday and get all fixed ahead I can. And you can look for me
soon after lunch Saturday. Don't fret, Mrs. Cortland, I'll fix everything for that dinner Saturday night." And Ivy had not fretted.)

Clay and Phoebe should have come by now. Hints of a dozen
things that might have gone wrong nagged at Ivy's mind. "I can't
imagine what's holding them up unless the plane was late," she said
to Naomi after they had gone over the dinner menu again. "I hope
Clay hasn't——"

"Mrs. Cortland," Naomi said, "with Mr. Clay in charge there's
just no telling what may have happened." She chuckled, her small
sharp face suddenly alight with the smile. "He's one more sight, that
man."

"Have you—have you heard anything about Clay's trouble?" Ivy
asked.

Naomi's face was sealed. "Seems like there was some talk over
in our part of town. I didn't pay it close mind. I figured it wasn't
true. You know how I feel about all your folks, Mrs. Cortland."

Ivy went out to the back porch and brought in a centerpiece of roses she had arranged early that morning. "It may or may not have been true, Naomi. None of us seems to know for sure what happened—not even Clay himself, unfortunately."

"That Hawk Williams," Naomi said, bending over a dish of apples she was fixing, still not looking at Ivy, "he was a bad-natured man through and through."

So she *had* heard all about it. Ivy wished that Naomi felt free to tell her frankly and fully all she knew. Good friends as they tried to be, treating each other with courtesy and friendliness and sharing little defeats and hopes and news of children, there was still this barrier, visible only at certain times, yet always there. Ivy took her bowl of flowers into the dining room. She had the impression that Naomi knew something she could not or did not want to tell her.

The telephone rang and Naomi answered it. "For Mr. Phil," she said, on her way back to his room. Ivy heard her knock gently on the door and tell Phil he had a call. When she came back to the kitchen, she said, "A girl. They not giving the young men a chance to catch they breath these days."

"Now, Naomi." Ivy smiled. "Just because we think Phil's handsome——"

"It was one of them satin-back voices," Naomi said. "I can tell when they're calling——"

A car door slammed. Ivy looked out the window. "Well, they've finally come," she said, and left off setting the table to run to the front door.

Clay and Phoebe walked up the path from the driveway separately. Phoebe moved briskly, with short, quick strides of her plump legs, ahead of Clay who came behind carrying her suitcase and a hat box. Ivy knew immediately that something was wrong.

"Never. I'll never ride with him again," Phoebe was saying rapidly as she came in. Her voice was high and quivering and her eyes, so dark they seemed black, were flashing with anger and tears. "He can kill himself if he wants to, but I've a few good years left, I hope, and I don't want them thrown away by some—some fool!"

"Oh, Phoebe!" Ivy went forward quickly and put her arms around her sister's shoulders.

"Why did you let him come after me in that high-powered sports car in his condition, Ivy?" Phoebe's little feathered hat was slightly askew. One earring was lost.

"I'm sorry, Phoebe. I didn't realize he'd been drinking that much——"

"He came through town and up the highway like a hot rod——"

"Now, Pheeb!" The object of their discussion entered, set the suitcase and hat box down very carefully and spoke very distinctly. "Now, Pheeb, how would you know how a hot-rod driver drives?"

"I don't have to know about them to know that you nearly killed us——"

"Oh, oh, oh." Clay shook his head in mock deep shame. "My sister Phoebe, you are nervous. You are overwrought. You've lived down there in that nice sleepy little South Carolina village for so long you've forgotten cars can do sixty-five now and not even break the speed limit. I swear I never once went over seventy."

Phoebe was composing herself. They were so quick to anger, all of them—but Phoebe had always been quick to forgive, too. "I guess you didn't really come near to killing us," she began lamely.

"Ah-ha!" Clay said. "Old Phoebe knows she acted the fool, squealing every time I went around a curve, I never saw any such damned carrying-on in my life——"

"All right, Clay," Ivy said. "You seem to have created enough excitement for one day. . . . Phoebe, it's so good to see you. Rutledge and the children, how are they?"

"Oh, Ivy, they're just wonderful. Lucy Kate loves Sweet Briar——"

"Tell me about it upstairs. Mama's counting the seconds till you come."

Phoebe was flustered. She kissed Ivy. "I'm so proud of Phil, too. My goodness, I read all about him, all I can find, and what he's doing in Washington."

"Well now, Pheeb," Clay said, just beyond the door, "it might be a race between the senator and me to see who can make the cover of *Time* or *Life* first. Would you settle for either your nephew *or* your brother?"

A silence fell on the room. Ivy said, "Come on upstairs to see Mama. You can rest a little, have a hot bath before dinner."

But Phoebe was looking around at each of them. "I couldn't get a sensible word out of him in the car. Is his trouble . . ." Her voice trailed away.

The grave expression on Ivy's face seemed to alarm her more than words. She sat down abruptly on the nearest chair. After a pause she went on. "All the way up on the plane I kept saying over and over, 'Please, God, don't let it be true. Let it all be some mistake.' Over and over."

"Poor Phoebe." Ivy tried to offer some reassurance. "Hugh Moore is Clay's lawyer. Phil is going to try to see him this afternoon. We'll know more after Monday morning."

"What happens Monday?"

"The preliminary hearing when the judge will decide about a trial for Clay."

"I'm so ashamed!" Phoebe blurted.

Ivy glanced at Clay. He was taking off his wide grey hat, bowing low from the waist. "Well, I tell you ladies how I feel. I feel just like an old hound-dog that won't tree. Ladies, this has broken me from sucking eggs."

"And what does that mean?" Phoebe asked. When no one answered she went on, to Ivy, "I haven't seen anything in the news down our way. Can we keep it out of the papers?"

"Oh, my God! 'Keep it out of the papers!'" Clay roared. "Somebody's been killed—killed, that is dead, dead, dead. And little Phoebe here is ashamed. She wants to keep it out of the papers. Sister, dear sister, the New York *Times* already has three top-flight men flying down to cover the story. The *Herald Trib* has pulled back their man from Moscow and assigned him with two photographers to——"

Phoebe's face was white. She appealed to Ivy. "It's not true? Why does he try to——"

"Be quiet, Clay," Ivy said sharply. "Of course, it's not true,

Phoebe. There's been only one brief item even in the local papers. This is no way for us to greet each other."

"Old Pheeb." Clay shook his head. He would not be subdued or put off. "Thinking about her reputation!" He whirled around. "No reporters are coming, Pheeb. AP and UPI haven't assigned a single man to the Clay Thurston story. Maybe we can hush it all up, get that poor bastard shoveled under the ground, get me off with a dozen or so years locked up—oh, my God! A few *years* fastened up, caged, penned in"—he strode across the room—"and that'll keep me out of sight and my big mouth shut. And maybe the nice tidy people who count with my sisters will never know anything about it, and those who do know can forget, bit by bit, what old Clay did, with new killings coming along every day or so and even little wars now and then."

"I didn't mean——"

"We know what you meant, Pheeb." He spoke more slowly. "I know exactly what you meant. You were saying that if nobody saw it or heard about it or printed it, it didn't happen. But it did. Oh, God, it did!"

Ivy, stung to anger by his first attack on Phoebe, was now stirred to pity by his misery. She had had no idea that his remorse at the death itself, not only his possible part in it, had bitten so deep. Even the destruction of miserable Hawk Williams could reach Clay, the way harm to living creatures had always touched him.

Phoebe sighed. "After all, none of our family has ever been mixed up in killing before."

Ivy bit her lip and turned aside. There were times when Phoebe displayed Mama's knack for saying just the wrong thing.

"Oh, I don't know about that," Clay said. "The family has been mixed up in killing,' one way or another, ever since Great-grandpa Moore and Grandpa McQueen were in the Civil War, and since Uncle Burn and Gib were out there in the Philippines and since Phil was in the Pacific, and a way on back before that I'd be willing to bet."

"Bloodthirsty lot, aren't we?" Ivy said, then linked her arm in Phoebe's firmly. "And now we must go up to Mama. Clay, if you want to bring Phoebe's suitcase up, you can put it in my room. Do you mind staying in with me, Phoebe? Frone's in the little front bedroom, she's had a headache today."

"I want to stay with you, Ivy dear," Phoebe said.

Phil had heard their voices, but when he came from his room they were already halfway upstairs. He started to speak, then changed his mind. He went into the living room, stood in front of the double windows that looked out into the woods and lit a cigarette.

The house was quiet except for the murmur of voices upstairs. Phil was thinking of the call he had just had from Sherry Austin.

"A little old bird told me you were here, darling." She was in her gayest Southern-belle role. Then, after the usual greetings, "How about taking me to the buffet supper at the club tomorrow night? That is, if you still remember who Sherry Austin is, Senator Cortland."

"I remember," he said. The tone of his voice created a momentary silence between them.

"Then I can count on you tomorrow night?" Her voice was lilting but insistent. He recalled that special quality so clearly.

"Why?"

That caught her breath, ever so briefly. "For old times' sake, darling."

"For old times' sake, let's forget it——"

But she interrupted with "Tell you what. I'll run out to your place tonight right after dinner."

"Lord, Sherry, you make it hard for a man to——"

"Just for a few minutes. To renew acquaintance. I'll blow the horn." She made him seem like a high-school senior again.

"O.K., Sherry."

"And Senator, darling, be a little happy about it?" She hung up. The click of the receiver was the sound of her heels, tapping down a long corridor, a long time ago (or was it a short while ago?), carrying her away when he thought he could not endure the loss. Click, click.

The cigarette scorched his fingers. He had not realized it was burning so low. Holding a heavy glass ash tray in his hand, he stood crushing the cigarette and remembering how it had been with Miles Austin's daughter. He forced himself deliberately to think of her as Austin's daughter because she had first forced him to think of her so. And she had been that girl in his life who marked the passage from adolescence to manhood, from romantic dreams of love to the conflict and glory and tenderness and brutality of sex.

Often lonely, always shy, Phil had waged the toughest battle of his life during the last years of high school, through college and law school, in that painful effort to make common cause with the rest of humanity, to establish a beachhead of casual concern and easy relationships with those others who seemed to find attention and affection so effortlessly. Then, at last, after agonies of awkwardness, his height had become fixed, his hands and feet had become familiar to him, his body had come under discipline, and gradually he had forced himself to the center with people—to the center of their acceptance and laughter and desires. To his astonishment he had discovered a deep unease among them, too, an unease which made them all akin. The knowledge was a great release. Suddenly, feverishly, he had made up for all the backward years. His assurance became doubly attractive because it was self-won and grew from within himself. Even more than his looks, which were good enough—brown hair that was almost curly, laugh wrinkles around mouth and eyes, lightly tanned complexion—that acquired assurance drew women's attention. It drew Sherry Austin's.

She had noticed him first because he was so sure of her disinterest in him that he had stayed aloof and therefore challenging. But she charmed him off his lonely perch easily enough, once she put her mind to it. After all, she was the carefully nurtured flower of Miles Austin's money and the leisure, pleasure, beauty, manners, it could buy. She was not Nantahala County's offspring so much as she was the product of all the mid-twentieth century's "advantages" and improvements and short cuts and beautification. There was much invested (not only cash but time, talent, care) in Sherry Austin's rich black hair, in that throat and shoulders like creamy velvet, in smooth round legs and arms and bright blue fathomless eyes under perfectly arched brows. Her beauty was a weapon, a wand, a miracle and a drug—as Phil discovered.

During Phil's last year at the state university, Sherry was finishing Pine Manor. Perhaps it was the geographical distance from each other that nourished their mutual attraction. They shared every long weekend the schools' schedules allowed, he going north or she coming south, and their holidays at home in Nantahala County came more and more to be devoted exclusively to each other. Ivy had noticed this and mentioned it to Phil. He had only nodded agreement. To tell the truth, if he had had to make a statement of his and Sherry's relationship at that moment, he could not have done so. Neither could she. She knew she could not because her father had asked her outright and she had been unable to answer. Instead she had merely repeated the question, mocking his best executive tones: " 'What does this Phil Cortland mean to you?' Oh, Miles, you dear old dear, that line went out with dueling pistols and hoop skirts!" When his seriousness had persisted, however, she reassured him. "He's a good playmate——" and then giggled to herself.

When Phil went to Columbia Law School, Sherry came to New York. "I've enrolled in some fancy school of design," she said to him the first time he went to her tiny apartment, "but my designs are really elsewhere, chickadee."

He had spent the night with her that night, for the first time. During all of their previous times together she had known and practiced a varied repertoire of tricks, tricks of enticement and evasion, arousal and refusal. Sometimes Phil had accused her of dishonesty; he had threatened to forget her; and twice he had proposed marriage to her. She accepted accusation, threat and proposal alike —with a kiss, deep and long. "*That* for all your words!" She would laugh up at him.

But there in her apartment their relationship had changed. For the first time Phil felt that he was now master of the situation. They were together often after that. He and Sherry Austin were strangers together in a vast wilderness of people on an exciting island of wealth and opportunity and temptation and loneliness, and they prowled the streets, tasted the museums, sampled concerts and night

clubs and all sorts of wild and peaceful corners of the city. Afterward they always came back to themselves, to the cave of their
own warm, eager, throbbing flesh.

Phil had assumed that they would be married before long. He
was studying with demonic fury at the university, as though determined to carry off the work of law with as much satisfaction as the
adventure of sex. But Sherry was not one to remain a stranger in
the city for long. Her father's friends, last season's college class-
mates, an assortment of people in her new world of designing and
decorating, began to enter the island of privacy they had created.
They were alone together less and less frequently. Sherry went out
often with the little coterie she was creating and she was playing the
role of Southern-belle bitch to the hilt, to Phil's disgust. On these
evenings he would not wait for her at the apartment. He went back
to his own sublet bedroom to work and try to reach her by telephone until late in the night. At these times the studies became
drudgery and his involvement with Sherry turned bitter.

One Sunday in midwinter he asked her when they should plan
to be married.

She was dressing while he lay on the bed, hands behind his
head, and watched her. Her fingers were nimble among zippers and
hooks and buttons. He enjoyed this leisurely looking at her skin—
no callus or wrinkle or scar to blemish it—contemplating the sheen
of her hair, the white evenness of her teeth, even the pink healthi-
ness of her fingernails, the easy relaxation of her shoulders and sway
of her hips in her hand-sewn underwear. "Married, chickadee?" she
said. "The old theory that two can live as cheaply as one? Which
one?"

"Don't turn mercenary on me, pretty girl."

"Oh, but I am mercenary. Mercenary as Caesar's Legions. They
were the ones, weren't they, chickadee?" She turned her blue eyes
to look at him. But there was a cutting edge to her voice.

"I won't be in law school forever," he said. "And then I'm going
back to Nantahala County and hang out my shingle. I'll make
money—if you can give me a little time."

Neither one of them spoke for a while. She gave a last little up-
ward stroke of the mascara brush to her eyelashes. Surveying her-

self in the full-length mirror—smoothing hair, waist, hips—she asked, very casually, "Phil, had you ever thought of going into the paper business?"

So this was it! He took a deep breath.

"Any special paper business?" His casualness equaled hers.

"Oh, yes!" Brightly. "The Universal Paper Company, whose president and founder happens to be Miles Austin, who happens to be Sherry Austin's father."

"How long the arm of coincidence," he said.

Suddenly she sat down on the bed beside him. "Why not, Phil? Miles likes you. I ought to know. You're the only one of my"—under the mascaraed eyelashes there was a glint in her eyes—"my chickadees that he——"

"I don't like that damned 'chickadee' talk," he broke in. He swung off the bed.

"Oh-h, he's angry!"

"I've told you before, cut it out." He strode across the room. "Don't call me any such silly nickname."

"Is it that, or my proposition, you're mad at?"

"Both," he answered promptly. "What the hell do I know about paper manufacturing?"

"That doesn't matter. A brain like you can learn paper from pulpwood in a little while. In this case, it's not *what* you know but——"

"Don't say it! That's exactly the point."

"Oh, Phil, don't ring in the John Wayne bit." She sighed impatiently. "Independence. Integrity. All that schmalz. I forgot my violin for background music today."

"So for you they're just words——"

"I'll tell you what makes you independent: money. I know. I've tried it both ways. Oh, yes, once I brought a Negro trumpet player to the hotel for Miles to meet when we were on a vacation in New York. It was purely a gesture of defiance, of independence, but Miles doesn't have much wit about him. He wound up getting that trumpet player a job in Chicago. And he cut off my allowance for six months. No funds. Do you know how long six months can be without any money? Especially when you've been spoiled before——"

But Phil was thinking how both of them, Miles and his daughter, used people. Trees for pulp, water for the mill, people for whatever need the Austins had of them at the moment. The arrogance of it made him laugh. "I'll bet that poor chickadee never knew what hit him."

"Who?" she asked, having already forgotten.

"The trumpet player."

"Oh!" She reached for a cigarette from the crumpled pack on the night table. "I haven't the foggiest."

"But you made peace with your father, with Miles?"

"Of course." She blew a long stream of smoke into the air. "Now I just take his cash and let the credit go, do as I please and don't tell him."

Phil nodded. "No more Negro trumpet players."

"It wasn't any fun, trying to scratch along without the green stuff. No fun at all."

"And you're afraid with me you'd have to scratch along without the green stuff?"

She made a gesture, with the cigarette between her fingers.

"Maybe not for always—but why at all?"

"Because I want to choose my own work."

She shrugged.

"Because I'm no slick-haired gigolo——"

"Don't be obsolete, darling. That word went out of circulation about the time 'speakeasy' faded."

"Maybe I went out of circulation then, too. Damn it all, Sherry, what we've had is good. You're not going to throw it all away——"

"*I'm* not throwing anything away!" she retorted. "Who's tossing aside the chance to come into a company halfway up the ladder? And when he pretended to like the boss's daughter, too."

"I'm in love with you, Sherry."

"All right, then, in love with the boss's daughter."

Before he knew that he was moving he had crossed the narrow room and seized her bare shoulders between his hands. "You. Sherry Austin. I've been loving you. Not the daughter of some damned paper company." He was shaking her so hard that her head bobbed back and forth.

She clawed at his hands holding her shoulders in a vise. "Stop it, Phil. Let me go."

"Can't you understand that? Can't you tell the difference between me and the others?"

"Don't—you—dare—hurt me!" The words jerked out stifled by surprise and anger.

Abruptly he loosed her. His fingers felt stiff and bruised. He was remembering those lonely times. With Sherry he had thought that all the old longing and terror was vanquished forever. But he had never felt so chilled with loneliness as he felt now.

"You're a pretty wild mountaineer when you're riled, aren't you?" she said in a tight voice. She was examining her shoulders, stroking the angry red imprints left there by his grasp.

He turned away to the window. "It's just that we . . ." There were no easy words for all he wanted to say. And there was no time to search for the right words. "We've loved each other. I'll never love anyone this way again." He looked down into the deserted street and sidewalk below. New York's Sunday streets were bleaker than any landscape he knew. A single Judas tree grew on the opposite corner. He could see its leafless branches from where he stood.

"Oh, Phil, really! Let's not have all this dialogue about 'the end between us.' Aren't you even going to think over what I've offered? You might like the business more than you think. Your law would come in handy——"

"Forget it, Sherry."

"——and we could build us a pretty home out near the golf links, take a trip whenever we were bored——"

"You think we'd grow bored?"

"Not with each other, darling. Just with those provincials we'd have to run around with. But it would go on being good between us forever after."

He shook his head. "It's already finished, Sherry."

"Don't be foolish." Something akin to fright flickered for a moment in her eyes. She came across the room in her stocking feet, in her white slip trimmed with a deep edging of lace. All her anger and archness had disappeared. She lifted her arms and circled them about his neck. Standing tiptoe she lifted her mouth to his. After they had kissed, he picked her up and it was easy to carry her to the bed, to lie there with her again, to obliterate for a while the sense of futility, the miserable aloneness that lurked, no longer waiting but already consummated, down at the core of his life.

When he left her that night, he said, "You really tolled me on, pretty girl. For a little while there I thought we were going to make it."

"Don't write 'finis' yet, Phil," she answered lazily.

"It's already spelled out, Sherry, in bold type." At the door he turned, looking at the small, dusky, overheated room, already feeling the nip and bite of the air that would greet him in the streets below. "Sorry I can't fit into the Austin way of life."

She laughed languidly, confidently. Because they had brought their bodies together again, she thought everything else was the same. Actually they were a chasm apart.

Phil had not seen her again for two years after that day—with one exception—and he had not *seen* her then. Once, that spring, she had come to his place, but he had heard her heels clicking on the hard floor as she approached his door and he had not answered, pretending to her that he was not at home, pretending to himself that he did not care. He felt like a fool, sitting on one side of the closed door, with the chilly spring wind blowing in a window behind him, while she stood on the other side and knocked half imperiously, half reluctantly, but he could not bring himself to open to her. And already he knew that part of his pretense was true: he didn't care any longer, not as he once had. In fact, his first reaction was impatience. He had to study for his exams (he had determined to be among the top in the class) and then during spring vacation he was going home (not exactly home, but to the state capital) where he wanted to talk with someone in the Wentworth legal firm and see if he might find a place there when he passed his bar exam. Unwittingly, Sherry Austin had provided his ambition with the cutting edge it had lacked before. She had rejected his lack of power (money) before he had had time or chance to acquire it; she had shown him how the favored-of-the-world use people—charmingly or ruthlessly, but to their own purposes always. Both lessons had been etched deep. And now Sherry was the pupil of her own precepts, the victim of her own existential catechism taught too well. Phil Cortland was going to Washington someday, and when he did, he would be unencumbered by any wife, one of those little creatures Mrs. Oliver Wendell Holmes had meant when she made her familiar statement that Washington was full of famous men and the wives they had married before they became famous.

Sherry had waited only briefly after her final knock on the closed door. Then Phil heard the high heels once more, receding now, clicking down the corridor, neat and rhythmic as the ticking of a clock or the turning of train wheels over a trestle. The sound faded and with it went the passage of another time, a lost and buried self, romantic love, a caring that would never come again. Her stylish heels tapped out the Morse-code message (but it was Phil's message, not hers) as unmistakably as a telegraph key: We are finished, but I have only begun; I take what I need and let the chips fall as they may; say "Yes" to me, to all I can demand and offer and cry out for.

Phil looked at the dead cigarette butt in the tray he was holding. The stale smell of ashes seemed alien to this room. He set the glass dish on the window sill. Sherry Austin and Ann Howard. His past and his future?

Upstairs he could hear the indistinct undercurrent of the family's voices as they talked in his grandmother's bedroom. He thought of Ann Howard's clear, chiseled countenance, the long clean lines of her body. He wondered how this encounter with Sherry later today might go. He felt the vague stirrings of a familiar, better-forgotten excitement, and he realized that he was looking forward to seeing her. The danger of it (he did not intend to be entangled in the web again) spiced his determination to follow a policy of noninvolvement.

He sighed. "The hell with it!" He could think about the girls any time. Right now there was Clay's meaningless mess to get cleaned up and rolling, that committee report to shape into something that would prove useful. He wondered if it would be fortunate or unfortunate for him in the long run that Senator Howard was chairman of the committee.

He had meant to call Howard during the afternoon and ask if it would be all right if he didn't get back to Washington until early next week. If he phoned now, to his house, perhaps he would get to talk to Ann, too. Mid-Saturday afternoon was no hour to make such a call; he was well aware of that. But he and the Senator had seemed to become close friends on their hard journey together . . . He strode back to his room and closed the door. He dialed Ann's private number.

Her voice was suddenly in the room, light and cool as Rhine wine, as summer dew, slightly heady, effervescent. "Phil. Where are you? I thought you might have been overwhelmed in some of the native harems."

"Then you did miss me? You were worried?"

"Scandalously."

"But you're not pining away?"

"Oh, I'm going out in a few minutes. One of those embassy affairs." She paused, and there was laughter in her throat when she added, "With father."

"Good girl! And remember, I'm on my way."

"I hope you're going to spur on your trusty steed. Your committee will need your services."

"You hinting me something?" Phil asked.

Her voice was totally serious now. "Why don't you talk with father?"

Then Senator Howard was on the line.

"Why, yes, Phil. Good to hear from you. . . . Anytime. No, no rush at all on your coming back because of our report. The two of us here will put a few ideas together. You can check them out when you get in your office. We'll see that that bright young assistant of yours, Jerry Stewart, keeps up to date. I thought we had a pretty good meeting of minds on our journey, similar feelings about what we found, what needed to be done, how to trim some of the fat here and there, all that sort of thing. Didn't you, Phil? . . . Of course. You stay there and say hello to your family. Now I'll admit there are friends here—I'm harboring the main party right under my own roof, I suspect—who won't understand your delay. But don't worry about this committee, Phil. . . ." All of his words were right. Somehow they didn't add up to reassurance for Phil, however.

After he had hung up, he sat on at the desk, unconsciously rubbing his thumb back and forth across his upper lip in a gesture carried over from childhood moments of concentration or worry. Howard had seemed casual. That was the fact which disturbed him. The old man was not famous for that particular characteristic. He was not approached by partisans or enemies as a casual person. And Phil happened to know that this particular chairmanship of the committee to study agricultural problems and innovations in certain underdeveloped areas abroad had been especially sought by him. Why should he be so relaxed then about timing on the report? Phil had heard from other colleagues that Howard was a driver, a demon for speed and accuracy and hard-hitting recommendations.

What about the "meeting of minds" he had mentioned, trimming the fat and all that? Phil didn't like it. The three of them had not even scratched the surface of their opinions and ideas. They had been on too tight a schedule for any real exchange of views, yet Howard had spoken as if the report were already agreed upon, as if recommendations were already drafted. Well, it was one hell of a thing and he didn't understand it. He was uncertain and suddenly depressed.

He heard Clay's heavy footsteps coming down stairs. At least he could get on top of this Hawk Williams business, and fast. "How about locating Hugh Moore and finding out what the score is?" he asked abruptly.

The briskness in Phil's voice brought Clay to attention. "Yessiree. I'll phone out to their snooty club here and see if he's around." After he had dialed, he held the phone with one hand and reached into his hip pocket with the other. He held his bottle up to the light and squinted at the level of amber liquid.

"Same bottle you had at noon?" Phil asked.

"Same bottle, different liquor." Clay's smile was as brief as his words. "Hello. Hello, there. Connect me with the locker room?" As he waited, he tilted the bottle to his lips and took a quick swallow. "Damned little sport. Guess he's out on the golf course. Or more likely, in that locker room getting soused."

"A heavy drinker?"

"Hugh Moore is so bottled in bond that if I ever get hard up for liquor myself I intend to look him up and wring a drink out of him."

Clay returned the bottle to his pocket and spoke into the phone again. "Is Hugh Moore around there? . . . Thanks." He closed his eyes a moment. "Hugh boy? This is your cousin-client Clay. Say, Phil and I want to run over and talk to you a minute."

"Here, let me speak to him." Phil reached for the phone. "Hello, Hugh. How are you?" There was a pause and then he said, "I'm anxious to see you, too. And you know, it might be smarter if we weren't sitting around at the club there trying to discuss Clay's case. Why don't we pick you up at the club parking lot? . . . Sure, we could run out to your house. O.K." He hung up.

"Lord, I hate this weaseling around like I had something to hide," Clay said.

"Sooner we get that hearing behind us, keep you from being bound over for trial, the better off we'll all be," Phil said. "Now let's make sure Hugh's on top of it all."

"You're calling the shots, Senator." Clay rearranged his hat. "Take me to our leader."

Hugh Moore's home was on Evergreen Circle. Evergreen Circle turned off of Laurel Lane, which led to the Nantahala Country Club. There were fifteen houses on Evergreen Circle. They were ranch-style and split-level and neo-colonial and the oldest was barely ten years old. Some were of lumber siding painted grey (three), white (three), green (one), two were partially veneered in mountain stone, and the rest were brick. Hugh's was brick. It sat thirty feet back from the street on a lot which was one hundred by one hundred fifty feet, exactly. A picture window faced the street. On a table in front of the window stood an imitation antique hurricane lamp.

"It's no estate," Hugh said, as he led Phil and Clay into the living room, "but it suits Flora May and me to a T. I tell her long as we're carrying the mortgages, we're the ones to be satisfied." He laughed, as at a joke.

"Hell, yes," Clay said.

"I'll go get Flora May," Hugh said. "She'll want to say hello."

When he was out of the room, Clay glanced around at the knotty pine paneling finished with a hard shellac sheen, the precise scatter rugs on the polished hardwood floors, the sofa and two chairs wearing flowered slipcovers, a television set against one wall. On top of the t.v. stood a pot of artificial African violets. (How he hated African violets! Kathleen had always been fooling with them in the kitchen windows of their various houses and apartments in New Jersey, New York, Oak Ridge, wherever they lived. And what kind of an idiot would want one of the damned things that was *artificial?*) A coffee table in front of the sofa held a large ceramic ash tray, a cigarette box and matches, and one magazine on home beautification.

"This is just about what Kathleen always wanted," Clay said, more to himself than to Phil. "Just this. Seems like I couldn't be satisfied till I tried to give her more." He lit a cigarette. "Of course I wound up giving her a hell of a lot less."

"That's the way it goes," Phil said.

"Is this all there is to it?" Clay asked, his hard and tender face lined with puzzlement and yearning. "Is this honest-to-God the real settlement, the best to hope for?"

Phil shrugged, pretending that he did not know what Clay was talking about. He did know. He had just remembered what Sherry Austin offered him years ago: a house on the golf course with a trip abroad once in a while when they grew bored. (Bored with their neighbors, of course; never with themselves, never with each other.) Their house would have been larger, with walnut instead of pine, wall-to-wall carpeting instead of scatter rugs, brocades instead of chintz—but would it really have been so different? Looking at the barren little room, he realized how much he would miss Washington if he had to leave. He did not intend to leave.

Hugh Moore came back. His purple-veined face wore an expression of irritable wonder. "Now where could Flora May a-gone? She honest-to-Pete isn't here now. You fellers like a drink?"

"No thanks, Hugh," Phil said quickly. "We just want to review Clay's case——"

Hugh held up one fat, stubby hand. "Whoa. Whoa, boy. Back up there. Don't take long to get onto those Yankee ways, does it? A-rushing and a-pushing. Reckon we could take time for a Coke?"

Phil, looking at him, thought how absurdly Hugh Moore's appearance contrasted with his reality. Adapted as carefully as some tailor could fit them to his paunchy middle and sloping shoulders and short legs were the sport coat and grey flannel slacks. In cut, material and detail they were careful and expensive. The button-down collar of his white Oxford-cloth shirt fit the thick fleshy neck closely, the maroon of his knit tie matched the grey-white-maroon Argyll socks.

When he spoke, however, this whole carefully constructed portrait of casual sophistication was dissipated. He became a small-time lawyer, trained in the practice of his profession but scarcely educated. He was the provincialism, shrewdness, cunning, chauvinism of one segment of the mountains and small towns everywhere, combined into one clever but never intelligent scheme of man. Wanting to participate in change and progress and prosperity, he dressed for the part, then spoke the lines of old greeds and prejudices and suspicions that were changeless. Because he looked like men in magazines and on billboards, some people thought Hugh Moore was like anyone else in Akron or Seattle, Hartford or St. Paul. But he was not.

He came back from the adjoining kitchen—a room of chrome, porcelain and plastic wood—dangling three uncapped Coke bottles from one hand. He gave one to Clay and one to Phil. He sucked a long drink from his own, then sat suddenly and heavily on the sofa. He placed the bottle carefully on the floor in front of him and surveyed Phil from shoes to necktie, missing no detail of appearance. "O.K., fellows, what can I do for you?" he said.

"How does the situation shape up for Clay?" Phil threw it to him directly.

"All depends. Far as the evidence is concerned it's bad—but circumstantial. As for the judge we'll have Monday, it's old Anders."

Phil looked at Hugh Moore sharply.

Moore nodded, as if Phil had spoken. "Tough break."

"Straight law, that's what we'll need," Phil said.

"Judge Anders has been a friend of our family for a long time, Phil."

"When he's hearing a case, that old man doesn't have any friends," Phil said.

Moore took another swallow of Coke. "He's not God," he said smugly. "Anders has got pressure points, just like everybody else."

"Are you telling me you've got special influence with Judge Anders?" Phil demanded.

"Not exactly," Hugh answered a little hastily, "but I'm telling you there are channels—before this case even gets to sessions court. For instance, there's the sheriff's testimony."

"And I guess you know Sheriff Doggett pretty well?"

"Let's say we're on speaking terms." The lawyer's face glowed with sly self-satisfaction.

"And?" Clay asked.

"And sometimes he can give testimony that influences Judge Anders' decisions," Moore explained patiently, as to a child. "He can testify to the character of the dead man. And for a special friend he'll help get the right testimony from some of the witnesses present at that shooting."

"What do you mean, 'the right testimony'?" Clay demanded.

Moore wiped off the narrow mouth of the soft-drink bottle carefully with the palm of his hand. Then he answered slowly, "Should I draw you a diagram, man? I mean that Sheriff Doggett gets the right facts for a friend's case."

"Seems to me we'd better get something cleared up," Clay said. "Do you think I'm guilty or——"

"Hold on, Cousin Clay." The fingernails on Moore's hand were carefully trimmed and buffed. He pointed a stubby forefinger. "It don't make one damn bit of difference what I believe! What I *know* is this: The law in this county is just like it is in most places, a pretty jealous little club. And it's rough going for anybody who tries to sail in from outside—even if he is a native-born outsider—and know all the ropes in ten minutes."

"Oh, hell, Hugh——" Phil began.

"Maybe you fellows don't recollect how folks back home in the country here like to run things our own way. And one way to win lawsuits is to know who you're working with: the judge, the sheriff, prosecutors, witnesses—know them inside out. Then you'll be onto the timing, when to sidestep, when to feint, when to lower the boom."

Clay set his full Coke bottle on the table. "This some kind of a big game to you?" he asked.

Hugh Moore's eyes were sharp under their heavy lids and above their flabby bags. "Somebody wins, somebody loses. The stakes are high."

"They're for keeps!" Clay bellowed. "And I'm putting up all the wagers. You're having your fun and games, but I'm covering all the bets. And a man's been killed."

"A Nigra," Hugh Moore corrected.

"A man, damn it!"

"Settle down, Clay," Hugh said. "Stop spinning your wheels."

"We've got to be realistic," Phil said. He frowned and rubbed a thumb along his lip. He wished Hugh wouldn't try to flaunt his influence and grubby knowledge so blatantly.

Hugh's face was resuming its familiar bland watchfulness. "Nigra killings are getting harder to fix all the time," he said slowly, examining his Coke bottle. "Guess it's the stir everywhere about all this 'rights' business. But"—he sighed—"there are still ways to keep everything under control, if a man's just willing to look."

"Well, damn your hide, I'm not so sure I want to be defended by some two-bit shyster tricks, behind-the-door deals," Clay said between clenched teeth. "I want to stand up like a man——"

"You want to stay out of the pen, don't you?" Hugh asked softly.

There was a silence. Clay turned away, slammed a clenched fist into one hand. "Oh, Lord, yes."

"Then be careful whose hide you're damning!" Moore said sharply. "And maybe you ought to know that I defend more Nigras than any lawyer in this county."

"Sure, Hugh," Phil broke in swiftly. "We know you'll do your best for Clay, too."

Clay snorted. "Aw, both of you make me puke! Two sides of the same coin. Two-bit lawyer thinks the whole killing doesn't really count because it was done on a Negro. Big liberal senator thinks it's more important because it was a Negro."

"We're pointing out realities——" Hugh said.

"Well, I don't know what the hell you're either one saying. I should have chosen my victim more carefully? If I shot Hawk Williams, it was because he was a son-of-a-bitch. And I didn't give a good damn about whether he was pink, blue, black or white. But his color makes a difference to you, and to all the others standing out there on the outside looking in."

Phil suddenly wished that he could forget he was a senator. He wished that he had no more responsibility than Clay. Then, by some unexplained paradox, he felt this could make him more responsible as an individual.

"Now let's not blow this up into more than it is," Hugh was saying. "Hawk Williams isn't the first bastard to be shot in a fight; reckon he won't be the last."

"A fight?" Clay asked. "Did we fight?"

"Sounds like it to me." Hugh drained his Coke and set the bottle on the floor. "I better tell you, since you won't see a psychiatrist, plead any temporary blackout——"

Clay gave a mocking laugh. "Not likely!"

"Then that's going to be our case: you shot in self-defense."

"But Hawk didn't even have a gun."

"He had that walking stick. And every man in this county, if it comes to a jury, knows how quick old Hawk could put out a steer's eye or break a bone with that locust stick. They know he was a bad Nigra." Hugh spoke with lazy authority. They were quiet a moment, then he asked, abruptly, "Now! You want me to be your lawyer or do you want to bring in some high-powered outsider?"

Clay and Phil glanced at each other. "You stick with it," Clay said.

Hugh grinned at him. "Well, O.K., fellow. Just want to set the record straight."

"And for that record," Phil said, "what does the sheriff say about Clay's gun matching the fatal——"

"Why the sheriff hasn't mentioned it, Senator," Hugh interrupted. "We oughta know something by Monday."

"Hell, we ought to know everything Monday. Now"—Clay resumed his pacing—"you know anything about a new witness, Mr. Attorney?"

The lawyer's eyes blinked slowly. "New witness?"

"Maybe you'd better get up off your big soft sofa there and circulate around," Clay said. "I've been waiting for you to mention it."

"Mention what?"

"Kin heard something at work today about a new witness that would change the whole case."

"A feller can hear anything." Hugh leaned back. "I'll check it out."

"You do that," Clay said. "You check it out damned quick."

"Think we can keep this from being blown up into a big national story?" Phil asked.

"We can try, Mr. Senator." Hugh winked at him, trying to recapture his self-confidence, but Clay's mention of new information seemed to have disturbed him. He joked weakly, "You hate to be roasted for a goose when you're only a sitting duck, Phil?"

"Nobody likes to wash his whole career down the drain," Phil said.

Hugh nodded. "One suggestion, Phil: come next election, when you make the race for Senate on your own, you get used to squaring up to the facts. Choose between Mister Right and Mister Possible."

Phil turned in surprise. "Maybe——"

"No maybe about it. First law of survival." Hugh spoke with startling decisiveness. He heaved himself up from the sofa. "I just can't figure out where Flora May got to. Wanted her to meet you, Phil."

"Maybe next time." Phil stood up.

"Maybe out to the club buffet tomorrow night,'" Hugh said.

"Why, yes. Word-of-mouth circulates by jet here, doesn't it?"

Hugh nodded. "Just heard Miles Austin, when he was starting out on his golf game, say that girl of his was bringing you."

"I guess so," Phil said.

"That Sherry"—the lawyer winked at him as if they had a private understanding—"she's stacked all right. They didn't skimp on a thing when they put her together."

"While all you gentlemen are there at your club"—Clay's voice was heavily sarcastic—"I hope you won't forget you have important business Monday morning——"

"Cousin Clay," Hugh said, "half of Monday morning's business is settled Saturday and Sunday night at that club."

"You and your penny-ante wheeling-dealing!" Clay muttered, turning away toward the picture window and its little hurricane lamp.

"You know," Hugh Moore said to Phil, "when our folks used to live out on Thickety Creek, everyone joined the church and made contacts, friends, prospects. Now the country club's taken that place around here."

"Lord, Hugh," Clay said, "you were jerked up a shirttail boy in the country, and ever since they threw you and roped you and wrestled some shoes onto you, you've been in this little flea-bitten burg. Last thing you needed was a *country* club!"

"Maybe so. But like my grandma Dolly Moore used to say, there's lots of ways to kill a cat besides choking it on hot butter. Lawyers got a lot of cats to choke, Clay."

"Well, before you choke in your own hot butter, you check out this new witness." Clay frowned. "I hope to God he knows something that's true."

After they had left and were driving out of town, Clay broke the silence. "How'd a pompous fool like that get in the family anyway?"

Phil didn't answer. He was pondering one of the oldest gaps in politics: between his constituents and his colleagues, between a full commitment to office and considerations of re-election. They rode in silence until Phil turned into his mother's driveway. He parked beside Clay's low-slung sports car.

"Looks as if we'll just have to sweat it out for a little while, Clay," Phil said. "Think you can make it?"

"I'd rather bust rock all day under a hot sun. But I can do it. Maybe I can even do it well." He had walked over to his own car, and was patting one shiny fender. "I can sure as hell give it a try. Tonight at Ivy's dinner I'm going to get along with every one of them. I'll take their bossing or their pity or their remembering—and I'll keep my temper. I will! Or there's not a jack pine in Georgia and that's a turpentine state, so help me God."

When the family came to the long buffet, Ivy and Naomi stood by to help with the serving. Ivy had put on a grey silk dress with a small silver fleur-de-lis pin on the collar, and Naomi's small dark face was less serious than usual. It gleamed with satisfaction. As the family surveyed the platters and bowls and serving dishes heaped with steaming food, they realized what their sister had done.

"Ivy," Frone said, "it's been years since I've had corn pudding!" Her severe face softened as she dipped a serving spoon into the luscious golden crust. "Do you remember how Papa always called corn old two-in-a-hill? How he liked corn and hot biscuits for breakfast?"

"Mama was speaking about that just this afternoon," Ivy said.

"Mama!" Frone interrupted. "What would Mama know about it? She wasn't making the biscuits, fixing the corn, grinding the coffee, building the fires. That was you and me."

"I guess there was always so much to be done," Phoebe said.

Kin had taken a helping from one of the long casseroles. "Sweet potatoes." He looked gratefully at Ivy. "You never forgot."

He had put on his black suit, the one he used for every funeral and wedding and Christmas dinner. He had stopped at the barbershop that afternoon and the fresh shave and cut (leaving a pale rim between his hair and sun-bronzed neck, a rim that matched the spreading bald spot on top) made his face appear open and innocent and vulnerable. He was wearing a new shirt. Only his hands —immense, rough, stained, with square, broken nails—had not been adjusted to this occasion. "I was always sort of partial to sweet potatoes," he said.

Ivy smiled at him.

"I recollect watching Aunt Tildy bake herself a sweet potato on the hearth. She'd lift it out of the coals so carefully, blow the ashes away, roll it back and forth in her hands. 'Cooly, cooly, cooly,' she'd croon while she was rolling it. And then she'd split it open and put a big chunk of fresh butter right in the middle. That was good eating."

"Selfish old woman, living off of Papa," Frone said.

Kin served his plate from the orange mound of potato.

Phoebe, plump like Mama but wearing a tight girdle as Mama never had done, and a flowered dress with gathered skirt that was too youthful for her matronly figure, looked at Ivy and smiled. At her round neckline she wore an antique lavalier that Rutledge's mother had given her on her twenty-fifth wedding anniversary. It suddenly occurred to Ivy to wonder if Phoebe had a single memento of Mama's, a single object from her own mountain family, in that great old house full of antiques in the Lowlands.

"I know the apples are for me, Ivy," Phoebe said, lifting the silver spoon carefully from the thick juice and tender fruit. "Smelling these apples takes me back to those long afternoons we spent slicing apples to dry on the scaffolding in our back yard. It seems hard to believe now that we spread four or five bushels out to the sun——"

"Four or five?" Frone said. "More like eight or ten bushels. We picked them up till my back was bent so crooked I felt like I never would stand straight again."

"And didn't they smell good when they were dried and we stuffed them in white sacks to hang from the rafters and use during the winter?" Ivy asked. "They were tough and stretchy as leather before we'd soak them overnight and cook them on a cold, snowy day!"

"We called it 'fruit,'" Clay said. "I don't know what the hell we thought peaches or bananas or oranges were, but apples were sure the fruit as far as we were concerned."

Kin nodded. "The hired hands used to say they liked Mama's fruit."

"And pork was meat," Clay went on. He stopped in front of the great crown roast of pork that stood on Ivy's big silver platter. It glistened with beads of juice, rich and succulent, its outer skin baked to a crisp bronze, and heaped in the center was moist, carefully seasoned dressing.

They looked at the splendid roast and remembered all the autumns of their childhood when the first cold snap had come and Mama said, "It's hog-killing time," and they took off days to butcher, dress, cut up, preserve, cure and prepare the porkers they had fattened through the year past. Hard, messy work it had been, from the first barrel of scalding water heated over an improvised stone fireplace in the back yard to the final rendering of the last drop of lard into storage crocks and cans. They ground out pyramids of sausage and seasoned it with sage from Mama's garden and stuffed it into the larger entrails they had carefully washed and cleaned. They made headcheese. They scraped the feet until they were pink and dainty and would cook to a sweet gelantinous mass. As Mama said proudly, they wasted nothing but the pig's tail and its squeal. And they ate heartily of the sweet, savory, fresh meat. They enjoyed crisp slices of ham or shoulder with platters of eggs for breakfast, liver or sausage for midday dinner and spareribs or loin baked for supper. It was rich, heavy food, but they did heavy work and the feasting lasted only a brief time.

Clay laid tender slices of meat and helpings of dressing on each plate and, as he did, he laughed. "I was thinking of that time when old Lazarus Shook decided he'd sell some beef to make a little cash, but all he had was one scrawny bull calf. So he butchered it and was selling meat in town when one man began to suspect it wasn't regular beef and he asked, 'What is this, anyway: a steer, or veal, or cow, or what?' And Lazarus rolled his eyes and answered, 'It was just a little innocent male brute.'"

"Law me!" Kin laughed aloud with the others.

They sat at the table and pealed forth laughter as they remembered bearded old Lazarus Shook, who lived beside the road on Thickety Creek. During the summertime his bare feet, propped up on the railing of his porch, shone like pale tender mushrooms never exposed to sunlight.

Phoebe patted at her eyes, her hair, and as they quieted, they became aware that no one was eating. "Should we have a blessing?" Ivy asked.

Then they knew that this was why they had waited. Mama's training, like the rings in a tree trunk marking the seasons of growth, might be covered over, but it was never quite eradicated. They were together again and old habits asserted themselves.

Self-consciously they bowed their heads for Phoebe's formal Episcopalian grace.

"Well, I guess that does the job, Pheeb," Clay said, when they had begun to eat, "but it's sure not any of the blessings I ever remember hearing on Thickety."

"A mite shorter." Kin winked.

They all began to smile again, each indulging his own private recollection of some special instance when a visiting minister or self-infatuated elder of the community used up large hunks of Sunday afternoons and other middays rendering oratorical thanks and blessings.

Phil alone was unable to enter fully into this merging of memory and the present. After the differences that had flared between them only a short while before, he wondered at their unity now. He had had little experience with the varied and shifting currents of a large family's life. Their angers could lash out and wound, and yet within a brief time their sympathies and affections would be protecting each other from outside assault. Their alliances altered, grew and waned in intensity, but their over-all allegiance to each other remained. And Ivy had used their common memory of big meals together to remind them of the old strong bonds. (Actually, Phil thought, it's like being part of the Senate. "We slash each other's arguments to bloody bits," Senator Howard told him once, "but we never cut each other's throats.")

"And Phil," Ivy was saying, "I made the green salad especially for you."

"An improvement over what I had last week at this time," he said.

Phoebe took another biscuit from the tray Naomi was passing. "What sort of food did you have over there in the jungle?"

Phil laughed. "It wasn't *all* jungle. But in this particular instance, our committee was invited back into the interior to have a meal with some native leaders. The other two senators were so tired after all our traveling that they pulled seniority on me and I was elected to do the dining honors. One of our government officials went along. After we arrived at the feast, I was seated at the head of the circle and passed the main delicacy. They had killed a goat in celebration of our arrival and I was to be favored with the eyes and head."

"Ugh!" Clay clutched his stomach. Frone and Ivy smiled, remembering how squeamish big swaggering Clay had always been about his food. "What did you do?"

"I remembered the honor of our country and gulped the best I could."

"Damn if you don't deserve the Purple Heart," Clay said. "Goat's eyes!"

"That was a bad moment." Phil grinned. Then he said, "There were worse ones though: seeing scrawny legs and bloated stomachs and cavernous eyes of half-starved people."

"Poor devils!" Clay said. His face was troubled and concerned.

"I never could stand to think of anything being hungry," Frone said. "Back on Thickety Creek I used to slip extra feed to the cows and horses."

Ivy looked at Phil. "You may find your family has all sorts of shortcomings," she said, "but one thing we're not. We're not indifferent."

"No," Phil said. "I can vouch for that."

Kin swallowed a bite and leaned forward in his chair. "I remember back during the depression, when we had that national relief program, one old man—he used to work with me sometimes in the woods—got a bag of groceries each week. One time there were a couple of grapefuit in with the other supplies. 'My woman,' he told me next day, 'boiled them things for three hours and they never did get fit to eat!' "

Phil laughed. They always had a story, some tale for every eventuality. "I guess some of our mistakes abroad today have been as foolish." The thought sobered him.

"Maybe foolishness isn't the greatest sin," Ivy said. "People have to make mistakes, they have to boil a grapefruit now and then, to learn, to change."

They helped themselves to seconds, enjoying the plain old familiar food of their childhood, all except Clay. He toyed with what he had taken on his plate, ate a few bits of the roast with a great flourish.

"Mr. Clay, let me help you to some more of that nice fluffy rice——"

"No, Naomi, thanks," he said. "I'll be around for more in a little while." But his hand stole to the bulge where his bottle rested in his right rear pocket. He was fooling no one. "If there's one damn thing I like, it's a bountiful meal. I've always admired folks who were good livers."

"That's the Thurston in you," Frone said. "Papa always loved to have bighearted people with big appetites around him. That's why he never liked Thickety Creek: he knew we'd never get ahead there. I can't see why Mama wanted that old farm anyway."

"It had been her grandpa Moore's——" Kin began.

"And because it was her grandpa's, I suppose that paved it in gold and fenced it in pearls! Well, if I'd been in Mama's shoes I'd have been a little more worried about whether or not my children were working their guts out on that mountain land."

"Let's charge that account to the dust and let the rain settle it," Ivy said.

Frone looked at her. "That was Papa's saying."

"Yes," Ivy agreed. "I remember he told us that once when we children got in a fight over which of us cost the most. Papa had paid the doctor five dollars when both Kin and Clay were born——"

"Well, I bet you one thing: you and I lost that fight," Frone interrupted. "Old Tildy brought us and she didn't charge anything but board and room, although counting all the bellyaching and bossing she did that was a God's plenty."

"The thing I remember best about our farm was Papa's barn . . ." Clay began, then hesitated. "Poor old Papa."

Naomi brought in a punch bowl and cups and Ivy served them delicate boiled custard topped with whipped cream and a sprinkle of nutmeg. There were also wedges of coconut cake, light and rich with the moisture of freshly grated coconut between each layer.

"Ivy, Papa would have traded his interest in heaven for a piece of cake like this," Frone said.

"We always wanted custard at Christmas," Phoebe said.

"Hell," Clay vowed, "when I come to think of it, I wouldn't take a million dollars for my past. And," he added, "I wouldn't give ten cents for my future."

"You know," Ivy said thoughtfully, "I believe it was one of the prettiest country places I ever saw in my life, our farm there on Thickety." She looked at her son and leaned forward eagerly in explanation, "Not that it was so grand or expensive, Phil, but it was a spacious, simple home and it was surrounded by a magnificent sweep of mountains. It was a rarely wonderful place to grow up."

"It was a narrow-minded little valley," Frone contradicted flatly, "shut off from the rest of the world——"

"It *was* the world," Ivy murmured.

"——and we had a big fine house we couldn't live up to," Frone concluded.

They ate silently for a brief space. The poles of their experience, in the same place with the same resources, had been suddenly defined: the pettiness and the majesty, the bitterness of unfulfillment at evening and the wonder of nameless joy encountered at daybreak, Had the mountain heights surrounding them, the Devil's Brow and all the other saddles and ledges, been oppressive barriers imprisoning them from life, or had they been pinnacles reaching up into a clearer atmosphere, challenging an experience more unique than was possible for those who lived on lower levels?

Their silence was broken by the sound of a motor in the driveway and the sharp tattoo of three taps on an automobile horn. Phil stood hastily, excused himself and strode from the room.

When he had gone, Clay leaned forward on the table and shook his head gently. "Lord, I'll never forget . . ." he began.

And Kin was asking no one in particular, "Say, do you remember the time . . ."

They were for an interval once more on the land, a unit together, the oldest unit in the world: a family.

"Not a million bucks for yesterday," Clay repeated absently, sadly. "Not a thin dime for tomorrow."

CHAPTER 4

Yesterday

T HEY CAME to the farm in the spring of the year during the first decade of a new century. A freshness of season rode on the wind.

The earth was spongy from winter's rains and snows. Willow trees were tinged with green as delicate as lace mantillas. Every watercourse—rivulets from springs high up in the hidden hills and hollows, Thickety Creek itself and the broad river beyond—rushed full and clear and cold between its banks. Moss on boulders and on fallen giants of slowly rotting trees was thick and lustrous as deep-piled fur. Early crows called in the stillness of high wild places and mourning doves were plaintive in open meadows and wood lots. Everything seemed new and beginning again, fresh as daybreak. It was a good time to leave old half-failures and doubts buried under rotting sawdust piles. It was time to face the first planting in other fields, acres of a family's own possessing.

"Now I tell you girls," their father said the first morning after they arrived, as they stood looking up at the waiting woods and un-pruned orchard, and over the fields and stream and pasture, "it makes your papa feel right gaily to know what we can make out of

this old place. Why, I wouldn't be a-tall surprised if this old lumberman didn't turn out to be the master farmer in Nantahala County!"

"You will, Papa, you will!" they shouted with confidence, with
eagerness for this new domain that was theirs to explore and know.

"I told you you'd like Grandpa's place, once you came here."
Martha beamed proudly at her husband.

"But it's not Grandpa's place any more." He frowned briefly. "It's
the Thurstons' place."

"Why yes, Tom——"

"Well, skip-to-my-Lou-my-darling, let's all get to our chores,
then," he said, making a little dance step. "You'll all have to move
lively if you're going to keep in sight of this man's tracks!"

Acquiring the farm had not been easy, but even Martha's family
often underestimated her determination. She was short and slight
and soft-looking with wavy brown hair drawn in a loose knot at the
nape of her neck and small brown eyes that seemed especially dark
in contrast to her white skin. Strong sunshine gave her sick headache.

She had lost two babies before Frone was born and there was
about her an air of frailty, of something less than enjoyment of ro-
bust health; friends and strangers alike sensed this immediately and
deferred to it. Not pretty—her nose was somewhat prominent, her
forehead was too low—Martha nevertheless received attention
wherever she went. She was educated (by her grandfather Jesse
Moore, by her mother Lydia McQueen, by such teachers as were
available when she was growing up, and by herself—her own reading, her own dedication) in a time and place when the majority were
scantily schooled. She was, from some source deep within herself,
gravely dignified and refined. These rare qualities, along with a
waist so small he could encircle it with his two long hands, had first
captivated high-spirited Tom Thurston. "My little Miss School-
teacher," he had called her when they were first married. And although he was adept at understanding many subtleties of character
in friends, he had not yet realized, or admitted to himself, that
Martha McQueen had not been as supple as she had appeared before
they were married, and Martha Thurston was as tough as a pine
knot when she chose to be. Martha had chosen Grandfather Moore's
place for her home.

She was sensible and reasonable and unswerving in that choice. Patiently she followed the labyrinths of family discussion and objections and agreements, the diversions into ancestral history and childhood memory, as her aunt and uncles tried to decide how they should meet the offer Martha and Tom made them.

Three of Jesse Moore's daughters, Lydia McQueen, and Annie Marie and Elizabeth, unmarried, had died before he did, leaving three heirs to his farm: Paul, who owned the mill and had lost one arm and whose wife was spoiled and fretful Dolly; Kate, who lived in another state and kept little contact with her family; and Robert. It was Martha's Uncle Robert who finally ended the family discussion and arrived at decision.

"I think we owe it to Lydia to let her daughter have this farm," he said quietly.

Greying hair gave him a distinguished appearance. Indeed, Robert Moore was distinguished. From Nantahala's county seat to the state capital, he was known as an incorruptible lawyer and a fearless one; fearless not only in his disregard of enemies—no matter their politics or power, if he felt he represented justice—but more subtle and more rare, fearless of poverty, too, his own poverty or his client's. He might have been one of the wealthiest men in the state if he had selected his cases by a shrewder measure. Instead, he lived on a modest income which scarcely reflected his ability or reputation, only his generosity. Since he had never married and his simple tastes influenced no one but himself, Robert Moore only smiled when his brother Paul, or his sister or a well-meaning friend sought to inspire him with his opportunity to make "a better living." And although Robert's family could not understand him, they respected him. They listened when he counseled. They listened when he spoke this time.

"Since none of us has special need or claim," he continued, "I think we ought to accept their offer and wish Martha and Tom well on these old acres."

The farm was a world of its own: part mountain, part valley, both wild and tame. On the summits of its three hundred acres there were pockets of virgin timber. Along its lower slopes were domesticated rows of apples, peaches, plums, cherries—the fruits Jesse

Moore had planted long years gone by. It was situated fair to the morning sun, yet winter snow lay deep and long in its upper coves.

In the middle of the farm sat the low frame house built a quarter-century before the Civil War. It's high loft had once served as church for Thickety Creek, when that community was only a handful of people. The boards of the house were weathered to the warm silver-grey of old pewter. Boxwoods grew at each corner and there were rose-of-Sharon, lilac and snowball bushes that bloomed in spring and summer.

Clustered behind the house and wearing the same soft patina of age were barn and smokehouse, outhouse, corncrib, woodshed. Nearer the house, at the base of a small rise, surrounded by a cluster of tall tulip poplars and beech trees and a thick growth of rhododendron bushes, sat the springhouse. Moss grew in its crevices and on its shaded roof shingles. Two stone steps surrounded by moss and ferns and tiny wild flowers led down to the natural bowl of water, scooped deep in the sparkling sand, chilled by the secret depths from which it flowed. The spring's overflow ran under a stone slab into the springhouse where a long wooden trough held crocks, pitchers of milk, pans of butter in the cool constant stream of water. The path which ran from the spring to the back door of the house was hard and smooth as concrete from the constant wear of generations.

There was more than land and buildings to the farm, however. There was a past, the presence of those who had turned this ground before, swept these floors and cleaned this springhouse during many yesterdays. Ivy had never before been part of this feeling of aged places, familiar paths. Her mother involved them in this sense of continuity and the children were captivated.

"This front room right here was where your grandmama and granddaddy stood up to be married," Mama said.

"During the silver war," little Phoebe said.

"The Civil War, stupid," Frone corrected.

"During the war." Mama nodded. "And in the kitchen here is where I first heard the name of Bludsoes. My grandma Moore had died and we came down from the mountain for her funeral and one of the Bludsoes brought a side of venison for us to eat. None of the others would take it, but my mama thanked the boy and brought the meat on in. I remember Aunt Dolly nearly had a fit."

"Who are Bludsoes, Mama?" Frone asked.

"Are they still here?" Ivy asked.

"I guess so, 'way up on the mountain above where I grew up," Mama said. "They stay to themselves. They're strange, dark-blooded people; nobody knows for sure where they came from. It's best to let them alone."

"Grandma didn't leave them alone," Ivy said.

Mama frowned. "Your grandma was different," she said. "Times change."

"I knew Granddaddy McQueen," Phoebe cried.

"I remember Granddaddy."

"Of course you do, foolish," Frone said. "He just died off last year."

"Frone," Mama corrected.

"Azalie says 'died off,'" Frone said.

"Azalie Shook's all right," Mama said, "but you can't pattern your talk after her. Remember, Frone. Yes, your granddaddy died, Phoebe, of that old stomach ailment he'd gotten while he was in that Civil War prison."

"And now"—Ivy fairly danced up and down—"tell us about the time Uncle Burn and Uncle Gib came home from the coal mines——"

"No more right now." Mama shook her head firmly. "Your papa's coming and you girls better carry in some stovewood so we can get supper started."

"Papa"—Ivy ran down the steps toward the tall figure, straight as a poplar as he turned in the gate—"did you know that a long time ago right here——"

"No, I wasn't right here a long time ago." He picked her up and swung her in the air and set her down. "But I'm here right now. That's what counts."

"But so much has happened——"

"Not what *has* happened, what's *going* to happen," Papa said. "That's what I want to know about!"

Ivy was puzzled and a little disappointed. Mama's way of look-ing and Papa's way of looking—why did they have to be at odds? She went out to the woodyard slowly, hearing Papa say to Mama behind her: "Guess what Cass Nelson was telling me down at the store just now? To his mind there's going to be big money in berries and fruits and all such. With tourists from down south and up north coming into the mountains, the hotels and boardinghouses will all be wanting fresh fruits and fancy foods——"

"Why that seems reasonable, Tom."

"And look here, Martha, with the head start of fruits we've got here on this place, Lord, in a few years we could be free and clear and sitting on easy street."

"Yes, Tom."

Ivy picked up the fresh-smelling sticks of green wood and laid them neatly along one arm. She didn't mind carrying in clean wood like this—oak or hickory or even pine although the resin sometimes made a sticky black spot on your arm—but she did hate old trashy wood that was buggy or had loose bark or was unevenly cut. She thought about others who might have carried wood from this self-same spot in years gone by. Were they like her in any way? she won-dered. "Your blood-kin," Mama would say, but that didn't always mean being alike. There were Mama's brothers, Uncle Burn and Uncle Gib, roaming the world, having high adventures, and Uncle Fayte, never going anywhere but teaching the school in Thickety Creek four months a year, living up under the Devil's Brow where Mama was raised: they were all brothers, the closest kin there is, and yet they were different, as different as eagles and crickets. Kin-ship didn't guarantee harmony. There was Mama, thinking back, remembering the good times, making links with yesterday. And there was Papa, forgetting yesterday, foretelling fortune, paving the way to tomorrow.

Papa's words created confidence just the way strong seeds blossomed into plants. He left no doubt that they could conquer these stubborn rocks and themselves and the hard world. "We'll build a master farm here, one that folks will stop to ask about years from now: 'Whose place is that? It's different from all the rest.' And some feller will say, 'The Thurstons'.'"

"But how will they know it's the Thurstons that are *you*, Papa?" the children insisted. "How will they know *we're* the ones?"

And he would answer wholeheartedly, "Because that feller will go on to say, 'Oh, it's that Tom Thurston has all those smart young ones—and they built it together!'"

With that vision they worked field or hill, garden or pasture, with all the strength and confidence of their being, rarely feeling the weariness of their muscles because they had a dream, they were "looking up." And this was the difference between Mama and Papa: for Mama they worked because they had to; knowing there were chores for everyone, they nonetheless grew bone-tired and sometimes resentful of the demands that seemed so ceaseless. For Papa they worked, but their spirits never flagged and the blisters on their hands, the aches in their legs were easily forgotten flaws of a long and major enterprise.

The move to Thickety Creek was more than a coming to new land and its past. It was acquisition of a family, an intricate design of aunts and uncles, cousins, grandparents, names and relationships made flesh and blood.

Frone and Ivy and Phoebe were eager and curious as small woods animals in these new surroundings and they sorted through their relatives with all the zest and skill of squirrels discovering mast for winter.

As they pulled and hauled at the Monday wash in the big black kettle over an open fire in the yard, they weighed and compared and chose favorites among these new-found kin.

"I like Aunt Dolly," Phoebe declared. "She always kisses me and sometimes she has peppermint——"

"Slobbering all over you. Always complaining," Frone said, stirring the boiling clothes. "It's Uncle Robert I like. He has such a nice sad smile."

"He treats us like grownups," Ivy said.

"None of this kissing and head-patting and 'How are these fine little folks today?' for Uncle Robert," Frone said.

"Next to Uncle Robert," Ivy cried, "I like Uncle Burn best."

"Uncle Gib is my choice," Frone stated.

"There's Uncle Fayte," Phoebe offered. "Mama says Uncle Fayte

would be content the rest of his life to sit up on that mountain before his fire and read his books."

"He'll be our teacher when school commences," Frone said.

"Oh, I'm wishing Grandpa and Grandma McQueen weren't dead
and gone." Phoebe went to get fresh wood for the fire. "I like having
kinfolks."

There were neighbors, too. Closest by—on the opposite side of
the creek and down the road—lived Lazarus and Ida Shook and
their three children, Vaughn and Verlee and Azalie, the youngest
girl Frone's age. Lazarus Shook was a dark-maned bearded man
who complained, as Aunt Tildy said, "of a weak back and a frail
heart, and he was born lazy to the bone and had a relapse." His wife,
Ida, was a big hearty woman with arms like fence posts and freckles
across her broad nose and over her arms. Her hair was reddish and
her bare legs were mottled down the front from the heat of many
open fires. She was generous and hard-working. Vaughn, their son,
had her features and freckled skin, but his father's slow ways. The
girls Verlee and Azalie were dark and thin and as work-hungry as
their mother.

Sickness and death, as well as work and make-believe, became
part of their lives. Late in the summer the girls overheard Mama and
Aunt Tildy and Ida Shook talking about Great-aunt Dolly Moore's
suffering.

"Vanity, vanity, all is vanity. Dolly never learned." Aunt Tildy
and Mama exchanged glances.

"You know what's a-happening to her?" Ida Shook asked, wiping
her broad forehead with the back of her hand. She had just come
from two nights and two days in neighborly service to Paul and Dolly
Moore. "She's plain rotting away inside!"

Her voice boomed easily into the kitchen where Frone and Ivy
and Phoebe were washing dinner dishes. They looked at one another with wide eyes and made no sound with pots or pans as they
strained to hear the grown-up talk.

"Oh, Ida!" Mama shuddered.

"It's gospel, Martha Thurston," Ida went on. "Rotting."

"Eh law," Aunt Tildy said, rubbing her gnarled fingers, "there's no need to be proud in the flesh. I've seen them borned and buried, raised up and brought low, and in the end the flesh was always a cheat and a deceiver."

"That's gospel true, Aunt Tildy," Ida Shook agreed.

In the kitchen Frone whispered to Ivy, "Well, she's carrying plenty of deceiver around on those big arms and legs of hers."

Ivy giggled. As she scrubbed the plates in her dishpan, she wondered about the proud flesh.

Aunt Dolly's flesh died slowly. There were terrible tales of her agony. Mama had morning-sickness again and was weak as dishwater and could not help out with the neighbors' nursing. Aunt Tildy hobbled down the last few days to brew the strongest herb teas she knew from the last roots she had dug on the mountains, but when Cass Nelson finally fetched Tildy home in his new buggy, she brought word of Dolly Moore's death.

The girls ran to tell Papa and Uncle Fayte, who were pruning apple trees up in the late autumn orchard. It had taken from summer until the threshold of winter for Aunt Dolly to die.

"How are my scholars today?" Uncle Fayte called out as soon as they came in sight. Through the thick-lensed glasses that were his special distinction he looked down at them from his perch high in an old apple tree, where he was sawing away a dead limb.

"Fine, Uncle Fatye," they panted. Then, in unison, so that neither one would have all the satisfaction of announcing important news, they said that Aunt Dolly had died.

Papa and Uncle Fayte climbed down from the trees. "You're a master hand to prune, Fayte," Papa said. "I'm much obliged to you for coming down here this cold weather and helping me out."

"Proud to do you a good turn, Tom," Fayte McQueen replied. He helped gather up saws and shears. "I always liked pruning, seeing a tree take the right shape and growth."

"We aim to make some money on fruit next summer," Papa said confidently. "Now why don't you come on down and take supper with us tonight?"

"Yes, yes," the girls begged.

"You could stay the night and go to the funeral with us."

But Uncle Fayte shook his head. "There will be people in plenty at Aunt Dolly's funeral. I'll remember her up on my mountain."

There were, indeed, people in plenty. Some came from town, friends of Dolly's children, Tim and Pru. There were those from over the county who had known the Moores since the earliest settlement and came to pay their respects to a family more than to an individual. There was all of Thickety Creek. Parents took their children. They let the children go up to the open casket and look on the face of the dead woman. None of the children made any sound or gesture. They were quiet and respectful and curious.

During the long sermon (and a short prayer by Uncle Robert) and the mournful music and finally the burial in the family plot, Frone and Ivy watched the woman named Pru and the big red-faced man named Tim as they sat by Great-uncle Paul. A little boy —he might have been the age of either Frone or Ivy, but he was the replica of his father in appearance—sat between Tim and Paul.

"That's Uncle Paul's grandson," Frone whispered. "I sat by him at the dinner table while you were with Mama."

"Oh." Mama had had to lie down just as dinner was beginning and Ivy had stayed with her to keep wet cloths on her forehead. "What's his name?"

"Hugh. Hugh Moore. He looks like a cry-baby face to me."

"The preacher's shoes squeak," Ivy said.

"There's Azalie over there on the other side of the room, trying to be solemn," Frone said.

When they found a dead bird under the lilac bush the following week, Frone and Ivy and Azalie, who had come to spend the day with them, gave it a proper burial. Frone made up a sermon and Azalie sang "In the Sweet By-and-By," in a high trembling voice, while Ivy gouged a shallow grave out of the frozen ground and spoke the prayer. The ceremony was an imitation of the one they had witnessed a few days before. When it was finished, they went on to something else.

"Race you up and over the orchard wall yonder," Azalie challenged.

"Watch out the blackberry vines," Ivy said. "Papa told us to be careful of all the fruits around the place."

"Whoever heard of watching out for blackberry vines?" Azalie's big round brown eyes shone with derision.

"We're going to sell fruits in town in the summer to big hotels and make money."

"Well, if there's money in blackberries, Pa's found his fortune." Azalie scratched her heel and grinned. "With all the brier patches we've got, I reckon the Astors better get ready to move over."

Azalie had cast just enough doubt in their minds to make the girls work harder than they had ever thought possible. Late in June early apples began to ripen, crisp and tart and ready to dissolve to tender sauce when they were hot through, and by the first week in July vines hung heavy with blackberries as sweet as sun and dew could make them. They picked, sorted, heaped up baskets of the early apples. Then, during one big day's push, they gathered pails full of blackberries, enough to fill out the wagon with a full load of fruit. Their arms and legs were torn by briers, reddened by chiggers and gnats; and in spite of the big hats the girls wore, their faces shone with sunburn as they picked juicy thumb-sized berries from shaded spots around the spring, along the creek bank, beside the old stone wall, and found smaller ones on the sides of hills and in the open pastures. They loaded up the wagon that night, covering the buckets of berries with cloths, so that Papa could get an early start in to town the next morning. He was taking Vaughn Shook along to help him.

They were all up in the dim grey dawn to wave good-by and call good luck and wonder at what the day might bring forth. "I hope I can have a new dress," Phoebe whispered to Ivy, but none of the rest of them dared say what they hoped.

The day's waiting seemed endless. Early in the twilight the wagon (Did it look lopsided?) came into view. The girls saw red-headed lanky Vaughn hunched on the wagon seat, and Papa, very erect, very square in the jaw, holding the lines while the mules kept to a brisk trot. They knew that something had happened. The children slowed to a walk before they came up to the wagon where Papa had brought it to a halt in the barnyard.

"You want I should put your team up for you, Mr. Thurston?" Vaughn asked in a voice that was barely audible.

"That would oblige me very much," Papa answered, as formal as his Sunday celluloid collar, "if you think you can see the job through."

"No, Mr. Thurston . . . I mean, yes, Mr. Thurston, I can see it through."

"And if you please, leave this wagon standing right here."

"Sure, Mr. Thurston."

All dressed up in his black town suit, now dusty and disheveled, Papa strode across the yard, but he did not go into the house. He stopped by the woodyard near the back door and laid his hand on the double-bitted axe lodged in a block of unsplit stovewood. He jerked it with such force that when it came loose, his arm flew back and upset his balance. He recovered and strode back toward the wagon. The children stared.

Now that the team was no longer hitched to the wagon, it listed crazily to one side. With his jaw set like Gibralter and fury in his eyes, Papa planted his feet squarely beside the wagon, lifted the axe over his shoulder and struck a merciless blow. Then he slashed again and again.

The flying splinters, the gaping holes in the wagonbed, the flashing axe, stunned the children. "Papa! What's happened, Papa?" Frone cried as they watched him attack the wagon.

Vaughn Shook came back from the barn and fled across the road toward home. Finally Papa threw down the big axe. The wagon was a shambles. Then the children followed Papa across the yard, careful at first to stay behind him and then to run ahead and open the kitchen screen and stand aside as he entered.

"Well, Tom, how did you make out?" Mama asked. She stood at the stove, her back to him. "We waited supper for you." She wiped her arm across her pale forehead, apparently oblivious to his mood or countenance until he began to speak.

"I've fixed that damn homemade wagon. At least I'll never make a fool out of myself in that way again." He pulled off his coat and hung it across the back of a chair.

"Tom, what's happened?" Mama stood with a spoon poised in one hand.

"Peddlers," he said. "That's what we were: peddlers!"

"Well, now, selling food you've grown is honorable work," Mama said briskly. "Nobody need be ashamed——"

"I *was* ashamed," Papa shouted. The children melted back into the shadows. "Don't give me any self-righteous Moore-McQueen talk about honor and honesty and heaven-is-the-goal-of-hell."

Mama's mouth tightened.

He began to roll up the sleeves of his white shirt and Ivy saw that his hands—long, fine hands which were his pride—and the cuffs of his new shirt were stained with purple blotches of berry juice. "In our damned ignorance——"

"Tom! The children."

"The children aren't beeswax, they won't melt at a little heat. In my infernal ignorance I reckon I thought the storekeepers would welcome me and my berries like Gabriel on Judgment Day."

"And didn't they?"

"Those griping weasel-faced city men! Two of them bought a bushel of apples and a gallon of berries apiece, and you'd a-thought it was charity they were handing out. The others . . ." He looked forlornly at his wife.

Martha sat down heavily in one of the chairs by the table. She still held a long cooking spoon in one hand. "Did you have any luck at all, Tom?" she asked wearily.

"Luck?" Papa had finished rolling up his sleeves and he ran both hands through his hair. "If I'd spent the last week walking under ladders, carrying hoes into this house, listening to a chorus of screech owls under our windows, I couldn't have conjured up the luck I had today."

"Something else happened?"

"Something else? Everything else. When we crossed the railroad tracks to sell to some of the Negro citizenry of town, that fool Vaughn asked if we were going to sell to them. 'Son,' I told him, 'I'm going to sell to green money, and I don't care whether the hand that's passing it is black or red, pink or white.' He buttoned up his mouth at that."

"And then?"

"I left him holding the team beside the tracks while I went up to a store on the hill. I'd no more than got to the top when I heard a freight whistle blowing and all hell broke loose. I looked down to the street. There was my team running away with the wagon bouncing along behind."

"Oh, no!" Martha's eyes were wide.

"Oh, yes! I don't know which that train scared worst, the mules or that fool Vaughn. They bolted down the street, up an alley and out of sight. Somebody caught the team. I found them after a while. There were fifteen or more bushels of prime apples, twelve or fifteen gallons of good old mushy ripe blackberries—by God, it seemed like twelve or fifteen *barrels*—all overturned and smashed and running together on that wagon bed."

Martha's voice was muffled. "And what did you do then, Tom? You never did have a feel for handling fruit."

He held out his hands. They were shriveled and purple from the stain of berry juice. "Well, I sure as hell got the feel today," he said.

They were all quiet. Only the fire in the stove made a small rustling as they sat and looked at one another.

"I gave it all away," Papa finally finished. "Every colored family in town is feasting on blackberry cobbler tonight!" He poured water from the bucket on the shelf into the granite washbasin, and lathered his hands with soap. "A man in my position selling fruit," he muttered.

"And what is your position, Tom?" Mama asked. There was an undercurrent of laughter in her voice.

"That's what I've been studying about all the way home!" Papa answered. "And I can tell you one thing: I'm no dirt farmer, raising a dib of this and a dust of that. I won't measure out my life in measly cups and quarts. I want what can be measured large. The only farming fit for a man is stock raising."

"Stock raising?" Mama echoed. The children paused carrying food from stove to table.

"I'm going to raise cattle. My mind's set on it, Martha. I'm going to build the damnedest barn in this country, the kind they have up north, fit for thoroughbreds."

"But, Tom——"

"And while I'm about it, I may just turn this house into a respectable dwelling."

"It's respectable enough now," Mama protested.

"It's not the *best*," Papa said. He took down the towel and dried his hands. "Don't you see, Martha, this could be the finest livestock farm in the county? We can plant all the fields to corn and hay, clear more pasture up there where it's good strong mountain land, build a stout barn. Fat and warm, that's the way I want everything."

"I don't know, Tom, I don't know," Martha murmured.

"Don't you fret yourself, Martha girl," Papa hung the towel on its rack. "We're going to be *farmers*. You get that boy baby here fine and healthy and leave the cattle growing to a man's man." The anger and dejection that he had brought from town were gone. His spirits were mounting, boosted by his own words. "Your old papa knows the lick it's done by, children," he said. "We'll make a barn and house here that this whole valley can boast of." He pulled his chair up to the table and Frone brought a hot plate from the warmer in the stove and set it in front of him. Papa dipped chicken gravy onto his rice. "We have to look up," he said.

When no one answered, Mama spoke. "Well, in a few minutes whenever you've finished supper, you might have to look somewhere else."

Papa's fork rattled on the plate. "As soon as you've eaten," Mama went on, "you girls can go over to Azalie's and spend the night with her. And you can tell their mama to come over here whenever she's ready." She planted the palms of both hands flat on the table and lifted herself up.

Ivy never forgot that the night Papa announced he would build the big house and barn was also the night Clay was born.

Papa was jubilant when the children came home the next afternoon. He met them in the yard. "You girls guess, and a dime to the one who wins. What came to our house last night?"

"A new baby," Phoebe said before he could finish.

"You're right, Phoebe Thurston, but what kind of a baby? Just tell me that."

"A boy," Frone said.

"A great big fine baby boy! Yes siree. Here's a dime for you, Frone——"

"I don't want it."

"Of course you want ten cents to buy a treat at Nelson's store."

"No." Frone shook her head stubbornly. "I don't want any dime for a baby boy."

Then Papa tossed Phoebe the dime, and she put it in her pocket. "Now come on in and look at your brother."

They tiptoed into the bedroom. The well-known room seemed to have been transformed into an unfamiliar chamber by the event that had taken place there during the night. The children saw the same old fireplace (littered with papers and ashes and ends of wood from the last fire, Ivy noticed, wishing it were clean) and the same little windows and the washstand with its mottled marble top and its white ironstone bowl and pitcher and Mama's hairbrush and comb (from which loose wisps of hair still hung where Mama had dressed her long heavy hair into two tight braids): the furniture was all the same and yet everything was different. During the dark quiet hours of night turning to morning, some strange ancient experience had taken place here. They did not know for sure whether it was something fearful or joyous, something to be welcomed or dreaded when it came into their own lives. They felt another presence, sensed a rearrangement of patterns in their living, and with children's conservatism they resented the intrusion, the change, and with children's resiliency they welcomed the newness, the change.

Mama seemed small in the big brass bed with her hair unbraided now and scattered all over the pillows. Her eyes looked out of deep hollows, glazed and tired. The room was sweet with the smell of soap and water, the freshly scrubbed floor and clean sheets.

Ida Shook took up the bundle on the bed beside Mama and folded back an edge of blanket. The girls' first impression was of wrinkled red flesh, a mass of hair and two fists beating the air. There was sound to match the furious fists—crying that was incredibly loud for such a small creature.

"You tell them, boy," Papa said, touching one tiny hand. "Don't you let them overlook you. . . . Say, is he all right?"

"Course he's all right," Ida said. She laid the baby back on the bed. "He'll quieten down once her milk comes."

"It had its little eyes screwed shut," Phoebe said to Frone and Ivy.

"What will we call him?" Frone asked.

Papa pointed toward the bed. "Ask your mama there. She does all the naming."

"His name is Henry Clay," Mama said slowly, "after his grandfather. We'll call him Clay. Clay Thurston."

"You're sure that's what you want, Martha?" Papa asked her.

"Yes," she answered.

"Paw'll be mighty pleased, Martha," he said.

"I always did like your father, Tom."

"Well, now, a feller like this one here"—Papa was listening to the loud crying still coming from the bed—"it's plain to see he's going to have big ideas about things. This old man is going to have to step lively to keep up with him. And when he gets to be a little bigger he can be a help with the stock——"

"Well, before you set him to driving the cows, reckon you better let his mama get some rest," Ida Shook said.

The birth of a son restored any remnants of Tom Thurston's pride that were still shattered from his fruit-selling experience. His ambition grew. During the weeks and months that followed he was busy, preoccupied, happier than his family had ever seen him before. He spent long days in town, went over every foot and inch of the farm "with a fine-tooth comb," Mama said. He poured over strange unwieldy blueprints and drawings at night, wrote laborious letters and received lengthy answers from livestock growers and dealers in many parts of the country. He sang ditties and verses of old ballads as he pursued his work, unconsciously enlivening the house or any other spot where he might be. All the crops, except corn and hay and a little wheat and oats, were abandoned. He tied a big team of mules to over a hundred peach and apple trees and jerked them out of the ground by the roots. "We'll have to stack hay in the fields," he said, "and put corn wherever we can. But by next winter we'll have us a barn and all the space we need for good animals and their keep."

His plan was to trade off the timber on one of the back parts of the farm (a hillside and ravine of tall white pines) for dressed, cured lumber sufficient to build his barn and remodel the house to more ample proportions.

"That stand of pines—it's so beautiful . . ." Martha said the day he told her his plans, the first day she came out in the yard after Clay was born. It was time for the baby to nurse; her breasts felt tight and heavy and she was nervous to go back inside. But she paused to look up toward the hillside towering off to the east beyond the Upper Pasture.

"Yes siree," Papa said, "just like it was put there waiting for us to make use of it."

"I mean it's so fine *growing*," Mama explained.

"A prime stand of pine any way you look at it," Papa said. "But I believe in things doing people some good. Besides, we'll be killing two birds with one stone when we cut that because we'll make that hillside and ravine into pasture, too. It takes grass and clover for cattle and we'll have to use all we can get."

"But what about——" Mama began.

"I've got it all straighted out, Martha girl," he said happily. "Man in town Paw used to trade with, the one took my lumber when we were over in the Smokies, he's going to buy the pines, let me have my lumber to start building right away. That way, we won't need any sawmill, just a few good loggers—I'll get old Gunter and his son Leck to head them up—and before you know it, skip-to-my-Lou, you're going to have a barn big as any of those up in old Penn-syl-van-i-a."

"I hope we can afford to build it, Tom."

"We can't afford *not* to build it! That's why they're rich up there in Pennsylvania and New York and those Northern places; they look up, they build a good barn, and then they just naturally work to make a good farm to match it. That's why they get ahead."

"But everything all at once . . . it's such a big undertaking,

Tom. Why not build just the barn now, and then fix the house the way you want it later on?"

"No." He shook his head. "I won't have my stock living in finer quarters than my family."

"But we're comfortable——"

"Sure we're comfortable. No reason why we can't be proud, too."

Inside the house the baby was crying. Martha clutched Tom's arm, feeling the weakness of her legs, but also needing, from some deep inner rebellion and fear, to remind him of her frailty, her dependence on him. "Don't fail me, don't fail me," her gesture begged. And she might have added, had she known the words or even her own need, "Leave me just a bit of land and house without grandeur, without worry, without debt, and I can love you; we can raise our children in the old ways——"

"Oh, we'll have plenty for that little feller to take hold of one of these days," Tom went on. The plea of her little gesture for help was lost in his own need for some large success. Their hungers were of such different proportions that each found it difficult to understand what the other craved. He helped her through the door. "Thank you for bringing that boy, Martha."

"Did a son mean so much, Tom?"

He nodded. "I'm the proudest in the world."

All the family was proud of Clay. The little girls rushed to be the first to see him awake each morning. They argued over which one should bathe him. And as he began to assume more human shape, they gazed at him and studied every feature, making careful comparisons that incorporated him into the family.

"He's got Papa's hair."

"It's curly, all right, but seems like the color is more Uncle Burn's."

"Babies' hair always gets darker."

"And it's Mama's nose."

"Maybe. There's a trace of——"

"Oh, its little nose isn't Mama's at all. It's just Uncle Fayte to a T."

"Just so it didn't get the Thurston feet."

And once again Ivy felt the links of a long chain reaching back and forward, holding them all—visible and invisible—together.

Uncle Burn and Gib came to live with them and help Papa build the grand house and barn. Old man Gunter and his boy Leck came up the valley to cut logs and snake them down the mountain-sides. School term came and went and Uncle Fayte passed the girls into the next grade. Seasons flourished and waned in the Lower Meadow where joe-pye weed bloomed lavender in fall and caught winter's snow in delicate traceries on its brown stalks, in the Sandy Field where corn matured and was harvested, and in the forest of virgin pine where the Gunters were laying on their axes with a heavy hand.

It seemed to Ivy no time at all until she looked up at the ravine and hillside far above the house and found the sky empty of its towering pinetops. Green limbs that had mantled the earth in winter and bent under heavy burdens of snow were suddenly gone. Massive logs on wagons pulled by two and three teams rolled through the farm gate and down the road. Ravine and hillsides showed more and more barren except for ragged stumps pockmarking the land. While Burn and Gib were tearing down the old barn and ripping the narrow front porch off the house, Tom Thurston decided to use dynamite to clear these fields quickly, once and for all, of the stubborn stumps.

And so it came about that the people of Thickety Creek grew more or less accustomed that spring to having the morning quiet or the afternoon's doze punctuated by blasts reverberating through the hills. If they looked up, they might see a cloud of dirt, leaves, twigs and bitter smoke catapulting into the air.

"Well, well"—Lazarus Shook wagged his big tousled head— "looks like Tom Thurston has set out to remake creation."

"Frone and Ivy say they're going to have a big fine barn and house to live in," Azalie reported for the seventeenth time.

"Pride goeth before a fall," their father reassured them hopefully. "They're trying to rise above their neighbors, the Thurstons are."

"Then why don't we all rise, too?" Vaughn asked. His father

caught him off guard with a slap that landed him against the wall.

"Already breeding discontent, disrespect of elders, this foolishness of Tom's," Lazarus Shook complained, and sat down in his rocker to watch for another blast across the road and up the mountain.

Papa was adding one big square room to the house downstairs, a full upstairs with gables facing in each direction and double gables toward the front along the big road and the end which faced down the valley. A regular "finishing" carpenter came to build the fancy gables, complete the rooms and the wide porch which ran all the way around the house. Another school season was ending its four months before this was done and each day, as the girls came up the road, they were overwhelmed when they saw the house taking shape. Tall and handsome with the pointed gables, broad and spacious with the additional room and porch on all sides, they could hardly recognize it as their home.

"It's the finest house in the valley," Ivy said as they walked from school.

"The valley? In the whole country!" Almost shyly Frone added, "Ivy, it could be an English country house like the ones in novels."

Frone had discovered the world of poetry and love stories. Her attention these days was only half on Thickety Creek. It ranged in English meadows, on estates of the peerage, where handsome men and winsome ladies lived dewy romances. It floated through drawing rooms in the gracious cities of the world, enjoying sweet encounters with learned gentlemen and gracious hostesses who loved her, who loved Frone Thurston for her wit and charm and grace and beauty. Her imagination was haunted by castles and battlefields, the cottages and moors of long, sad, romantic poems. Frone had found a secret life. She lived it, breathed it and, most wondrous of all, she had discovered she could create it through her own words, her own writing.

Once, as she read aloud one of the long tragic epics from an anthology Uncle Fayte had loaned her, Mama and Ivy found themselves crying at the sadness and beauty of it all. Their hands trembled as they shelled big ears of corn Papa would take to the grist mill the first rainy day. When Papa came in from work on the barn, he halted at sight of the tears. "What's wrong?" he asked. "What's happened?"

"Elaine is dead," Ivy sniffed, and her eyes filled again.

"Elaine?" Papa turned to Mama, subdued, his face grave. "Elaine? I hadn't heard of anybody on the creek dying."

"She was so fair," Ivy whispered forlornly.

"Somebody at school?" Papa inquired.

"It's a poem," Mama said.

"A poem?" Papa stared at them.

"Frone's been reading to us——"

"You mean"—Papa's face flushed—"all this sniffling is over something in a *book?*"

"One of the greatest poems——" Frone began.

"Almighty be! Sitting around crying over a pack of lies!" Papa's eyes flashed. "Why, I'd throw those books away and get to living myself instead of fretting about that Elaine what's-her-name."

And by the time Mama and the girls had finished laughing, there was no more room for tears.

One who shared Papa's low opinion of the literary life was Aunt Tildy. She followed Frone through each day, not on foot but with remarks, suggestions, advice.

"Eh law, straighten up your shoulders, girl. No need to go all knotted over even if you are getting your growth early."

Or, "Frone, I'd be much obliged if you could get your nose out of that book long enough to fetch a bucket of fresh water from the spring. This warm stuff has been standing in the house since daybreak; it's plumb brackish."

Or, "Frone, don't be absent-minded. Eh law, it's downright aggravating to be around somebody walking in a daydream."

Once Ivy overheard Aunt Tildy talking to Mama. "Law, Martha, you ought to pay some mind to that oldest girl. She's asking for disappointment."

"I hope not, Aunt Tildy, no more than most of us know."

"Folks got to live in this world. Can't make one of their own choosing to live in."

"Girls dream for a while, Aunt Tildy," Mama said.

Ivy thought about that conversation later, but there was little spare time for thinking during the months in which the house and barn were being finished. And when Tom Thurston decided to paint both of them, his extravagance became the topic of talk for miles around. "Paint's high as quinine," Lazarus Shook said, and Martha Thurston could not help resenting every drop of the precious liquid, for she knew that it had been bought by mortgaging their richest piece of creek-bottom land to Cass Nelson.

Both the house and barn grew white—dazzling, immaculate, conventional white—with a dark green trim. Their home seemed a mansion to Ivy now, a building worthy to match the mountains surrounding them. The barn was even more fantastic, looming between the old barnyard and the Lower Pasture. One night when Ivy could not sleep, she went to the bedroom window to see the splendor of full moonlight in the quiet night, and there—dominating the landscape, floating in unreality—was the barn. It might have been a great ship riding undulating waves of earth, moored by an unseen anchor. She wondered that Papa didn't put it to some greater purpose than housing cattle.

The last few weeks of work, after winter broke and spring rains let up, had been hard ones on the men. Papa and Uncle Burn and Uncle Gib worked hardest of all. They ate breakfast and supper by lamplight and were on the scaffolding at the barn from first daylight till the last streak of sunset faded.

"Eh law," Aunt Tildy sighed as she tried to follow their activities, "everybody living at a gallop."

"Not like the old days, Tildy," Tom Thurston answered. "Now a feller has to run to stand still." To Burn and Gib he said, as he had several times already, "He'll be arriving any day now. We've got to be ready."

"Who'll be arriving, Papa?" the girls cried.

But he would not answer them. "You'll see." He would only smile knowingly, proudly. "You'll see." His face was thin and seldom without lines of fatigue, for if he persuaded his men to extra effort, he drove himself to double labor. At breakfast he looked scarcely more rested than at supper. As his buildings grew larger, he grew leaner. Sometimes in the evenings or on Sundays he simply walked around the veranda and then went and sat in the barn enjoying the clean fragrance of new lumber and his plans for the bounty of cattle and feed that would soon fill these stalls and bins and runways.

"And that's for him." Tom gazed to the end of the corridor at the big stall surrounded by stout boards. "The big feller. The quality feller."

When the children were about to lose hope of learning the secret, Uncle Robert rode out from town and told Papa there was a shipment for him down at the railway station. "And you'd better get it soon," Uncle Robert warned, "or you might wind up having to build Nantahala County a new railway station."

Papa's excitement infected them all. When he left the next morning, while it was still dark, he brushed aside Martha's repeated warnings to be careful. "This old boy and me, we're going to have an understanding right from our first 'howdy.' He cost me a plumb legacy in cash; not likely I'll let him harm me or himself. Besides, we've got work ahead: to lift this whole valley up."

"But I've heard of so many men gored, disabled, even killed . . ." Mama said.

Then the girls knew what the surprise was: the pedigreed bull Papa had been talking about all winter.

While Papa was gone into town, Mama told them that he had bought a thoroughbred male brute by letter from a dealer in up-state New York. Uncle Robert had loaned him the money for its purchase. "If only your Papa could be satisfied once to make a small beginning," she said, biting her lip, thinking aloud. Then, ruefully, "If only your Papa could be satisfied!" And there was a wistful expression on her face.

"Menfolks!" Aunt Tildy snorted from the corner, peering at the new patch she was sewing on a faded threadbare shirt. "They've always got to be out resurrecting the world when they've got more problems at home than they can say grace over."

But when the cart Tom had hired—which was nothing in the world but a heavy mule-drawn pen on wheels—pulled into the yard just at nightfall, Aunt Tildy hobbled out on the porch while the others ran to meet it. Tom Thurston sprang down from his seat beside the owner of the wagon and held up his hand.

"Don't storm the gates, boys." He walked around to the pen and patted one side of the wooden enclosure. "Well, folks, here he is. Old Kingsridge Knight II."

Through the slats they could glimpse a massive head and shoulders and heaving black sides. Above all the commotion they could hear angry fearful panting and sharp snorts. A chain through the ring in the bull's nose was snubbed short and fastened to the side of the wagon. With little freedom to move, the powerful animal stood quietly enough, but Ivy crept closer to the front of the cage and peered up into the wild red-rimmed eyes and foam-flecked mouth and flaring nostrils. All the pent-up anger at the heart of the universe seemed concentrated in those fierce searching pupils peering out of their tiny slits. Ivy stepped back so quickly she stumbled and fell.

"Careful, girl." Papa helped her up just as Mama came out of the house.

"Frone! Ivy! Phoebe!" Mama's voice was sharp with annoyance. "Come inside right this minute."

"But, Martha," Tom began, "this is the feller that's going to send these girls through college."

"It's not proper for young ladies to be looking over male brutes."

Uncle Burn and Uncle Gib and the Gunters and the other men shuffled their feet self-consciously and their attention was suddenly engaged by some invisible substance in the distance. The girls walked slowly to their mother and entered the house. As the door slammed behind them, Ivy could see the men gathering closer around the wagon and Kingsridge Knight II. After a while the wagon rolled on up to the barn and Ivy heard the shouts and noise of unloading.

During the weekend people came from all of Thickety Creek, men who traded in livestock rode out from town, and farmers from throughout the western end of Nantahala County gathered to look at Kingsridge Knight II. Tom Thurston was in his element. He liked owning the best. He liked sharing his happiness with friends. He liked to be among people, swap judgments on cattle and horseflesh, politics and the general foolhardiness of mankind. Some of the men brought their wives, too, and the women admired Martha's spacious new home, gleaming with paint (the Nantahala White House, some called it), and surrounded by her luxuriant shrubs and roses, spring lilacs, summer hydrangeas, beds of lily of the valley, lavender (to dry and crush for sachets) and flamboyant prince's-feather. Among themselves, the men speculated on Tom's chances for success.

"Looks to me like old Tom's boring with a mighty big auger," Cass Nelson said on Sunday afternoon, remembering—even as his beady eyes surveyed the dimensions of the barn and the thoroughbred quality of the imported bull—the size of Thurston's bill at the Nelson General Store.

The other men who were there spat and nodded reflectively.

Martha's Uncle Robert came out from town later that afternoon. He went with Tom to inspect Kingsridge Knight II, and he agreed that this was a fine prime animal in every respect.

"All we need, here in these mountains, is some first-class stock," Tom said eagerly; "pure blood to give our old scrawny cattle quality."

"That's right." Robert Moore clasped his hands behind his back and stood for a moment as if he were in a courtroom instead of a barnyard. His face was troubled and he gazed at the ground intently. "Tom, have you ever thought some of your plans might be ahead of the times?"

"I don't follow you, Robert," Tom Thurston said. "You telling me something?"

"Maybe asking, not telling, Tom. Is the time ripe for raising prime stock in this hard mountain country?"

"How in God's name will we know if we don't try and——"

"Oh, it'll come someday." Robert Moore nodded emphatically. "And everybody will be better off when it does. But right now, it calls for such a heavy investment, before there's another purebred milch cow or beef steer in Nantahala County, and no first-rate veterinarian, and even grass seed for pasture is——"

"Hold on, hold on. You've already got me halfway to the poorhouse." Tom tried to laugh, but the lines were gathering in his face. "Look here, Robert, this could be bigger than any kind of farming ever done around here. It would bring Thickety Creek, Nantahala

County, more than money. We could take new pride in our land, in looking after our livestock. Why, folks around here don't know how to half take care of a cow or a horse. It would help this whole valley look up."

"I'm not arguing that, Tom," the older man said gently. He looked across the yard toward the little stream flowing in the distance and sighed. "It's no river-bottom farm, Tom. No big market handy. Caution: don't make too heavy an investment before you know the odds."

"I reckon neither me nor you are too clever at calculating odds." Tom smiled slowly. "I've never known you to shy away from risk, Robert."

"Maybe it's easier for a man that doesn't have a family."

Tom was plunging on. "You've never taken just the big lawsuits, the sure winners, the fat fees. Now I ask you, how does a man know he's alive if he doesn't play for the big stakes sometimes? How does he keep the juices running in his belly if he doesn't risk everything once in a while for something big, something beyond himself?"

Robert Moore did not answer. He looked at the woods and meadows and fields where he and Martha's mother had worked and played and grown up. There seemed to be nothing more to say just then.

The next morning before he went back to town he spoke briefly with Martha, out in the back yard where she had gone to feed table scraps to the chickens. He thought how neat she was, trim as one of her Dominecker hens. "Tom taught me something yesterday, Martha." He chose his words carefully. "There's something worse than failure, and that is not even trying."

She thought a second. "Well, Tom's turning mighty scholarly——"

"Oh, he didn't say it like that. But that was the meaning of what he told me."

She looked up at him, her small brown eyes alert and alarmed. "You think this barn, this high-priced purebred—oh, I knew from the beginning there wasn't a chance——"

"Martha, Martha." Uncle Robert took her by the shoulders. "You didn't hear what I was trying to tell you."

"I know your meaning clear enough: Tom's courting disaster."

"I'm just trying to warn you——"

"You needn't warn me, Uncle Robert. I've lived with dread gnawing away at me——"

"Martha——"

"This time he's put all we have—and a lot we haven't—into his plans." The words tumbled over each other. "We've traded off our finest stand of pine, signed notes to get cash to pay carpenters and Burn and Gib; we've mortgaged our best creek bottom to buy paint, and he's borrowed from you to get a fancy male brute, who'll never pay back half his worth."

"Martha, Tom told me, 'For one time, I want to do one thing absolutely right, show my children, this valley, the lick it's done by.' "

"He cares more about showing other folks than protecting his family's welfare, Uncle Robert."

"No, Martha. You and the children, you're the ones he's building for."

"But we don't want it. Not this way, with debts and uncertainty——"

"We can't always choose the gifts folks give us," Robert said to her slowly. "They have to give what they can—and we have to accept it. Martha, we not only take what we need in this life, sometimes we give what we need to, too."

"I don't understand. I don't understand at all! We could be so happy here on Grandpa's farm, growing our food, raising a few market crops for a little cash, pasturing a few cattle, contenting ourselves with what's at hand . . ." Her voice trailed off.

"Martha," her uncle said, "you must try to be happy anyway. The world, even this farm—it's big enough for both your way and Tom's."

She tried to understand. She tried to be happy. But these were not qualities to be secured by effort alone.

With the work on house and barn finished, Uncle Burn and Uncle Gib departed in their usual sudden, secret way. One night they were there, the next morning they were not. The children grieved that they had gone.

"I hope they're not headed back for the coal mines," Mama said. She wiped her eyes and forehead with the hem of her apron, as if she were hot, but Ivy knew that it was too early in the day for Mama to be that warm, and besides it was a foggy cool morning.

Tom Thurston and a hired hand fenced pasture, enclosing the mountain slope that had been so laboriously cleared. Several farmers brought cows to be bred to Kingsridge Knight II and, with the money they paid him, Tom began to buy a few cows of his own. Cattle prices had soared during that spring, however, and the animals Tom could afford to buy were rangy, raw-boned, shaggy-haired. He felt demeaned—for himself, the barn, the arrogant bull—that they should have to make-do with such a motley herd. He vowed to replace them as soon as he could scrape the next few dollars together.

Meantime, the sleek, broad-shouldered bull dominated the farm. Sometimes during the day Ivy could hear him snorting in the lot, or she saw him with head lowered as if attacking the very ground itself. Sometimes at night she could hear his fury pitted against the timbers of his stall as he butted and bellowed in the darkness. Increasingly the farm seemed to Ivy to be a male domain. From the first confident cock crow in each day's pre-dawn to the midnight rage of Kingsridge Knight II, the waking hours seemed dedicated to male needs. The old boar in the hog lot was ill-tempered with sows and shoats alike and, at feeding time one morning, he bit off a young pig's ear. Frone and Ivy took the pig to the house and poured turpentine on the bleeding stump of ear and tried to bandage it without success. It was healed in a few days, but Frone was still furious. "One more meanness from that male-brute boar and I'm going to fix a master dose of physic in his food," she vowed.

Papa's heavy sweaty work clothes and Clay's diapers dominated the washings that Frone and Ivy and Phoebe boiled up and beat and scrubbed and rinsed in the yard each week.

Ivy began to watch Papa and Mama and consider them as a husband and wife. How did a man and a woman ever find each other and come together in marriage? She looked at the boys on Thickety Creek, and those in town the two times she got to ride in with Papa (to have a tooth pulled and buy some July Fourth shoes), and she even looked at sickening, lazy Vaughn Shook, but she could not unravel the mystery between "male and female created He them," as the Bible said.

Some months later, Frone and Ivy and Phoebe went to spend the night with Azalie Shook again, taking Clay with them. When they got home the next morning, they found another "big fine boy." Ivy was both happy and dismayed. Mama looked too pale. Papa laughed too loudly. But the baby was big and healthy and was not even crying when they came to look at him.

"We'll name him William McKinley and call him Kin," Papa said, "if that's all right with you, Martha."

"Yes." She nodded, gazing at the baby, not seeming to care about a name.

"Who knows? He might grow up to be President of the United States," Papa persisted.

"Yes, and he might get shot, too," Frone whispered to Ivy. They had listened with greedy curiosity to every tale and ballad about President McKinley and his killer, Czolgosz, and the dreadful assassination.

"Just as long as he grows to be a good Christian man," Mama said.

With another son, Tom Thurston was spurred on to even greater efforts in building up his herd. He advertised the services of Kingsridge Knight II in the *Nantahala Weekly Chronicle*, but the widespread response he had hoped for did not materialize. A few progressive citizens made the journey to Thickety Creek, but most of the reactions ranged from ignorance ("All this talk about blooded stock don't make any difference far as I can see") to apathy ("My cows done give down all the milk I need, I reckon") to outright hostility ("Why'd Tom Thurston have to go all the way to New York State to buy him a bull? What our daddies and granddaddies had isn't good enough for him?"). Tom nursed along the calves his own cows dropped, proudly showing off any improved features that revealed the mark of the thoroughbred bull.

Then, in midwinter, disaster struck and altered the course of all their lives. It started with such deceptive simplicity and pyramided so swiftly that the whole episode seemed like some desperate improvisation. Gradually as the slipping of sand down a mountainside before a landslide, the incidents gathered and gained momentum.

There were the quarrels between Aunt Tildy and Frone. The old woman could not seem to tolerate Frone's romanticism, her escape into an imaginative world created by words and dreams alone. She picked and pried, and Frone, always quick in anger and tenacious in grudges, self-conscious and unsure of her talent, her body or her own worth, lashed back. They hurled words as neatly as death-tipped spears and because the old woman and the groping girl were of the same blood and tormented spirit, because they were more alike than they were different, each knew the other's vulnerability and sought it out. The sharpened darts of their words embedded deep in old wounds.

"You're a gawky goose of a girl," Aunt Tildy hissed at Frone one day, "a goose who won't ever change into a swan, mark my words."

"And you're a useless old hag," Frone cried out.

"Gawky" and "useless." These were what each most feared, resented, despaired of. A raw nerve had been bared. For weeks they did not speak to each other. Then one day Aunt Tildy found a poem of Frone's. It had been hidden among some dress patterns in a drawer of Martha's sewing machine. Before she told anyone what she had found, Aunt Tildy read and reread the half-dozen lyrical sentimental stanzas.

When the family were gathered at supper that evening, Aunt Tildy spoke up in one of the silences. " 'Delicate as cobwebs and sweet as love my breath . . .' " She paused.

They were all silent, astonished at the strange words repeated in the old rasping voice. Only Frone did not look at Aunt Tildy and Ivy heard her sister's quick suck of breath.

" 'Delicately and sweetly it engages me till death.' " She finished, mockingly, triumphantly, slyly.

"Why Aunt Tildy," Mama began, "where on earth——"

"Ah ha!" she cackled, patting her apron pocket and staring at Frone. "Cobwebs and love indeed. Who's the one around here has time for such fancying——"

"You had no right!" Frone shrieked. "You stole that and read it when you knew——"

"Don't you call me a thief, Miss," Aunt Tildy answered.

But Frone was rushing on. "You read what wasn't ever intended for your wicked old eyes and that's the same as stealing something that wasn't meant for your pocket. You're a——"

"Hush, girl." Papa stopped her, almost teasing but caught between the two pairs of challenging eyes. "Don't get so worked up. It's just a little verse. Tildy must have worked hard to memorize some of it. That's a compliment."

" 'Sweet as love . . .' " the old woman mocked. "Eh law, looks like we've got experts on love we never even suspected——"

Frone had pushed back her chair and stood up. Ivy could not bear to look at her face, it was so white and contorted with pain. "I hate you," she said in a deadly quiet voice to Aunt Tildy. Then she looked around at the others who were staring at her, even Papa and Mama, unsure of what they should do. "What do any of you know about—about my 'little verses'?" She rushed from the house. The stillness she left behind was the quiet at the eye of a hurricane.

"What a damned mess!" Papa sighed. He pushed back his plate. "I just can't figure out what ails that girl."

"Fayte says she's got a rare mind," Mama said. Her face was troubled. "He says he never had a scholar read the classics so easily, so well."

"Aunt Tildy shouldn't have repeated that poem Frone wrote," Ivy said softly and clearly. "It was Frone's private——"

"Too much private about her," Aunt Tildy said. "Sooner she gets that poetry knocked out of her the less likelihood she'll get hurt."

"She's hurt now," Ivy said, surprised at her own audacity, but compelled to speak for her older sister who could use so many words yet tell her family so little that really mattered about herself.

"Go find her, Ivy, will you?" Mama said. "I don't like for her to be roaming around in the darkness in that state of mind."

"I'll fetch the lantern." Papa nearly turned over the chair in his haste to get up.

"Can Phoebe come with me?"

The two girls searched all the familiar haunts—the fern-filled corner on the far side of the springhouse where they sometimes went for secret talks or to hide, and the stone wall at the old orchard, the upper pasture which opened off the barnyard but stretched far up the mountainside to many corners where they liked to sit and take in the view of the farm and Thickety Creek winding below. They called and called. No answer came and they did not find Frone. When they went back to the house, Papa and Mama looked at each other. Papa reached for the lantern, but Mama stopped him.

"Maybe we'd better let her alone," she said. Ivy could not believe that this was cautious, fearful Mama speaking.

"Whatever you say, Martha," Papa answered in a subdued voice. It was a night of astonishments.

Ivy could not go to sleep in the bedroom she shared with Frone, whose absence made her more present in the room than ever before. Ivy wondered if Frone would have the courage to stay out all night by herself. Or perhaps it wasn't courage at all but hurt, desperation, alienation, that drove her out there in the darkness wherever she was and held her there. A screech owl uttered its lonely little tremolo in the big catalpa tree at the edge of the yard. Awareness of the strangeness and sadness and separateness of all their lives surrounded Ivy. It was their separation—no matter how close the kin, no matter how keen the wish for oneness and understanding—that most depressed Ivy. She undressed and put out the lamp and lay a long time thinking and listening to the screech owl. She wondered if Frone could hear it too.

Sometime deep in the night she heard Papa go outside.

The next morning Ivy went to the milk-gap by herself. She went earlier than usual. It would take her a long time to fill both pails by herself. Dew was heavy on the grass. Then all at once Frone, pale, disheveled, tired, appeared on the path beside her and pulled one of the milk pails off her arm. Frone fell in step, making an effort at nonchalance.

"Frone! Where were you all night?"

She did not look around, but kept her eyes set straight ahead. "It doesn't matter," she said.

"But weren't you scared?"

She only sniffed.

They milked the cows in silence. The swish of the warm milk streaming into the buckets was the only sound in the early stillness of woods and pasture and barn. Even old Kingsridge Knight II, Ivy thought, was not stirring yet. Once she tried to start conversation—"I'm glad it's a beef herd and not a dairy herd Papa wants to build up"—but she received no reply from her sister.

When they got back to the house, Frone washed at the basin on the back porch and combed her hair and helped fix breakfast as always. No one said anything to her. In fact, very little was said to anyone. Aunt Tildy did not even come to the table. Ivy took coffee to her bed and the old woman gulped it down gratefully.

Frone and Ivy were alone in the kitchen, ironing, a short while later when Papa came in at a run. "Frone! Were you around the barn last night?"

She looked up from the shirt she was smoothing. "No. Just in the lot. I——"

"That's what I mean. Did you go through the barnyard?"

"I cut across through the gate." Her eyes widened as some realization came to her. "There wasn't anything——"

"Did you leave the gate open, Frone?" Papa asked in a level voice.

"I don't know, Papa! I can't remember fastening it. But then I can't remember opening it either. I guess I just did whatever I had to to get through. I wasn't thinking——"

"But did you leave the gate open?"

"I'm not sure!" Frone cried.

"You must have. It was open when I went up just now. And our bull is gone."

"It can't be. It's in the stall at night. It wasn't in the lot when I went through——"

"Lately we've been giving it the run of stall and yard both at night. It got out through that gate sometime in the night."

"Oh, no, Papa!"

"Oh, yes." Worry made his face miserable. With three strides he crossed the kitchen. His wet shoes made a slight sucking sound at each step. With the full force of his open palm he slapped Frone on the face. "You and your daydreams and foolishness! If they've cost us Kingsridge Knight II and all that's invested in him . . ." He could not finish the thought and neither could they.

Frone's face was worse than pale now. It was the color of cold ashes, Ivy thought, cold damp ashes that could never be rekindled to warmth or life. The only hint of color was the blaze of her eyes and the mark Papa's hand had made on her cheek. For the first time in her life Ivy realized that there were hurts beyond tears.

"But she didn't mean to——" Ivy began. The words seemed as childish and inadequate as if she had brought an infant's pacifier to comfort a dying grownup. Papa turned and strode out of the kitchen. "We've got to find him," he muttered. Frone and Ivy were left staring at each other over the irons that had grown cold.

They did not find the big black bull that day. By the following morning neighbors on Thickety Creek had come to help carry on the search. Kingsridge Knight II was on the high ridge that led around to the Devil's Brow at the head of the valley and when the men found him, he was sick.

Stretched out on the ground, huge sides heaving, he let out a muted bellow now and then. His eyes rolled, trying to focus. A thread of white saliva drooled from his mouth to the ground.

"Lord, what ails him?" Tom Thurston asked, down on his knees, rubbing the bull's neck.

"Hard to say," one man shook his head.

"Milksick," Lazarus Shook volunteered. "That's the trouble with these high-bred creatures: they're never hardy." He shook his grizzled head and spat. "Likely the old brute nibbled some ivy leaves before the dew had dried, and it acted on him like poison."

"Ivy? . . . Dew? . . . Poison?" Tom repeated dazedly. "What the hell are you talking about? I never heard about——"

"Well, you've heard now," Lazarus Shook rejoined sharply. "Seen, too."

The bull lifted his head, made motions to struggle to his feet, fell back. Spittle oozed from his mouth. "I've got to do *something*," Tom Thurston said.

He came off the mountain, told his family what he and the men had found, and made ready to ride in to town to find a doctor who would come or tell him what to do for his expensive and ailing animal. After he had gone, a backwash of consternation and helplessness engulfed the family. Mama's lips moved silently and the children knew she was praying.

Frone crept to a corner of the yard under the comforting shadow of the oldest lilac bush and promised in solemn, private guilt and appeasement to an unknown god: "I'll never write another silly verse. Please let Kingsridge Knight be all right. I'll never moon over another foolish dream." Over and over she repeated the vow.

Ivy and Phoebe tried to carry on with the kitchen chores, but they moved in a trance. "Poor Papa. Poor, poor Papa."

Just before midday Aunt Tildy came into the kitchen wearing her heavy old brogan shoes and a stout bonnet.

"Aunt Tildy," Martha said, "what on earth——"

"Whatever grows in the woods to kill, there's something grows nearby to heal, if we've eyes and wit to find it. I'm a-going to the mountains to find the herb that will save that male brute's life."

"Aunt Tildy, you're not able. You've not climbed a step in years. The doctor said——"

"Eh law, the doctor!" she snorted. "Let me alone." And she picked up a bleached sugar sack, the sort she had gathered herbs and leaves and plants in years before.

"She's as determined as rain." Mama sighed.

"I aim to be useful around here," she said loudly as she started down the steps. She was halted by Lazarus Shook. His shirt was sweaty and torn. He shook his head gravely. "The old feller didn't make it."

"Eh law!" Aunt Tildy said and sat abruptly on the top step.

Ivy, in the kitchen, had heard what he said and so had the others. They stared at each other, but no one spoke. What was there to say?

Papa's silence was worst of all. When Mama met him at the door and took the package of livestock medication a druggist in town had recommended and slowly shook her head, tears running down her cheeks, he only said, "Lord Almighty!"

He sat down at the table and covered his face with his hands. Ivy looked away, aware of the intrusion of her gaze, her sympathy, on his private despair. Mama motioned to the children to leave the room.

They huddled on the porch. Presently they saw Papa leave the house and go to the barn. He walked wearily, with stooped shoulders. He came out of the barn carrying a sharp heavy shovel and mattock and they watched him climb the mountainside till he disappeared into the woods.

When the men came down from the ridge, they went their separate ways home quietly, having nothing to say to the family or to each other. The mattock and shovel were dirty when Tom Thurston brought them back to the barn and he spent a long time cleaning them, wiping and polishing the shovel as meticulously as if it were a valuable Swiss watch.

No one ever spoke of Kingsridge Knight II again. In a couple of weeks, on a warm, thawing day, Papa plowed up the new-ground pasture.

Ever more insistently the barn and all it stood for became a burden to them, while the house and its spaciousness grew in meaning for them. It provided room for privacy and growth. It became the place where visitors who came to the valley from town—school superintendents, religious leaders, politicians running for office—stayed overnight and made their headquarters. Their talk drew Tom Thurston gradually out of his humiliation and depression and brought him into the heat of argument and discussion he had always relished. The children loved these nights when there were strangers from town bringing them new ways, new thoughts, reviving Papa's vision.

Everyone was aware of the failure of the stock farm. Cass Nelson closed the mortgage on the bottom land Tom had pledged for money to buy the white paint. Martha had little to say for days after she and Tom signed the deed for those precious acres along the creek. Gradually Tom sold the rest of his livestock and used the money to pay most of his debts.

Papa's barn was a disaster and people in town spoke of it as "Tom's white elephant" or "Thurston's folly." None of the family looked at it without feeling sad, embarrassed, miserable. The half-empty stalls, the almost empty hayloft, the many unused troughs:

they were mute testimony to a prosperity that had never material-
ized, a dream of quality that had never existed anywhere except in
Papa's mind. They had to "live down" the barn.

But Papa's house was different. The house was something beautiful and splendid in their lives. They could look at it as they came
up the valley and their spirits lifted with the buoyance of a leaf before a west wind. The house stood for hope and pride, free-handed
hospitality, a confidence in life that would not be denied—circum-
scribed and discouraged sometimes, but never completely denied.
They had to "live up to" the house.

And with all their building and working, succeeding and failing,
the seasons turned in orderly design. Galax and Solomon's-seal
bloomed in the woods. Squirrels nested in the treetops. Lichens
grew on boulders along the mountainsides. Ivy breathed and
touched and lived in this world, too. She felt the sweep of time
over everything around her.

She knew that Papa would have some answer when Mama
finally asked, "Tom, what are we going to do now?"

CHAPTER 5
Today

SHERRY AUSTIN was still pretty. Her face was without a blemish. Phil came out of the house and across the lawn and driveway up to the long white convertible where she sat smoking. He stopped at the window beside her and in the light from the gadgets on the dashboard he could see how pretty she still was.

"Hi," she said, looking up at him directly with the full impact of those blue eyes and the dark mass of her hair framing her white face and throat.

"Well, hel-lo, Sherry." He smiled, trying to make the words fit a tune as he hummed.

She flung away the cigarette and held up her face, eyes half closed. Phil pretended not to notice the invitation. He was determined not to touch her. Not even in the most casual or perfunctory manner would he contact again that cool flesh which could turn warm in an instant, a breath, a pulse beat. He laid both hands along the window sill and leaned toward the car, leaning and withdrawing at the same time.

There was a momentary pause. Just beyond them the creek splashed, running silver in the night. Its sound in the woods and darkness seemed to isolate them on a trembling island. Phil might have come miles from the family eating dinner back there in the house behind him.

Sherry pressed the handle on the door and it swung heavily open with a movement as smooth and practiced as her own slide across the seat to the opposite corner of the car. "Come on in, darling," and she patted the upholstery beside her.

He sat where she had been, under the steering wheel, and he half-turned toward her, laying one arm along the back of the seat. "You look wonderful, Sherry, as if . . ." He lifted his shoulders in an almost invisible gesture of frustration. "Words fail me."

"Bad precedent!" she laughed. "How will the Senator ever lead a filibuster if words fail him?"

He shrugged wearily, not playing any games tonight.

"I didn't realize I had such a lock on you," she persisted, teasing, leaning ever so slightly toward him until the soft curve of her shoulder was within easy reach of his hand.

"Who else?" he asked.

She frowned petulantly. When she frowned now, Phil noticed that the crow's feet between her eyes came more easily than they once had and did not disappear as quickly as they once did.

"All right, Phil-baby," she said.

He was surprised that he could still be so annoyed by her latest nickname fad. "Sherry, I'm not trying to argue with you or make you mad or hurt you," Phil said, looking directly into her beautiful eyes, determined to ignore them. "I'm tired. I've had a fantastic day after a fantastic week—and I'm tired right up to here."

"And I'm bored right up to here," she answered blatantly. Apparently she thought him the same man she had known several years—several existences?—ago: no need for subtlety, for wit.

"So?" His eyebrows lifted quizzically and for the first time she looked at him sharply, seemed to be studying his face. He moved slightly. "I'm sorry, Sherry. You're bored and I'm tired. Could be we're growing old?"

She shifted approaches ever so invisibly. "I'm not tired, Phil-baby, and I'm not really bored either. I'm lonely."

He looked at her a moment and then laughed aloud. "You? Lonely? Good Lord, Sherry, remember who this is. This is not one of your latest beach boys. This is Phil Cortland who knows you from a long time back, remember?"

"I remember very well, darling," she said, her eyes turned away from him, looking past him, over his shoulder toward the lighted house. And in the dim glow from the dashboard Phil seemed to detect a new emotion in her, hinted ever so slightly by the tension around her eyes and mouth, the quick nervousness of her hands. All at once he sensed that she was frantic.

Sherry Austin was frantic in the cool, controlled style that would not give her away, would not reveal how deeply she despised the surroundings of her life or how desperately she was resolved to get away. At the moment, Phil Cortland seemed her best possible means of escape. Escape from provincialism and her own limitations into the world of large affairs and sophistication and purpose. She had invested hours of time and attention pouring over the Washington columnists that appeared in the local newspaper each Sunday. None of them was first-rate, but any one of them was more knowledgeable than she in the ways of the capital city. The society columnist was naturally her favorite. Sherry had read carefully the breathless-style descriptions of embassy dinners and society matrons' cocktail parties and glittering gala occasions, and she knew that given such opportunities *she* could make *her* place in such surroundings. Consideration of how and why these people had gathered in Washington in the first place never occurred to her. There was a vague realization that they were there to participate in government, but what that meant, either in large philosophical attainments or in specific personal ambitions, was beyond her interest. If she thought of the governmental or career aspects at all, it was in romantic terms in which Washington became a sort of streamlined version of the court at Versailles, and her home became the Petit Trianon (with modern plumbing). Hard and realistic as asphalt in all else, about government and the people who guided its destiny Sherry Austin was sentimentally fanciful.

Washington—a Washington no one knew but her, a Washington

that existed nowhere except in her mind—was Sherry Austin's goal,
her salvation she would say. And how ironic could you get when
Phil Cortland was the only presently available means by which to
achieve that dream! At the country club she could show him how
skillful she was with people, how adept in social situations, as a
successful senator's wife would have to be. (What might happen if
she succeeded in winning Phil again, and then his stay in Washington should be suddenly terminated—by defeat at the polls or even
a decision not to enter the race—she had not taken into account.)
She knew that she wanted to get away from the drag of Nantahala
County, not just on a vacation or a leave of absence from her father's
pocketbook, but permanently—and now.

"I'm lonely, Phil," she repeated. She laid her arm along the
back of the seat too, so that their hands touched. The deep-scooped
neckline of her blue dress stretched tautly over her firm round
breasts and pulled unevenly lopsided so that one fold fell low, dis-
playing the tender whiteness where sun-baking of the summer past
had not penetrated or toughened. Phil remembered how sweet and
ripe she was to touch. He did not take his hand away from hers
along the cushion-top.

"I'm sorry, Sherry," he said. "It just seems so unlikely that you
would ever be——"

"Unlikely?" Her laugh was clear and brittle as an icicle. "All
sorts of unlikely things happen, Phil-baby."

"No rebuttal," he said, holding up his hand in mock surrender,
wondering why she had insisted so urgently on seeing him tonight.
What was she up to?

As though reading his thoughts, she said, "Like the summer after
we broke up . . ."

He did not know what she meant, so he waited for her to go on.
He was positive she had something to say, but she retreated from
saying it. She reminded Phil of a gambler playing for high stakes,
who looks at the cards on the table and then finds in his hand the
wild card that will add up to the exact winning total. But she did
not lay it down.

Instead, her mood, her approach, shifted suddenly. She tilted her head slightly until the dark hair swung softly around her face and throat and when she laughed the evenness of her white teeth made her lips appear full and warm. "Will it be such a burden to take me to the club buffet tomorrow night?"

"Come off it, Sherry," he said. Abruptly he reached into his pocket and drew out cigarettes, lit two, and gave her one. "It's a matter of time—and timing——"

"The people there have votes, too," she said.

"That's right, appeal to my better nature." He smiled at her. The smoke from their cigarettes floated in blue wisps through the car windows.

"Up there in the big city, you don't want to get completely out of touch with Nantahala," Sherry said.

Phil thought of the day he had just experienced and he laughed aloud. "Not much chance of it."

"Or your old 'great and good friends,' " she continued half-mockingly.

"Perhaps I hesitated to see you, Sherry, because I was half afraid. As my Uncle Clay often says, you can't warm over cold potatoes."

"So who's a cold potato?" She laughed throatily. Triumph flushed her face. She mashed out her cigarette, glanced at her tiny ruby-studded wrist watch and sat up on the edge of the seat. "I'd better run now. It's wonderful to see you again, Phil. And bygones are bygones, agreed? It's such a drag, dredging up the past."

He nodding, killing the light in his cigarette, too, and depositing the stub in the ash tray.

"You're an old darling to take me tomorrow night." She leaned over and gave him a brief, warm kiss on the cheek. Apparently she had found what she came searching for.

When the sound of her car had faded in the distance, Phil took a deep breath of the clean night air and walked back to the house. He found the family upstairs in his grandmother's room. Naomi had just brought after-dinner coffee and set the tray on a table beside Ivy's chaise longue.

"A mighty fine set of children paying you court tonight, Mrs. Thurston," she said. She rearranged the bed-rest against which the aged woman leaned, half sitting, half lying among the white pillows and blankets of her bed. The white softness of the covers made the skin of her face and neck appear as dry and faded as parchment.

"Yes, Naomi." A thin weak hand with swollen arthritic joints reached out and grasped the strong dark hand. "They're all good to me. Every day I thank the Lord for letting me live long enough to see them grown and my grandchildren."

Naomi pulled her hand gently, firmly from the old woman's clutch. "You have a good visit now with all your fine folks, and then a good night's sleep, Mrs. Thurston," she said, and went quickly downstairs.

Ivy began to pour the dark fragrant coffee. She enjoyed the soft luster of her pewter service, the round graceful simple lines of the pot and the sugar and creamer as she handled them. They reminded her of a far-away day in London (the rain and fog were the color of this pewter), and a distant street (the antique shop had been run by a friendly civilized man who reminded her of Cort when he showed her a few volumes of rare books he had acquired only the day before). The afternoon had been pleasant. She was glad that she had yielded to the impulse to buy these pewter pieces and make them her own.

"That Naomi makes me nervous." Frone's voice, as she accepted a cup, drew Ivy back to Nantahala County from London. "She looks like a little dried-up high priestess, seems to know too much——"

"She does," Ivy said.

"I mean about us."

"That's what I mean, too," Ivy said. "She knows all about us— what we eat, wear, talk about, do, how I keep my house, what's on Mama's mind, where and how all of you live. And we don't know a thing about her except what she wants us to know about her children, Juanita who's a nurse, or Norwood the boy, or the youngest, Melvina. . . . Here, Kin, with sugar and cream." She handed him a cup. It seemed as thin and fragile as tissue in his powerful hands.

"Thank you, Ivy." He went to the straight chair beside Mama's bed and sat down carefully.

"Well, that would get on my nerves," Frone continued. "I never did know many Negroes anyway."

"Oh, you're just an old Connecticut Yankee now." Phoebe bustled into the room, pleasant and excited. "You don't *have* to understand them."

"And I guess you do, now that you're a native down in the big planter country."

"Yes, I guess I do, Frone. I've never had any trouble getting help. Old Aunt Hettie, who was there when Lucy Kate and young Rutledge were both born—she still comes by every so often and makes us an orange spice cake or a pan of rolls. The children love her like part of the family. Yes, I think I understand Negroes, Frone—at least the ones around us."

"Is it pretty much like understanding people in general, Pheeb?" Clay asked. "Or is there some special trick to it with Negroes?"

Phoebe looked at him a moment, then shrugged. Ivy paused, coffeepot in mid-air, and looked at Clay in astonishment and approval.

Ivy dreaded these differences in the family, the large and obvious ones which had existed since they were each born, and the subtler differences which were products of experience and locale and contrasting marriages. They had spent the afternoon and early part of the evening becoming adjusted to the calamity which faced them as a family, becoming readjusted to one another. They had asked about each other's families and the lives they lived apart—interested but not involved, not able, really, to imagine Frone's sons or Phoebe's Lucy Kate and young Rutledge, or even Jud and Rutledge Senior, but trying to be human and care.

These formalities finished, a meal together accomplished, a shift in their attitudes, their feelings, subtly altered the atmosphere and exchanges between them. Like the settling of undersea mountains unseen and unheard which brought sudden shifts of tide or shoreline that were visible, so their relationships formed and reformed and the surface stirred from the flow of deep currents they neither recognized nor directed. When Ivy handed Phil his coffee, she was thankful for her son's smile, brief and distracted as it seemed.

"Well, I just talked with Rutledge on the phone," Phoebe went on to the others. She fingered the soft yellow gold and amethyst lavalier at her throat. "He always wants to know if I've had a safe trip, even if I'm just a few miles from home." She smiled. "He was asking about each of you. . . . Mama"—raising her voice—"Rutledge sent you his regards."

The old lady nodded. "Rutledge always had nice manners."

"Lucy Kate's home for the weekend," Phoebe went on brightly. "We'd bought her dress for the Harvest Ball before she went away to school. . . . When your call came Wednesday, Ivy, I thought, first thing: Well now, isn't it a good thing we went ahead and bought Lucy Kate's dress? That's one thing off my mind——"

"Oh, my God!" Clay turned toward the window.

Phoebe looked around at them puzzled. "It's a very important dance——" she began.

"And if there's a prettier girl there than your Lucy Kate, I don't believe it," Ivy said hastily. "Here's coffee, Phoebe." She reached out to her.

"Oh, how nice, Ivy." She accepted the cup. "And isn't it nice for us to have it up here with Mama, all together——"

"Yes, it's 'nice,' Phoebe——" Clay began.

Ivy interrupted him. "And your coffee, Clay."

He looked at her. "Old Ivy, playing at the grand dame," he said. "Well . . ." He turned and set his cup on the window sill, sloshing drops of coffee on the white draperies that were drawn back in heavy folds. As he disappeared through the door and downstairs they heard him call, "Back in a flash—with a flash."

When he did return, he had an armful of packages. He put them on a dresser, pushing aside his mother's comb and brush and mirror to make room. Then he turned toward them as though they were a vast audience. He flipped his hat over one eye and reaching up into the air received an invisible walking stick in his grasp. Twirling the imaginary cane with jaunty ease, he strolled the length of the large room, half singing, half speaking. "Hel-lo every-body. This is your old friend, Ted Lewis."

Phil stood in the doorway and watched Clay as he transformed the bedroom into his stage, singing hoarsely, softly.

"Come to me My Melancholy Baby,
Cuddle up and don't be blue. . . .
Smile my honey dear,
While I kiss away each tear
Or else I shall be melancholy, too."

Then he went through a brief imitation soft-shoe shuffle, flicked the invisible cane under his arm and tipped his hat in a gay good night to some breathless audience. Phil applauded. The others joined him.

"Thank you. Thank you, Senator—and ladies and gentlemen." They all smiled. "You ever see Ted Lewis, ever hear old Ted in person, Phil?" Clay asked.

"I guess his heyday was a little before my time. But when I was in college I collected some old records——"

"Old records. They're nothing. You couldn't know anything about how it was from old records. It was seeing him with your own eyes, hearing him through your own ears, with all the smoke in your lungs and the booze in your belly, young, dressed up fit to be the Prince of Wales and twice as happy, and old Ted up there full of music and dancing that seemed to flow right through the soles of his shoes. That was what made it good, made it anything at all."

They were quiet. Then Mama spoke, louder than her usual high whisper, from the bed. "If you children are going to sing, I wish someone would sing 'A Land That Is Fairer Than Day' for me."

Clay waved his hand. "All together now. Remember old Lazarus Shook and the way he used to raise the rafters on old Thickety." Hunching his neck down into his collar and peering at them over imaginary glasses, Clay held his fingers to his mouth as though blowing on a pitch pipe. "All right, saints and sinners, in old Lazarus' name."

They sang together, smiling at one another. Phil did not know all the words, but he hummed along with the tune:

"There's a land that is fairer than day,
And by faith I can see it afar,

For the Father waits over the way
To prepare us a dwelling place there."

With no effort on their part the words and tune came back to each
one of them. They sang with gusto. Frone kept time with one foot,
a slight frown troubling her face. Phoebe looked at each of them in
turn as she sang in a clear, high soprano. Kin was self-conscious, yet
his words came clearly. Ivy threw herself wholeheartedly into the
singing.

Phil studied them with amused disbelief as they went without a
halt or hesitation through the long stanzas to the end. "Whew! That
was quite a performance," he said.

"Well now, we've had a song for Mama," Clay said.

"As Phoebe told the visiting minister once, there were Papa's
songs and Mama's songs." Kin's sturdy face spread in a reminiscent
smile. "And when the minister asked her what she meant she said,
'Mama sings "Beulah Land" and "No Dark Valley" and Papa sings
"Little Brown Jug" and "Shanghaii Rooster Got No Comb." ' "

When they had finished laughing, Clay said, "Now I guess it's
time for me to give you all a little surprise."

Ivy had collected their empty coffee cups on the tray. Now she
picked up Clay's full untouched cup of cold coffee from the window sill. She set them all on a table in the hallway.

"I haven't remembered my sisters and brothers and mother at
Christmas or birthdays for a long time now, and this afternoon while
I was downtown I slipped by Nelson's Boutique, or whatever the
hell he calls it, and tried to make amends."

Frone and Ivy glanced at each other as Clay took his stance beside the cherry dresser where he had laid his packages.

"Dear family all, old Clay wants you to know how much he ap-
preciates your rallying around him in his hour of need." The dark
eyes suddenly brimmed with tears and the deep-lined face grimaced
between a sob and a grin. "As good old Rudyard the Kipling wrote,
'Yes, it was Din, Din, Din——' "

Again Ivy's and Frone's glances met. Frone shut her eyes and
shook her head.

" '——Though I've belted you an' flayed you, by the livin' Gawd that made you, you're a better man than I am, Gunga Din!' "

"You know, Clay, you should have been an actor," Phoebe said. "You really should." Her plump little face was serious and sincere.

Clay swept the soft fine hat from his head and made a low, unsteady bow. "Thank you, sister mine."

"He's eaten almost nothing all day," Frone said in a low voice to Ivy.

"I did hope the supper would appeal to him," Ivy said.

"It wasn't the supper," Frone said, "it's just that bottle——"

"And what are you two dear old crones discussing there?" Clay asked. "Resume your seat, sister Frone. The Barrymore of Nantahala County would now like to present each of his sisters with this token of his affection and esteem."

The three square boxes were lavishly wrapped in thick gold-flecked paper tied with white satin ribbon.

"Oh, Clay, you shouldn't have," Phoebe murmured as she unwrapped her package eagerly. Ivy could not help wondering wryly if Phoebe knew how truthfully she spoke, especially when she saw the square bottle of golden-colored perfume.

"What's yours?" Phoebe was asking her.

Ivy looked at the label. Half-hysterical laughter bubbled in her throat and she swallowed before she replied. "Velvet Midnight."

She saw Phil glance around quickly. His expression was of that rare sardonic humor that had lighted his father's face in memorable moments. She, who loved sun and air and breezes blowing and light drenching through first leaves in spring or scarlet leaves in fall, she wearing the fragrance of Velvet Midnight!

"Mine"—Phoebe looked again—"mine is Nostalgia. Oh, Clay, I've heard of that. It's very expensive." (And Phoebe, Ivy thought, always immersed in the moment, wearing Nostalgia!)

"Buy the best: it's always been my motto," Clay told them. "Whether it was a saw or a set of hinges or a suit of clothes—or a pair of teddies for a girl."

"Teddies!" Phoebe cried. The sisters looked at each other and doubled with laughter.

"And what's your perfume, Frone?" Phoebe asked.

They all looked at her. With the self-deprecating satire that she had acquired long years ago on Thickety Creek, Frone held her heavy square bottle at arm's length and appeared to be studying it awkwardly. Then, plucking at the high formless neckline of her loose dress, she said flatly. "Tahiti Temptress."

They rocked with laughter. Clay led them, slapping his thigh. "I told the damn clerk to wrap up the three costliest perfumes she had," Clay tried to explain. "Tahiti Temptress! Old Frone! Oh, my God!"

Finally they subsided. "Here, Kin"—Clay staggered as if from exhaustion across the room—"did you think I'd forgotten my favorite brother?"

Kin tore the tissue paper as carefully as if he were handling one of his woods flowers or mosses. The tie he lifted from the long box was a custom-signed original creation of Italian silk. Over Kin's broad rough hand it hung like some limp exotic trophy. "A tie," he said.

"Yes," Clay answered. "What did you think it would be, an elephant stick?"

"Why, now," Kin went on lamely, "this is about the finest tie I ever had."

"You like it?" Clay asked. They could see he was aware of the incongruity of this small masterpiece of workmanship compared with Kin's suit. "By God, I wanted you to have one really good piece of clothing sometime in your life——" He broke off.

"You'll have to find somebody to court," Frone said, "when you get dressed up in that finery, Kin."

"Now that's right." He grinned at them good-naturedly.

"And, Mama, here's a present for you, from your eldest son, from the black sheep namesake of old man Henry Clay Thurston er-ah the First."

"Clay!" She looked up at him. Wisps of her white hair had come loose from under the net she wore and created a sort of halo around her shrunken face. Ivy could feel the pathetic eagerness to make some contact with this son whose ways were so alien to her. Ivy went to the bed and helped her sit up straighter against the bed-rest as she slowly opened the package Clay had given her. A pair of gossamer stockings fell on the bed. "Clay—son"—she handled them carefully, without familiarity—"maybe I can save these fine stockings to be buried in."

"Oh God!" Clay cried with a final roll of his eyes. He strode across the room, then stopped in front of Phil. "Senator, my apologies. Somehow I forgot to include you in my little production——"

Phil waved his hand to include the whole friendly disheveled room, so filled with good intentions and misunderstanding. "You've given me enough with just—this."

"He was remembering only the underprivileged countries this time," Frone said.

"I tell you, Clay, you have the touch," Phil said. "You really put on a good show, man."

Clay again set his hat at an angle above one eye and did a few dance steps and turns. "Sometimes I used to think if I'd had a chance I could have been better than any of them. Old Ted Lewis, Al Jolson, the lot. I had a kind of style all my own——"

"Coming from Thickety Creek, you couldn't have been any singer, any entertainer," Frone said. At her tone and words the atmosphere of the room altered. "Narrow, ignorant, inbred people suspicious of anybody who wanted to improve himself, look up."

"Oh, Frone," Mama said. They all looked at her, startled. Mama shook her head. "Frone, Frone, you looked at us too hard. Thickety Creek folks were God-fearing people who tried to keep the Ten Commandments——"

"Yes, and every other good thing they could get their hands on!"

"O.K., Frone," Clay said. "Don't start harping on Thickety and the people back there."

"Now I tell you children"—Mama looked at each one of them dramatically—"I may not be with you much longer. I've been talking to the Lord——"

"Mama, don't start that," Frone said.

"You can talk to the Lord for eternity, Mama," Clay said. "You'd better talk to us now. And you know what I'm going to do, Mama? As soon as I'm out of this trouble I'm in——"

"Trouble?" Mama was alerted. Like a doe, Ivy thought, at scent of danger to her young, Mama froze at that word. "What trouble, son?"

"I mean"—Clay fumbled—"I mean this troublesome moving back down here from up North and all . . ."

"Oh!" It was difficult to tell from Mama's face whether she was convinced or not.

"Anyway, once I get everything straightened out, I'm going to look after you, Mama. What I'm going to do is get me a farm."

Mama reached a hand toward Clay. "Son, I'm so proud you want a farm. It's the best way of living——"

"Or starving," Frone said.

"No, Frone. Man does not live by bread alone." A smile trembled on Mama's lips. "Did I ever tell you children about the time at my mother's wedding when her father—your great-grandpa Moore that would have been—assured his friends that man does not live by bread alone. . . ."

They looked at one another. Clay and Frone closed their eyes and shrugged their shoulders. They all knew each syllable by heart.

"My mother used to tell me about it and laugh," Mama went on happily. "A man who lived in the valley, Burke was his name and he was a miller, sort of rough, unlettered fellow, and he answered Grandpa, 'That's right, Mr. Moore. A man don't live by bread alone. He's got to have a little meat to go along with it.'"

They smiled dutifully, half in exasperation. Mama nodded and seemed satisfied by their reaction.

"Phil, you'll have to remember that for your committee studying foreign countries and their needs," Ivy said.

He nodded. "Could be."

"Oh, we never wanted for anything while we were on the farm," Mama said.

"Except a little rest," Frone said under her breath.

"All the apples we could eat——"

"As long as we ate specked ones," Frone added. "We'd work all fall in the Spanish needles and cockleburs till our backs were broken picking up apples, then never enjoy a whole one the winter through."

"Why, Frone——" Mama seemed puzzled and bewildered.

"I'll never forget one night I went out to that apple house and got the biggest, soundest, reddest Winesap I could find. Then I cut a little round hole out of it so that when I came inside and you asked me, Mama, if that apple was one that had a bad spot and needed eating, I said, 'Yes,' and showed you and Papa the place I'd cut out."

No one said anything.

"The next day Papa said to me, 'That apple wasn't specked, was it, Frone?' And I told him no. I didn't know what he'd do. He just waited a minute and then he said, 'Well, Almighty be! Go ahead and eat the good ones then. No need to wait for everything around here to spoil before we begin to take any satisfaction in it.' "

"Did you eat good ones after that, Aunt Frone?" Phil asked.

She shook her head very slowly. Her face was sad. "No." She didn't continue.

No one spoke for a moment. Then Phil said, "I can remember Mother telling me about those evenings around your fireplace, when she was a child, Grandma Thurston." He was taken aback at how loud his voice sounded in the muffled room.

"Papa had the knack," Frone said. "He could make a fire seem about ten degrees hotter than it was, or a breeze in summer about ten degrees cooler."

Ivy nodded, absently looking at Phil. "He made a room in winter seem cozy, like the best place on earth to be that moment, just by the way he drew his chair up to the hearth and crossed his legs and held one foot out to the fire."

In the silence of the room as they meditated on Papa they could hear Naomi moving around downstairs. Outside a dog barked on a distant hill.

"I guess maybe I should lie back down," Mama said in a small voice. They all rose at once to help her. Kin, siting closest to her bed, took away the back rest and helped her stretch out. Ivy fluffed the pillows and put one under her head and one beside her.

"We've tired her out," Phoebe said.

She looked up at them, small and wasted and yet in some way, it seemed to Ivy, stronger and more enduring than any of them. "I'm afraid I failed"—her chin quivered—"I'm afraid somehow that none of my children are as religious——"

They avoided looking at one another. Frone made a stab at humor. "Well, I guess none of us would ever be mistaken for preachers."

"Now, Grandma Thurston," Phil spoke soothingly, moving nearer the bed, "you've not raised such a bad set of offspring——"

"That's not enough, Phil," she answered.

"You're not on the Hill now, Senator," Clay said. "No need to try to fool her."

"Indeed, I wasn't." Phil was irritated at their rejection of his effort.

"They've got to know," Martha Thurston said, "you've all got to know, and I'm not sure you do"—her chin no longer quivered—"we belong to God—and to each other."

They shifted uneasily. "Well hell's bells," Clay muttered on the other side of the room, "I don't even belong to myself."

"I reckon we all believe—maybe in different ways, Mama," Kin offered hesitantly.

She closed her eyes. "It was something your papa and I could never see alike on. Talk of religion or our immortal souls or eternity always made him uneasy. We never could . . ." She turned her head on the pillow and did not finish.

As if she had to tell them! As if each of them in that room—except Phil who was exempt from the experience and its memory—did not bear within something of that mortal schism. It occurred to Ivy that not one of them actually had any present knowledge at all of the other's basic beliefs—sturdy or hazy, the code, the formula, the pattern, the thrust (as Phil, in his Washington jargon, would say) by which they lived. The few times they came together, from Connecticut or South Carolina, New Jersey or right here in Nantahala, they had other things to talk of, to give. And they discussed and shared everything but this.

"Mama, you must get some rest now," she said matter-of-factly. She took tablets from a bottle on the table and handed a glass to Phoebe, who brought fresh water. Mama kept her eyes closed while she swallowed the medicine, allowed them to take off her bed jacket, and lay back down. Ivy motioned them out of the room. Phil left first, but he heard his grandmother say, "I'm so proud you could all be here with me, together, one more time."

Behind him, Clay spoke. "That Mama, she's not going to be up-staged by anybody. I love every hair on her dear old head, but she's got showmanship plus and there's no damn use denying it."

In the hall at the foot of the stairs Naomi stood, buttoning up her slightly oversize coat.

"I'll run you home, Naomi," Clay said. "Wait just a sec——"

"That's mighty nice, Mr. Clay, but no thanks." The little woman looked at him seriously. "I'll just walk and catch me a late bus——"

"No, no"—Clay waved his hand—"won't hear of it. No walking for somebody who can throw together a dinner and a roast like that one we sat down to tonight. Phil here, he'll go with us."

Phil, startled, looked around.

"You've been drinking, Mr. Clay," Naomi said. "I'd be afraid to——"

"We'll let old Phil here drive." Clay laid a heavy hand on his shoulder. "O.K., boy?"

"I guess——"

"Besides, there's an errand I want us to do."

"Look here, Clay, it's been a long day——"

"It's for Naomi—and old Clay. You'd do something for us, wouldn't you, Senator?"

"Sure, sure," Phil said wearily and Clay disappeared into the ad-joining room.

"It's all right, Mr. Phil," Noami said. "I know how it is. I'll catch my bus——"

"No, Noami, I'm glad to drive you home. It's Clay's 'errand' that bothers me. Running by a bootlegger's when he's already had more than——" He broke off as the others came downstairs.

"Poor old Mama." Kin was shaking his head. "What can we do?"

When Phil told them he was going with Clay to take Naomi home, Ivy brought him the keys to her car. "I know you must be tired," she said. "I'm sorry."

"Forget it." Phil winked at her. "We'll be home before the rest of you have got around to saying good night."

Clay had come up behind him. Now, flourishing his hat, he recited in loud, oracular tones: "We shall be home with the yellow gold before the morning light—though *hell* should bar the way!" And he threw open the front door for Naomi and Phil.

After they had gone, Kin followed his sisters into the living room. "I've got to be going on home," he said, but still he stood there by the fireplace. "It bothers me to see Mama so—so worried about us."

"Law me, Kin," Frone said (and Ivy thought to herself how the mountain words, the old phrases, reasserted themselves despite half a lifetime of living in New England), "you know she's always been like that. Mama never did think anybody was going to heaven but old Lazarus Shook who was too lazy to commit any sin, and Aunt Tildy who was too old, and the preacher who was too scared."

Phoebe giggled weakly.

"I never did think it sounded like a very lively crowd up there on the golden streets," Frone finished. "Nobody you'd want to spend eternity with!"

Phoebe laughed outright and Kin and Ivy joined.

But Kin was still troubled. "Seems like I always felt—working with the flowers and shrubs and earth, trying to keep things alive, make them grow where folks could see them—that I was on pretty close terms with some kind of religion."

"Of course you were, Kin," Phoebe said.

"You know"—Kin looked at them eagerly—"I was thinking just the other day about some of those Bludsoes and how I used to meet up with them in the woods and they'd take all morning or all afternoon to show me where a stand of mountain ash grew or a hive of honeybees was swarming or where there was a bed of trillium high as my knees."

"How awful," Phoebe gasped. "Why, I never knew Mama let you run around with any of those Bludsoes."

"Mama didn't know anything about it." Kin grinned like a little boy, a little boy aware of some sweet secret he must not share or he would be deprived of it.

"What was so bad about that, Phoebe?" Frone asked.

"They were trash, just trash," Phoebe replied.

"Wasn't it because they were supposed to be partly colored?" Frone demanded. Ivy thought wearily that it was a funny way to put a question, "partly colored"—like an Easter egg? Wasn't everyone colored, one shade or another?

Phoebe flushed as pink as the flowers on her dress. "Maybe so. After all, when we were growing up, Nigras and whites——"

"It's Negroes, Phoebe, N-e-g-r-o. I declare, you talk just like Rutledge," Frone said.

"Well, that's every bit as good as talking with that Yankee accent of Jud's. And if you lived where I do, you'd understand that Negroes——"

"I'm fed up—fed up, Phoebe, with your 'understanding,' like you had some special knowledge——"

"Come on, Frone, Phoebe," Ivy pleaded. "No more differences tonight."

"All right. All right."

"Why, those Bludsoes," Kin went on, recalling softly, "they were as much at home in these hills as ever the Cherokees were."

"About this religion," Phoebe said, after a moment, "Mama's just judging us all by Clay. And that's not fair. I belong to St. James's, where Rutledge's family have always been, and Lucy Kate and young Rutledge were confirmed there. But I guess Mama's still suspicious of anything not Baptist or Methodist or Presbyterian."

"No." Ivy did not look at them. She was putting Phil's pipe and tobacco pouch in the drawer of the little smoking stand where his father had once kept tobacco and pipes and cigars for after dinner. "I don't belive it's membership Mama's talking about."

"Maybe not,". Frone agreed, "but I can remember when membership meant a good deal to her, when she made it important"— there was an awkward pause—"to all of us."

"She wanted Papa to think more of the spirit," Ivy said.

"Or what the community thought," Frone added.

"Well"—Kin moved toward the door—"I'll go on home. It was a good dinner, Ivy."

"Thank you. You and Clay come on over for Sunday dinner about one tomorrow."

"I just hope Clay's eating by then," Frone said anxiously.

"He'd better be. He's got to get straightened out for Monday morning," Kin said.

"That," Frone agreed sharply, "is what I'm thinking about."

Phil and Clay drove Naomi home in silence. Only once they talked, when Phil asked her, "What about your family, Naomi? How are they doing now?"

"Fine. Just fine," she answered. "All getting themselves up in the world. My oldest girl, Juanita that is, she's in a hospital up in Philadelphia, taking her nursing; and my boy, Norwood, he's up in Detroit, Michigan, working in one of them automobile plants. I just hope these machines they been writing about so much don't close down his job there."

"Your boy wouldn't be the first one, Naomi," Clay said. He half turned toward where she sat on the back seat. "Did you know they got something automatic to take the place of my work, a god-damned machine to cut out homes—no, I mean houses—to cut out houses like paper dolls."

"And your other girl, Naomi," Phil went on, "where's your baby?"

"She's going to secretary school. Melvina, she's got ambition to spare." Naomi gave a short laugh edged with bitterness. "I don't know whose secretary she's planning on being."

"There'll be openings," Phil said.

"Your mama helped get her in that school, you know."

"No. I didn't know."

"Your mama"—Naomi paused—"not many like her, like Mrs. Cortland in this world. She don't say so much, she *does* a-plenty."

After Phil had thanked her, he drove silently, thinking about his mother, grandmother, the whole web and fabric of family, and somewhere along the way, in the end-of-day weariness, to his surprise he found himself wondering if Ann Howard and Ivy would like each other if they became well acquainted.

When they came to Naomi's little house at the edge of town—neat imitation brick with a fenced-in yard the size of a pocket, and chrysanthemums in bloom—she thanked them quickly. "I'll be seeing you folks tomorrow."

"Sure, Naomi."

As Phil drove on down the street, Clay pulled the flat pint bottle from his pocket and took a long, raw drink. He pursed his lips, shook his head, and with great precision put the nearly empty bottle back in his pocket. "Now," he said, "let's go on our errand, nephew."

"Look here, Clay——"

"No need to look anywhere, Senator Phil. I found out a couple of days ago where she lives. I couldn't get up my nerve before this."

"What are you talking about, Clay?"

"I should have gone to see her before this." He shook his head in heavy self-reprimand.

"Who the hell——"

"Watch it, Senator." Clay looked at him seriously. "I'm surprised you hadn't thought of it yourself. Why, I'm talking about going to see Mr. Hawk Williams' widow."

Phil sucked in his breath.

Clay did not seem to notice. "I think it may be my duty to call on the woman I made a widow—*maybe* I was the one widowed her—and the little devils I orphaned—if she and Hawk had any—any f-fledg-lings." He was tangled in the word, repeated it, then gave up. At last he said, "I've got to see them."

"The ones we'd better be seeing are those fellows that were with you on that damned hunt, or steak fry, or whatever it was. Besides, it's late."

"It's Saturday. Never too late in that part of town on Saturday night."

"But you've had since Wednesday——"

"I told you, damn it, I couldn't get up nerve before! What if they hate me, want to—to lynch me?"

Phil could not keep from laughing. "That would be a new angle," he said. He could not help it if a visual image of the improbable newspaper headlines crossed his mind: "SOUTHERN SENATOR'S UNCLE LYNCHED BY MOB OF NEGROES!"

"You're a mighty cocky little bundle of guts and go-get-it, aren't you?" Clay said. "Well, the hell with you——"

"Hold on. I'll take you to see them," Phil said. It was obvious to him that it could not hurt to know the attitudes of these strangers before Monday morning's confrontation. "If they're still up, we'll talk to them. That is, if you can direct me to the street."

"I can get you there, son. It's not a hard street to find. Just four blocks from the majestic seat of government in this worthy county. Four blocks back and down and under—the narrowest, dirtiest, crowdedest alley outside Harlem, N.Y."

When they came to it, Phil felt the full impact of the accuracy of Clay's description. Unpainted, soot-grimed houses tumbled beside one another like pasteboard cracker boxes and were linked together by a rutted dirt alley strewn with every sort of trash and debris cast off by daily living. There was a slow, watchful sort of activity on the corner where the alley joined the street and a dingily lit Pool-Eats parlor poured forth a bedlam of shriek and wail. The car crawled along its narrow passage, making room for an occasional couple walking in the near-total darkness or simply lounging along some sagging steps or on a little stoop that reached almost into the alley-way. Phil drove carefully, dodging the worst ruts, managing only by inches to avoid hitting the people who stepped aside so casually, carelessly.

Hand-printed signs written with school crayons on random-size pieces of cardboard were pasted in the mud-splattered window of a store that was no more than a cubbyhole. "Chicken Necks and Gizzards, 15¢ a lb." "Meat Skins, 10¢ per lb." "Fresh Collards."

"Old collards wouldn't taste bad right now, with some good hot cornbread and fresh buttermilk," Clay said, and Phil knew that he had been reading the signs, too. "But meat skins—good Lord! It sounds like the old depression days."

And Phil was thinking of the bills he would be voting on up in Washington this session, bills that would be proliferating for years to come, whose roots and ultimate meaning lay right here in this dim alley.

As though reading his mind in some weirdly casual way, Clay asked, "These some of your constituents down here, Senator Cortland?"

"Sure." Phil nodded.

"This precinct pretty heavy on the votes during an election?"

"Nothing remarkable. About forty-five per cent of those registered voted, last senator's race."

"What's the matter? Going price for votes too low that day?"

Phil shrugged.

Clay laughed and stretched his legs as far as he could across the car's floor board. "Up north, in that office where Kathleen works, for instance, about two-thirds of the damned fools believe every place below the Mason-Dixon line lynches every black man who wants to vote. Boy, if I didn't set a crowd of them straight one night. I told them we didn't worry about the Negroes voting in my state. We weren't Black Belt South. We just threw a goat-wobble and made sure our Negroes voted the right way. 'What's a goat-wobble?' they were all screeching, and I told them it was just a hoedown where somebody provided all the roast goat and rotgut anybody could eat and drink—and got a little old vote in return."

Phil didn't answer. He was thinking about next year—if he should run for the seat he now held. No, he knew that "if" was dishonest: *when* he would run for the Senate seat. Was he going to come down here and talk about some of the nice points of the law and the international relations he had studied in college? Or would he get one of the courthouse boys, one of Hugh Moore's friends, maybe Hugh himself, to quietly throw a goat-wobble, or a more civilized-sounding counterpart, for "the Negro vote"? Already Jerry Stewart, his administrative assistant, was talking about "the women's vote," "the farmer's vote," "the Negro vote," "the labor vote," and although Phil relished the political game, the challenge, the struggle, while he was in its midst, when he stood off—as during this weekend—and looked at it, some sub-self rebelled at the fragmentation these categories implied.

"Roast the goats literally down here. Go uptown and roast your opponent figuratively. Make the fire hot and the swallowing easy. Formula for winning elections," Phil said.

"You go to it, boy," Clay commended.

They were near the end of the way. "Here." Clay held up his hand. "This is the house. Stop here."

They climbed out of the car. The house—two rooms wide and

two rooms deep, made of rough, unfinished, unpainted lumber, covered with strips of tar paper for a roof—was perched on the side of a slope. A long slim pole at each of the front corners of the house provided unconvincing support to the foundation. Its back rested in the bank. A half dozen planks laid along cinder blocks formed steps of varying heights. A dim light shone through the two windows facing the alley.

The clay path up to the steps was slippery. Phil could see refuse scattered under the house: a jumble of discarded pasteboard boxes, broken bottles, empty tin cans, rags and a small heap of soft lump coal. As he went up the steps, he saw the tin flue of a stove jutting out from one end of the boxlike house. The flue's creased elbow turned it into a dark round arm grasping toward the sky.

"Poor people get poor ways," Clay said, as he kicked a dirty soft-drink bottle out of his way. "That damned Hawk!" he muttered. Phil wondered which of the two statements—one in sympathy and one in anger—he meant. Both, of course, Phil decided.

The door slowly opened to Clay's loud knocks. A big woman in a dark green silk dress and a tall black hat stood squarely in the narrow entrance. Her arms were large and muscular under their tight silk sleeves. Behind her there seemed to be a confusion of people frozen in sudden tableaux. Not a sound came from the crowded little room.

"Look here——" Clay began loudly, out of the darkness.

"We were looking for Hawk Williams' house," Phil interrupted.

"You at the right place," the big woman said. "This used to be his house." She did not alter her squarely planted stance, barring them entrance.

"We wanted to see his wife," Phil said. "My uncle and I, we're——"

"I know who you are, Senator Cortland." She turned her head aside and called, "Lorna . . . ?" Then, "You come on in."

The heat struck them like a wave. The night outside was only mildly chilly, neither Phil nor Clay had worn overcoats, but the pot-bellied stove in one corner of the room was stoked to capacity. A single bare light bulb hung from the ceiling by a length of electric cord and in its harsh illumination the faces crowding the room ap-

peared bleak and immobile, dark and shining. A queer sense of
familiarity, of some cycle completed, overtook Phil. He might not
be home at all, but back on his journey to strange countries. As he
had wondered so often on that trip, he wondered now even more
strikingly: What was the key to unlock the door of centuries of silence between them? Where lay the common ground on which they
could meet and become part of a common world they had experienced so differently?

Children of assorted age and size scurried over the bare floor,
dragging two empty chairs to the fore. A very old man with a cane
between his legs and toothless gums showing in a tentative, meaningless grin sat beside the stove. A half dozen other adults, including
the stout woman in the hat, who had gone back to a place beside
the table—the only other furniture in the room besides the stove and
chairs—watched the two strangers intently.

A thin woman with narrow stooped shoulders and enormous eyes
out of all proportion to the size of her small sunken face came
through the door into the adjoining room. A heavy smell of food
drifted from this room behind her.

"Take seats, Senator Cortland, Mr. Thurston," she said. Her voice
was surprisingly deep and throaty coming from such a spent and
weary body. She indicated the chairs. Her arms, below the short
sleeves of her black formless dress, seemed to be only one long bone
covered by a drapery of tough dark skin.

"Look here," Clay said too loudly, "are you Hawk's wife?"

"That's right." She nodded. Her face was impassive.

No one else spoke and Clay seemed suddenly wordless. Phil felt
overwhelmed by the hot, shut-in, crowded house. Its smell was the
smell of poverty: stale air; grease, splattered and grown cold from
a hundred hurried fryings; cheap clothing saturated with the scent
of food and sweat. And overlying this everyday layer of kitchen and
bedroom smells, which had seeped into every crevice and pore of
their lives, hung now the sweet, the cloying odor of carnations. Phil
saw, on the table, like a centerpiece, a small wreath of imitation
greenery boasting six lonely-looking but live carnations. They were
a brilliant red.

The woman saw Phil looking at the wreath. "We held his funeral this afterooon. Somehow they forgot to carry his wreath out to the burying."

As she spoke, two of the children walked over to the table, leaned their elbows on it and stretched to smell the red carnations. They moved as gracefully and precisely as if they were following the ritual of a ballet.

"Take chairs," the woman said again.

"Look here," Clay began anew, as they sat down on the edge of the straight ramshackle chairs, "I don't know what you've heard——"

All at once the old man beside the stove spoke up. His lower lip worked against his bare upper gums and muffled his words. "If you're the Thurstons I'm thinking about, then I'm of a mind you were some relation to old lawyer Robert Moore."

"That's right," Clay said quickly. "He was my great-uncle."

"Lord! Lord! Now ain't that something! Your great-uncle and one of the finest friends I ever met up with. He done kept me off the roads back years ago when I was young and just sprouting my tail feathers. I got in a little trouble—nothing bad like they tried to say, just boy foolishness—and he believed me. When I said I hadn't taken no hand in big trouble, he believed me; made the judge believe me, too. Lawyer Moore believing me that time did more to keep me straight the years since than ever' sermonizing I ever heard." The weak, aged eyes looked up, searching him out in the blurred mist and images of half-blindness. "And you his great——"

"Nephew," Clay provided.

"That's right, great-nephew. Now ain't that something, Lorna?" The old head swung around like a buffalo's, the eyes trying to focus again. "Lorna, this here's a good man. No matter what they try to say he done or didn't do, you listen to him. He's got lawyer Robert Moore's blood running in his veins."

"All right, Papa," Lorna Williams said. She went over and stood by his chair.

"Him trusting me that once, standing up there in the white courtroom talking for me just the truth that was, when all I'd been able to look forward to in my mind was that old rock pile waiting out there for me . . ." His grey head wagged back and forth. "It's something I'll carry to the grave."

"I remember Uncle Robert from the time I was just a little kid," Clay said. Then he turned to Phil. "The old man's right. He was one unselfish fellow. Died when I was ten years old, right in his prime, of pneumonia fever. He caught it going way back in the mountains during a snowstorm to find some damned witness he needed in a mental commitment case."

The ancient Negro man nodded his head and rubbed his lip along his bare gums. "That's him, that's lawyer Moore he's talking of, all right——"

"I remember Mama saying Uncle Robert worked all over this country and state trying to get some provisions for poor old idiots and crazy folks locked up in back rooms and smokehouses and wherever their folks could keep them," Clay went on. "Something had made him a plumb fanatic on the subject."

"Sure," Phil said. "They still remember him once in a while over at the state capital, when they're fighting over a mental-health bill, something of the sort."

"Hell, he knew more about folks, had more humanity in his heart——" Clay halted as if recalling all at once where he was, and why. "I'm damned sorry about Hawk," he blurted forth.

"Thank you, Mr. Thurston," Hawk's widow said.

"I don't know how the hell it happened. If I did, I'd tell you the whole truth about it."

She nodded.

"And no need for me to lie to you about how I felt toward Hawk." Clay plunged on. "I thought he was a mean son-of-a—a mean actor. I didn't like him a little bit. He hurt every animal that came around him, and that's just something I can't forgive in any man: mistreating dumb animals."

"Then why'd you take him with you on that big hunt?" Lorna asked.

"Why, he was the only one could cook us up a batch of food to eat——"

"And get you a jug to drink?" she asked.

Clay flushed. "Both, I guess."

"Oh, it's all right, Mr. Thurston." She sighed. "You trying to be honest with me. I'll tell you the truth, too. Nobody around here to miss anything from Hawk but slaps by those big leather hands he had on him, kicks by those heavy boots he wore."

The children crowded near the table listened with wide expressionless eyes. Phil watched them and wondered what they might have seen and known here in the narrow confines of these hivelike rooms. From their faces it was impossible even to be sure which of the children were Hawk's, familiar with those stinging slaps and wounding kicks, and which were neighbors', knowledgeable only through rumor and occasional eyewitness.

"Nobody here able to cry because Hawk's gone," Lorna Williams went on. Her fingers, thin and deft as pincers, absently, mechanically stroked the old man's bent shoulders.

Clay looked around the room. The woman who had let them in nodded at him. "Mean as a cobra to all of them, Lorna the worst," she said.

"Can't feel bad because he's gone," Lorna went on softly, steadily, "but can't help feeling bad for what he was."

Phil looked at her sharply. No one spoke.

"Somewhere, way back, things happened to Hawk," she said, and her words fell insistently, like rain in the night. "There was his no-count daddy. All he ever done for Hawk was give him breath and teach him how to butcher. He let that young'un go with him when he used to make the rounds to different farms butchering whatever kind of meat come to hand around the countryside: hog, beef, sheep, veal. Then the old man froze to death in the snow, drunk, one night and Hawk took over his trade."

"Sure," Clay nodded. "I heard about old Hawk getting to be head butcher down at that little meat-packing plant moved in here five, ten years ago."

"'A fine handler of meat,' the head of that plant called Hawk. And I reckon he knew what he was talking about. Hawk knew right where to stick a pig so it would bleed to death just as clean as could be. He knew how to lay a blow on a steer's head to bring it to its knees without no plunging around——"

"Oh, my God!" Clay groaned.

"It was the job he could do," Lorna said. "All the kicking about he'd had, there wasn't no way to learn nothing but what come to hand. And killing had come to his hand early. He didn't choose it. It was just there, and nothing else was. Why, he was given up to be the champion crow and hawk shooter in these parts when he done quit school at thirteen. Course, in all truth, I figure anybody would have to say Hawk liked killing."

The old man sitting beside her nodded his head gravely.

"There was something riling around in him . . ." She paused. None of the others in the room, except Clay and Phil, were looking at her. They were staring at the floor or the ceiling or their fingernails.

"You know, I recollect him coming home one Saturday night and he was in a pure rage. I never did find out what was behind his raging, just that it was there. And he spent the whole fore part of the night yelling around. 'It's meat, Lorna, just meat, on hoof or claw.' Those big hands of his would grab hold of my shoulders so I couldn't move while he talked, pounding his words into me. 'Buy it by the pound, sell it by the pound, eat it up, spew it out. All meat. It don't count for nothing, on or off that hoof, but what the price of sausage, chops, gizzards, selling for that day. All that squealing, bleating, cackling don't get nothing nowhere—nobody listening, just that meat all that matters.' Oh, he was wild that night," she said. Her large deep eyes looked past them all into that dark memory.

"'I swing that hammer,' Hawk yelled at me like I was deaf or across an ocean from him and not right there in the room under his hand, 'I swing that hammer or I push that knife and all the time I'm talking. All the time I'm saying, "Looky here, animal, you up against a man now." I ain't just meat, Lorna. I'm a man. You hear? A man.'"

Phil was spellbound by her voice, her words uncovering an abyss around them all, by the heat, the silent watchful eyes.

And she added, almost inaudibly, compulsively, "'A man, you hear? A man.' And then he felt like he had to prove all over again to me he was a man. I reckon it wasn't so much me he was showing. But he was rough on me, rough as on any of those cattle he knocked with a hammer."

"Poor devil. Poor devil." Clay wagged his head. Phil wondered whether it was Hawk or Lorna he spoke of. Or both.

"All kinds of ways to be sad, Mr. Thurston," Lorna said.

"It's a damned shame!" Clay stood up and the jerkiness of his movement tipped over the chair. One of the little boys, six or seven years old, ran to set it straight. Clay did not elaborate on what was a shame. He thrust a hand into his pocket and pulled out some change. "Here, son," and he gave the boy a quarter.

Other small faces moved suddenly in the room. Without seeming to come forward they made Clay aware of their presence. "Here." He laid a dime in one small hand. "And here." Another dime. "And this little tyke." A nickel. And then two more dimes and seven pennies. "Is there anything you're needing?" he asked Hawk's widow, like a thunderbolt.

She did not seem astonished, but as if she had been expecting his question.

"No." She shook her head. "Thank you."

"Lorna, she's had a rough row, Mr. Thurston," the old man mumbled, but she silenced him before he could go on. "Hush, Daddy," and her fingers pressed into his shoulder.

Phil had stood up now, too. "You go down to the county welfare office Monday morning, Lorna," he said. "That's why they're there, to help you out. And if you run into any difficulty, tell somebody to call my office. We'll vouch for your need."

"All right, Mr. Senator," she said.

There was a moment of uneasiness in the room.

"You folks have something to eat?" the big woman said from the kitchen door. She held a plastic plate with half a caramel cake on it.

"No—no, thanks just the same," Clay said hurriedly.

"A piece of cake and some coffee?"

"It's late"—Phil glanced at his watch—"and we've stayed longer than we intended . . ." He could see that they were disappointed at the rejected invitation, but Clay was suddenly nervous, intent on leaving.

When they were halfway out, Lorna Williams said, "Mr. Thurston, we know you didn't do it."

Clay made her no answer, but flung himself on down the path to the car.

While Phil started the motor, Clay pulled the bottle from his pocket. In two long gulps he drained it. He rolled down the window beside him and hurled the bottle out into the darkness. They heard it crash on a rock and break into many pieces.

"They're always so damned polite," he said. " 'We know you didn't do it.' What the hell kind of courtesy is that, with old Hawk out there in the ground?"

"I don't know," Phil sighed wearily. "I only know that woman—well, she's seen hell."

"They all have," Clay said. He rolled his window back up. "Boy, when we first went in there"—he was regaining his self-control now, as the hot whisky surged out into his pulses—"I thought there for a minute we were in no man's land."

Phil nodded.

"Then old Grandpa, he spoke up and got to remembering around." Clay gazed through the windshield at the street they had turned onto from the alley. At last he said, "Lord, you never know who you got working for you or against you. That's the difference between being down here and up in one of those big cities: folks remember. Things you don't even know about, relatives whose names you can't get straight. Why, I barely know how Uncle Robert Moore looked. But here he is helping me out years later . . ." His voice trailed off.

Phil nodded. "Sometimes things are petty tangled up, all right," he said, "especially family problems involving——"

With a sudden shift of mood, Clay turned on him. "Yeh, yeh, I know how you'd handle everything, you and your 'advanced' city folks: Mama could go to a 'nursing home'; I'd be put away in a sanitarium; we'd get Hawk's widow and kids on relief right away—and then everything would be all neat and cozy, no problems around to clutter up the view every day, to sweat over and cuss at."

Phil felt a tired sort of resentment rising in him at these words, although he recognized the accuracy of much that Clay said. If his mother had said the same thing, he knew that he would have agreed with her, for she was one of the few people of his acquaintance who refused to institutionalize her problems. But for Clay—who not only did nothing to correct any of their problems but, in fact, compounded them—for him to ascend to the pulpit irritated Phil sharply.

"If everybody," he said, "and I mean everybody, would stop rejecting their responsibilities and creating a vacuum into which 'outsiders' and institutions and governments have to step, then we could have everything more like you want it."

"Like I want it? Look, you little burp in the buckwheat, all I want is to be left alone. I just don't want to interfere in anybody's life or have anybody interfering in mine."

Phil laughed shortly. "Interference? You've just shaken up the whole family with your carryings-on, and you have the gall to talk about being left alone? Look, I've noticed that the ones who holler loudest about interference, whether they're individuals or countries or states or whatever, they're the ones who've helped create the very conditions that permit—maybe demand—interference."

"Is that what you've noticed, Senator Cortland? Well, I've noticed that you're getting to be a high-and-mighty pile of muckety muck since you took up office in Washington, D.C. But I have news for you straight off the hot line: You ain't learned quite all there is to know about—about people!"

Phil considered how foolish it was to argue with his uncle now —or ever. To Clay he would never be a rational, possibly capable, adult; he would always be an awkward, inarticulate nephew somewhere between childhood and adolescence. "Forget it, Clay," he said.

"I don't want to forget it. I want to know how you really feel toward me. I want . . ." He gazed out of the window as if searching for whatever it was he wanted. Presently his head sagged forward. His shoulders moved with the motion of the car. He was lulled into momentary sleep. One moment, thought Phil, he's settling the problems of the world, and the next moment he's asleep.

Phil pondered, as he drove, on the friendliness Hawk Williams' family had shown Clay. No resentment. No revenge. Maybe that could help him some way Monday. Damn it, Phil thought, he ought to be awake right now fighting for his life, instead of leaving it to me and the others. But Phil knew that he himself was fighting not so much for Clay's life as for his own. It was a chilling little admission of selfishness. It reminded him of Sherry Austin's visit right after dinner.

They were out of town now and driving up the valley. Phil noticed for the first time the great new disc of a moon that hung in the sky and flooded the dark mountains with pale light. "Harvest moon" he murmured. " 'Shine on, harvest moon. I ain't had no loving since January, February . . .' "

He wondered if Ann Howard, in Washington, had come home from her dinner party yet. The contrast between his evening and Ann's made him grin sardonically. He could almost smell those sick-sweet carnations again. "Be damned if they 'forgot' to take that wreath to the cemetery," he said to himself. "That woman just decided flowers are for the living." He thought about the wild tale she had told, so intimate in its savagery that it could be told only to family or utter strangers. And it seemed to him that there was some message, some truth hovering at the edges of his consciousness if he could but concentrate on grasping it. Too fast, everything moved too fast: the jet he had come home on, the complications of family and career, the crowding of emotions. He needed time to sift and choose, evaluate and plan. But there was no time.

Phil parked in the driveway close to the walk so that he could help Clay into the house. Ivy was still up, sitting by the last embers of the fire. She had put on her bedroom slippers and her face was pink from the warmth of the fire. After the dwelling Phil had just seen, the harmony and glow of this room, of his mother, brought him relief and gratitude.

"I didn't know where Clay is staying," he said.

"Since the rest of the family came, we fixed his room over at the other house, with Kin," she said. "But bring him on in here now. He can sleep on the couch tonight."

"My dear sister . . ." Clay tried to stand straight, without Phil's aid, and failed. "I accept your hospitality." They guided him to the couch and he sat down heavily. "Well, where's the Lord Mayor and the key to the cupboard?"

"Be quiet, Clay, everybody's asleep," Ivy said. She looked at her son and laid one tentative affectionate hand on his arm. "And I imagine you, from halfway around the world, are a little weary . . ."

He smiled at her and put an arm around her shoulder. Ivy did not move. She did not want to shatter this instant. She would have liked to kiss him, loudly, on the cheek, as she had done when he was small, oh, not so very many years ago, but she rejected the impulse. It sometimes seemed to her these days that she had a great horde of affection stored up within her waiting to be spent, to be given to someone who wanted it, needed it, would take it. She had love to spare and she needed to give it in a kiss, a caress, touches and glances that would make life pulse richly with joy.

"You're a wonder, Ivy," her son said, and she glanced up at his unaccustomed use of her given name. He smiled at her again; she noticed once more how the lines around his eyes and mouth had deepened during the past year. "Strangers, the Hottentots or Eskimos, I'll cope with, but this family—well, you're what's known as ambassador without portfolio. State Department would be a breeze for you after . . ." He motioned to include the house, the day, all of them.

"O.K., Senator, O.K." Clay revived momentarily and looked up at them, trying to focus his vision. His hair was disheveled, his eyes dark and unseeing, and his skin was a deep blotchy red. "You needn't be trying to write me off, flush me down the drain. You remember what Papa used to tell us, Ivy? 'I'm not a has-been and I'm not a will-be; I'm an is-er!'"

Ivy laughed. Phil moved toward the door. "If he'll be all right there tonight, I'll——"

"Yes, you go on to bed, Phil. I'm doing the same in a minute. It's good to have you home." They smiled at each other and Phil left the room. Ivy heard him walk down the hall to his study-bed-room.

"An is-er. That's me, Ivy," Clay muttered. "Don't let them tell

you I'm a has-been. And I don't give a rap for will-be. Is, right now,
that's what——"

"Yes, Clay, I remember Papa saying that," Ivy said. She moved
around the room turning off switches on several lamps until only
one light remained. She shook out the soft hand-woven coverlet
that lay across the back of the couch and handed it to Clay.
"Put this over you, Clay. You want me to help you with your shoes?"

"Old Clay doesn't need any help," he said. Tears suddenly
brimmed in his eyes. "Let old Kathleen leave him. Let his brothers
and sisters be ashamed of him. Old Clay can stand on his own——"

"Old Clay can't even stand right now," Ivy said, and they both
broke into a laugh. The tears overflowed and made rivulets down
the tough skin of his face. She helped him lie down, his highly polished shoes propped on the delicately colored upholstery of her
couch.

"'Is-er' . . . That's what Papa said." Clay's eyes dropped shut.
He was not asleep, but he was by himself now.

Ivy turned off the last lamp. Through the long windows looking
out on the hillside, moonlight flooded into the room. Behind her,
around her, the house was silent. But it seemed to Ivy that unspoken
words lay over each room like a dense atmosphere, invisible yet
suffocating. They charged the air around her, the pale light, beautiful and treacherous yet more honest in some ways than the spot-
light of day. Unspoken words above, rip tides of memory below;
need and forgiveness, hope and fury and tenderness.

Clay breathed heavily on the couch. Ivy picked his hat up from
the floor where it had fallen when he lay down. Holding it in her
hand she looked out again at the weird familiar world of earth and
moonlight. Phil would be voting on a space program . . . Did he
have time, too, for this face of the moon? she wondered. She looked
at the hat, turning it slowly in her hand. Tomorrow would be
Sunday—and then Monday, dreaded Monday. What verdict would
that day bring for Clay, for all of them? Especially for Phil. It seemed
to her that she had lived with this fear and foreboding for months
instead of only the days and hours since Wednesday.

This year, she thought, has been so much less than it might have
been; tomorrow will be better, if I give it everything. Her hands

clenched the brim of the soft felt hat and crushed it. "My God, my God," something deep inside her cried out, "has been, will be, what is it hinders us so? Who hobbles us? If we don't have joy of this world we can see and touch and breathe, how shall we ever take it in another we cannot see?" She thought of their faces as they had been together tonight—Mama's, Frone's, Phoebe's, Kin's, Clay's, Naomi's, and her own and Phil's; the ghosts as well as the flesh she could touch. She wept briefly.

After a while she went to bed. On the stairs she smelled a faint odor of pipe smoke and she knew that Phil was not asleep, either. She yearned to go and talk with him, but she kept on up the stairs. Better to preserve the illusion that they might have talked than to face each other and find no words.

"**N**O SIREE, there's two things this sawmill doesn't need." Tom Thurston rocked back on his heels in the sunshine and his strong white teeth shone in a smile at the men scattered in the yard before him. "It doesn't need a has-been, and it can't use a will-be. I want an is-er!"

The men laughed. One or two nodded their heads as if to say, "That's old Tom, all right." And, nudging each other in the ribs, "Listen to that Tom Thurston."

The children stood on the porch and watched him talk to the hands he had hired for the new sawmill. They beamed with pride at Papa's easy command of these big burly men who had gathered under the towering oak and maple trees inside the picket fence around Mama's yard.

"We'll make good this time," Papa had said the night before, as he watched Mama enter neat notes of the workmen's names in his pocket-size payroll book. "Before we know it, we'll be free and clear of debt. Then you just watch your old papa's tracks."

Free and clear! The words lifted their spirits like fog rising from the valley in the morning. Frone and Ivy felt hardly less responsible for the fortunes of the family than Papa and Mama. "I see a straight smooth road ahead, Martha girl, with the wind at our back." The children could almost feel it lifting them now. The world was good again.

"I wasn't cut out to work the land," he said. They had been through this discussion over and over until Martha came to agree with him automatically, nodding her head as she sewed together pieces for a quilt or bent over the girls' tablets in an effort to improve their penmanship. But in the back of her mind she was wondering what had gone wrong, why she and her little family were being punished when all they wanted was to grow the goodly fruits of the earth, raise sturdy livestock on their own acres and live seemly lives. Such wondering left her absent-minded and little interested in any new plans. Even worse, it gave rise to doubts that troubled her more than the actual loss of farming.

"Tom"—she might interrupt his figuring or reading of the weekly paper by the lamp at night, her pale face grave and preoccupied as she fixed her gaze on something behind or above or beyond him— "Tom, do you think there's any way that a Creator who marks the fall of a sparrow's feather wouldn't know about our stumbling around here?"

"I couldn't say, not being taken into confidence as to what's on His mind," Tom would reply, trying to sound cheerful and hearty, "but Almighty be! if we're not more important than a whole flock of sparrows we might as well look to the Lord and be dismissed right now."

"Maybe we were doing it all for our own glory, Tom," she persisted, the far-off look in her eyes distracting and disturbing him. He liked for people to look at each other and deal in concrete facts and plans. "The fine cattle, the big buildings—maybe we were building too much for this world, Tom, and not enough for the next."

"I couldn't say about all that, Martha," Tom cried in near-exasperation. "All I know, if a man wants to eat high off the hog, he's got to bring home the bacon. I'm trying to wrestle out a living for you and the young'uns any way that comes to hand, and we happen to be living in this world, not the next. Nothing would do you but for us to move here to your grandpa's place and turn our hands to farming. Well, Lord knows we did our best and we fell flatter than flounders. Now I'm going back to timber, to something I know firsthand."

"And glad to go back, if I'm any judge!" Martha flared. "You love every bit of it: strangers crowding in, men all over the place, teams to drive, saws and axes noisy on the mountains, the scream of the mill from daylight to dark, a big excitement all the time, tearing up creation!"

"You do make it sound lively, Martha." He grinned at her.

"You think deep down in your heart there's something more important about sawing down trees than growing a good crop——"

"I think it's a rare sight quicker," he answered. "Getting tangled up in farming is like trying to swim in a barrel of molasses. You spend a third of your time planting a crop and another third of your time nursing it to come up, and the last third explaining why it didn't grow and how you can do it all over next year. But a man cuts a tree, he can see the stump right there on one side and the pile of lumber it makes on the other. At least he knows where he stands without all that infernal waiting!"

"Maybe so, Tom." Martha retreated into herself, arguing no longer, yet by no measure defeated in her viewpoint. She reminded Ivy of a terrapin Kin had found down near the springhouse one day last week, and when they prodded it the creature had simply withdrawn its head with the bright beady eyes back under its tough yet delicate shell.

The moment she seemed to yield, however, Tom Thurston was all contriteness and consideration. "Martha girl, we'll live on here at your grandpa's old place," he said. "You and the girls can have you a good garden. I'll cut the rest of the timber here on the land we own and then I'll try to buy the tract on up the mountain at the head of the valley—there's a fine virgin stand still left up there—and I count on getting it cheap. We'll still have this home, it won't be as if we were moving——"

"But it won't be the same, Tom." Martha would not look at him.

"Things are never the same, Martha!" He flung out of his chair and paced the long room. "Take these young'uns here. They grow like Jimson weeds and one morning they're not the same as they were

the morning before and they're not the same as they'll be the morning to come. You can't hold them. You can't hold anything. The old
ball spins, Martha, and nothing you nor me——"

"But I want some permanence in my life, Tom!"

He looked as if he could laugh or cry with her, either way she
wanted. Finally he shrugged in exasperation. "Well, I didn't make
this world; I can't overhaul it."

And thus they had come to this morning when Tom Thurston
was standing on the porch in the sunlight (the men out in the yard
before him, eager and fresh too for this new promise, this work they
needed) and Grandpa Thurston's money was invested in the new
sawmill that was sitting ready, waiting, in the Lower Pasture.

"Men," Papa continued, his voice as keen and clear as his twinkling eyes, "we can set the timber cutters and loggers to work tomorrow morning. Looks like we might be in for a stretch of fair weather
and we better all turn in and pile up a master raft of logs
while the clear spell holds. Then when we get up a head of steam on
that sawmill and begin ripping out those boards come next Monday
morning, we'll have something to chew into."

"That's right, Tom Thurston, give 'em hell and high water," old
man Gunter called out. "My boy and me, we'll be behind one of
them ox teams afore daybreak tomorrow."

"We'll set this old valley humming," a bearded fellow near the
steps said. Other voices joined in.

Ivy took notice of the "we" that her father used in talking to
these men, no less than to his family. Instinctively she realized that
he involved people totally in his undertakings, so that not only their
work, their muscles and sweat, were demanded and used, but their
pride was stirred too, and their concern. And for this, she could
understand that they liked him, that even the men who had not
worked with him before were already caught. They looked at him
with respect because, in some subtle, genuine way, he gave them
self-respect. Because he spoke to them as separate individuals who
were whole men—not fragments for his use and needs only—because he called upon their total use, they yielded up to him their
total allegiance. He said "we" and the men who lived on Thickety

Creek and those who had come from farther away throughout Nantahala County knew what he meant.

Sunlight shone on the water surging by. Ivy's gaze followed the first green of spring where it had begun creeping up the hillsides. Across the road at some little distance below them stood the Shook's weather-beaten house. Ida Shook's feather beds, flung across the back fence, were airing in the sunshine. The Shook house was little more than a tight cabin built of ancient hand-hewn logs, but Ida's energetic dedication to her everyday tasks kept its interior shining. The boards of the floor were bleached and smooth from many scourings; her cookstove gleamed, her hearthstones were clean and unstained, and despite an indolent husband and awkward son, her house was always fresh and sweet—and Ivy admired its every corner. She wished she might have time today to haul Mama's feather beds out into the spring sunshine too. She looked up at the sky. It seemed to hang very near, a hazy blue, soft and indefinite as the mourning dove's call she could hear in the distance. A sweetness —blended of grass, earth, sun, leaves, everything purified—drifted on the air. The sound of her father's voice, of the men's laughter, was as good as the morning itself.

"Fellers, there's one thing we've got to watch out for while we're on this job. Martha, my wife in there"—he nodded toward the door —"she's laid down the law. She says there's to be no cussing around her home or children, no matter how big this sawmill operation grows. She's asked me to tell you that she'll personally fire the first man lets a swear word loose on these grounds."

The men nodded, grinned sheepishly, shuffled their feet. "She'll do it, too," one of them muttered to another.

His companion spat a rich brown stream of tobacco juice. "That's right. She ain't named Martha McQueen Thurston for nothing."

Then Tom Thurston fixed his wide blue devil-may-care gaze on them, and added, "Just remember, men, if there's any swearing done around here, I'll do it myself!"

They slapped their thighs and winked and nodded knowingly and laughed deep male laughter. Ivy enjoyed the sound of it—free of malice, full of the vigor of life. Then the group broke up. Those who lived in the valley went back to their own homes to make ready for an early start on the next day's work. Four of the men would be boarding at the Thurstons—the head teamster Gunter and his boy Leck, sleeping in the barn feed-room, a fresh clean room smelling of raw lumber, and the sawyer, Amos Knott, and his fireman, a cousin, Isaiah Knott, who had the big back bedroom on the second floor of the house. Now Amos and Isaiah went with Tom Thurston to finish setting up the boiler for the mill. Gunter and Leck went up into the woods to finish laying out their logging trails.

Phoebe stayed on the porch rocking Kin, hoping to put him down for an early nap so that she could help fix dinner on this first big day of the sawmill venture. Clay sat on the steps near where Papa had stood; tears rolled down his cheeks and fell on his bare feet, not yet tough and brown but still pale and tender from winter's confinement. He had wanted to go with the men to the enormous, shiny, new mill, had trotted along beside them until Amos Knott spied him.

"Don't want no chaps around," the short, bearded man growled. "Better send him home, Tom."

"Clay here's a pretty dependable feller." Papa laid his hand on Clay's shoulder, but the sawyer would not listen.

"A mill's a dangerous place," he said, and his voice rasped like sandpaper on a board. "I've watched those blades take arms and hands and more fingers than I'd care to count, take them quicker than a jaybird gobbles a junebug. Grown men's limbs they were. I ain't hankering to have no young'uns chewed up by this mill."

"You run on home, son," Papa said gravely. There was no use protesting against that finality in his voice. But, to Clay, how dull and tame this house, these steps seemed compared with the excitement down there in the Lower Pasture.

Frone and Ivy hurried back to the kitchen. Papa had said at breakfast that able sawyers and firemen were hard to come by and hearty men liked hearty food. "Thurston folks have always been good livers," he said. "You girls step lively and help your mama set a heavy table at this house." Then he added, "Fact is, I'm sort of proud of my girls and their way with victuals. Glad to show them off. Right now, Frone there can turn out as light a pan of biscuits as her Grandma Thurston ever did, and nobody on this creek can beat Ivy molding a firm sweet pound of butter with all the water worked out and no strong taste. Yes siree, I'm just anxious to show off my girls' cooking."

They stopped in the doorway. The kitchen was blue with smoke. Mama leaned over the door to the firebox on the stove. Her face was flushed from blowing at a handful of coals under the mound of sticks she had jammed into the stove. "I let the fire get too low," she said, "and this green wood won't catch at all." Smoke stung her eyes and made them water.

"Here, Mama." Ivy opened the back door so that fresh air could flood the room; she pushed the damper on the stove and smoke no longer seeped from the top of the stove. "I'll get some kindling."

The woodbox was empty and she went out to the back yard. As she picked up bits of dried chips and twigs in her apron she considered how satisfying it would be if they could ever have a wood-yard where there were always piles of wood already chopped and seasoned and waiting in neat tall stacks and rows. Neither Papa, nor Uncle Burn nor Uncle Gib when they were here, ever laid in wood ahead for the cookstove or fireplace.

"When I'm away from here, grown up and on my own," Frone had told Ivy one day as they searched for bits of pine hearts they could hoard to start next morning's fire, "I'm going to have heaps and heaps of wood ahead, enough for a whole year or more, and when it snows or rains or weathers up any way a-tall, I'll just build me the biggest blaze I can and be warm and cozy, knowing there's all the wood I'll ever need waiting to be used."

Ivy could hardly think of a nicer dream. She carried her apron full of kindling back into the kitchen and opened the stove door. With her free hand she pulled out all the big green sticks that would not burn and threw them back into the woodbox. Carefully she raked the handful of scattered coals into a heap and laid on some dry twigs. She blew gently until the coals glowed a deep red and the bits of wood burst into flame. Then she filled the stove with the rest of her kindling and laid a couple of sticks across each other above the hottest part of the fire.

Mama, smoothing back her hair and rubbing her temple with

round gentle strokes, watched Ivy and said, "The fire didn't seem to hold at all this morning. It burned down so quickly. Oh, sometimes I do long so for poor old Aunt Tildy to be here and help look out for us all!"

Neither Ivy nor Frone, washing dishes, answered. They were reminded of the bleak day, two months before, when they had buried Aunt Tildy up on the hillside, among all the old familiar graves. She had been a link from a lost world.

"I was in the bedroom resting for a minute—I'm afraid one of those sick headaches is about to come again—and I was just marking that passage in the Bible where we're instructed to multiply and replenish the earth."

Frone, setting a kettle of water to heat on the stove, rattled the lid with unnecessary noise. But Mama did not seem to notice. "I want your papa to read that verse. It doesn't mean just multiplying your own kind, I know it doesn't. It means to replenish the earth of all you wrench from it, multiply the fruits instead of just subtracting them. Oh, I feel somehow that this timbering of his is all wrong. He can't just take and take from the land and never give back."

"You can't say Papa's stingy," Frone broke in. "He gives all the time. He's the most generous person on this whole creek."

Mama looked startled. "I didn't say anything about your papa being stingy. This doesn't have anything to do with generous or not, Frone. What I'm talking about is the creed we live by. It's our relationship to our Creator and the world He made. And He said to replenish it."

"What do you want Papa to do?" Frone demanded. She was tall for her age and coming into awkward years and her shyness and pride combined to expose her to every nuance and inflection of a word or gesture. She reacted twice as sharply as necessary to every encounter. "Should he go around planting acorns every time he cuts a tree?"

"Maybe so." Mama nodded seriously, rubbing, rubbing at her temples. "But that's not like your papa. He wouldn't do that. He'd have to find his own way." She sat down beside the table. Ivy did not look at her, but laid more sticks on the blazing fire, watching the lick and leap of its flames. As it grew in intensity, after she was

sure the wood had caught, she drew the damper shut. The fire settled to a slower, surer burning.

"Maybe the new minister"—Mama was talking on—"will bring
us help. We need somebody beyond ourselves. It's not good for a
community to be without a man of God in its midst. Sometimes I'm
afraid you children are growing up no better than pagans, out of
contact——"

"And what about all those visiting preachers who stop here to
eat and sleep?" Frone asked. "I've plenty of contact with them, passing them chicken and gravy, washing their sheets and towels——"

"Frone!" Mama was truly hurt and angry now. "It's not the same."
She pursed her lips and Ivy was abruptly aware of how much
Frone and Mama looked alike when you studied their faces.

"Talking of eating"—Ivy interrupted them—"what can we fix for
the men's dinner today, Mama?"

"I put dried beans on to cook, but I doubt if they'll get done
after the fire got so low." She stood up and went to the white bowl
and pitcher on a washstand near the door, where she dipped a cloth
in cold water, squeezed it gently and pressed it against her forehead.
"I'll have to lie down a little while, girls," she said. "My sick headache . . ."

How Ivy dreaded the words. She hated the darkened windows,
the hushed house, her mother's misery during those long gloomy
hours of nausea and pain. And why did the sick headache have to
come this day of all days, when there was such excitement and hope
and everything was to be special? "You girls fix whatever you want
to for dinner," Mama said. "Oh, the dizziness . . ."

Ivy helped her get to the bedroom. After she lay down, Ivy
pulled off her shoes, spread the faded wedding-ring quilt up over
her legs and laid the cool damp cloth across her eyes and forehead.
Then she drew down the shades on the windows, closing out the
early spring sun.

Back in the kitchen, Frone stood with her soapy wet hands on
her hips. " 'Fix whatever you want.' Well, I *want* tenderloin and am-
brosia, but I'll be dogged if I can find anything to fix it with. Ivy,
whatever can we cook? Papa said for us to set a good table."

"I know." They looked at each other, stricken for a moment by

the weight of this responsibility. Then Ivy said, "We'll get the last of
the winter cabbage out of the garden hole in the back yard. I'll slice
the biggest pieces left on that last ham in the smokehouse and you
can bake hot biscuits and stew a pan of apples. We'll make out."

Tears of frustration glistened in Frone's eyes. "She oughtn't to
run away and leave us to face all these strangers ourselves. I hate the
thought of them being around all the time, Ivy. Nothing we have—
the farm, the house, nothing—will be ours for our very own any
more."

"Why, you're just like Mama," Ivy said in surprise. "You don't
want the sawmill either."

"It's not the sawmill," Frone replied hastily. "Papa wants the
sawmill. I'll stick by anything Papa wants. But it's the men, those
outsiders who come in and want to be part of our lives——"

"Well, you can't have one without the other," Ivy said.

The kitchen was quiet except for the crackling of the fire in the
stove. Frone wiped her hands on her apron. "Just wait! I'll have a
home of my own someday," she vowed.

When the men came to eat at noon, soaping and rinsing their
hairy arms and hands at the washbowl, scraping their chairs noisily
to the table, devouring great mouthfuls of steaming vegetables and
meat and hot bread, washing it all down with glasses of cold buttermilk and cups of scalding coffee, they emptied the dishes without
comment, pushed back from the table and went out into the yard
where they stood around for a little while under the big white oak.

"Well, we know one thing," Frone said wearily, handing little
Clay the last biscuit left in the pan, "they're not going to starve to
death. At least not before suppertime." She and Ivy laughed. Clay
was buttering his biscuit. He put half in his mouth at a bite, the way
he had seen the men do. "You little old copycat," Frone said, and
hugged him to her.

"I love you, Fwone," he said, his mouth full of hot bread.

And so the strangers came into their lives—the wanderers, the
woodsmen, the workers and taletellers, the sawyers and cattle
drivers and axemen. They invaded by invitation this private domain

of clear waters, clean woods and gentle grass, trampling it to their own shape and need—imperative, rough, impervious to all patterns not of their own creation and to all needs beyond their own consumption. The little family was wrenched out of its intimate intensity of self and land into other relationships both larger and lesser than those they had accepted as the foundations of existence. As Burn and Gib McQueen had opened to them years before, through experience of the Spanish-American War, a door that could never be closed again, so these strangers brought them to a crossroads that could not be evaded. They might choose the pace and pattern of their change, but they could not repeal the change itself.

Through the long days of spring and summer the high scream of the sawmill filled the Lower Pasture and echoed up to the big white house. The heap of honey-colored sawdust grew to a pyramid and stacks of straight new board increased across the only level acres left with the Thurston farm. On the mountainsides there was a constant din of axes, saws and crashing trees as ancient monarchs trembled on their stumps and then went down with a great tearing of limbs and undergrowth and saplings. Shouts of the loggers at their rebellious mules and plodding oxen tore through the woods from early morning until nightfall. Tom Thurston was in his element, as Martha's brother, Fayte McQueen, pointed out to her one day in July. Crops and gardens in the valley had been laid by and school had started. It would last four months, until cold weather set in in November. Fayte had stopped by to leave a Latin book for Frone.

"Caesar will come as easy to Frone as timbering does to Tom," he said in his low, kindly voice, adjusting the glasses that kept slipping down the bridge of his nose. "She's like our people in taking to books, Martha."

"Don't let her hear you say that, Fayte," Martha sighed and shook her head. "Frone's got her heart set on being a Thurston through and through."

Fayte smiled. "Well, sometimes she seems like a pure reincarnation of Aunt Tildy, whether she likes it or not."

Martha nodded. "The other night Frone came in from the milk-gap, weak as widow's porridge and twice as pale, vowing she'd

heard a screech-owl near the barn and there was bound to be bad
luck in store. The very way she said it took me back to when you
and I were children at home . . ."

"Aunt Tildy and her night birds and all her omens," Fayte mused.

There was a pause. The only sound was that of the sawmill
in the distance, changing voice as its blade bit into a thick log and
buzzed through slowly, steadily.

"Well," Fayte went on, "Frone's not an easy girl to know, Martha,
but she's smart. All three of your girls—they're a little different from
most of the others in my school . . ."

"They're your kinfolks," Martha teased him.

"No," he insisted, "it's not partiality. Most of the children on
Thickety are bright enough, but yours and Tom's—they've got ambition, Martha. And pride."

Tears sprang to her eyes. "Oh, Fayte, do you remember how
much Mama always wanted for us, for her children?"

"You know then why I'm content to hold this school here, don't
you, Martha?"

"Why yes, brother Fayte. I've always known why you stayed
here. Bless you." She patted his arm.

After he left, turning his quick long steps up the road that led to
the meadow under the Devil's Brow, she sat on the porch for a little
while longer. Her mind this afternoon was like one of those grab
bags stuffed full of quilt scraps she collected. Bright, dark, little,
large, new, threadbare. She thought about her girls: Frone too sensitive and shy and angry; conscientious, loving Ivy; Phoebe full of
quickness to either anger or love, reflecting whatever was given her;
and the little boys—Clay, his father's shadow and vanity, straining
toward school already, toward grown-up ways and the men's world
of the sawmill; and Kin, even though still a baby, perhaps the keen-
est and most adventurous of all her children. She thought about
their school. Would Tom have money by year after next to send
Frone in town to boarding school? And Ivy would be ready the following year; then after a little while the three younger ones. Certainly they would all have to finish high school. She wished she could
think of college for them, especially for Frone—and maybe Kin. It
was a big wish. It could stand or fall only by Tom's sawmill.

She thought about the sawmill. Unconsciously she had shut its sound out of her ears, but now she heard it again, insistent as a great fly droning over the valley. She wondered what it might bring to them next, after that dreadful day two weeks ago when Leck Gunter was fastening a log chain to a big old poplar his oxen were to snake down the mountainside and the log broke loose, catapulting over the slope, smashing into the boy and leaving him, miraculously, with only a broken leg before it careened on down the mountain and finally jammed into some other trees. Tom had taken Leck to the doctor in town and then on to the boy's home at the other end of the county where his mother and younger brothers and sisters could help him get well. The trip had cost Tom a full day away from the mill, but he had given it ungrudgingly. He had not trusted anyone else, not even the boy's father, to see that the doctor set the leg properly. On their way in to town in the little one-seated buggy with Leck stretched out beside him, one shard of broken bone sticking up through the skin, he had held the boy's attention with a dozen funny tales and songs and after that day no one by the name of Gunter would listen to anything but praise for the person of Tom Thurston.

Scarcely any of the timber-cutting or logging was going as smoothly as they had hoped it might. Amos Knott was a fine sawyer, but Tom's difficulty lay in finding men who could handle the animals. He had a big investment in four strong-shouldered pairs of prime oxen and three stout teams of high-spirited young mules, but outside of the Gunters none of the men he hired seemed to be able to work them to the limit of their capacity without beating them up and wasting more hours with balkiness than with actual work. They lost time and tempers, the recalcitrance of men and beasts held up the hungry sawmill. And yesterday, just when everything had seemed to be moving more in harmony, one of the mules had developed such shoulder sores that when Tom discovered them he ordered the mule left in the barn lot till the bleeding rawness could be healed. Furious at the careless, heartless teamster who had allowed such a condition to grow critical, Tom fired him then and there—the third logger he had fired in as many weeks—with a little of the swearing he had promised to do for all concerned when necessary.

Martha smiled to herself. Maybe a strong word or two was necessary just that once. The smile disappeared. Swearing had certainly
not be necessary the night before, however, in front of the children,
when she had told him about Preacher Grey's arrival.

"Be damned if I care when you have him to dinner, Martha,"
Tom had said in the kitchen, after the other men had gone outside
to enjoy the cool of the evening and the girls were washing dishes
while Martha bathed the baby for bedtime. "With that high-powered
schooling he's supposed to have had, I expect he'll be more your
breed than mine anyway, Martha. Probably squeezed all the sweat
out of everyday living, got his problems packed down and salted
away under a lot of big words a long time ago. I'll just be damned
if I've got time for all that right now."

"Tom, you needn't talk like that." Martha had bitten her lip
until it was bruised, but she had spoken no other words as she patted
a towel along Kin's wet legs.

"It's all I can do to keep things on the track out there." He
nodded. "You'll have to take care of the church and your preachers,
Martha."

She thought about this now, on the porch, as she planned for
dinner tomorrow when they would meet the preacher and for Sunday when they would all go to church together—she hoped—and
hear his first sermon. She knew with a vague unease that there was
something she must do for her children and soon. It was something
that would remain important through the rest of their lives. But because the feeling of her task was better defined than the form of the
task itself or its purpose, she assumed it concerned religion and she
was ready to let Preacher Grey help her with it all he would or
could.

Abruptly Martha arose and walked down the steps from the
porch. She went around the house to her vegetable garden. The season had been good and the children had worked the garden well.
Neat rows of beans, cucumbers, tomatoes, hung heavy, ripening on
stout vines. In one corner of the picket fence a thick patch of rhubarb was marked by its profusion of broad green leaves and long
red stems. Martha pulled an apron full of these stalks. She wrung
off the leaves as she went along, throwing them outside the fence.

She was counting on Tom's taste for deep-dish rhubarb pie. If his stomach could be put to good use to save his soul, she saw nothing wrong with that.

By the time the girls were back from school, loitering behind their Uncle Fayte to talk with Azalie and some of the other girls and tell "tales that ain't so," as Azalie called the stories Frone made up for them, Mama had peeled the rhubarb and cut it in small chunks ready to cook the next morning. "With the preacher coming to take dinner tomorrow," she said to Frone and Ivy, "I thought maybe you'd like to stay home and help me with the cooking and serving."

Frone would not hear of missing school. "Uncle Fayte says I might win the English prize for all Nantahala County if I can finish reading *Pilgrim's Progress* between now and the end of the month and write a good report. I won't, I won't stay home——" Her voice was rising.

"All right, Frone." Mama put her fingers up to her forehead and rubbed her eyes wearily.

Phoebe, on the other hand, was eager to help entertain the visitor and miss school. But her mother told her, "You're too little to do much of what needs doing. You'll be of better use to yourself and everybody else in school."

Frone volunteered to take Clay with her to classes, pointing out that this would relieve the work at home a little. Mama let him go, for although he was too young to take up his books regularly with the others, Frone and Ivy had taught him the alphabet and he was already making letters into words. He scrubbed his small stone-toughened feet eagerly when he learned he could go to school with the big children the next day, and Frone put an extra biscuit and jelly sandwich and apples in her lunch pail.

Ivy, then, was the only one to stay home, except for the baby. And she became the first one to meet Preacher Zachariah Grey. She was sweeping the walk that led from the veranda to the gate in the picket fence, between Mama's red rambler roses, when she saw him coming up the valley on his proud black horse. And from her first glimpse of the powerfully built man, with a broad-brimmed black hat pulled low over one eye, Ivy knew that Thickety Creek would never be the same again. What the change would be she couldn't even imagine, but she was certain that it would be different from anything any of them had ever known before.

She watched him ride around the curve, slow down long enough to take one sweeping glance of the countryside and then turn onto the road toward her house, and all at once he was there, in front of her, before she could prepare herself. Seen so close, he appeared even larger, more overwhelming. His shoulders were massive. The coat he wore seemed too small to contain him and the long string tie around his neck was made into a loose bow as though otherwise it might choke him. The Western-style boots he wore had narrow high heels such as Ivy never had seen on a man's shoes before. They were polished as brightly as Ida Shook's windowpanes.

"The Lord make His countenance to shine upon you—good day!" he said, and his voice was like him and like the horse he rode: strong, controlled, full of energy waiting to be tapped.

Ivy spoke to him, shamed that he should have found her in her oldest faded work dress. She knew the house inside was not tidy either. Why had he come so early?

He leaned down and held out his hand to her, gravely, as to an adult, while the horse tried to shy but could not, for his master held a firm rein with the other hand. "Zachariah Grey. Preacher for Thickety Creek Church," he introduced himself.

His grip was strong and sure. She remembered what Papa always said about a first handshake: "Take any stranger. I can tell in a minute whether he's a man with a grip on life or whether he's just a cold codfish wearing pants." Papa would like Zachariah Grey's handshake.

As though he had read her very thoughts in some uncanny way, he straightened in the saddle, after she told him her name, and said, "Where can I find your father, Ivy Thurston?"

"Papa's not here now. He'll be back at dinnertime. He's down at the sawmill." She nodded toward the Lower Pasture and the whine and buzz of the saw confirmed her direction.

"That's where I'll see him, then," Zachariah Grey said. He turned the big horse sharply. "I'll be back with your papa for dinner, Miss Ivy." He was gone along the road.

Ivy watched him out of sight, then ran into the house. She felt the same exhilaration that she had found a few times before—once in winter walking by herself under tall pine trees during the hush of the first thick snowfall, and again last spring the afternoon she had found a bed of white trillium tall to her knees in a damp hidden ravine up on the mountain.

Mama was dismayed to learn that the preacher's introduction to her husband would be at the sawmill. She and Ivy set about airing and dusting the dim, unused parlor. Ivy thought all the while how the musty horsehair smell of this room bespoke long Sunday afternoons and the crowded mournful hours when neighbors had come, in such great numbers that there were not even chairs for all, to sit up with Aunt Tildy's body before her funeral. It was a formal, dismal room and Ivy was glad to be finished with it and leave it to the sightless stares of the stiff-necked bearded men and solemn women whose pictures hung along the wall. She felt more at home scrubbing the kitchen floor and dining room and spreading Mama's white linen cloth on the long table where they would eat dinner. "Clear off the kitchen table," Mama said, "and for once we'll let the sawmill hands eat to themselves while the preacher has a chance to get acquainted with our family in the dining room."

But Mama had reckoned without Preacher Grey and Papa in her planning for privacy. They came up to dinner walking briskly, as if the July heat did not simmer in the fields around them and make little clouds of dust that rose around their feet in the wagon ruts where they walked. Preacher Grey led the black horse behind him, and a little farther behind came the sweaty, weary crew. The newcomer's black suit stood out strangely among the grimy work clothes of the other men. Down the front of his coat and trousers, however, flecks of fresh sawdust already clung. There was even a slight film on his wide hat. He hitched his horse to a limb of the black walnut tree in the back yard and he and Tom Thurston came on into the house.

"Tom! You should take the preacher to the front," Mama cried, as they appeared in the kitchen door. She and Ivy had put on fresh white dimity dresses and clean aprons, but the heat of the stove, the steam from pots of cooking food, and the sultriness of the day had wilted their freshly combed hair and brought beads of sweat to their faces. Mama patted her forehead with the edge of her apron now, and in embarrassment held out her hand to the newcomer.

"Don't fret yourself, Mrs. Thurston," Preacher Grey said. When he removed his hat, his shoulders seemed even wider than before, and his broad deeply lined face became suddenly arresting because of his eyes. He looked at Martha. "I didn't come to see your house. I'm here to meet you and your family, and it appears you're right here where it's best to find you, at your work. I'm happy to make your acquaintance."

"Oh, Preacher Grey"—Martha Thurston looked up at him with wide, hopeful eyes—"we've looked forward so to this day, to your coming up our valley." She laid both hands in his. "We want you to be happy and have a fruitful ministry here."

Tom Thurston, dipping water into the bowl on the washstand, cleared his throat loudly as he sometimes did when he was annoyed or embarrassed. "Now, Martha, I've not had a chance to know the preacher here for very long, just the little while since he came walking up to me where I was helping off-bear boards for Amos, and he stuck out his hand and told me he was the new preacher. But if I'm any judge of men, you won't have to use your literary talk with him. Just plain old everyday words will do. Here, Preacher, care to wash up before we eat?" and he handed their visitor the fresh towel Ivy had put on the rack.

Preacher Grey caught them both in his quick glance—Tom with his wide easy smile under the brown curly hair and laugh-crinkled, wide-set eyes, and Martha with her small anxious face, direct brown eyes and slightly pursed mouth. "Any word a friend speaks is good to hear," he said, "whether from book or field. And"—he smiled at Ivy by the stove, the first time she had seen him smile—"I've already met one of the nicest Thurstons."

She blushed, quickly turned to the stove and stirred the thickened chicken gravy.

"That's so," her father said, rescuing her, at the same time compounding her self-consciousness. "Not a one of our children that doesn't have her—or his—own special little quality." He winked at Ivy.

Preacher Grey, washing his hands with a big new bar of Mama's homemade soap, watched Ivy and her father. Ivy decided there wasn't much happened around this man that he didn't see.

"Frone, that's our oldest girl," Papa went on, "she's at school today, a regular bookworm, smart as a a judge but temperish. And Phoebe, next youngest after Ivy here, she's our home body, quick as a cricket, looks just like her Mama. Clay's our oldest boy, not quite old enough for school but he's high-powered anxious to be a man already. I'm hoping maybe he'll make a doctor one of these days. Kin's the baby. We haven't settled that little feller's future yet."

"You're a fortunate family," the Preacher said as he dried his hands carefully, and the way he said it carried special conviction to them.

The sawmill men who had washed outside came into the kitchen and Martha explained about the two tables.

"Now hold on a minute, Martha," Tom said before the men could take their places, "there's room enough for everybody at the big table in yonder. The preacher would like to know these men and they ought to get acquainted with him."

The crew looked uneasily at one another and one or two protested. "The places are done laid in here, Tom."

"Bring your plates on in here." He would not hear their excuses, and led the way into the adjoining room. "We ought to all eat together."

"I would rather eat with all of you," Preacher Grey said. "That is, if it's agreeable with Miss Martha's plans."

What could she do but agree? And listen in amazement as her husband and the preacher talked throughout the meal, while Ivy passed platters of crisp fried chicken, bowls of rice, green beans, a plate of thick red tomato slices and pungent garden lettuce wilted with hot bacon and onions, biscuits and a boat of rich gravy. The others ate heartily, silently, but they were attentive to all that was said. Listening, Ivy knew why they were so interested, for Preacher Grey's history, or as much as could be drawn from him by Papa's skillful, interested questions, was like a book.

He had been born in eastern Pennyslvania and, when he was still a boy, had come to the Southern Appalachians with his father, a poor but excellent schoolmaster. Both parents and a younger brother had died in a cholera epidemic and all alone the boy had struck out for experience, an education, a livelihood. He told them that in a lifetime of wandering he had accumulated a great deal of the experience, enough of the education to whet his appetite for more, and enough of the livelihood to be sufficient for his needs. He was a man grown for many years before he found God and decided to be His minister to other men.

"Your reputation has run ahead of you," Martha said. "We've heard of your power and conviction in the pulpit."

"Even more so out of the pulpit, I trust," he answered slowly.

Martha was slightly taken aback, but Tom Thurston looked up from the breast of chicken he was finishing and gave a quick approving smile. "I couldn't have said it better myself, Preacher."

Preacher Grey made a brief mock bow toward him. "I'm glad to learn that you're a man of religious concerns, Mr. Thurston."

It was his turn to be ruffled. "Now—now look here, Preacher . . ." The men at the table glanced up from their plates for the first time and grinned at one another and waited to see what old Tom would say. "I tell you, Preacher, I leave the biggest part of the church doings to Martha." He nodded toward his wife. "She's got a leaning that way."

Ivy, in the door to the kitchen, fetching hot biscuits, paused for the preacher's reply. There was a long pause and it seemed that he might make no answer. Then he said, "It's a leaning we all come to, soon or late, Tom Thurston."

No one said anything. There was a scraping of plates as the men lowered their eyes and finished the meal. Men of their acquaintance did not talk about such things, especially on weekdays.

Then Martha spoke. "That's true, Preacher Grey, oh, so true. But many wait too long to find it out."

The preacher leaned back in his chair and confronted them directly. Ivy saw then why his gaze was strange, for all its compelling force. He had a cast in one eye and when he faced another person it appeared that the sight of one large hazel eye was penetrating to the very marrow, while the vision of the other eye was turned irrevocably inward. "We all come by our own way," he said. "Some find the high road early. Others have to flounder along side roads and detours." He looked around at each of the men. "The more of a man, the earlier he climbs out of the muck and seeks God's face."

They did not answer him, but it was obvious they were impressed by what he said. Like Martha, they found it difficult to reconcile this big man, whose rugged muscles of arm and thigh and shoulder had surely not been developed in any pulpit, with his words, which spoke of such a private thing as faith, such an unseen unstated substance as hunger after God. His words, in their own way, were as muscular as his limbs.

When they finished eating and went outside, Ivy sat down alone at the table and nibbled on a chicken wing. Kin crawled to where she sat and she took him on her lap, absent-mindedly gave him the stopper from the vinegar cruet to play with. "Kin," she whispered, "Preacher Grey's come. And as old Aunt Tildy used to say, 'a quare enough coming it is.'"

But the whole valley, no less than Tom Thurston, was caught up by this newcomer's paradoxes and by his power. His Sunday sermons stirred them to take new, often uncomfortable, looks at themselves, and even the men came inside to hear him instead of standing outside waiting for their wives, talking in low voices, as had been their custom. The preacher's everyday encounters with them—in fields or woods, on wagons or porches, at home or gathered at Nelson's crowded old store—left everyone puzzled and pleased. No one ignored him.

Lazarus Shook was the only person who even tried to belittle him. "Ah-h me, just another busybody lazy spouter of Scripture," he grumbled as he aired his soft white feet during the summer afternoons of late July and early August, seeing in others those faults most obvious in himself. But Preacher Grey overcame him simply and swiftly by remarking on Lazarus' new glasses. Then Lazarus' attitude changed. "Ah-h me, a fine citer of Scriptures, a deep-sighted man. Said right off, 'Mr. Shook, I can tell you're a leader in this community, just the way you wear your spectacles. I'd like for you to give me help here whenever your time allows.'"

Azalie Shook told Frone and Ivy as they walked to school one morning that her pa had decided he was going to help the new

preacher get Tom Thurston into the fold of the church. Frone and
Ivy agreed, as they went home that afternoon, that they would not
mention what Azalie had told them. "Papa would never go to church
if he knew what that Lazarus Shook had said," Ivy warned her
sister.

Frone promised she wouldn't tell, but a gleam of laughter came
into her eyes when she thought of it. "I'd like to hear what Papa
would say if he knew Lazarus was going to save him!"

All through the long summer days Tom Thurston's cutting, logging, sawing, continued. Wagon loads of lumber rolled into town.

"Why, Martha, we might be buying back that creek-bottom land
before next summer. We need more corn to feed these teams."

Martha's eyes shone.

As Ivy sat in the little schoolhouse where all the pupils met in
one room and Uncle Fayte gathered each grade of readers in turn
around his desk while the others studied back on their benches, she
could see, through the wide-open door, heavy loads moving down
the dusty rutted road. She marveled that there was so much lumber
in the whole world and she knew that there would be an even
swifter flow if Papa could find two or three other teamsters who
would do their jobs.

Sometimes, early in the mornings she heard the loggers taking
their oxen and mules out from the barn lot, yoking or hitching them
up for a new day, and sound of their blows made her sick inside.
One mule especially, a bright brown one, was stubborn early in the
day till it had settled into its collar and harness, and she wondered
if the men took turns beating, prodding, gouging it. At church on
Sundays she heard Preacher Grey speak of kindliness and gentleness
to God's creatures, but six days a week she heard whips and curses
and saw bruised flesh if she dared look. Her allegiances and anxieties seemed stretched between Papa's sawmill on one hand and
Preacher Grey's church on the other.

She sat in Uncle Fayte's schoolroom, while the children up front
droned away at their spelling, and she wondered what darkness and
brightness was buried in people. What lay inside herself? In bed at
night recently she had wondered about souls and their reality, and
once or twice she had cried herself to sleep because she feared the

lostness Mama sometimes spoke of so sadly to Preacher Grey. And because, too, she knew abut the cuts and bruises and pain of the animals lying out there in the barnyard in the darkness and she could do nothing to ease the poor creatures. She thought of all the calves and lambs, pigs and chickens, bobwhite quail and squirrels, that had died to feed her own small family and families around the world. Beyond their flesh was the flesh of wounded people, and that was worse. She brooded over the inevitable cannibalism of life.

Then, early in October, Great-uncle Robert Moore came out from town one afternoon and brought a stranger with him. Ivy would never forget that this was the year when both Preacher Grey and Nye Blankenship rode up the valley and into their lives.

Uncle Robert hitched his horse and buggy in the back yard and when Ivy and the rest of the children, followed by their mother, rushed to him from the wide brass kettle where they were stirring apple butter over an open fire, they hugged and exchanged greetings and talked for a few minutes before the family even noticed the slightly built man who stood on the other side of the buggy. He was not watching them but looked up toward the barn and the mountains beyond where a raw gaping scar was spreading across the slopes.

"Nye, come on over here and meet these folks." Uncle Robert's voice, it seemed to Ivy, was even kinder than usual. He reached out one hand, as if to a child. With his hair heavily turning to grey and his good city clothes and a manner that was enormously self-assured but not assertive, Uncle Robert appeared to Ivy as the model of all that was best to have or learn in faraway town.

The stranger came around the buggy, patting Uncle Robert's horse on the neck, watching them all as though they might spring a surprise, an unpleasant surprise, on him at any moment. His age would have been hard to guess, perhaps fifty-five or sixty, but he was tough as whang-leather. He was poorly dressed in faded shirt and trousers that hung loosely on his thin frame, and his shoes fit so ill that they made a slight slapping sound against the ground when he walked. Under a shapeless, stained hat pushed to the back of his head, wisps of greying sandy hair were visible. The slight stubble of beard on his gaunt face was sandy too, but under the beard his skin was pallid. It accentuated the catlike greenness of his watchful eyes. He nodded as Uncle Robert introduced them.

"Nye Blankenship here," Uncle Robert went on, "is one of the finest men I've ever met. He's as honest as daylight itself; and he's already forgotten more knowledge about the ways of woods and woods' creatures than most of us will ever know in our lifetime."

The man was shy and embarrassed. He looked away, up the mountain again.

"I heard that Tom was having logging trouble and I brought him Nye Blankenship," Uncle Robert said.

Martha did not know what to say. She could not hire a new man for her husband's work. And the stranger still hadn't spoken a word to them. "Tom will be in from work after a little while," she said. "You two come on in and wait and then we'll have some supper when Tom comes——"

"Oh, yes, yes, Uncle Robert." The girls seized his hands and Phoebe jumped up and down.

He looked at them and smiled and shook his head. "Well, I'm glad my sweethearts haven't forgotten me yet. But I can't stay this time. Martha, there's a case to come before the judge at nine o'clock in the morning and I have to search out one of my witnesses this evening. But I'd like to have one thing: a drink of good fresh buttermilk right out of a crock in your spring-run, if you'd give it to me."

Ivy started to get him the drink, but Mama called her back so sharply it hurt her feelings.

Mama and Uncle Robert walked down to the springhouse and an uneasy silence settled over the yard. Then the man named Nye Blankenship suddenly asked, "The mule in the lot yonder—why isn't she up on the mountain a-working?" He had a soft voice, not at all like the rough skin of his thin face and hands.

"Old Kate has a bad shoulder," Ivy said. "Back in the summer there were sores and they didn't heal right and the men kept having to use Kate anyway when the work was pressing. Now Papa says her shoulder is probably injured for good and none of them are to touch her again—she's so mean now . . ."

But Nye Blankenship was already on his way to the barn lot. He had a countryman's long, free, easy stride, even in his slightly flapping shoes. Frone and Ivy looked at each other, then back at him. Phoebe watched them. When her older sisters started following the man, she trailed after them. He was already over the fence and in the barnyard when they reached the barn. Ivy started to call out to him, then paused. The mule stood by the opposite fence, motionless, head raised, ears pointed, eyes white and wild. Any noise or alarm could make it bolt.

"Mister," Frone whispered loudly, panting after they ran the last few steps, "watch out! Papa says Kate's dangerous."

But the man was walking toward Kate, hand outstretched, talking softly, steadily. When he came almost within reach, the mule backed up, head still raised, nostrils flaring, eyes rolling. Nye Blankenship did not falter. He walked on without breaking his stride, speaking quietly, and this time he reached out slowly and deliberately laid his hand on the mule's neck. Ivy heard Frone suck in her breath.

Old Kate stood and did not break away. The man talked on, his hand rubbing the big neck with long firm strokes. All the while his catbird eyes were looking at the animal's shoulders, at its back and legs. Frone and Ivy did not move but watched intently the little drama before them. The man and the mule stood in a sort of tableau of tension and ease and after a time that seemed almost interminable to the girls, with everything quiet except the stranger's low voice and the dry ticking of insects in the tall October weeds, they heard Mama call.

"Don't you want to tell your Uncle Robert good-by?"

They looked at each other and at Nye Blankenship. Rubbing, rubbing that neck with strong gentle hands, he made no sign that he had heard. The girls drew away from the fence and ran back down to the yard.

"He's tamed old Kate, Mama," they cried. "He's up there patting her right now, talking to her like she was somebody."

Martha glanced at Uncle Robert. "Why, that's fine, girls——"

"Now Martha, you're not to worry," Uncle Robert tilted her firm little chin up toward him with one forefinger. "You tell Tom what I've told you and then forget it. Take poor old Nye for his value now—and I believe, Martha, he'll mean a lot to Tom's work."

"Thank you, Uncle Robert," she said. "You've always been a help beyond compare——"

"Sh-h." He shook his head and hugged them each good-by in turn.

When Tom Thurston came up from the sawmill, he found Nye Blankenship currying the mule. "Scared me out of a year's growth," he said laughingly to Martha that night as they made ready for bed, "till he told me how he came to be here, that your Uncle Robert had brought him—and I saw how he'd gentled old Kate."

"The girls were very impressed," Martha said. She was sitting on the edge of the bed in her white nightgown plaiting her rich brown hair in two long braids. It seemed that the only time she and Tom could talk together any more was at bedtime, when there were no outsiders around, but by the end of the day Tom was often either too tired to talk or too eager to blow out the lamp and reach for her and make love in that high-spirited, abandoned way he did everything. Sometimes on these nights their animosity grew even as their passion increased—she fearful of the seed in which he exulted, for she did not want to bear any more children, and he resentful of her cautious acquiescence when he wanted total enjoyment and fulfillment. Tonight they needed to speak about this newcomer.

"The girls weren't alone in being impressed," he said, unlacing his high shoes wearily. "The men watched him like he was a ha'ant, straight from the nether world."

Martha frowned. "That's what I have to tell you," she said. "Uncle Robert took me to one side before he left and told me that Nye Blankenship had just finished serving time in prison."

Tom paused, one shoe half off, and whistled softly. "Prison," he repeated. "I don't know about that."

"I didn't either, Tom," she said, "till Uncle Robert told me how he came to be there." In and out and around she wound her hair with dextrous fingers, her words keeping time to the steady plaiting. "He was working down in the next county for a man who had a big tobacco acreage. Something happened one day, there was an argument, the men exchanged blows and Nye quit. Walked off the farm and it was right in tobacco-cutting time, the busiest season of the year. The man was short of help, he lost some tobacco that could have been saved if Nye had stayed on. At least that was what he told the court when he brought Nye up for breach of contract. When Nye couldn't pay any fine, they threw him in prison."

Tom shook his head. "Seems like a kind of hard thing."

"Uncle Robert said that farmer was a powerful political leader over in his section; he was using Nye as an example for other farm help who might take notions about walking out."

They were silent until Tom asked, "How do you feel about having him around, Martha? Looks like he knows how to handle stock and God knows that's somebody I could use right now, but if it goes against your judgment to have him——"

She threw the two braids back over her shoulders where they hung down to her waist. "It's all right. Uncle Robert would never have brought him if he'd harm our family in any way."

He nodded and finished taking off his shoes. He chuckled. "Between retired wrestlers and released prisoners, Thickety Creek's getting right——"

"Who's a wrestler?" she asked quickly.

"Why, Preacher Grey. He was telling me about it the other day when he rode in town with me to take a load of lumber."

She frowned doubtfully. "Seems strange for a preacher to ride on a lumber wagon."

"Martha, you're just too damned prissy sometimes." He stood up and unloosed his suspenders. "That's what I like about Preacher Grey. He don't think this earth, or heaven either, is made up of a lot of pious old maids and choir leaders. He's willing to get out in the mainstream——"

"I guess that's why he was a wrestler?"

"No." He looked at her sharply. "He wrestled to make a living, out West, while he was still a young buck. And then one day he had a match with an Indian boy, a Cherokee out in Oklahoma, and the first good hold he got, that Indian fell out cold. When they went to help him up, he was dead. There'd been something wrong with him for years, he shouldn't have been in a contest a-tall. But Zach Grey had killed him. And the preacher said he looked at his own hands and for the first time in his life he couldn't take pride in himself. Memory of that feller's eyes followed him, and his own strength was a burden to him—that's what he said. Somewhere along the way, when he was sick to death of himself and everything else, he heard a sermon about losing your life to save it. The preacher said if you lost your life in something bigger than yourself, you'd save yourself and others, too. And Zach Grey got the call to God, the call to preach."

"Well, I never——" Martha began, then stopped.

"I tell you, he's the only preacher I ever heard since I came to manhood that made religion seem like anything real, for this world."

Martha leaned toward him eagerly. "Can't you profess it in church, Tom?"

He frowned, started to speak, then waited. After a moment he winked at her. "Can you just get me roped and corralled in church all nice and safe, and can I just find me somebody who'll look after my work animals with a little heart and care, we'll be walking in high clover, won't we, Martha girl?"

After they were in bed, he said, "We won't mention anything to the others about Nye Blankenship having been in prison. He might be touchous about it."

They need not have worried about Nye, however, for he himself told all the other men—and consequently the children, too, since they absorbed every scrap of conversation that took place at mealtime or anywhere else around the house—about his term in prison. He spoke of it unself-consciously, as the most remarkable experience of his life from which he drew scraps of remembered conversations, knickknacks of knowledge, and insights into characters of other men. His year and a day in prison was all any of them ever knew about his past.

"Old Blankenship never speaks of anything that happened yon side of his prison days," Amos Knott said to Tom at the sawmill one day.

"No," Tom Thurston replied, and the conversation died right there.

By the time winter settled over the valley, Nye had Tom Thurston's mules and oxen in good condition. Salves he concocted, and rubbed on patiently day after day, gradually healed old Kate's shoulder and toughened tender spots on other hides. Long before daylight every morning Nye was in the barn feeding, talking to the mules and oxen in a low soothing garble of sound, and by the time the other men came to work he had the harness and yokes all on and adjusted. His Sundays were devoted to currying the animals until, after several weeks, their coats lost cakings of mud and matted hair and they began to look as sleek and well-tended as "show critters."

Nye had been at work less than a month when a brush with one of the loggers led to an upheaval among the men and as a result Tom fired or lost all of his logging crew except Nye and old man Gunter and his son, Leck, who had hobbled back to work in late October. Icy rains and snowstorms slowed down the winter cutting and logging so drastically, however, that Tom was glad to have the smaller crew and payroll during this season.

"Poor old Nye, seems like he has a rough time getting along with the men," Tom Thurston told Martha. "The very things that make for his easy ways with livestock seem to cut him off from folks. But the Gunters and Nye get along together. They can turn off the work of six quarrelsome hands."

Martha nodded hopefully.

"Seems like things are looking up for us for a change, Martha," he went on happily. "No better sawyer in this country than Amos Knott, and old Nye has all the animals working and looking decent. He was a godsend."

"Then you won't forget to thank God next time the preacher holds service," she said.

"Why, I thank Him every morning when I go out and see my teams all lined up in first-class order and Nye there easing them into a new day's work," Tom answered, both shaming and puzzling her. It was hard for Martha to be sure when he was teasing and when he was in earnest.

The winter seemed interminable. There were long rain- or snow-bound afternoons when the sawmill men sat around the fireplace in their heavy winter shirts and coats and mud-caked boots, lethargic and slow as hibernating bears, and Clay sat on the edge of the hearth looking up at them, absorbing every story, every word they uttered. Early mornings and late afternoons were drudgery for Frone and Ivy and Phoebe—carrying water from the spring, drawing into cold pails clutched between their knees streams of frothy bluish milk out of the cows' udders, bringing in stovewood, fetching meat from the smokehouse, fruit or vegetables from the dirt cellar. School was closed until next summer, but the children kept at work on their studies. They read every printed word they could find, from Mama's magazines to Papa's *Toledo Blade*, from Preacher Grey's Concordance to Uncle Fayte's set of Dickens and Victor Hugo. They were not selective. They were hungry to devour all the words available.

Spring finally opened for good. Redbud burst into a lavender froth on the hillsides, dogwood bloomed pure white, the earth thawed and streams ran full and fresh down the slopes. Stacks of lumber grew tall again as one long workday followed another. And late one Saturday afternoon, when the sawmill men were all out at the barnyard pitching horseshoes, Martha and Tom Thurston figured up the lumber finances. They found that there had been just enough workdays during winter to keep a trickle of lumber flowing into town and, although Tom had sworn at the roads that were like gluepots of wet clay and thawing mire, he had made enough money to finish paying for all his livestock.

"By the end of summer, Martha, if everything goes along this way, we'll be free and clear," he said. The children's hearts rose with joy. "Come here, Clay, to your old papa," he said gayly, and when the little boy raced across the room to him he took this oldest son on his knee, looked at him steadily a moment and asked, "What are you going to make of yourself when you grow up, son?"

The boy's bright brown eyes were fixed on his father's face. He was intent with adoration and an effort to please. "A sawmill man like papa?" he half asked, half stated.

His father laughed and bounced him on his knee perch and tousled his curly hair. "No, son, not a lumberman. You want to look up, be something better than your old papa."

The eager eyes searched his father's wind- and sun-toughened countenance, asking silently if it were possible to be anything better.

"Maybe you'll follow medicine——"

Frone, near the door, rolling lamplighters out of strips of newspaper, winked at little Clay. "He'll have to get over puking at the sight of blood."

"Or be a lawyer," Papa went on, "like his great-uncle Robert. I tell you, Martha, there's nothing these young'uns of ours can't do. Their old papa's going to see that they get all the education they can take—and then we'll just turn them loose to see how far they can go!"

Ivy felt the lift of his spirit. She would go beyond this valley, beyond these mountains, beyond herself even, to build something good and beautiful and indestructible.

"Papa," Frone asked, reddening, not looking at any of them, "could we have a piano sometime?"

"Almighty be! A piano? Of course we ought to have a piano for all these girls." He looked at the three of them. "They're growing into young ladies. I guess I've been so busy with the farm and then the timber . . ." He looked at them again and shook his head, not sadly but in a puzzled sort of pleasure. "Just as soon as we're out from under these debts, we'll order us a piano."

"They'll have their chance," Mama said calmly, "if it's the Lord's will."

"We'll help make sure it's His will." Papa winked at them.

"Don't blaspheme, Tom."

"I'm not blaspheming, Martha. Preacher Grey would agree with what I mean. He's for folks bettering themselves. You know what he told me yesterday?"

She shook her head.

"He's about talked a couple of the Bludsoe children into going to school down here, come July."

"He's what?" Martha asked.

"That's right—the Bludsoes and Thickety Creek's school are about to get together. Funny, I had to tell the preacher I'd just never thought about any of that family's schooling before, living up there on the mountain the way they do. We don't hear much about them until they've shot one another or raised a ruckus with some of their liquor."

"It will make trouble." Martha bit her lip sharply.

The children looked from one parent to the other. They were unsure about what their own reactions should be to this news, having
seldom even seen the swarthy, silent strangers who lived high up
on the mountains at the head of the valley. The Bludsoes were self-
contained, powerfully built outcasts whose origins were shrouded
in mystery and stigma. Aunt Tildy had told Frone and Ivy once
that when the first Matt and Vashti Bludsoe came up to this valley,
they claimed it before anyone else settled in Nantahala County, but
because they were rumored to be partly Negro and never denied it,
and therefore their children and their children's children and on
and on were partly so too, they were pushed farther and farther up
the slopes. The girls could have listened all night to these tales of
"olden times," but Aunt Tildy didn't like to talk about the Bludsoes.

"Your grandma tried to help them and I reckon we ought, too,"
she'd say. "But they're a proud people and hard to help." And so,
all that the Thurston children knew firsthand about the Bludsoes
was sight of Young Morg, white-haired but still called Young, riding coldly down the valley, silent and withdrawn as a bronze
statue; or Black Matt, the second or third Black Matt from above
Devil's Brow, when the sheriff arrested him for shooting a man and
hauled him away to prison where he died within the year. They remembered the length of the wooden coffin on the bed of the wagon
that jolted back up Thickety valley and hauled Black Matt Bludsoe
as far up the mountain as a trail climbed before the other men of
the family came and carried him to the ridgetop Bludsoe burying
ground.

"I told Preacher Grey that as a rule around here the preacher
didn't take much concern for the school," Tom Thurston said. "He
told me it wasn't the school but the children that ought to be in it
that were his concern."

"If only those Bludsoes would go away!" Martha shook her head.
"Seems like, for as long as I can remember, they've just been up there
waiting . . ." She did not finish, but sat rocking Kin back and forth
in her arms.

Tom threw back his head and laughed heartily. "And where

would you like for them to go away to, Martha?" he asked.

"Oh, I don't know—somewhere among their own kind."

"Well now, there may not be many of their kind"—he began gathering up the payroll notebooks and the papers on which he had been figuring their finances—"but we won't fret about that now, Martha. I believe by the beginning of summer, when I've finished timbering our land here, my trade for that tract the banks owns will go through——"

"Does the bank own a lot of timber, Papa?" Ivy asked.

He nodded. "Just about the rest of the mountain above this valley, except for the rocky ridge of the Bludsoes. Why, there are yellow poplars in some of those coves that would saw out enough board feet to build a house!"

"They must have been growing there when Columbus came to these shores," Mama said.

Ivy looked at Frone to share the marvel of that fact. She would put it away in her mind to contemplate tonight after she was in bed and everyone else was asleep and she could enjoy privacy and quiet to think. Tall, straight, leafy poplars so ancient that they cast a perpetual green twilight on the ground below, growing through seasons and cycles and centuries of flood and drought, storm and stillness. She would go and see them for herself before they were cut.

By the time Fayte McQueen's school opened again, everyone in the valley had heard of Zach Grey's plan to bring in Bludsoe children. Thickety Creek had been impressed by the fine black horse, the powerful muscles, the unflinching sermons of their preacher. At the same time, they had been a little taken aback by his spirit's fire, which was not banked on Monday for the rest of the workday week, but burned as zealously as on Sunday. They were awed by the energetic past which had obviously been his, but they were apprehensive about the energy which he might expect from them in the future. And they were not happy about his having anything to do with the Bludsoes.

"Eh me!" Lazarus Shook sat on his porch and fanned his bearded face and tangled hair while his wife, Ida, swept the front yard with a sturdy broom she had made from her own broomcorn. His girl, Azalie, and Ivy Thurston were at the other end of the porch cutting out brown-paper covers for the new schoolbooks they would begin using next week. Frone had already started studying her books; she would not even take time to make the wrappers for them. Ivy could not help smiling to herself when she heard Lazarus Shook's complaining voice. "If I had my young man's strength back, I'd go up there and tell them Bludsoes straight out to pay no mind to a preacher who tires to interfere in school affairs. We don't need their kind down here."

Azalie and Ivy were disappointed. They had looked forward to something new in the school routine.

But when Preacher Grey rode by a short while later and stopped to enlist Lazarus' support, neither Ida nor the girls heard such big talk from Azalie's father.

"Brother Shook," the preacher called, refusing Ida's invitation to come on the porch, swinging one leg loosely around the horn of his saddle as he relaxed and let the horse crop the grass along the roadside, "how is your health today?"

"Poorly. Thank you, Preacher, but poorly." Lazarus touched his chest lightly with one stubby, dirty fingernail. "An aching here in my breastbone."

"I'm regretful of that. But I know you won't let your ailment interfere with support of your preacher while he needs a good right arm to uphold him."

Lazarus Shook did not look directly at his visitor, but studied intently some distant object beyond his left shoulder. "I do what I can," he said uncertainly.

"Then you can help me make sure there's not a lot of talk when a couple of the Bludsoe children come down to the school here next week."

Lazarus did not answer, but spat over the edge of the porch.

"Have you ever been up there to the Bludsoes, Brother Shook?" Preacher Grey asked.

"Never had any business with them."

"Well, I went up. And it's my belief, Brother Shook, that this valley will never prosper as it ought till the Bludsoes are raised up, too."

There was a silence. Ivy watched Preacher Grey's face and the eye that seemed to look inward and the eye that focused ever more intently on squirming Lazarus Shook.

"The way we can raise them—all of us—is through our school here——"

"I thought you come as our preacher, not our schoolmaster," Lazarus muttered almost inaudibly.

"I came as a whole man, made whole by the grace of God," Preacher Grey said, "and that means I've got a part in all the life of this place."

"Yes, eh me—yes." Lazarus Shook retreated before the intensity of the other's voice.

"To save ourselves we've got to save the Bludsoes, and we've got to give them a chance to be decent human beings. How can they be civilized if we don't give them any of the tools of civilization—words and figures and knowledge of this earth?"

"That's right, Preacher."

"I'll depend on your support then, should there be any opposition, Brother Shook."

But Lazarus Shook was a weak reed on which to depend, and others of Preacher Grey's congregation were no more sturdy. They did not oppose him outright, they simply did nothing. Indifference had won them many a skirmish against change in the past. They did not use it as a conscious weapon; it was simply their mode, their instinctive reaction to any bold alteration in their pattern of living. They knew that apathy could triumph again and again over the force of good intentions.

The real opposition to Preacher Grey's effort came from the Bludsoes themselves. After his first startling visit to them, Young Morg and Little Euell (who stood only six feet six inches), the family's leaders since Matt's burial two years ago, had eased their suspicion and permitted this stranger to visit freely. Young Morg's very dark wife, who had come from farther south many years before, asked him to preach for them and Preacher Grey had twice conducted services on the mountain. When Morg himself gave first off-hand agreement to the preacher's school proposition for their children, and said his oldest boy and girl could go and have a try at book learning, no Bludsoe had thought that the people of Thickety Creek would agree to their coming. They had been too long accustomed to rejection and separation. Faced with Preacher Grey's insistence that the boy and girl could actually attend school, they were forced to deny him bluntly. In their primitive, unpainted cabins they sat like lords and told him, "We don't aim to send our young'uns out to be laughed at."

"We don't have much, but one thing no Bludsoe's ever been without: that's pride."

"We know what them young'uns down at the school would do to ours——"

"You don't know anything about it," Preacher Grey pleaded, "until you've tried. Of course, you're proud. But where's your courage, too?"

"We don't push our babies out to do our fighting."

"You're pushing them out to do some growing," he answered.

But they shook their shaggy heads, hunched their shoulders like cattle heading into a storm, and were adamant.

Preacher Grey talked over his setback with Tom Thurston. They had finished a summer Sunday dinner and were sitting in the yard on straight-backed chairs tilted against the tree trunks. A warm quiet pall lay over the afternoon. In the distance a hawk hung in the stillness above the hills, circling slowly, with no visible motion of its widespread wings. There was no sound from barnyard or pasture or woods. Inside the house, Martha Thurston had darkened her bedroom against the afternoon glare, and Frone and Ivy, having failed to trade each other out of washing the Sunday dishes, now worked lethargically on the stack of plates and crusted pots and pans. Phoebe rocked Kin and sang, "Go Tell Aunt Rhody," over and over, in the hope that he might doze off into a long afternoon nap. Clay had gone to the spring for a bucket of fresh water and was delayed there by a crawfish he felt called upon to examine. It was cool in the deep shade beside the spring and when his bare foot crushed a stem of mint beside the spring its fragrance filled the air.

"Preacher, I've got troubles of my own," Tom Thurston said amiably. He loosened the tie around the celluloid collar of his white shirt and leaned back comfortably. "Here I am, just ready to start on another big timber tract and my two main men, my sawyer and my best logger, are still feuding with one another worse than game roosters in the same pen."

Preacher Grey looked down the dusty road beyond this green flowery yard and sighed. "Man's surely a creature born to fighting," he said, "and the path to any kind of peace is up hill all the way."

"I couldn't dispute you there."

"But that can't keep us from trying." His powerful hands clutched each other as he leaned forward in his chair. "Tom Thurston, could you but see those two little children of Morg Bludsoe's, a girl about the size of your two oldest, and a chap about the age of little Phoebe, bright-faced and open to learning as any of your own, I know you'd stand with me on their having a chance."

"Look here, Preacher, I'm not braced against you. It'll suit me just fine if they come to school down here. Why Almighty be, I wouldn't mind giving Morg a job at my sawmill! But I thought it was the Bludsoes themselves scotching your way."

"If I could convince them their children wouldn't be made the butt of jokes or teasing . . ."

They talked on under the trees. Clay came slowly up the path from the spring and carried his bucket of water into the house. The men spoke of the past of the Bludsoes, myth woven with fact, and of the valley. "They've provided Thickety Creek with liquor and legends for a long time now," Preacher Grey finally said.

Tom was silent for a moment, staring at the ground and his feet thoughtfully. He stooped and picked up a twig and turned it in his hands. When he looked up at the other man, there was a glint in his eyes. "I believe I know how you could get those children in school," he said.

"Well?"

He hesitated, then said clearly and deliberately, "You and Morg Bludsoe could wrestle it out."

The minister stared at him. A stem of grass he had been chewing suddenly hung limp between his lips. "You don't know what you're talking about," he whispered hoarsely.

"You could wrestle it out on these terms: If you win, those young'uns would come on to the school and nobody—Bludsoe or otherwise—objects. If Morg wins, you're to leave them alone and forget about their schooling."

"No! My wrestling days are over. After I saw that Cherokee lying there . . ." He shook his head.

"You said yourself that man's a fighting critter. You and Morg could settle it for all of us."

The preacher's big hands were clenched so tightly that their knuckles stood out like white granite rocks. "By taking all the others' anger and objection onto ourselves," he said softly, "by wrestling this thing out fairly and openly, we just might overcome the obstacles. I don't know."

But the more they thought about it, the more certain Tom Thurston was that this provided the answer. "Folks respect a man stands up for his convictions. And when you put your muscles behind your belief, you're speaking to this valley in a language it understands, Preacher."

"I'll turn it over in my mind, Tom. I'll bring the proposition to God and seek His guidance."

"You'd be wrestling against the Bludsoes and the valley alike, Preacher. For once, they'd be standing together. All that would be on your side are maybe those Bludsoe young'uns who'd be having a chance at school—and a few renegades like me."

"It wouldn't be a vote-getting contest, Tom," the preacher said. "It would be a match of endurance. And I'd count on the Lord to strengthen my muscles."

Tom grinned. "Well, you've provided Him a pretty good head start."

The news spread through the length and breadth of Thickety valley like green on the hillsides after summer rain. Preacher Grey rode up to the Bludsoe stronghold and made the proposition for a wrestling contest, and Morg Bludsoe was caught by such surprise that he agreed to every term of his children's schooling and guaranteed his own attendance at Thickety Creek church if he should lose. On the other hand, if he won, he would get Preacher Grey's thoroughbred horse and assurance that his children would be let alone to grow up any way they chose.

Preacher Grey's past career as a wrestler became common knowledge and stories of his exploits were circulated and enlarged. Some of his church members were deeply disturbed at discovery of their minister's worldly past. On the other hand, men in the valley who had not warmed a church bench for years suddenly appeared in his congregation and their wives rejoiced, although some of the faithful contended that these latter-day candidates for grace were more intent on sizing up Preacher Grey's weight and form than on hearing the scripture interpreted. Little else was talked of at the Nelson store, at homes and in the fields, at Tom Thurston's sawmill, or at the school where Fayte McQueen was trying to collect his pupils' scattered attention from the crops they had just helped lay by for the summer and direct it to gathering a harvest from books.

The Thurston children had to discuss the future wrestling match while they were at school, or at least away from home, for although most of the people were more pleased than shocked to have some diversion and drama brought into their daily lives, the difference of reactions was at its sharpest between Tom and Martha Thurston.

"It seems heathenish," Mama said, while the children listened in the kitchen. "I never heard of a similar thing: our preacher wrestling with some ruffian that doesn't know anything but making whisky, running foxes and fighting." Her voice quivered with grief and exasperation.

"Then Preacher Grey's talking to him in his own language," Papa said. "And if he wins and gets Morg Bludsoe's young'uns in school down here, your brother Fayte can teach them something different from foxes and liquor."

"But there's a proper way for things to be done——"

"Well, if the proper way doesn't get it done, I say try something else."

"You wouldn't care about the church anyway. You don't even belong."

"And maybe that's why I don't. I've been waiting these years for somebody with blood and guts to give it life in this world as well as the next."

"You're not at your sawmill now, Tom. You don't have to be coarse."

"I'm trying to be honest!"

"Well, I don't want to talk about it any more." Ivy, listening, knew that Mama's lips would be white and pursed, and her forehead pale above her flashing brown eyes. "Zachariah Grey came to this valley with the highest prospects any preacher ever had. We'll wait and see how this wrestling comes out, and if it destroys our church, Tom, I'll never forgive you."

"Almighty be, Martha! You're burdening me for——"

"I won't talk about it any more." And the children heard her cross the room, begin humming a tune. "'There's a land that is fairer than day, And by faith I can see it afar . . .'"

Ivy felt her stomach tighten with tension and she went to bed a short while later miserable with uncertainty. Did Papa and Mama no longer love each other? What was it, anyway, some awakening consciousness within her demanded to know, this relationship between a woman and a man? She had lived with animals on the farm all her life and she knew as the other children did both the terror and ease, the total mystery and complete naturalness of birth and its processes of creation. But Frone grew sharp and disgusted and buried herself in reading Sir Walter Scott whenever Ivy wanted to talk to her about all that she did not understand. Mama was somehow unapproachable on male and female questions, and in her presence the doubts and fears and dreams stuck in Ivy's throat and would not shape themselves into language. Azalie Shook winked and whispered odd words behind her hand and Ivy could talk with her least of all. She felt desperately ignorant and she yearned toward knowledge so that she could separate love from fear, accept the urges stirring within her freely and gayly, or reject them harshly, whichever way was "right." But how could she learn from Mama and Papa when they rejected each other? For she loved them both deeply.

She liked Preacher Grey, too. Ever since that first day he had ridden up the road with the black hat slouched over his brow and his kind gaze had seen her, really seen her and liked her, although she was only a girl and no pillar of the community at all, she had hoped for a transformation of Thickety Creek dwellers into his image. But how should she pray for him now, when it seemed that, if he won this strange contest, he would somehow lose; and if he lost, he might lose all?

The sawmill hands made bets with each other on Preacher Grey's and Morg Bludsoe's wrestling, but they did not mention the contest when Martha Thurston was in earshot. One Sunday, Amos Knott and the Gunters went to church with the Thurstons, but Martha, who would have been joyful over their interest a few weeks before, accepted them with quiet reservation. Nye Blankenship won the only smile from her on Friday evening at supper when he broke his accustomed silence and asked Ivy, as she made sure he had some hot cornbread, "You going to that ruckus tomorrow?"

Silence fell around the table. Ivy looked at her mother and shook her head reluctantly. "Girls and ladies wouldn't be proper there," she said, sounding just like Mama.

Nye snorted and crumbled a piece of cornbread in his glass of milk. "Just thought I'd ask. You might be wanting to use one of the mules in the buggy——"

"The match is going to be right down here in Mr. Thurston's lower field," Leck Gunter said. "No need to ride."

"Well, I hadn't kept track of it," Nye blurted. "I don't aim to be wasting my time at such fool carryings-on."

And Mama looked at him and smiled and nodded.

"A man don't deserve as fine a horse as that big black of the Preacher's," Nye went on, "if he'd risk it up against a little book learning for some drippy-nose young'uns."

No one answered.

Ivy watched the men and boys of Thickety Creek gather in the distant field the following afternoon. She longed to be with them. She was tempted to slip out of the yard and look for some closer place where she could see and yet not be seen. Right after midday dinner, as soon as Mama had set out a jar of water for Papa to take to quench the wrestlers' thirst, Mama had taken Kin and a big basket and announced that she was going up into the woods to get some rich dirt for her flowers. Ivy knew Mama would probably be away all afternoon, winding back around by the little family cemetery to leave a cluster of ferns or a handful of green moss on Grandma McQueen's grave. But Ivy could not completely disobey her, even at this distance.

Watching from the edge of the yard, she saw Preacher Grey's black horse arrive. A muffled sort of cheer went up from the crowd of men already gathered and Ivy smiled to herself in wonder that they should be opposed to the thing for which he wrestled and still they could not bring themselves to hope he lost.

All around her, the yard and flower beds and house were silent in the summer afternoon's heat. One Dominecker hen wallowed in the dust under a rosebush, but there was no other activity. From the barnyard in the distance she could hear the occasional cry of guineas as they prowled the quiet farm and raised momentary alarums. Inside the house Frone was reading *Ivanhoe*, which Uncle Fayte had loaned her yesterday. Phoebe was down near the spring playing house with some cracked teacups and bits of old bottle and a bent spoon. Clay had slipped away with Papa and the other men when they went down to the meadow. Ivy felt as if the day had stopped or been suspended here in time and heat and immobility while in some other place life went on at some bold pace.

She climbed a beech tree and found a low-hanging limb where she could perch and have an opening to look out between the thick green oval leaves. The shade was pleasant. She laid her face along one bare brown arm and smelled the pungent, salty warmth of her flesh. No matter if all her family and even Azalie and girls at school made fun of her skin because it wasn't milky white and tender as apple buds in spring, she liked the sun on her arms and neck and face. She would never submit to those burdensome bonnets and stockings pulled over hands and arms while she worked outdoors. She would be free to move and open to breezes and heat alike. If there was some silly boy somewhere who wanted to marry a lily of a girl, then let him take Frone, whose hands were almost as fine as Papa's; or Phoebe, whose skin was as white as Mama's;

or even Azalie, who caked her freckled face and arms with butter-milk baths. Romantic sadness at the thought of love passing her by settled momentarily over Ivy's afternoon.

Sounds of hoarse cries and excited shouts floated up from the meadow. She could see a great ring of men moving and milling around there. She wondered if any other of the Bludsoes had come except Morg, who was pitting his strength against any change in their lives up on the mountain above the Devil's Brow. She wondered about his boy and girl, the ones Preacher Grey wanted to come to Uncle Fayte's school. Would they be fierce as bobcat kittens raised in the ledges, or would they be frightened and innocent as untamed fawns? She remembered seeing the boy once—she supposed it was the same boy—when he had come down with his father fetching corn to Great-uncle Paul Moore's mill. He had been a slim, black-haired lad with a jaw like iron, clenched and tight. Somehow she hoped he wouldn't be coming to the school, not because of herself or other children, but because of himself. Yet it seemed a shame that anyone should grow up and not be able to write his own name.

The sun moved down the sky. Afternoon shadows scooped deep hollows out of the mountain sides and Ivy's beech tree cast a long shadow. She strained unsuccessfully to see what was happening in the distance, and all the while her thoughts rambled like the cow paths that laced the pasture slope.

Then, suddenly, the ring of men broke, flowed together and began to walk up through the field toward the house. The only single object she could make out distinctly was the big black horse.

They were almost below her beech tree, leading the horse with Preacher Grey's body lying across it huge and limp, before Ivy jumped down to the ground. The preacher was stripped to the waist and his back seemed vast and white, glistening with sweat.

"What happened?" She caught Amos Knott by the sleeve, for her father was leading the horse and he had already reached the picket fence and was unlatching the gate.

Amos Knott looked at her and shrugged.

"But you were down there. What happened? What's wrong with Preacher Grey?"

"I couldn't say. He'd been getting the best of Bludsoe. All of a sudden he just crumbled like beeswax. Shook his head two or three times and couldn't seem to throw off Bludsoe's hold or get any grip of his own—then he crumbled." The men around Amos nodded their heads in puzzled agreement.

"Ivy!" It was Papa calling her. "Run in there and fix one of the beds. A couple of you fellers help me get the preacher in the house."

They did not know what to do after they laid him on the bed. They could feel his pulse and see that he was breathing with most astonishing regularity. Many of the men waited in the yard a little while, recalling every detail of what had taken place, then they went on home. A few drifted into the back yard and were still there talking, going over the afternoon that had started with such excitement and ended so curiously, when Martha Thurston and little Kin came home. Under her split-bonnet, her face was flushed from the afternoon's heat and exertion. It flushed even deeper when Ivy took her into the bedroom where Preacher Grey lay. Tom sat by the bed.

"Almighty be! I'm glad you're back, Martha." He sprang up and pushed her into the chair. "See if you can tell what's wrong with him."

She sat down. She felt the preacher's forehead, held the big wrist lightly in her fingers for a moment. "Ivy, wring me a washcloth in cold water," and to Ivy's astonishment it seemed to her that her mother smiled.

"Where's Morg Bludsoe?" Mama asked.

Papa seemed startled by her question. "I reckon he went on home, I'm not sure," he said.

"Then he was all right? Did he win the wrestling?"

"Yes." Papa was puzzled by her manner.

She applied the cold cloth and after a while Preacher Grey stirred on the bed. His eyes, the one with the cast and the other one, gazed up at them. "I must have been asleep," he said slowly.

"Yes," Martha answered briskly. "We'll fix some supper now with a pot of good strong coffee and you'll be as good as new."

He stared at them in a sudden wave of recollection and embarrassment. "He outwrestled me."

"No," Tom said soothingly, "I reckon it was a draw——"

"It was no draw. I lost. Those little children . . . my horse . . . everything." He turned toward the wall.

"Nonsense," Martha Thurston said. "We can just be thankful the whole thing's past and behind us."

The girls had already built a fire in the kitchen range when Mama and Papa came out of the bedroom where the preacher lay. Frone was making biscuits; little puffs of flour came up each time she cut one out with a quick hard twist of a water glass turned upside down. Ivy was putting fresh coffee beans through the grinder on the wall. Phoebe had gone down to the springhouse for butter and milk and cream.

"I tell you I was scared there for a few minutes." Papa grinned at them in relief.

"It's dangerous doings, egging men on to fight," Mama said.

"I didn't egg them on." Papa went to the washstand and poured water in the basin. "I was trying to keep from having real trouble by letting them act it——" His elbow knocked a little bottle off the edge of the stand. "What's that doing perched on a corner anyway?" He picked it up, squinted at the label. "'Godfrey's laudanum.' Why, I just bought that bottle last week when Kin was crying at night." He held it up. "Lord, it's empty already. I pay for it by the drop and these young'uns swig it by the bottle——"

"Don't blame the children, Tom," Martha said quietly. "Kin only had a few drops."

Ivy stopped grinding coffee and looked at her mother and the others in the room did, too. Suddenly they all knew the same thing.

Mama didn't mind their knowing. She wanted them to know. "I emptied it in the jar of water," she said.

"What water?" Papa asked, although he knew.

"For your wrestlers."

"But how did you know which one would drink it?" Papa asked.

"I didn't. I didn't care. I thought maybe they'd both drink it. Just so it put a stop to their foolish exhibition."

"But why, Martha?"

She turned to look at him and her words were ready. "Things of the spirit can't be settled by the flesh!"

Tom Thurston stood by the washstand and shook his head. "Martha, when will you understand? They can't be separated. Body, mind, spirit—they're all one, one great big whole, or we're nothing."

They looked at each other.

Through the kitchen door they heard the sound of Amos Knott's voice talking to a couple of other men as they came across the yard.

"Don't you ever tell a word of this, you young'uns," Papa said. "Understand?"

They nodded, impressed by the sternness of his tone.

"I wouldn't mind." Mama's chin tilted defiantly.

"Well, I would. Good God A-mighty!" he shouted, and suddenly swept the ironstone pitcher, half full of water, and the big round bowl and soap dish off their stand. "Maybe that'll keep everybody busy awhile cleaning up," he said, as he plunged out of the house and turned back the men headed toward the kitchen.

On Sunday morning Preacher Grey walked into his pulpit. Most of the seats in the church were taken. Even Tom Thurston was there, on the back row but nonetheless there. With great dignity shaded by sadness the preacher told his listeners, "I am not sure what happened yesterday. I am not sure that I did the right thing. I am sure of only one thing: that I thought I was doing God's work and I had hoped that by today I might help win a new set of lives into our school, our church, our community. I had hoped our community might be made whole. It did not come to pass. The fault was surely mine, for our God is without fault. Let us pray."

Just before they bowed their heads, Tom Thurston looked at his wife. "How do you feel about the laudanum now, Martha?" his look asked. She closed her eyes.

The text of the sermon was that Jacob wrestled with his angel all the night through.

When the congregation came out from church, they found a wagon stopped along the road, waiting quietly. A team of little grey mules pulled the wagon which carried some household furnishings

—bed, stove, straight chairs, quilts, a broken trunk—and four people: Morg Bludsoe and his wife on the seat, two children, a boy and a girl, behind. They sat like statues, staring straight ahead, except for Morg who watched with unchanging sternness as everyone who came out stared at him and his family a moment and then stepped aside to wait and see what would happen. Presently someone told Preacher Grey of Morg Bludsoe's presence and he came down to the road.

"You're going somewhere, Morg?" Preacher Grey asked in surprise.

The dark, erect man nodded briefly. "We're moving off the mountain," he said.

"Well, before you go I believe I owe you a debt," Preacher Grey said clearly. "One black horse, and one acknowledgment of defeat."

"Keep your horse," Morg Bludsoe said. "Something ailed you, there in that last grapple——"

"You're a strong man, Morg. You bested me."

"Figured last night I bested myself," he said. "I set and pondered it: a stranger thinking enough of my young'uns to wrestle it out for their right to take up schooling. Least I can do is give them as good a chance."

Preacher Grey nodded. Ivy could see the light rekindling in his eyes. She looked at the girl and boy in the back of the wagon. She didn't even know their names and all at once it seemed odd to her that this should be so.

"It's hard for a man to move out of the country he's knowed from birth up," Morg Bludsoe said, "but we done it this morning. Somewhere around town yonder there'll be a way for us to live, I reckon." He looked out at the scattered people. "I'm a-cursing this valley for making us leave our mountain to go out yonder and find a school that'll take my young'uns. The rest of my folks think I'm stark mad. But I'm thankful too, thankful for this-here wrestling preacher who made me see that my chap and girl get a chance." He picked up the reins lying across his lap and gave a sharp cluck to the team.

"Thank you," Preacher Grey said to him. No one else spoke or moved. The team jerked forward and then the wagon began to move. "God bless you, Morg Bludsoe," the preacher called.

Morg sat erect and unyielding and the woman and children looked straight ahead. To Ivy they appeared as stiff and brittle as icicles frozen in an alien world, and she wondered if, like ice, they might not break at an unexpected touch, or melt down under a sudden warmth. Then she heard Papa call, "Good luck, folks!" She was glad he had called. She could tell by the faces of the others that they were glad he called, too.

And she had no possible way of knowing, there in the sun on that summer morning when all the world was opening around her and the grey team of mules with its shabby wagon was disappearing down the dusty road, that she would ever again welcome the sight of any of Morg Bludsoe's family.

When they got back home and were eating Sunday dinner, Papa said, "Well, tomorrow we begin cutting that new timber tract. It's even finer than I'd figured on at first, Martha."

"Will we be able to buy our creek bottom back?" Martha asked.

"Will we be free and clear by this time next year, Papa?" Ivy asked.

"And have our piano?" Frone urged.

"Next year?" He laid down his knife and fork and looked around the table. "Well, it wouldn't surprise me if we see daylight before the snow flies." They looked at him with happy confidence. "I tell you folks, you needn't think your old papa is a has-been. And he's not a will-be, either. I believe in is-ers!"

CHAPTER 7
Today

PHIL awakened to the sound of rain. Sunday morning, and rain beat on the dying leaves of trees and bushes beyond his open windows, sustaining a muffled stir and whisper among the undergrowth. It ran in rivulets down roof and pane, stirring memories of long days when he had been a boy in this same house and the raindrops had splattered outside on the same rhododendron and galax and oak and pine. Or nearly the same. The evergreens out there now might be wholly fresh, with shiny leaves and new growth from recent seasons, but he wanted to remember that they came from old roots. He stretched, smiling to himself, thinking how much his mother was reflected in that thought—and how little it reflected Jerry Stewart and Washington and everything he knew most closely now.

The thought of Stewart erased his smile and brought him fully awake. He glanced at the stack of papers on his desk. His administrative assistant had done a good job while he was away. Last night before he went to bed, while the house was quiet, Phil had checked over the material Stewart had forwarded from Washington.

As usual, there wasn't an unnecessary report in the batch, or a

request that could be postponed. Phil noted replies on the margins
of the letters and slipped them into his brief case. New statistics
supporting a bill that would reach the floor early in the session were
of special interest to him. Slouched in one of Ivy's big comfortable
chairs he had committed the neat columns to memory. There was
satisfaction in dealing with precise, firm figures after a day of con-
fronting a situation in which nothing seemed precise, where everything was fluid, defying analysis, permeated with contradiction,
nuance, paradox. And the day's final episode still disturbed him.

His expedition with Clay to see Hawk Williams' family had
been both foreboding and ironic, a climax not only of this day's
return home but of the past weeks' journey around the world. The
careful, guarded faces; the eyes that took in everything and told
nothing; the gestures that concealed more than they revealed—
these were the barriers Phil found more formidable than brick walls
or geographic boundaries. And he knew that he had helped build
those barriers, he and every other person who had grown up in any
corner of the world half blind and deaf and unaware. Yet there
was the pragmatism of politics, and he felt that this pragmatism
had made its feeble symbolic gesture when Clay had handed out
all the coins in his pocket to Hawk's children. A gesture of charity,
easy and self-righteous, solving nothing; indeed, saying nothing.

Old guilts and new ambitions: How could they be reconciled to
each other? He was supposed to be, at last, in a position of power,
and yet he had never felt more powerless. Especially before the
eyes of Hawk Williams' widow (and those of the tribal chief in the
heart of Africa who had looked at him and asked in perfect Oxford
accents, "How do we move from the stone age of my country's tech-
nology and your country's morals, out into the space age?").

And there sat the tidy brief case this morning. Phil lay and considered it. He considered it as a symbol of power with all the subtle
handicaps and advantages and leverages involved. He pondered
the powerlessness that made him no larger or lesser than the others
in this family when they came together with all their stresses and
strains. Yet in the short time he had been in Washington he had become convinced that its power was one of the basic problems his

country must acknowledge. This included power to cope with its own needs as well as the expectancies of others, power to abstain as well as participate, necessity to be wise as well as generous. He felt that given time and tenure he could make some useful, some practical suggestions on how to meet these necessities. But how did you win that time, secure that tenure? He hoped that one of his first steps could be by participation in the report on conditions and recommendations for assisting those countries he and the other senators had just visited. His ideas could be reflected publicly there, could be given the test of workability. Perhaps later today he would call Senator Howard and they could talk over the general direction their recommendations would take.

When he thought of Senator Howard, he thought of Ann. The heavy rain outside, the opaque dullness of the morning light, made him aware of an unaccustomed loneliness. He wanted—well, what did he want, or whom did he want, to share and understand that participation and anger and frustration that were becoming the pattern of his life? Ever since one night last winter he had suspected it was Ann Howard he wanted.

They had gone to dinner at a little restaurant over in Virginia where the service was unobtrusive, the food was adequate if not superior, and the atmosphere of log fires and lamplight was rare and leisurely. They had talked more than they had eaten. As they drove back to Washington, snow began to fall. The big soft flakes piling thickly through the stillness slowed their driving. By the time they reached Ann's home all the Georgetown streets were blanketed with white stillness. When Phil turned off the motor they sat, by mutual unspoken consent, and listened to the whisper of the snow falling over and around them.

As easily and slowly as the snow drifting, he laid an arm around her shoulders and turned her to him. He had kissed her before but never like this.

After a while they drew apart. "I have to go in," she whispered.

"Ann," he kept his mouth so close to hers that they were almost touching, "I'm coming with you."

She shook her head, the bright hair falling loosely around her face as she drew back to look at him. "No, Phil, you can't."

He sat quite still, looking at her clear dark eyes, her flushed cheeks, aware of the loosened pearl pin at the black silk plunge of her neckline. "Ann, for God's sake, we're not going to play fun and games, are we? Like high-school sophomores?"

"I'm sure the high-school sophomores could teach us a lot about making out these days."

He reached for the door handle.

"I'm a lot older than that—and more naïve," she added.

He didn't say anything, but he let go the handle. He did not take his eyes from hers.

"If you knew me better," she said, "you'd know that candor is my chief virtue—or my worst flaw. According to how you look at it."

"I know you pretty well, Ann——"

"Well enough to know that I don't want an affair with you?"

That halted him for a moment. "No," he admitted. "I guess I didn't——"

"It was a misunderstanding," she said. "It's a common misunderstanding. I run into it all the time. Love and kisses with the senator's daughter, the one who's been around Washington so long she's knowledgeable and eligible as hell."

Phil laughed in spite of himself. "The tough talk just doesn't come naturally to you, Miss Ann."

"Neither does the bed-hopping," she said, with a purposeful ugliness.

They were quiet a moment. The snow swept down through the trees and lights, between the closely adjoining old houses, and over their car. "That wasn't quite fair," Phil said.

"No?" She was looking out of the window.

"I suspect I'm in love with you," he said. "That makes a difference. Or should."

"Maybe." Now she looked at him again and her utterly serious expression gave her a little-girl look that was lovely and appealing. "That's why I won't ask you into the house tonight. Perhaps I'm more afraid of myself than of you. But I have a quaint notion that sex and love should be part of each other, that I'm not to distribute them lightly, that the sanctity of myself is the best I can really give in marriage. Even better than all the Spode china or Jensen sterling or Steuben glass such occasions collect. Quite mad, isn't it, such an obsolete idea?" But the plea in her eyes belied the flippancy of her question.

"No, Ann, not mad at all——" he began.

"Just quaint!" she said. Abruptly she kissed him, deeply, thrust open the door beside her and swung out her long silken legs. "Find another playmate, Senator Cortland. That's one resource our capital has in ample stock pile."

The street was slippery as he walked around the car to help her out and by the time he reached her Ann was already at the door with the key in the lock.

"I'll be away over the weekend," he said. "Dedication of a new bridge back home. Governor Wentworth wants me to come. I'll call you when I get back in town."

"Of course. And thanks for a perfectly lovely dinner. I guess it was that big log fire and the second brandy and then the snow that nearly carried us away." She smiled.

"No," Phil answered. "It was you that nearly carried me away."

On the way home Phil had admitted to himself that night that her attitude surprised him. Ever since college he had found it easy, if somewhat impermanent (which was the way he wanted it), to have girls who were not so much unconventional as the creators of a new convention. Ann was neither as free and matter-of-fact, nor in another sense as confined, as they.

During the rest of winter and summer they had seen each other frequently, but always they had kept the light touch, enjoying parties and receptions as co-conspirators against pomposity and boredom, careful not to touch hands or lips too often or too long. Ann knew everyone and Phil found her a marvelous combination of sophistication and naturalness. She possessed that urbane international know-who and rural courthouse know-how that seemed to Phil the epitome, the balance, the dichotomy, of success in Washington.

Thinking about her now, this rainy Sunday morning in the mountains, Phil experienced a twinge of homesickness for Ann Howard's low, pleasant voice, her quick glance, her physical presence.

All at once he was annoyed with himself for not having married several years ago.

He was buttoning his shirt when he heard the doorbell ring. As he went down the hall, he smelled coffee percolating in the kitchen. He and his mother met at the front door.

"I thought maybe you could sleep late this morning——" she began.

He laid an arm around her shoulder and squeezed her. "Thanks for the thought, but I need to catch up on some work."

The doorbell just beyond them chimed again. Ivy smiled. "Well, let's see who our early bird is," and she opened the door.

The old man stood there in the rain quietly—straight-backed, shy and self-possessed. He wore a threadbare Sunday suit of blue serge. The hat he held in his hands was the same one he had had at the airport the day before, with tiny cracks in the creases of the crown. His white shirt was buttoned up to the frayed collar, but he wore no tie.

"I hate to be bothersome . . ." he offered tentatively.

"Hello, Leck." Ivy opened the door farther and motioned him inside. "Phil, this is Leck Gunter. He was down at the airport yesterday just before your plane arrived. He's an old friend of your grandpa Thurston's—and mine."

Phil held out his hand and gripped the other's hard, bony fingers. "How are you, Mr. Gunter?" he said.

"Leck," Ivy went on, "this is my only chick—little Phil I was telling you about yesterday."

He looked up at the tall young stranger. "Just a mite of a lad for sure." He smiled. "I'm the proudest in the world to make your acquaintance, son." There was diffidence, eagerness and honesty behind his every word and glance. "I knew your mama here when she was just a little feist, growing up over on Thickety——"

"And if you don't want to catch your death of cold and forget it all, you'd better come on in and get dry," Ivy urged.

She hung his hat on the brass stand in the hall. In the living room the couch where Clay had spent the night was marked only by the tousled coverlet he had left behind. Ivy drew the draperies back from the windows, exposing the view of drenched trees and their dark shining trunks and freshly fallen leaves on the hillside behind the house. She folded the cover and took it with her as she left the room. "I'll let you men talk while I fix more coffee." Then Phil knew that she had been pouring that first percolator of strong coffee down Clay's throat. He would be miserable this morning.

"Sit down, Mr. Gunter," Phil said, wondering what cousin the old fellow was wanting appointed postmaster at some crossroads, what road he wanted built up some remote hollow.

Gunter sat down on the little cherry rocker near the fireplace and leaned forward with his elbows on his knees. His blue eyes were intent on Phil and what he had to say. "I never was one to be forward in my dealings with any man," he started, as though he had gone over the words in his mind beforehand, "especially a full senator of these United States. But the time comes when folks have to speak out, and I'd never rest easy if I felt I hadn't raised my voice when it was needed."

"Certainly, Mr. Gunter." Phil had remained standing, leaning against the bookcase beside the fireplace, in the hope that this posture would keep their talk from stretching out interminably. "You're absolutely right in considering it your duty as well as privilege to say——"

But his visitor, as if sensing the cant behind the easy flow of his phrases, interrupted a full senator of these United States. "We've got to have your help here in these mountains!" he said.

Phil suddenly had a vision of all the reports, analyses, statistics, plans, documents and bills on the Appalachian Mountains that had accumulated in his office during a few brief months past. And here before him was the flesh and blood behind that river of ink. "Tell me all about it, Mr. Gunter."

"That be beyond my power, Senator. I don't know all about it." (Phil paid grudging tribute in his mind to Leck Gunter's preciseness. He wished that the trained researchers on their safaris into the darkest hills were as precise. And as modest.) "But I can tell you what it's like with me and my folks that still live on Thickety Creek."

Phil sat down on the sofa and crossed his hands behind his head. "I'd like to know, Mr. Gunter," he said.

"I reckon your mama's told you about how it used to be on Thickety——"

Phil nodded. "A little——"

"Her papa had his big sawmills there, kept half of us in the valley in good jobs. For the rest, they planted their little creek bottoms to corn, tobacco, whatever brought the best price. Everybody had cows, chickens, a hog or two, gardens in summer and canned stuff in winter. Nobody lived very high, but there was comfort for the most part." He paused.

"I understand," Phil said.

"But nowadays," Leck went on, "like good seed run out, seems like it's all come to naught. The timber's been gone many a day. It takes might' nigh all of a hillside to pasture one good cow, and outside the tobacco patch there's nothing we can grow to bring us decent cash profit. Azalie and me had six young'uns, all of them up North now but two."

Phil nodded. "I've heard my mother talk about Azalie Shook."

"If I do say so myself, Senator Cortland, she was a bright girl; way ahead of me. But we saw all of our two girls and four boys, excepting one, finish high school. That one, he always had a rambling foot, and one year he lit out for Illinois . . . Iowa . . . that corn country. And from what he's told me, I know my little grubbing around by mule and hand can't run a fair race with them big tractors, planters, harvesters and the like. Now that boy of mine is home: no farm work for him to do full time out there in that plentiful country and nothing worth a decent living back on our poor land. He don't know no other kind of work. My oldest boy, he went up to the coal mines in Kentucky and Pennsylvania—and he hung on long as he could against them machines, but it's better than a year now since he was laid off and come on back to Thickety. He don't know how to follow any other work."

Phil shook his head. "It's happened to tens of thousands of other men, Mr. Gunter——"

"That don't ease the pinch a particle when it's happening to you," the old man replied.

"I know it doesn't. I only meant that it's a big problem——"

"Best put some big men to tackling it then," he said.

"We are. The Government and private agencies have been investigating——"

"It's about time they finished up investigating and started doing something for us. Four of my young'uns gone already, and only old Lazarus, Azalie's daddy, he lives with us now, is sure to hang on tough as saw briers. He come ninety-four last month."

"Now look here, Mr. Gunter, I want you to understand that I'm utterly in sympathy with your problem." Phil wished he'd had some coffee before this conversation began. "It's not just one problem, it's many interrelated ones. And they're all big. They're all tough. And the Government's big and sometimes it's cumbersome, too. It's hard to set in motion. Meantime, emergency measures, welfare——"

Leck Gunter's face flushed. "What do you know about welfare, Senator Phil?" He looked down at his big work-scarred hands. "A man takes it to keep his body from breaking, and first thing he knows it's a-breaking his spirit."

Phil looked at him, astonished at the fervor of this reticent mountain man.

"My pappy would a-turned in his grave to know I ever reached out and took money I hadn't earned. But a man's got a right to stay alive as long as he can, I reckon. The thing that worries me is my boys, fear they may come to expect it——"

Phil nodded. "It's a bad situation. Second, third generation——"

"Getting without giving: a man worthy of the name can't hold to that pattern and keep his manhood. Senator, find us a way to give something back for what we get. For God's sake, help us find a way for the young'uns back in our hills here to grow up with a man's dignity and hope!"

"New patterns." Phil sighed. "Everywhere the need's the same."

Ivy had come in while he was speaking. She set a tray on the table and handed a cup of steaming coffee to each of the men. Phil was startled to see tears in her eyes as she gave him his cup.

"You're a pretty eloquent advocate, Mr. Gunter," Phil said. "With many like you around, I can't believe this region has a thing to worry about." He was trying to re-establish a little distance between them, for the older man's plea had caught him off balance. He was more moved than he wished to be. He tried to remember an appearance he had made before one of the Senate subcommittees drafting legislation on the economic problem spots in the country: the boredom, the ignorance, the outright hostility revealed by that committee's questions would be an astringent, cooling any emotion aroused by this outburst.

Yet he knew the truth of Leck Gunter's words and he wanted to hold on to that core of reality. He had long since convinced himself that his desire to be in the Senate, his elation when Governor Wentworth had appointed him there, his growing determination to remain there, sprang from his desire and determination to do the greatest good for the greatest number of people possible. He had the imagination to hear Leck Gunter's plea as louder than a single voice and larger than a single valley. He would try to respond.

"But there aren't many like Leck or Azalie," Ivy said.

Leck Gunter flushed and took a great swallow of coffee. "Lots that are a sight smarter, I reckon," he said; "maybe a few that are dumber. But we're in a box down here right now. We can work our way out—but we need leaders somewhere along the way. I reckon I'm asking you to find a way to help us help ourselves."

"A way—or ways," Ivy said.

The old man nodded. He gulped the coffee, sitting stiffly on the edge of his chair. "If we could just get some new industry here—"

Phil stood up. "Believe me, Mr. Gunter, you have my attention. Not only mine. Abler men than I am are working on just the things you've been talking about."

"Then tell them to hurry!" he said.

Ivy looked up at Phil. There was triumphant laughter in her eyes.

The phone in the hall rang. She went to answer it.

Leck Gunter stood up. Handling Ivy's fragile china with gentle care, he set the cup and saucer back on the tray as she returned to the room.

"Long distance for you, Phil," she said. "I took the operator's number and told her you'd call back. It was from Jerry Stewart."

"Thanks," he said. "I could have taken it now."

She did not answer.

"Much obliged for the coffee, Ivy," Leck Gunter said. "You know, it's not just everybody can make a real cup of coffee. I reckon you've come up to be as good a cook as your grandma ever was."

He shook hands with them as he left and accepted his battered hat from Ivy with grave courtesy. "I'm sorry for butting in on your Sunday morning," he said, "but I was bound to come and speak about Thickety and all the rest——"

"Quite all right," Phil said. "I'm glad to have had this little visit with you, Mr. Gunter." It seemed to him that the old man went away satisfied with their conversation. When he went back inside he said so to Ivy.

"Are *you* satisfied?" she asked.

He looked at her. "No, you don't," he said, trying to make it a joke. "You don't get me into a single debate, at least before breakfast."

She picked up the tray and empty cups.

"I like the old fellow," he said.

She hesitated, but said nothing.

"I'm just glad he finally realized there are other places and problems besides Thickety Creek." He put his hands in his pockets and stood before the window.

"If Leck Gunter had hurried a little faster, you'd have had more time for your report on those underdeveloped countries?" she asked.

Phil looked around, but she was carrying the tray out and he could not see her face. "Ouch!" he said. He grinned. "Aren't we full of irony this morning?"

"Not I," she said, going to the kitchen. "The irony is in the situation." He followed her and when he came into the kitchen, she said, "It's always so much easier to sacrifice people than principles."

"That has all the earmarks," he said, "of a wise saying. Does it mean something?"

"It means"—she reached up and pulled his hair lightly in mock annoyance—"that it's easier to dictate reports on distant lands than it is to talk with Leck Gunter, our friend."

"And so?"

"And so maybe Leck Gunter and Thickety Creek have something in common with your hosts abroad; maybe they've something to teach each other."

"I could recommend you as chairman of the next emergency committee on domestic problems——"

"You could, but won't." She winked at him. "One kibbitzer to every household, you know." She took her whisk and a crockery bowl out of the drawer and began to break eggs for an omelet. "If you make your call to Washington now, I'll synchronize it with your breakfast and a perfectly respectable omelet won't be spoiled by waiting."

"For your omelet," Phil said, "no sacrifice is too great. People or principles. I'll even talk to Jerry Stewart on an empty stomach." As he went toward his room he called back to her, "What happened to Clay?"

"He's upstairs shaving," she said. "That is, if he can face the mirror. We had a pretty rugged couple of hours just after daylight."

When he closed his door and dialed the operator, he put all of them out of his mind. He'd have to concentrate on his own life just now. Jerry wouldn't have called this early if he didn't have something urgent to say.

"Senator?" Jerry Stewart's voice fairly crackled on the line.

"Right."

"What the hell is going on down there in the mountains?"

"What are you talking about?"

"*I'm* not talking about anything. The wire service man that called me in the middle of the night *is* talking—about a murder trial coming up tomorrow in your old home town."

"They've made quite a story of it?"

"They'll make quite a headline of it," Phil's administrative assistant said, "unless I can tell them something quick. They say you're under wraps, won't see anyone——"

Phil laughed. "I'm so under wraps that I've seen half the town, already had a conference this morning with an ambassador from Thickety Creek, Appalachia, U.S.A. As for that wide-awake reporter I suspect of putting out the story, he's due here in a little while for an interview. This is being under wraps?"

"Just give me the facts, Senator, and we'll scotch those head-lines——"

"But I wanted to explain——"

"Damn it all, you know by now no one reads the explanations, Phil." Jerry Stewart's sigh was barely audible. Phil could visualize him leaning back in the big chair and propping his feet up on his cluttered desk.

"All right. All right. To begin with, there's no trial tomorrow, but a hearing——"

"Don't quibble over words."

"Simmer down, Jerry. Here are facts." And he recounted briefly the situation he'd found when he stepped off his plane and into his mother's car.

When he finished, Jerry said, "I'm sorry as hell that that corpse is a Negro."

"I'm sorry as hell he's a corpse," Phil replied.

"Yeah. Well . . ." Phil could hear the grunt as Jerry swung his feet off the desk and pulled up his chair. "Thing for us to do now is tell the news fellows they're riding a pretty dark horse—no pun intended—and if they'll string along with us till tomorrow we'll give them the full story. Straight from the horse's mouth. O.K.?"

"If they'll go along——"

"They will. After all, it's not a world-shaking item. You're not directly involved and when you branch out to uncles and cousins, that sort of thing runs thin pretty quick up here." Jerry was back on beam now, his easy patter of talk covering the efficient motions by which he went about getting things done.

"And when my eager-beaver reporter here in Nantahala arrives at the door in a little while——"

"You tell him, Senator, just to hold on to that pencil clutched in his hot little fist and by tomorrow afternoon when you have some real facts, you'll give him an exclusive interview."

"And if Clay is found sufficiently suspect to be bound over for trial . . . ?"

"We'll give it some thought. Meantime, during the interview to-day, why don't you take the young fellow into your confidence about this trip you've just made? Give him a gory tale or two about your firsthand observations. Throw in some pearls of wisdom. Get a little mileage out of this committee assignment, Senator."

"You make it sound very simple," Phil said. Sometimes Jerry's expediency set his teeth on edge.

"Nothing's simple," Jerry said. The way he spoke made Phil realize again, however, that it was easy to underestimate a man like Jerry Stewart.

"No," Phil said, "not even the help I can give my family in this trouble. If I've learned one thing during my short stay in the Senate, it's the treachery of power."

Stewart made no answer, waiting for Phil to go on as he so obviously intended to do.

"The greater the power, the greater the self-control. You don't use a tank to kill a mouse. Too little use, too much use of power— they're equally dangerous. And there are places where the certain kind of power you may hold is useless. Impotent."

"Write a think-piece on it, Senator." Stewart wasn't kidding. His tone was attentive and respectful. He was just in a hurry. And that was the difference, Phil thought, between being in Washington this morning and being here in Nantahala County. "I'll jot down some notes and leave them in your private file," Jerry said.

"All I'm saying is——"

"You're saying that folks think you can pull strings when you've got to give your attention to pulling levers. It may be, Senator, that you'll have to learn to use both."

"If I hadn't learned that some little time ago——"

"I like Washington," Jerry Stewart said. His words only seemed irrelevant. "Don't you, Phil? Like olives or oysters or avocado, the taste grows on you."

"I suppose so."

"Of course"—Jerry changed tone—"as far as your immediate problem is concerned, you could wash out one headline by making another one."

"Oh?"

"If a handsome young freshman senator and the elegant daughter of one of our nation's best-known senior senators should announce their engagement, that would be news."

"News to the Senator and girl, too," Phil said.

There was a pause.

"She called me last night, Senator. Asked me when you'd be back."

"But I talked with her myself yesterday afternoon," Phil said, puzzled.

"She wanted to know if you were planning to help write the report on your junket."

It was Phil's turn to sit straighter. "What the hell—of course I'm planning to help write it."

"I told her I'd heard some noises to that effect."

"Why'd she ask? What was on her mind?"

"I'm fresh out of tea leaves, Senator," Jerry said, "and my crystal ball is at the pawn shop. But I can guess that whatever was on her mind was something she'd picked up from her father. She and the old man aren't always on the best of terms, you know."

"I gathered, from things she's——"

"Oh, yes, she said to tell you to call if you had a chance—and the inclination."

Phil said nothing.

"I told her I thought you'd find both. . . . Well, when you talk to her, don't get caught in the cross fire."

Phil laughed. "Now that you've straightened out my public relations and my love life, is there anything else you'd care to arrange? Or may I go and re-enforce myself with an omelet and a second cup of coffee?"

"You're dismissed, Senator," Jerry said, but he managed to insert just the right amount of deference into his flippancy. Phil smiled at the bit of diplomacy, enjoying it even as he recognized it for what it was. He knew that Jerry used the same tactics in his behalf in tough dealings with many of the people a senator never even saw, and that was why he was a good administrative assistant.

"Jerry, I'll try to get back to the office tomorrow on a late afternoon flight. Leave the appointments open, though. It may be early Tuesday."

"Right."

Phil was ready to hang up when Jerry said, "And, Senator, even if I had talked with Miss Howard before, I'd call her again, right away."

Phil sat at the desk and watched the rain outside for a long pause. . . . No, he'd better call Ann after he'd eaten.

Clay was setting an empty coffee cup in the sink when his nephew came into the kitchen. "Morning," Phil said absently. "How are you?"

"I dropped dead exactly one hour and thirty-two minutes ago."

Snatched out of his preoccupation, Phil did a double take and noticed that Clay, again this morning, was wearing the grey felt hat in the house.

"Oh, Lord A'mighty," Clay groaned and leaned against the sink. "How am I for a fact?" He nodded toward the dining room. "They're all in there at the trough," he said. "You better join them."

Phil could hear his aunts' voices. "You're not eating?" he asked.

"Not for a little while, bright boy. The world may be your oyster, but right now I don't have any stomach for it. . . ." His voice trailed off.

"Oyster or clambake," Phil said, "I want Hugh Moore to get his carcass out here this afternoon. I want to find out where we stand— not ifs, ands or buts. You get the message to him, Clay."

"It's my bad day for running business errands——"

"Well, it damned well better turn good right away because it's *your* business you're errand boy for."

"Whoo-ee!" Clay looked up—pride, shame, respect, resentment, mingled in the look. "That's talking to them with the bark on, Senator. That's walking softly and carrying a big stick."

"You could phone Hugh." Phil was not to be sidetracked. "But however you do it, you get him out here today."

"I'm as mean as he is and twice as smart; I'll get him," Clay said.

Phil went into the next room and greeted Frone and Phoebe.

"We had to start without you," Ivy said. "The omelet was just right, but it's still hot if you'll hurry."

It was delicious and he ate rapidly, a habit he had acquired since he left Nantahala County. The room lifted his spirits. With no sunshine outside this morning, Ivy had managed to make the room create its own glow. There was the warmth of a yellow linen table-cloth and flowered crockery and a centerpiece of ripe tempting fruit —red and gold apples, yellow bananas, rusty pears, a cascade of green and purple grapes. It was a light, good room. He wished Ann Howard could see it.

"Sounded as if you might be getting brother Clay whipped into shape this morning," Frone said.

"Not especially," Phil replied. "We just have to find out where we are in this whole foggy affair. And it doesn't seem to me that Hugh Moore's acting with the greatest energy in his handling of it."

Frone gave a short laugh. "Can you imagine anybody from Thickety Creek acting with 'the greatest energy' on anything?"

Phoebe smoothed the napkin in her lap. "How did we ever stand it there?" she asked.

"There was nothing wrong with Thickety," Ivy said. "We stood it because it was our world. We found a good deal of living in it as I remember."

They were all quiet for a moment.

"Poor old Clay! I guess he did well enough to turn out as normal as he is," Frone said, seeking an excuse for her brother. "After Papa died—it was hard on all of us, but it was just plain hell for Clay. Papa was the only person he'd ever really looked up to——"

"I guess it was harder on both the boys than on us," Ivy said softly.

"How's Grandma Thurston this morning?" Phil asked.

"I think she seems brighter, don't you, Ivy?" Phoebe asked.

"Maybe, a little. She slept well. I guess she was tired out after all the excitement last night."

"Poor old Mama," Phoebe said. "Seems as if she's had so much in her lifetime to worry her. Isn't it a shame she can't have a few years of peace?"

"Peace?" Clay asked from the door. They were startled by his voice. "Why, that little lady's the only peaceful soul I know. She's settled the account with her God and she's settled the account with herself. Who could ask for more than that this side of Jordan?"

"We didn't mean anything like that," Phoebe protested, not explaining what they had meant. "We'd just like to keep your—your scrape to ourselves as much as possible."

Clay shifted in the doorway. His eyes were bloodshot and his cheeks were leathery and bloated. He still wore his hat at a jaunty angle, however, and he tried to speak carelessly. "I'm sorry, dear sisters——"

Phoebe laid her pretty plump hands on the table cloth. Her rings glittered. "I don't think you're very sorry. You don't know how to be."

"Phoebe, sister mine," Clay said, "I won't argue the point with you. In fact I won't argue any point with you right now. I'm in need of somebody to stand by me, and if it's not my family why, then, *who* will be there?" Tears flooded his eyes.

His sisters were no less quick to respond.

"That's why we're here, Clay," Ivy said in a rush of pity and concern. "We're here to help each other."

The others agreed. Phoebe's lower lip trembled for a moment. Phil felt a mixture of impatience (because they seemed so anachronistic in the world as it was that moment) and affection (because they did not care if they were anachronisms). "Let's not be too gloomy about the situation," he said. "Let's hope Hugh Moore has found a way to clarify the muddy waters." He pushed back his chair and stood up. "If you'll excuse me, I've another phone call——"

"Sure, Senator, sure," Clay said. He laughed shortly. "And any time things need livening up around the capital, you just let your family know. Among us I reckon we've broken every commandment but the eleventh."

"And that one?"

"Thou shalt not be dull."

Phil nodded. "You could be right, Clay." He smiled at all of them. (The smile, reflected in his deep-set grey eyes, brought a lump to Ivy's throat. In that moment Phil had looked just like Cort the first time she ever saw him—saw him alone, to speak with. They had been standing near a tall old magnolia tree. And now here was this man, this son . . .) As he left the room, Phil said, "You won't forget about Hugh Moore, Clay?"

Before Phil had finished placing a call to Ann Howard, Ivy came to say that the young reporter had arrived and was waiting in the living room. Reluctantly Phil canceled his call and replaced the receiver on its hook. He went through the papers on his desk and selected one or two which he took with him into the living room.

The reporter was a decent-enough fellow, overworked, underpaid, eager to be in on some big news, participate in some of the important happenings in the big world outside this burg. "Big" was an overworked word in his vocabulary.

Phil knew exactly how to handle him. They sat down together like two men of large affairs, and putting himself off the record Phil sketched in the muddled background of the hunt, Hawk Williams' death, Clay's surrender as a suspect. When he had finished, the young stranger agreed that the news story would have to ripen with the developments at tomorrow morning's hearing. After all, the local paper had already carried a two-line notice of Hawk Williams' death "under suspicious circumstances."

"I used to know old Hawk, see him around," the reporter said. "Sometime I'd like to write up his case history as a classic example of Negro deprivation and frustration. Or maybe a novel."

Phil then offered a few of the high lights of the research trip from which he had just returned, along with two typed memos from which his visitor could quote—exclusively—if he wished to. Before he left, Phil asked him to drop by the office in Washington whenever he was in town. They shook hands on the steps. It had stopped raining, but the sky was still overcast. Phil stood outside a few minutes, enjoying the fresh clean air.

When he went back into the house, Ivy was just coming downstairs. "How did you and young Pulitzer get along?" she asked.

"Fine. Today he's going to write about my impressions of certain foreign countries and tomorrow we'll see what develops at Clay's hearing."

"Fine, indeed." She nodded. He always liked to watch her face when she was not certain whether to laugh or be serious. It was a very expressive face, wearing few of the reticences of age and masks of caution. She could be hurt—he hated to think of how many times she probably had been—but she could be happy, too, and God knows there seemed to be little enough of that capacity around. Just this morning he had begun to realize more distinctly how simple and hard a thing it was to be happy, even momentarily.

"That reporter says he'd like to write a case history of Hawk Williams." Phil sat down in an easy chair and stretched his long legs their full length across the carpet. He knew he was needling his mother even as she had needled him earlier in the morning. "Says he thinks it would be a classic study of Negro frustration."

Ivy was sweeping the hearth with her stout little fireplace broom. "Poor Hawk!" She sighed.

"Why poor?" he asked.

"That would be the final insult to him. Not to be thought of in life as a man but as a black sledgehammer with a killer instinct, and then not to be thought of in death as a man but as a Negro case study."

"Makes a person larger than life, doesn't it?" Phil said. "Carrying a whole race on his back?"

"And less. Carrying nothing of your own along the way. Your own guilt—or your own triumph." She had finished sweeping and she laid a small stick on the fire. It blazed in bright contrast to the iron-grey skies and dripping tree limbs just outside. "I wonder, will he do a case study of Clay, too?" she asked.

Phil lifted his eyebrows in surprise. "Why?" He knew she had some reason for asking.

"If he's going to 'explain' Hawk's brutality, then he must 'explain' Clay's, too. If Clay was capable of killing Hawk, then we ought to know both victims. If you're tolerant, you have to be tolerant across the board, all the way. That's a hard lesson to learn. I didn't understand it until just a few weeks ago, Phil."

"What happened then?"

She drew a footstool to the edge of the hearth and sat down on it, gazing into the brisk fire. "I discovered one day, soon after Clay returned from New Jersey, that I liked Naomi Henderson better than Clay. She was kinder to me, she understood me better, she helped with Mama and loved her—and she made no demands on my emotions. I thought this was so tolerant of me at first—and then I realized it was easy for me to like Naomi. The color of someone's skin has never made any difference with me. But I saw that it would take real tolerance and effort for me to like Clay—like him in the way I must like any person if I'm to understand him. And it dawned on me that if you're really trying to understand, you have to go all the way. Anything less is just an hypocrisy more fashionable than the old church hypocrisy. When we try to understand one person, do we have to compensate by hating, misunderstanding someone else?"

"I couldn't say." Phil felt that any answer he might make to these meanings she was forging for herself would be too glib.

"You shouldn't have quoted that young man's jargon to me." She smiled. Absently, she smoothed out the pleats in her grey tweed skirt. "I always look forward to your visits, Phil: our bull sessions on Important Subjects."

"So do I." He stood up. "I never did finish making my other call," he said.

"I'll hold your constituents at bay this time, I promise," she said.

"I'm calling Ann Howard," he said casually.

"She's the girl I wanted to ask you about," Ivy responded not at all casually. "The one who had lunch with us the last time I stopped in Washington? The old Senator's daughter?"

"The same."

"Then don't waste a minute," his mother said. Her eyes lit up with delight and she smiled. "Matter of fact, I wish you didn't have to call her at all. I wish she was right here with us!"

Slightly taken aback at her enthusiasm, Phil went to phone.

Ann's voice, when it finally came on the line, was not as poised as it had seemed yesterday. They exchanged pleasantries and then she said abruptly, "Phil, do you remember that night last winter . . ." She hesitated.

Of course he remembered, but he would make her spell it out. He would see if she remembered it as he did.

"We went to eat out in the country and when we came home it was snowing . . . and I wasn't very hospitable . . ."

"Yes. I recall the evening.

"Well, that's the reason I called Jerry Stewart after I heard a conversation here at the house last night."

He failed to understand the connection immediately, but he could figure that out later.

"I thought," she said, "that you should know Father and the other senior member of your safari committee spent yesterday afternoon and part of the evening drafting their official report and recommendations."

"What the hell—are you sure, Ann?" He knew the question was silly, but he felt as though he'd been hit in the belly. He had to have a minute to get back on his feet.

"They're bypassing you, Phil."

"So I gather. But why? They invited me in on all the discussions along the way, had me appointed in the first place——"

"Do you really want to know why, Phil?"

"Of course I do." His stomach was tight and his mouth was dry. The thought nagged at him that he had built this up too much in his mind, made it larger than it was. "Level with me, Ann."

"You were in that group as 'filler material,' Phil. Father and his crony had the committee's spots sewed up months ago—except for one place, and when your governor appointed you to the Senate, they latched on to some nice young filler material."

"In other words, a rubber stamp?" he said.

"Not exactly, Phil. Partly that, partly the routine, the ritual, the test by which you learn to be part of the club, get along with the boys."

"To hell with the club. I'm doing a good job, Ann——"

"Of course you are. The point is, Phil, you're a beginner. They've got to show you you're not running the United States yet."

"I know that. But even a beginner wants to begin——" Whose side was she on anyway? he wondered.

"Sure, sure." She actually sounded like some of the men she was quoting. "You write out your recommendations, son, but just don't work up such a steam about them. Don't get so personally involved."

He had to laugh in spite of the jab he felt. "Aha, my knowledgeable friend, there's where the water strikes the wheel. In suspicion of commitment, of enthusiasm. Play it cool, keep the volume down, don't blow a fuse. What the hell, you might be wrong and make a fool of yourself. Worse, you might be taken in, be laughed at. Either

way, why all the steam? Why the risk? That's what they're really suspicious of, isn't it?"

Now Ann was laughing. "Why, Senator, you might just be right.
Right or wrong, you might give the old hill a tremor or two yet. If
you had the chance."

"Well, I come from a long line of involved and vocal people. I
seem to have just discovered that," he said. "Besides, you prodded
me to that outburst. You asked for it."

"I got it! That's the point," she said triumphantly. " 'That's where
the water strikes the wheel.' " She chuckled softly. He was alerted
by the change in her voice. "You remember how lovely the snow
was that night?" she almost whispered.

"And cold," he added.

There was the pause of a breath. "And cold," she agreed. "Well,
I'm not sure I wasn't unduly frosty myself that night. That's why I
wanted you to know about this report. I want you to have a chance
to be part of it."

"I'm glad."

"You talk with Father; sometime before Monday afternoon perhaps you can call him. Tell him you want a chance to discuss your
recommendations."

"Of course I do."

"It's up to you then, Phil."

"Thank you, Ann." Neither one hung up. "When will I see you?"

"As soon as you get back—if you want to."

"I want to," he said. And they hung up.

He took out the notes he had made last night and went over
them, making changes here and there.

When he went at last to rejoin the others, he found the house so
quiet it seemed empty of all life and motion—suspended in time and
space. No one was downstairs. The fire in the living room had been
fed a green log that would last during an absence and the brass fire
screen had been set in front of it. Pages of the Sunday-morn-
ing paper were strewn in casual abandon over the long couch.

He went upstairs quietly.

". . . and if he hadn't had such a big heart for every derelict in the country"—Frone's voice was raised so that her mother could hear—"he wouldn't have had to die the way he did or when he did, and Clay would have had a father as he grew up."

"Clay and Kin, both of the boys."

"And we wouldn't have had this . . ." Frone halted. "Things would be better for Clay, for all of us, today."

"And how is my favorite grandmother this morning?" Phil asked at the door.

Frone was helping her mother into a knitted bed jacket, guiding the stiff, wizened arms into the sleeves. Frone's motions were quick and impatient. "She's suffering some with her arthritis this morning. I declare, I don't know how Ivy manages when she's here alone with Mama." Frone sighed. "She just does the impossible, I guess."

"Good morning, Phil," his grandmother said.

"Morning, Grandma Thurston," he answered. Then, to Frone, "I think we should get a nurse to help. By the way, where did Mother and——"

"She and Phoebe went to church," Frone said. "Clay tore off to see someone in town. Kin came over to check on Mama, but then he went back home." She settled her mother in the bed and then went over to a chair by the window. There was a brief silence and Phil knew that his aunt was continuing her thoughts where they had been when he came.

"Jud, or my boys, Phoebe's Rutledges and Lucy Kate, even you Phil, can't have any idea what it was like back there on Thickety. On a rainy day like this, old Nye Blankenship and the other sawmill hands with their mud-crusted boots and their endless talk around the fire. . . . Working or idling they could eat like horses—with Ivy and Phoebe and me to wait on them."

She paused, not going on to recall the irony of having known this and yet married Jud Mather and had his four sons. For they were every inch Jud's sons: solid and deliberate in judgment, certain beforehand that whatever they undertook had immediate cash value. The younger one had come through a few wild years with airplanes and stunt flying, but now he could sell real estate better than Jud. Oh, they were all Connecticut Yankees, all right! They had never even visited these mountains, the place where Frone had lived be-

fore she went to teach in a school near that World War I army training camp in the middle part of the state and met Lieutenant Judson
Mather there. She had left her life sharply divided ever since, and
sealed the two halves off in tight compartments—unaware that they
were identical in several basic ways. Seeking to flee the narrowness,
the confinement, the provincialism she found in the hills of her an-
cestors, she had fled into another narrowness, confinement and provincialism of strangers.

"Nye Blankenship," the old woman whispered. "Poor old Nye
was our Job. He attracted affliction——"

"Like a lightning rod attracts lightning," Fróne finished for her.
She sat looking out of the window at the soaked lawn and driven
leaves and the leaden sky. Phil felt that the two women had entered
into some private world where he could not follow. It was the um-
bilical cord of memory that bound these vastly different people together now. And although he, too, was joined with them, there were
areas where he was a stranger. He left the room quietly.

"We all had to go on living," he heard his grandmother murmur
behind him.

Downstairs Phil lit his pipe and stood before the window for a
long time. He was glad that his mother liked him to smoke the pipe.
They could both remember his father standing in front of the fire in
this room and drawing on his pipe, then pulling up a chair and sitting for long hours absorbed in contemplating the view of mountaintops outside and the firelight inside.

The jangle of the telephone tore across the quiet. He went to
answer it.

"Phil?" Clay's voice blasted along the line.

"That's right."

"I took your gentle hint. I came over here and got Hugh Moore's
little red wagon rolling. He's had news all right."

"I'm listening." Phil gripped the receiver.

"There's not a new witness, but new evidence." Clay's voice was
tense, worried. "Burl McHone is ready to swear he saw me shoot
Hawk Williams."

"Who is Burl McHone?"

"One of the bastards on our hunting trip last week."

Phil whistled. "There goes the ball game."

"But, Phil, best I can remember about the other night, by the time old Hawk was shot Burl McHone couldn't have seen a white egg on a coal pile. How could he have made out——"

"But then your best isn't any too good on remembering the other night, is it, Clay?"

"No . . ."

"Then why don't you just shut up? Can't you understand what an eyewitness does to your case?"

Before Phil could say any more, Hugh's voice, concerned yet reassuring, came on the line. "Don't be too hard on him, Phil. He doesn't know law——"

"You fake little pipsqueak!" Clay shouted at the same end of the line. "I'm acquainted with the law enough to know that a lawyer is supposed to keep his client informed——"

"But I only learned about Burl McHone this morning," Phil heard Moore answer him. "Sheriff Doggett told me."

"Doggett? He still sheriff?" Phil demanded. "I thought they were going to oust him last summer when the League of Women Voters and the Jaycees——"

Hugh gave a sour chuckle. "It'll take more than a handful of do-gooders to pry Doggett out of office. He watches them come and go. While they're a-coming he 'jes lays low,' like Br'er Rabbit when the foxes are out. And when they're a-going he eases back into the routine again. Doggett survives."

"Apparently," Phil said drily.

"He helps his friends survive, too," Hugh Moore went on. "The word came in to him last night that this McHone had come down with an acute case of diarrhea of the tongue, was running around telling tales about what he could testify . . ." Hugh sighed heavily. "So Doggett went on out to check."

"And what did the lying son-of-a-gun have to say?" Clay demanded, so close to the phone that Phil could hear him as clearly as Moore.

"The sheriff didn't tell me quote for quote," Hugh replied, "but he did say McHone was having second thoughts about what he'd seen out there on the mountain."

"Second thoughts?" Clay cried. "That walking idiot never had any first thoughts yet!"

"And"—Hugh Moore made an obvious effort at patience—"Doggett suggested it might be worth our time if somebody could run out and see McHone before the hearing tomorrow."

"Is it a matter of choice?" Phil asked. "Of course we'll run out and see him."

"Good boy," Hugh said. The condescending approval in his voice set Phil's teeth on edge.

"Tell him we'll be out to Ivy's to pick him up in twenty minutes," Clay instructed Hugh.

"And you tell Clay," Phil said on the other end of the line, "not to drink another drop if he's going to drive us anywhere—and I'm not just beating my gums."

Clay's silver-grey sports car swerved off the highway and lurched to a halt. The early morning rain had stopped, but the air was still damp and heavy; fat drops gathered at the ends of leaves and twigs and splattered steadily to the wet ground. Like some smaller species of jungle animal returning to an ancient graveyard to die among its own kind, Clay's small sleek car came to rest on the hard-packed dirt of a yard choked with automobile carcasses. Eyeless, with windows gone and headlights smashed, stripped of wheels or naked of fenders and doors, sinking to rust and rot, tumbled on one side or completely upside down in huge and helpless surrender, a boneyard of wrecked, discarded, disintegrating cars filled the space in front of the house where Hugh Moore indicated that Burl McHone lived.

Hugh climbed out quickly. "I'll see if Burl's here," he said, and picked his way between the disemboweled cars toward the porch.

The house stood on a narrow strip of land between the road in front and a hill that seemed perpendicular behind it. It was an unpainted shell of a building that had once served as a store. The door stood open and there were no screens on either the door or the two square windows that faced the road, so that the spavined quilt-strewn bed, broken overstuffed chair, gaudy picture on the wall, and three dirt-caked children playing on the bare floor were all visible to passers-by. The porch sagged under a burden ranging from a once-white porcelain washing machine to mattresses losing their tangled stuffing, soggy cartons of empty soft-drink bottles and small heaps of sawmill slabs and lump coal for stove fuel. Under the steps and porch, in dank rot, was an unidentifiable mass of junk; and immediately to the rear of the house, under a cluster of rhododendron bushes, was piled the scattered accumulation of years—used cans, broken jars, plastic containers. On the unpainted outhouse, the door swung crazily by one hinge.

Phil looked at the steep hill just behind the house. Once green with a cover of sturdy balsam and delicate birch, thick mosses and vines, it was now a mass of rubble and devastation. The hillside had been completely cut over, the large logs snaked away and sold, rich humus and topsoil destroyed, and then everything abandoned. Dead limbs and lops of trees lay where they had fallen. In half a dozen spots loose soil had run off with the heavy rains so that the fingers of several gullies stretched down the slope. The few rhododendron and laurel bushes that had escaped ravishment served only to highlight the general holocaust on the hillside. Somewhere in the distance a crow cawed shrilly and received raucous reply from another crow.

And dominating all the other squalor and waste and decay of this place was the autombile graveyard, littering with rusty wheels, torn tires and twisted pipes the cementlike dirt which could hardly be called a lawn.

From among the steel and chromium carcasses, suddenly there came a sound of tapping. Hugh Moore, on the porch—where he was talking to a woman in faded chartreuse pedal pushers and pink flowered blouse, her hair rolled in tight plastic curlers—turned quickly and looked in the direction of the noise. He hurried down the steps and out to the Model-A Ford. He reached the man working underneath a moment before Clay and Phil caught up.

"Burl?" Hugh said.

The man pulled himself from under the car, surveyed his visitors a moment, and then got to his feet. "Sure thing." He spat, making a thin stream between his two front teeth.

He was of medium height and weight, stoop-shouldered, round-bellied, with a sallow face and eyes that were watchful, but could not meet another gaze. His glance shifted continually. His black hair was cut, or uncut, in ducktails around his ears and at the back of his neck, and it had known more hair tonic than shampoo. When one loose oily lock kept falling over his eyes as he talked, he smoothed it back in place with a careful hand. His long fingernails were caked with grease and grit.

"Reckon *he* knows me." He nodded slyly to Clay.

"Like the south end of a northbound mule. How you doing, Burl?" Clay said.

"Making out," he said, shifting eyes from one to the other of them.

"I'm Hugh Moore." The lawyer spoke too heartily and held out his hand, which Burl McHone seemed not to see. "We've met before —you might not remember."

"I remember O.K.," McHone said.

"And this is Clay's uncle, Senator Cortland," Hugh said, with all the pompousness he could muster.

McHone took Phil's outstretched hand in a limp grasp. A flick of the eyes and then a quick return to looking at the ground. A mutter of greeting.

"Well, this is quite a layout you've got here," Hugh went on, indicating the hulks of cars.

McHone's glance was sharp with suspicion, his voice whiny. "It ain't much of a garage, but it's all I got."

Clay looked at Phil and winked. Did McHone think they really might believe these cars were his business and not a front for the moonshine whisky he undoubtedly made up some narrow cove nearby? Which of these cars did he keep ready to run a fresh haul of the white stuff to adjoining states every few weeks? The Model-A with souped-up motor certainly, and maybe one of the two-door Chevvies over there at the side.

"Looks to me like you got it made, man," Clay said, wanting to mock this shifty, slinking creature, but restrained by knowledge of why he himself was here. At least he could be forthright and be done with Moore's and McHone's weaseliness. He took out cigarettes, offered one to McHone and then to the others. "Now, Burl, what the

hell is this I hear-tell you got dreamed up about Hawk Williams'
killing?"

Hugh Moore flushed with anger at Clay's impudence, his im-
prudence in snatching the conversation away from his lawyer's direction, but he waited for the other man to answer.

"Nothing much," Burl McHone said.

"Nothing much?" Clay repeated. "Way I heard it, it was pecker-
wood plenty——"

"Let's let Burl tell us himself what's on his mind," Hugh Moore
interrupted. "Come on, Burl . . ."

The man shuffled his feet, fixing his look on them as if they were
curious new appendages he had only just discovered. "Nothing much
in mind. Just recollecting best I could——"

"Best for who?" Clay demanded.

"Not for nobody," McHone went on. "Any judge get to poking
around at me with questions, I got to recollect the very way it was."

"Of course." Phil spoke for the first time. He had leaned back
against the twisted fender of a pick-up truck and now he crossed
his arms and said casually, "How was it, Burl?"

The man's unshaven face was even more suspicious and guarded
now. "A lot of fooling around . . ." He stopped.

"How many went along Wednesday night?" Phil asked.

"Me and my brother Doc that lives down the road a piece, and
Arley and Ranse Putnam, and him." He nodded toward Clay.

"How about Hawk Williams?" Phil asked.

"Sure. Sure, him, too. He"—glancing at Clay again—"asked the
nigger."

"And you sure hogged down his liquor and the meat he cooked,"
Clay said.

"Wait, Clay," Phil said quietly. "Then you built up a fire and
had some steaks—and drinks?"

Burl McHone nodded.

"Not much hunting done?"

He grinned and did not even bother to answer that question.
"We listened to the dogs run."

"Everybody got pretty drunk?"

"Some more. Some less. And some was target practicing."

"At night?"

"We had the car headlights all turned on and the fire was pretty high. It was all in fun anyway. Till him and the nigger set in to fighting."

Phil raised his eyebrows. Hugh was watching Clay and McHone with furtive attentiveness.

"Fighting?" Clay's face was pale. "You know damned well that Hawk and I didn't fight. I never laid a hand——"

"Arguing then——"

"There's a hell of a difference between fighting and arguing," Clay said tensely. "You better be careful what words you choose, man."

"Arguing loud and mean over Plott hounds and blue ticks——"

"Oh, hell!" Clay laughed shortly. "That wasn't more than a razor's edge difference of opinion between Hawk and me . . ."

There was a brief silence. The woman in bright pants had come back out on the porch with a baby, and now she stood watching them.

"Whose side you on anyway?" Clay asked abruptly.

Burl McHone kicked at a pebble on the ground and said, "If worst comes to worst, I'd try to see my way clear to be on your side . . ." He left the thought dangling.

"And what is the worst, McHone?" Phil asked.

"The worst," Hugh answered for him, "is if he saw Clay actually fire at Hawk."

Phil nodded. "And did you see this, McHone?"

He did not look at any of them, but at his wife on the cluttered porch, wearing her hair curlers like Medusa's serpents. "Not exactly . . ."

"Louder, please."

"Maybe just take aim. Not fire——"

"Oh, you bastard! You lying——"

Burl McHone's sallow face turned red as a turkey's wattles. "I don't take that off no man . . ." His right hand balled into a fist.

"Men, men." Hugh Moore came between them and his plea was

so quiet it seemed positively self-satisfied. "Let's talk this over . . ."

"Nobody asked him to come out here and I don't aim to be talked to like a dog——"

"Hell, McHone, I don't guess you meant to lie," Clay said, "but I don't see how you're sure you saw me take that aim at old Hawk when I can't even remember one hazy bit——"

"Seems like that's what I saw," Burl persisted, but weakly.

In a flash the whole situation became clear to Phil. He looked at Burl McHone and at Hugh Moore. He wouldn't be able to prove half of what he suspected, but he could test the other half right now. He looked at the butchered hillside behind them. "Say, McHone," he asked abruptly, "how did you come out on clearing that hill?"

Caught off guard, Burl McHone turned to look at the barren slope in surprise. His fist relaxed. "Didn't come out a-tall." Then he went on, more craftily, "No money in timber these days for a little operator like me. Hard to find any way to make a go——"

"Would a loan help you get on your feet?" Phil asked.

The dirty hand pushed the long forelock out of his eyes. "Government loan? I hate to get tangled up with——"

"Personal loan. Long term. No interest."

Relief settled into McHone's face. He had taken a long gamble and it was about to pay off. Hugh Moore's face was bland and impassive, but his small eyes were watching Phil. Clay had followed the conversation with anger, surprise, and slowly dawning comprehension. Phil decided to go the whole way.

"And if your mind were on that loan tomorrow morning, you probably couldn't remember as clearly as you thought you could when you talked to the sheriff last night?"

McHone shook his head. "Seems like I have these spells"—his grin was like a possum's, a night scavenger's—"when sometimes my remembrance is clear as day, and then overnight it turns plumb muddy. Reckon it's my high blood."

Up on the porch the baby began to cry. The woman dealt it a sharp slap and carried it into the house where it continued to cry, but now the sound was muffled. When the woman reappeared, she was fastening one of the curlers that had come loose over her forehead.

Phil turned to Hugh Moore. "There's the witness," he said.

"What do you mean, Phil?" the lawyer asked and then Phil knew positively that not only Burl McHone but Hugh—probably Sheriff Doggett too—had hatched up this little subplot as a scheme to pick up a fast buck.

"I mean there's the state's great witness," Phil said. "Unshakable as a mountain of gelatin. If you can't tear apart his faked-up evidence in about two minutes flat, you ought to be disbarred."

Clay was furious. "You mean this—this varmint was trying to gouge us for some money to keep his——"

Burl McHone's face was both angry and fearful. He looked from one man to the other.

"Looky here"—his voice rose—"I'm just a poor feller a-trying to get along. I done nothing wrong."

"I never did like blackmail," Phil said. "No deal." He turned and walked toward Clay's car.

"Now I ain't shouldering all the blame for this. Before you accuse me you better know who come to me——"

"Take it easy, Burl," Hugh Moore said smoothly. "Nobody's accusing you of anything. Senator Cortland and the rest of us just believe some of your evidence is a little shaky."

"But Sheriff Doggett——"

"I'll talk with Sheriff Doggett, get it all straight. You might not even be subpoenaed tomorrow."

"Who the hell you working for anyway?" Clay suddenly demanded. "You protecting this s.o.b. or me?"

"Shut up, you," Hugh Moore hissed so that Phil could not hear. "Shut up and get out."

"All of you'uns get out," Burl McHone snarled. His narrow eyes, under the lock of greasy hair, were sullen and resentful. As Phil and Clay and Hugh Moore left the junk-clogged yard, Burl McHone kicked the side of one of his wrecked cars. His wife, wiping one hand on her bright, stained blouse, offered them a casual gesture of utter vulgarity.

They drove back to town in silence. Embarrassment, fear of what they might say if they spoke in their own rashness, preoccupation with McHone's withdrawal (or revenge, if he should reconsider and decide to try to brazen out his fictitious tale tomorrow) absorbed them in their own thoughts.

Phil felt some slight relief. At least no eyewitness to Clay's killing (if Clay had killed) was yet known. But the encounter with Burl McHone and his sluttish wife and the degradation of their once-magnificent surroundings had left Phil depressed. Here was poverty —not poverty of cash alone but poverty of mind, hope, spirit, the senses—that equaled all but the most abject he had confronted in foreign lands. And they're my own people, he thought grimly, then wondered what he meant by the phrase.

Even more grimly, he wondered how many times in other years he had passed that house and never seen it until now, when its presence threatened his own security. Burl McHone had not managed to create that wretched place in a few months, or even a few years. It had been in the making for a long time. But Phil could not remember ever having noticed it before. Was he afflicted with a certain poverty, too?

When they came to Hugh Moore's house, they parted stiffly. Hugh made an effort at recovery. "I'll see you at the club tonight, Phil. And Clay, buck up. I'll talk to Sheriff Doggett. We'll find a way out of this jigsaw——"

Before Clay could reply, Phil cut in. "You do that, Hugh. And while you're at it, you tell the sheriff I won't be happy at all if he doesn't present evidence for this case straight down the line."

"Doggett will do right by us," Hugh Moore said and slammed the door.

"That man's got the brass of a government mule." Clay shook his head, for once more amazed than angry.

When the two of them were almost to Ivy's, Clay said, "Thanks, Phil, for catching on to their little con game out there."

"We don't *know*," Phil said. "Forget it."

"For now," Clay agreed. As he plunged his car into the parking space and braked it to a skidding halt, he said to Phil, "I'm sorry we brought all this on you right now. Honest to God I am."

"Forget it, Clay. Tomorrow morning ought to tell the tale."

"To hell with tomorrow morning. I'm not thinking just about my hearing. I'm talking about all the remembering that seems to come out whenever there's a death or trouble in the family."

Phil nodded.

"It's hell," Clay said with mock pomposity, "but it's life."

"It's also raining again," Phil said, making ready to run to the door and rejoin the family.

CHAPTER 8
Yesterday

THE SUMMER evening that Uncle Burnett McQueen came back to the valley, Frone was in the parlor playing the piano. She had learned "The Merry Widow Waltz" while she was away at school last spring.

Ivy sat beside the big lamp in the kitchen working buttonholes on a dress she would take with her to Nantahala Female Institute when she entered classes there the last of August. The other children were spending the soft evening hours intent on their own interests. Phoebe was brushing her long thick hair as she gazed out of the window at the white half-moon which grew more visible as night came, a moon like a burnished brass boat swimming on the jagged frozen waves of the dark mountains. Clay, out on the wide front steps, played with squares and ends of lumber from Papa's sawmill. He built them into elaborate structures. Kin sat out under the maple tree on the ground beside Nye Blankenship. The boy's posture—elbows resting on his knees, hands dangling loosely between his legs—was an exact copy of the older man's. Nye and Kin sat a little apart from the Gunters, who lounged on the deep cool grass near the house.

Everyone was resting after the excitement, just before supper, when Tom Thurston had returned from town driving a long glossy surrey. Hitched to it was a smart-stepping roan-colored horse. The four black wheels of the surrey were high and sturdy and shiny with only the lightest film of brand-new dust on their spokes. The sides and seats were painted black, too, but its top—a fringed, spacious canopy over the two upholstered seats—was a warm rich yellow.

Martha, drawn by the children's excited calls, came out of the house. "Oh, Tom, what have you bought now?"

He had left for town early that morning with a half-load of lumber on one of the old wagons pulled by Kate. Now he had returned, late for the evening meal, riding in high style. Ever since he had paid off the last of their debts on the farm and sawmill and had celebrated by buying Frone a piano and going straight into debt again at the music store in town, Martha had waited hopefully for him to say something about buying back the heart of the farmland they had lost years before, but he never mentioned it. The shrill hum of the sawmill ran on day after day; great gashes of paths where logs were ball-hooted down steep mountainsides grew longer, deeper, wider; and Tom and the men worked with demon drive each day until they were bone-tired. And they had paid for Frone to board in town and go to the Institute for a year. (This year, with two girls going, the cost would be doubled, of course.) They had helped pay their share of Uncle Robert's funeral expenses last winter. (On his books were records of law fees due—accounts of a lifetime spent fighting injustices both petty and large—but none of his family had assumed the job of their collection. They could not even assume he wanted those debts forced.) They helped pay Preacher Grey so that he could be a full-time minister on Thickety Creek. They paid their share of Fayte McQueen's small salary as a teacher at the little valley school.

And when the traveling photographer came through the countryside, they all dressed in their best and had a family portrait made. Tom ordered a separate picture of Martha enlarged and tinted. There were ornate gold-colored frames to buy, too, and when— months later—the finished pictures came, they were hung in the parlor. The children for weeks afterward took turns sneaking in to contemplate their familiar countenances frozen there on the wall for all time. (Clay alone seemed natural, in his Sunday suit with hair slicked down, tie knotted—and barefooted! His brown eyes looked directly forward, as if challenging the man hidden under the big black cloth: "Do you see me? I'm here, right now!")

The sawmill had brought them money; they had bought both necessities and luxuries, but they had not bought Martha security, relief from this world's anxieties. She could not fully enjoy Tom's surprises. They might be "free and clear," as he said so often, but the shadow of debt threatened constantly, like the wings of a summer hawk above nervous chicken flocks. Martha looked at the new horse and conveyance and sighed.

"Martha, young'uns, your old papa has gotten us the best surrey money can buy. A man in my position can't let his family ride around in just any old contraption." He jumped down from the seat and pointed out the vehicle's best features to them, but the children were already all over it, testing the seats, climbing over the wheels, stepping from front to back. "Whoa, whoa, steady!" Papa gentled the uneasy horse.

"And what become of old Kate?" Nye Blankenship asked from the edge of the yard.

"I traded Kate in on this fine piece of horseflesh," Papa answered. "Come and take a look."

"Can that fine piece of horseflesh work in timber?" Nye asked.

"I'm not expecting him to," Papa said. "He's our carriage horse, for Martha here and the young'uns."

Nye Blankenship snorted. "You had a good worker in old Kate, but you traded her off for something fancy." He came closer. "And if I'm any judge you've got yourself a sight of trouble with this feller."

Papa frowned. "No siree, Nye. We've got the prettiest——"

"Pretty is as pretty does." Nye walked around the animal slowly. It did not move. He spat. Ivy had never seen him so aloof with an animal before. "Some creatures are born evil, with evil destinies. That's all there is to say or know about them; then keep your distance. My pap was one such creature. This-here's another." He went back to the edge of the yard.

They could all see that the old man's pronouncement had thrown a pall on Papa's surprise. But Amos Knott, sauntering up for his turn to look at the new horse and rig, slapped Tom on the shoulder. "Did some men know all they think they do, they'd be driving teams of their own instead of ground-hogging it around from one job to the next. That appears like a thoroughbred to me, Tom." And Nye Blankenship snorted from the shadows.

But the children's enthusiasm soon revived Tom. They begged to take a turn down the road right that moment. "I want Azalie to see our new surrey," Ivy said.

"We'll bow politely but formally to everyone we meet, the way it is in the ladies' magazines." Phoebe jumped up and down.

"I wonder how fast we could go?" Clay panted.

"Hold on! Hold on!" Papa motioned them into the surrey. "We'll drive up to the barn and then we'll have supper. You'll have plenty of time to rare back and ride like ladies and gentlemen a little later."

"Can't we stack the dishes till tomorrow morning?" Ivy asked, after supper, and Mama and Phoebe agreed. They drifted to their various refuges. When Kin sat down by Nye, the silent man patted his head and transferred something from his own pocket. Crushed heart leaves—green, juicy, fragrant.

The windows and doors of the house stood wide. A faint breeze moved the curtains hanging at the windows. It stirred the leaves and touched the face of each one of them as they waited, rested, thought, played, dreamed. The light of the half-moon grew more luminous.

In the parlor Frone was playing softly. The music was as limpid as the evening itself. It enveloped the men under the trees and Clay on the steps and Phoebe at her window and Papa on the porch. No one even paid any special attention when the picket gate swung open and someone stepped through. He came slowly up the walk as though studying the big house. Finally Papa stood up, walked toward the newcomer.

"Who is it?"

"Why, what kind of welcome is that, Tom Thurston?"

"Almighty be! It can't be Burn—is it you, Burn McQueen?"

"Why not, Tom?" the familiar voice asked him. "You old rascal."

And their hearty greetings and laughter ended Frone's music abruptly and brought them all to welcome Uncle Burn.

Martha rushed from the house, laughing and crying. Then she looked around. "Gib?" she asked, as soon as she had hugged her brother. "Where's Gib?" The children stood aside. Ivy remembered that she had never seen Uncle Burn and Uncle Gib apart before.

"We'd better go in the house, Martha," Uncle Burn said. His voice was not as carefree as they had always known it. As far back as the children could remember, Uncle Burn and Uncle Gib had been wandering in and out of their lives—arriving without announcement or luggage, leaving without farewells. Now Uncle Burn was alone.

Inside, they sat down, stiff and uncomfortable, and he told Martha in the only way he knew, directly and without preamble. "We've been up in Kentuck for the better part of a year now. There was an accident in the mines——"

"Oh, no," she whispered, "not down in the black dank pits, not Gib——"

"There were five men killed in that cave-in, Martha. Gib was the only one didn't have a wife and children. I tell you, there's always something to be thankful for. It was a pitiful sight there in that holler the day the whistle blew at midmorning."

"How long ago, Burn?" Tears washed down her face. "Why didn't we know? He should have been buried here among his own——"

"It was last month." Burn paused. "They never brought up the bodies, Martha. We'd been working a vein that was about run out; that's why the owners hadn't put out the cost for any new ceiling supports. And after those tons of earth slid down, it would have taken days and days to unbury them—and maybe bury some more." He stood up and strode across the room and the family could see the bitter pain in his face and hunched shoulders. "I wanted to dig them out myself—I tried—they put a cross up over that place so people would know it was a graveyard."

"Burn, don't fret yourself," Papa said, running his hand through his hair. "You can't whip yourself. It doesn't matter where a man's buried. You and Gib had good years of living."

They sat in the lamplight and shared his sorrow because they, too, remembered the humor and carelessness and freedom of Gib, whom they had loved. After a while they began recalling special times during Gib's life, Martha going back to years of his boisterous boyhood, Burn telling of times in the army and jokes on buddies and their wandering since the war, Tom reminding them of the year Gib and Burn had helped build the big white barn.

"Since you've been away, we've had our troubles here, too, Burn," Martha said. "Did you get my letter about Uncle Robert?"

He nodded. "It was forwarded on to us in Kentuck. I hated to hear it. He was one prince of a man, even if I do say so of our own blood-kin."

"We buried him next to Mama," Martha said.

He nodded. "But your own chaps, Martha"—Uncle Burn looked around at their grave, attentive faces and he tried to smile—"they've seen good growing weather."

"Yes. Only Kin's had a bad sickness," she said. "Last fall we nearly didn't bring him through the typhoid fever."

Burn looked at her and shook his head in sympathy. "I didn't know——"

Tom spoke quickly. "It was a bad time there for a few days, with Martha remembering how her mother died of the sickness, and Kin raging with the fever. If it hadn't been for old Nye Blankenship, that boy might not have made it."

Frone sniffed. "He wouldn't let any of the rest of us around Kin. Acted like he owned him."

"The doctor thought Kin might have got the germ from an old spring down in the pasture when he went with Nye to hunt persimmons. I reckon Nye felt responsible," Tom said.

"At first, yes," Martha agreed. "But ever since it took him so long to get well and Nye got in the habit of bringing him special delicacies to eat—squirrel and wild raspberries and even quail once and the first watercresses in spring—there's been a rare bond between them."

"Nye has time to fool with him, learn him all the ways of the woods," Tom said. "That fever burned out some of the boy's quickness; he's not recovered from it even yet, but Nye and the woods let him amble along at his own speed."

"Gib and me, we used to talk about your young'uns. When we were out in the Philippines, old Gib asked me one day, plumb out of the blue, what I reckoned little Frone and Ivy were doing right that minute."

Ivy, remembering the silver dollars, the gifts and jollity of these two uncles, felt the tears rolling down her cheeks. So quickly did people disappear from life, without any message or stated meaning, without any tidying up.

And with all the stray ends dangling—explanations unoffered, affections barely suggested, fears and hopes buried under a carefree easy jauntiness—Uncle Burn left them two days later. He had spoken of the West, of perhaps looking up his and Martha's younger sister Jessie who had never written any of her family a word since her marriage and move "yon side the big Mississippi," as Aunt Tildy had put it. He told them he wanted to see cattle on an open range and fruits hanging heavy as in the Garden of Eden and feel space stretching out around him again. But when they came to breakfast and discovered that he had left in the night, they could not hide their surprise and sadness that he was gone so soon.

"Someday I aim to see that country myself," Papa told them as he ate his eggs and dipped a hot biscuit in ham gravy. "Ar-i-zona, Col-o-rado, Cal-i-for-nia. Don't the names just roll off your tongue?"

The girls nodded.

"All right, son," he reprimanded Clay who was picking over the biscuits, "remember the rule around here: touch and take." Clay took up the last biscuit he had touched, and Papa returned to his thought of the West. "I've heard that out there it's a land of tall timber."

But he was cutting his own tall timber right there on Thickety Creek now. And all their lives rushed on. They could not pause overlong for either grief or remembering.

At the end of August, Ivy went away from home for the first time. Papa and Mama took her in the surrey with Frone and their two small horsehide trunks, and all the way to Mrs. Enoch Madron's boardinghouse her throat was tight and dry.

Azalie came out to the road to tell her good-by. "Mama and I made this for you," she said, handing up a little package. Ivy unwrapped the bit of tissue and found a bar of rough homemade soap, delicately fragrant. "We crushed out some wintergreen oil and stirred it in with the lye and grease," Azalie said, "and it scents up the soap so nice."

"Yes." Finding it difficult to speak, Ivy nodded and held the bar to her nose.

"I'll bet it's as nice as any girl there will have," Azalie said. And then she blurted out, "Oh, Ivy, I wish I was going, too."

Ivy squeezed back the tears. "Yes, Azalie, yes. Maybe you'll come next year."

Azalie shook her head. "Pap says some folks think they're eagles, soaring higher than anybody else, when they're just old turkey buzzards that climb and climb and look all over and then finally settle on a cow pile."

Tom Thurston threw back his head and laughed until the surrey shook. He had always enjoyed Azalie's innocent repetitions of her father's jealousies and disgruntlements.

"But, Ivy," she went on, "I'd rather be a turkey buzzard believing I was an eagle than spend my days a little titmouse knowing just what I was!"

"Now, Azalie, you're a smart girl," Papa said. After they had said good-by and driven on, he added, "That old Lazarus Shook, he's too no-account to get his own breath if it didn't come natural. Azalie ought to be going on to school. A damned shame."

Frone nudged Ivy. "Lazarus Shook's so lazy he wouldn't go to his own funeral if he could get out of it."

But Ivy was smelling the fresh wintergreen fragrance of the soap and remembering how nice Ida Shook had always managed to make her shabby linens look, stacked on their neat open shelves.

The Nantahala Female Institute was located at the edge of town, a single brick building which had come into being just after the Civil War when an elderly Major, C.S.A, had tried to found a boys' military academy here with more vision than money, more tradition than education, more wistfulness than success. After the Major died, his school disbanded for there was not even the vision, tradition or wistfulness left then. A few years later a pair of Presbyterian sisters from "up North" opened their girls' school in the abandoned building. Most of the pupils came from town, for there were no boarding facilities at the school; but girls of high-school and junior-college years from all parts of the mountains were encouraged to attend if they could find an approved place to live. Mrs. Madron's boardinghouse, separated from the Institute only by a wide green pasture, was one of the favored places. Uncle Robert, before he died, had seen that Frone found a place at Mrs. Madron's. Now it was Ivy's turn to meet the dozen girls who lived under that good lady's sharp scrutiny and bustling care. She enjoyed fussing over the girls who stayed with her and went to school. She also enjoyed catering to strangers who came from far distances for a visit in the mountain resort town, and she usually had one or two such guests along with the girls. She liked being an important part of others' lives.

Ivy's homesickness during the first few weeks was almost intolerable. Frone was at the school, too, but she roomed alone this year, having especially asked for the third-floor cubicle with the sloping ceiling and narrow windows where she could perhaps feel she was Jo in *Little Women*, with her ink and papers. None of their classes were together. Ivy did not even dare tell her sister how miserable she was. She longed to hear Mama's familiar footfalls along the hall at night, or smell the oily machinery smell of the sawmill at noon or the clean tang of freshly sawed boards on Papa's clothes at the end of the day, or see Phoebe's bright pleasant little face as she offered to relieve Ivy of some chore or share some secret. It was truly a sickness, this longing for home, and while it lasted she ate little, slept less and adjusted poorly to her classses.

Gradually, however, the variegated beauty of autumn, her natural humor, interest in the people around her, reasserted itself. She began to like the school, the two sisters who ran it and taught Latin and embroidery, rhetoric and polite literature and piano. She also liked the other teachers on the staff.

Most of all, she liked Mrs. Madron and the cheerful, busy boardinghouse with its quicksilver laughing and crying of the girls and the interesting presence of two older outsiders who had no connection with the Institute. One of these was a heavy-set, shrewd man from Atlanta who had come to the mountains in search of minerals, clays, any natural resources that might be buried on the slopes or in the valleys, awaiting only the capital and a developer's foresight to yield rich returns. The other stranger was a tall, quiet, straight-shouldered Northerner named Henry Hudson Cortland.

Cortland had arrived at Mrs. Madron's in mid-July, saying he would remain there for a summer holiday, and then he had stayed on through August and into September. No one knew exactly why he had come to the mountains or this particular place. His manner did not invite personal questions. That manner balanced friendliness with aloofness, dignity with casualness, ironic humor with sympathy. His features were craggy but not forbidding: clear jawline and cheekbones, straight Roman nose, deep-set grey eyes. The grey eyes went nicely with his dark brown hair greying at the temples, Ivy thought. He was away from the house most of the time on trips into the mountains, but when he was there Ivy grew into the habit of watching him as he talked with the girls or Mrs. Madron—or, more correctly, as he drew them out and listened to them talk about their homes, their families, the part of the county where they lived. One night, after supper, when it was raining and everyone had gathered in Mrs. Madron's parlor because it was Saturday and none of the girls wanted to study or go walking, Mr. Cortland asked them to sing for him. "I wish I could hear some of your old ballads," he said.

So one of the girls sang "The Twa Corbies" for him—full of murder and mourning, and he was delighted. Others sang, too, and as Ivy and Frone heard the old familiar pieces, they winked at one another, remembering Aunt Tildy, Uncle Burn and Uncle Gib, Papa, other nights.

After a while he looked directly at Ivy and asked, "What about you, Miss Ivy? Don't you have a song?"

She flushed. All at once she recalled a foolish little ditty Papa sometimes sang:

"I'm as free a little bird as I can be,
I'm as free a little bird as I can be,
Sitting on a hillside,

Singing all the day,
I'm as free a little bird as I can be."

There were other verses, and the gay tune lilted along in contrast to the heavy sorrows of the other music they had heard. Ivy, all the time she sang, was recalling Papa's mischievous blue eyes and his patting foot, as though it fairly itched to dance in time to the music when he sang his favorite pieces, or walked along the worn path to the sawmill, whistling in a fresh day's beginning.

"Now that was a bright tune," Mr. Cortland said. "What would you call it, Mrs. Madron?"

"Peart," she said. "Folks around here would say that was a right peart bit of music-making."

"Peart," he repeated, and smiled at them. "Thank you for some fine music-making." He excused himself from the room and returned presently with a box of sweets which he passed to them. "Maple candies from my part of the country," he said. His firm mouth softened in a smile as he looked at each of them directly with a hint of sadness and a hint of humor, too, it seemed to Ivy. "Now we've exchanged riches of our regions."

The girls laughed and ate their candies, but they were more at ease after he had left them and gone up to his room. All except Ivy. Whenever he was around, she felt alert and stimulated, and she liked to watch his lively eyes. She had never before known anyone like Mr. Cortland.

Her classes went well. She studied conscientiously, remembering how hard Papa worked for the money that paid for her to come to this school, how thrifty Mama was in everything. (Ivy could see her peeling potatoes or apples, cutting the skin paper-thin to preserve all the substance possible. No one could peel as carefully, as finely as Mama.) Ivy did not lead her class, although Frone had already been acknowledged the best Latin student ever to attend the Institute, but she remembered well and her grades were good and with every passing week she became more of a favorite with both the teachers and girls.

One day at the end of September Ivy stood on the well-worn lane that led through the meadow between the school and Mrs. Madron's. She was gazing back at the dark green leaves of a large magnolia tree that stood in the yard of the Institute.

A voice suddenly spoke behind her. "Quite a sight, isn't it?"

Startled, she turned to see Mr. Cortland watching her with that expression compounded of secret amusement and quiet friendliness. "What is?" she asked, and was furious at the stupid words.

"All this." He moved his head slightly, but managed to indicate the countryside surrounding them. It was a countryside burning with color, especially in the late afternoon sun. The nearer trees were separately flamboyant, but the ripe shades of the distant mountains flowed into one long backdrop as of a palette dripping with all the red and yellow pigments run together.

"I was looking at the magnolia," she said.

"Do you like it?" he asked.

She was surprised. "Why, yes . . ." She halted. "No. No I don't really like it. It's too artificial-looking, with leaves like wax—slick and stiff. It doesn't seem to have any juice in it."

His eyes twinkled. "Now that's just the way I reacted to that tree the first time I saw it," he said. He looked off across the meadow to a clump of hickories near the road. "What kinds of trees do you have around your home?" he asked.

"Almost every kind you can think of," she replied. Eagerly she told him about the various places on the farm: the hill where great-bodied chestnuts loosed a heavy rain of nuts this time of year and wind in the night brought down a thick harvest for morning's hunting; the ravine where poplars and beeches blazed with gold; the ridge where pines traced a green line all the year long; and the tall mountainsides with their variety of trees Papa was cutting even now.

"It must be a good place, your home," he said.

She flushed, realizing that she had responded just as all the others at Mrs. Madron's did when he drew them out. "I didn't mean to say so much——"

"But I wanted to hear." He was quite straightforward now. "As a matter of fact, I'd like to see your farm sometime. I've heard people in town speak of your father."

"Papa likes company." She smiled. "You'd be freely welcome to come."

"Perhaps—sometime. Meanwhile, would you have time to walk with me down to that little clump of bushes beyond the fence? There's a shrub growing there I've never seen before. I'd like to make its acquaintance by name." He looked at her impersonally, pleasantly. "I have a feeling you could introduce us, that shrub and me."

She was happy to walk in the warm, smoky, silent afternoon across the grass. It was not a moment for books but for breathing in the heavy-laden air of Indian summer that would soon be gone. Her hair was piled in a soft mass of chestnut waves. Even the flow of the long brown skirt she wore and the sleeves of her delicate blouse seemed part of the languid, peaceful atmosphere.

When they came to the place he had mentioned, she looked at the little shrubs. "Do you know what they are?" Mr. Cortland asked.

"Yes, we have lots of them at home. They bring a little bloom in late spring. I guess you could really say it's more like a berry, bright red and sort of broken open with a little petal hanging out."

"But do you know its name?" he asked.

"Not the proper name."

"What do you call it?" he insisted.

She could feel the pink mounting in her cheeks. "Hearts-a-bustin'-with-love," she said. She wondered why just the simplest thing these days made her flush up redder than the blooms on this bush.

After that day it seemed to come about naturally that they often talked of plants and mountains and the outdoors and that they frequently walked together around the school and Mrs. Madron's, which was actually a country place with space and woods. The days seemed warmed by a light more golden than Ivy had ever known before. Mornings and evenings were tinged with chill, but at midday the summer's heat persisted and there was the dry sound of late insects among the brownish grass and weeds. Once, in the acres that stretched behind the Institute, Mr. Cortland and Ivy came

upon an old apple orchard. The unpruned trees had grown into a
tall tangle of limbs covered now with ripe apples. Ivy picked up a
firm one off the ground and wiped it on her sleeve. "These are good
old Limbertwigs," she said, offering it to Mr. Cortland. "They're
Mama's favorite."

"Thank you." He took the apple and turned it over and over in
his hand as if examining some fine gift or rare specimen. "I never
heard of this variety before."

"You never heard of a Limbertwig?" She found one for herself,
disturbing the yellow jackets that were buzzing over the juice of
other apples rotting in piles.

He shook his head.

"What kinds do you have up North?" she asked.

"Gravensteins, Pippins, McIntosh and Spies."

"Spies?"

"Northern Spies. They're fine. Hard and full of juice and flavor.
I used to eat them by the peck when I was a boy."

"Did you live on a farm?" she asked.

"Yes. Up the Hudson River from New York City. It's called
Dutchess County."

"What a lovely name. Did your folks live there for a long
time?" She was amazed at her own audacity and yet somehow these
questions seemed natural for her to ask.

He almost smiled. "For a long time. A generation or two before
the Revolutionary War."

She was impressed. "Is that where you live now? Do you farm
that land?"

He frowned and looked away. There was a long pause. Ivy bit
her lip and regretted her impulsiveness. She pretended to be searching the ground for other good apples. After a while Mr. Cortland
said, "Yes, that's where I live and farm now. My father died when
I was fifteen, my mother a few years ago. Since there was no one
else—my brother in Seattle couldn't come home and my sister in
Manhattan wouldn't—I took over the place. And now you know
my situation," he said.

"But I don't know anything," she wanted to cry out loud. "I
don't know the way your house sits to the morning sun or its size

or how the country lies thereabouts. I don't know whether your sister 'in Manhattan' is old or young or married—and most of all I don't know you in that house. . . ."

Instead, she walked on through the abandoned orchard, bedraggling her skirts with beggar-lice and Spanish needles and all sorts of weed dust. She stopped under another tree. "I'll take a handful of these Winesaps to Mrs. Madron. Maybe she'll let me make a pie."

That night she wrote to Mama and Papa and mentioned for the first time the stranger named Mr. Henry Hudson Cortland, who also stayed at Mrs. Madron's. She repeated his remark that he had met friends and acquaintances of Papa's in town, and that he would like to go out to Thickety Creek Valley sometime.

The very next Sunday, Papa's surrey pulled up in front of Mrs. Madron's boardinghouse. The girls were all just leaving, with the two school headmistresses, for church services in town.

"Ivy, look yonder," Frone whispered and they saw the high-stepping roan coming down the drive and Papa on the driver's seat. "He must have gotten up before day to get here this early. I wonder what's wrong at home."

But there was nothing wrong. Papa's bow to the schoolteachers and his hug for both tall daughters revealed only good spirits and great expectations. After assuring them that all was well with the family, he told everyone that he had come after his girls and the man from up North who had told Ivy he wanted to see Thickety Creek. He proposed to take them "out home" for the day.

Mrs. Madron glanced at Ivy. "I'll go and get Mr. Cortland," she said.

Frone and the other girls were looking at Ivy, too. She was miserable with embarrassment. Whatever possessed Papa to come like this and propose to take a stranger to their home? And if he went . . . ? She could not help but wonder if the rooms would be tidy, if Mama had given her full attention to the dinner or if she would be thinking about Preacher Grey's sermon and let the rice overcook perhaps, leave the lower layer of cake not quite done, serve the coffee a little less than scalding, the salt on the meat forgotten? She had heard that up North the women were perfectionist housekeepers and cooks. And how would their little mountain farm appear to a person who owned vast acres—she was sure they must be vast—in a place called Dutchess County on the mighty Hudson River? (Why, he himself bore the name of the river's very discoverer!) She wished she had chopped off her hand with Mama's meat cleaver before she had written that last letter home mentioning Henry Hudson Cortland!

The teachers were protesting to Papa that Ivy and Frone should not go home today. "We have an official four-day autumn recess in another fortnight," the elder one explained "and then all the girls boarding here will be returning to their homes for a visit. But this afternoon they have Bible reading and piano and voice practice, and this would disrupt their schedule."

Papa was clearly taken aback, but his blue eyes fairly glistened with secret laughter at the maiden lady's precise language. When Mr. Cortland appeared and they were introduced, Papa regained his voice. "Well, if I can't have the whole load, maybe I can settle for half," he said. "I'd be proud to bring you out to our little valley, Mr. Cortland, and have you take Sunday dinner with us. You a stranger to this part of the country?"

"Oh, Mr. Cortland's been here since late July," Mrs. Madron volunteered. "He's no stranger now."

Papa grinned. "Know all about these mountains yet?"

"I think not," Mr. Cortland said, and he smiled, too. "I'd welcome whatever you'll show me."

"That would take more than one day," Papa said. "But we can make a startation before I bring you back this evening."

"Oh, I'll walk back," Mr. Cortland said. "I'm used to——"

"A pretty far piece," Papa said. "It'd take you the better part of a day."

"I came here to walk," Mr. Cortland said, "to get acquainted with the country at close range."

"In that case, you could spend the night and walk back in daylight tomorrow, get an early start," Papa said.

Mr. Cortland turned to the girls. "Thank you, Miss Ivy, Miss Frone, for bringing me this great pleasure."

"Oh, I didn't know anything about it," Frone said. Her blue eyes were wide and solemn, concealing, Ivy knew, the laughter and teasing that would break forth shortly. "Do you know what he's talking about, Ivy?"

But Mr. Cortland interrupted quickly and firmly. "I'll be with you in a moment, Mr. Thurston. Just let me fetch my walking stick and pipe and tobacco." He disappeared into the house.

"He seems like the pattern of a man I could like," Papa said.

"Oh, he is, Mr. Thurston," Mrs. Madron assured him. "A gentleman, a true Yankee gentleman if ever I saw one."

"Well, you girls behave yourselves now. Your mama will be glad to have you home for that autumn holiday. I'll have to say you're looking like the bloom of life itself."

The teachers assured him of their good efforts at school and of Frone's classical excellencies. Papa beamed as Frone and Ivy walked down to the surrey with him. Only then did Ivy notice the white cloth bandage on his hand.

"Almighty be!" he said in answer to her question and grinned guiltily at his exclamation. "An accident the other day. Old Amos Knott and Nye had been quarreling all week like two sore-tailed cats and we'd fallen behind on our sawing. I was helping Amos out, running the edger while he ate dinner——"

"Papa, what happened?"

"That edger caught my thumb. Sawed it half in two——"

"Oh, Papa!"

"It's getting better now. The doctor says that thumb looks like it might grow back together."

"Oh, it has to, Papa."

"If it don't, I reckon you'll just have to put up with an old stump-thumbed papa!" He tried to make them laugh, but suddenly both Frone and Ivy had realized that they were not a daily part of the family now, that this crisis had occurred without them, without their even knowing, and this new awareness of separateness made them sad.

Mr. Cortland came down the walk. Papa kissed both girls good-by and Mr. Cortland shook hands with them. Ivy felt sure that his eyes were full of laughter when he looked at her, but it was

all right as long as it was her and not her family at whom he
smiled.

He arrived back at Mrs. Madron's sometime Monday night. Ivy,
meantime, had survived Frone's teasing.

"You and Mr. Cortland aren't getting up a case, are you?"

"Don't be a silly, Frone. He's an old man."

"Not any older than Mr. Rochester was to Jane Eyre, remem-
ber," Frone said, appealing to her most recent literary romance.
And Ivy did remember. Secretly, she borrowed *Jane Eyre* from her
English teacher and began rereading it.

During that Sunday and Monday she was surprised to discover
how much she missed Mr. Cortland when he was not at meals.

At breakfast Tuesday morning his face was slightly wind-
burned, but he looked very fit. He told Ivy that his visit to her home
and his return walk through the valley and into town had been one
of the most pleasant experiences of his life.

"Around here we would call the Thurstons clever folks," Mrs.
Madron said, as she refilled his coffee cup and wiped away with
her freshly starched apron the drop that gathered on the spout of
the percolator.

"Clever?" Mr. Cortland asked.

She nodded briskly. "Good-natured. Freehanded, Mr. Cortland.
Generous."

"Oh! Well, you're a clever soul yourself to share all these words
with me, Mrs. Madron; to take the trouble."

"Not a-tall, Mr. Cortland. I know you're truly interested, not just
poking fun."

One by one the others left the table, but Ivy stayed on, trying
to appear hungry, stuffing herself until she thought she might choke,
hoping he would speak to her again. He ate quietly, folded his napkin and slipped it into its napkin ring. Not looking at him, she saw
every movement Mr. Cortland made. "He's neat, but not prissy,"
she noted in her mind. Somehow the orderly gesture of folding his
napkin seemed very important just now. Then he leaned back in
his chair and began naming each one of her family, mentioning why
he had liked Phoebe or Clay or Kin, Papa and Mama, even old

Nye, and he said simply that her valley was the most scenic place he had discovered since he had been in the region. A feeling of intense relief and happiness let her leave the room, and she rushed to avoid being late for morning chapel.

During the day's classes she wondered about that relief. Finally, in midafternoon, as she walked from school to Mrs. Madron's hearing the cries of blue jays in the background, she was forced to admit to herself that Henry Hudson Cortland had become a part of her life.

Several days after that long and trying weekend, she confronted him face to face unexpectedly on the carriage road in front of the big old magnolia. Her throat constricted as if squeezed by some merciless invisible hand. The blood throbbed from her chest to her finger tips. She felt more alive, more miserable, more ecstatic than she had ever thought possible. For the full moment they looked at each other there on the lane, with the smell of dust and leaves strong in the air, she wondered if by some miracle of self-control she had managed to keep her stormy feelings hidden from him. But the grey eyes looked at her very directly and they were not laughing now. When she rushed on past him, he did not speak or try to detain her.

She ran to her room and closed the door and her crying and laughter came together in a rush. Was she such a ninny that on her first journey from home she could fall in love with the first man she encountered?

When Frone stopped by the room on her way up from supper, she gave a mocking smile after Ivy told her she had an upset stomach and didn't want food tonight. But Frone said only, "We heard from Mama today," and laid the letter on the bed.

"Are they all right at home?" Ivy asked.

Frone nodded. "We're going to be rich again. Papa's bought another stand of timber."

"Has he cut all that mountain above Thickety?" Ivy asked.

Frone shook her head. "I guess that would take till doomsday. But Mama said they were getting into such rough logging that Papa was losing money on every load of lumber that comes into town. The new tract has lots of pine on it, and Papa's heard word that a paper-pulp mill might come to Nantahala County, and if it does he could sell them pulpwood."

"Would that pay well?" Ivy asked.

Frone shrugged. "I guess Papa thinks so. Anyway, this new boundary is closer to town. Papa wants to build there and let us move off Thickety."

"Did Mama write that?" Ivy asked.

"Well, how do you think I'd have known it otherwise? By mental telepathy? Ivy, sometimes lately you act downright foolish."

Ivy did not want to see anyone at breakfast the next morning and she went down to the dining room so early that Mrs. Madron and her cook were only fixing the first pan of bacon. She ate a few bites and rushed back upstairs to wait till it was time for morning chapel.

When she came back for lunch, Mr. Cortland was already at the table. Ivy took food on her plate and tried to eat it. She made a poor pretense.

Frone told some silly thing that had happened in Latin class that morning and the other girls giggled. The man from Atlanta who was interested in minerals ate steadily and helped himself to seconds from Mrs. Madron's generous serving dishes.

Across the table sat Mr. Cortland, silent, his head bent over the plate before him, his eyes never looking at Ivy, yet he loomed so large before her that the others seemed only shadows. She felt that she might choke if she tried to swallow. He poured vinegar from the cruet onto the tomatoes on his plate. With elaborate care he cut a chunk of butter and spread it, melting, on a hot corn muffin. He took a bite and chewed it slowly, then washed it down with a long drink of milk. Not watching, bent over her own plate and its little mounds of food, Ivy knew everything he did. And by some perception she could not explain, she knew that he was aware of her presence, too. Abruptly, irrevocably, everything between them had changed. A lump hard as stone filled her throat.

"Guess it's this unseasonable warm weather that's taken everybody's appetite," Mrs. Madron ran on as she cleared the table for dessert. Ivy rose to help her, carried away dishes from Frone's end of the table, as far from him as possible. "Well, these warm days may be just a weather breeder. I look for winter to set in early this year. You can't tell, though . . ." She disappeared into the kitchen, still talking.

"Reckon warm weather's taken everybody's tongue, too?" Frone asked solemnly as Ivy passed her chair.

Ivy helped Mrs. Madron set dishes of canned peaches at each place, but not his. She struggled to eat one of the two tender halves of fruit before her. Frone and the other girls and finally the mineralogist left the room. Mrs. Madron gathered up empty glasses and dessert dishes and went to the kitchen.

"Ivy——" Mr. Cortland was looking directly at her. She met his gaze and all the blood in her body gathered and rushed to her throat and face. "Ivy, meet me this afternoon after your classes. Down in the meadow."

There was no subterfuge or bargaining or delay in her. "Yes," she said. "Yes."

He stood up and came around the deserted table. They heard Mrs. Madron's steps crossing the kitchen. "And Ivy, wear something white?"

She had no time to reply. He was gone and Mrs. Madron was there. Whatever it was the good, cheerful, busy woman said, Ivy did not hear as she fled the table, the room. Whatever it was that the school's precise younger headmistress taught early that afternoon about the geography of Persia and surrounding exotic lands, Ivy did not hear, for her mind was already where her body would be in another hour or so.

She went down to the meadow alone wearing white, with her head high and her feet unmindful of rocks or thistles and her eyes bright with first love.

She came up from the meadow with him—with Cort, as he had asked her to call him in the first good moments when they came together—and her feet were heavy as rocks and her eyes were bright with salt tears.

He had held her so close and kissed her so long that she felt she might joyfully smother. Then he had put an abyss between them. "Oh, Ivy . . . Ivy, how can I tell you about Susannah?"

"Susannah?" she repeated, looking up at him.

A gust of wind brought down a flutter of brilliant leaves unnoticed around them.

"My wife."

The word plummeted into her consciousness like a wounded bird plunging to earth out of the autumn sky. The air choked her. Once, long ago, when she had smelled Mama's ammonia salts, she had experienced this same black suffocation.

"Your wife?" she repeated. "Up North, in Dutchess County?"

He nodded. "For twenty-seven years. Longer than your entire lifetime." As she pulled away from his embrace he went on, miserably, irrevocably, "Susannah has been a semi-invalid for fifteen years. We have no children. She doesn't like living in the country, and I'm not a city man. When she goes to visit her family in Boston three months each summer, I go looking for my Walden."

"Walden?" she asked.

"It's a pond where a man named Thoreau lived for a while and wrote a book——"

"Yes, I've seen that book at Uncle Fayte McQueen's."

He appeared surprised and pleased. "How little I know about you or your family." He paused. "You read *Walden* and you'll know why I came to your mountains."

"But what can I read"—suddenly she was sobbing—"to tell me about—her?"

His grey eyes seemed sunk even deeper in their bony sockets as he took her again in his arms.

The woods around them grew still and no leaf fell and no bird called.

When at last she drew away from him and stood up, he grasped her by the shoulders and held her for a moment in the vise of his uncontrolled grip. "Protect yourself, Ivy," he whispered. "Build some protection against the world. Get a wall."

She stared at him, pale and uncomprehending.

"Oh, there are all sorts of walls we build: the low ones we can hide behind but still look over and believe we're part of the world; high walls are for full retreat when we're wounded. Most of them are poor-enough affairs, I suspect—full of chinks to let through light and air, just enough to let us hope that somewhere, sometime, we can walk out from behind our cover and live."

He paused and looked down at her. It seemed that there was in that look all the tenderness and unhappiness any person could endure. "No! Don't listen to what I say. Give the way you do now, Ivy." His voice choked. He drew her to him again. "Ivy . . . Ivy . . . Ivy Thurston."

The next day the wind shifted and blew from the northwest, chilly, foretelling winter. Leaves fell in hectic masses and up in the old orchard the last apples thudded to the ground and lay in piles of bruised ripeness. Ivy did not see Hudson Cortland when he went, for he settled his account and paid his farewells to Mrs. Madron the night before, and left at daybreak carrying his own valise into town and the railroad station. At breakfast Mrs. Madron told her girls that her nice Yankee guest had gone, and she told them, too, about the change in the wind that might bring sharper weather.

Ivy heard every word she said and ate every bit of food on her plate and walked to classes with the other girls and never looked up toward the rise where shrubs grew in the meadow. Aunt Tildy and those other old-timers had known the right name for that silly plant, she thought. And she knew just how it felt, that blossom or fruit, whenever it grew so full of itself it couldn't be contained any longer but burst its narrow shell and spilled out into the sun, reaching out —and there was nothing, there was nobody there waiting for all its beauty and richness. Nobody accepted the gift.

Frone and Ivy went home from the Nantahala Female Institute for their "autumn recess." Papa overflowed with talk about the new paper mill, the tract of timber he was planning to buy, and about their possible move to the "more progressive" community "closer in to town." He was ready with questions about Mr. Henry Hudson Cortland. When Frone told him that Mr. Cortland had gone back up North he was openly disappointed.

"I'd sort of counted on his coming back out to see us again. Wanted him to meet Preacher Grey. Mr. Cortland was a rarely fine gentleman. Mighty good company."

"Ivy thought so," Frone said, blandly innocent.

"Ivy?" Papa frowned. "What do you mean?"

"She doesn't mean anything, Papa, except trying to get every-thing all stirred up," Ivy said, glaring at Frone.

"Of course not." Ivy was surprised when Mama spoke up and dismissed the whole subject so resolutely.

"But Ivy and Mr. Cortland . . ." Papa was still troubled. "Why, he's old enough to be her father, older than me!"

"All right, Tom," Mama said. "Don't fret so. He was a friend to all of us. He's gone home now, you heard the girls say so."

"When would we move, Papa, if you did build at that new place?" Frone asked, trying to make amends to Ivy by changing the subject.

"I couldn't say, Frone. Maybe next summer or fall, depending on how all my plans worked out."

"I'd like to live closer to town," Frone said, "away from this back-woods creek, wouldn't you, Ivy?"

"I wouldn't care." Ivy was crying. "Whether we're here or there, or whether we're living at all, I wouldn't care much." She ran out of the room.

Later that night on her way to the kitchen for a drink of water she heard Mama cautioning Papa to give someone time. "She's had a deep hurt, I'm afraid. She's young and tender and needs time——"

"She's only a child," Papa said. "Maybe we shouldn't have let her go to that school yet."

"There are all kinds of school, Tom. You can't keep her from going to the one she's learning in now."

"Almighty be! Martha, stop beating around the bush."

"Ivy's not a child. She's almost grown. Let her have a little stretching room for a little time and she'll be an adult. Now that's plain-out."

"Yes ma'am," Papa said. "That's plain talking."

So they were sorry for her! Everyone knew how she had felt toward Hudson Cortland, and they thought he had left her be-cause he did not share her love. Well, she had the best secret of all, the sweetest meat at the heart of the kernel, and she was going to keep it to herself forever. No one would ever find out the truth.

She rather enjoyed their efforts at solicitude during the next three days, but they were all so busy with living of their own to follow and the energy of each day as it unraveled work and conflict and always the unexpected, that they simply could not remember to sustain this deference.

Papa's hand healed badly and he still wore bandages while the thumb knit back together. Mama was distressed by his plan to move from Thickety, for she had hoped they might spend the rest of their days right here on Grandpa Moore's acres she had known since childhood, where her mother had grown up. She had asked Preacher Grey to talk to him, to see if he couldn't be persuaded to make another effort here, but unfortunately after they had talked awhile Preacher Grey came away convinced that Tom was right.

"It will mean new advantages for all of you, Martha," he said. "Especially the young ones."

"Maybe, Preacher Grey, maybe. But in this world I've found there's nothing ever gained without something lost, too."

"Yes, Sister Martha. I know. Schooling for children or church membership, or whatever."

"I meant things of this world, Preacher," Martha said.

He sighed. "Things of this world and another world aren't so sharply divided sometimes. Each is part of the other." This was the first time Martha had been disappointed in him. After a pause he said, "Old Thickety Creek won't be the same without the Thurston family. Tom's a real earth mover."

The sawmill men teased Frone and Ivy about their fancy school. "Be dogged if they can even talk plain any more. 'Spewn' they say for 'spoon.'"

"And asking me to pass the applesauce when all they mean is danged old stewed fruit."

The girls were secretly pleased at the end of the four days' vacation to go back to the neatly ordered world of books and Mrs. Madron's and a measure of independence. Ivy felt that she was gradually recovering from a long illness and although she was not yet cured, she had emerged into a sort of numbness. Winter came early and sharply and for the first time in her life she felt no responsibility for fires or food or house and she was free to read all she wished, study without interruption, savor the cozy afternoons or long evenings in luxurious warmth when the first icy rains and snows came.

School was work and it was also adventure because Ivy began to feel the stretch of her mind, began to sense the enormity of the world. The possibilities before her suddenly seemed limitless. She discovered that although one part of life might shrink or be wounded, the rest could go on reaching out and out.

Early one morning, after the first heavy snowstorm of the season, Ivy was the first one to leave the boardinghouse and walk across the intervening yard to the Institute. No path was visible. Familiar landmarks were transformed into white silhouettes. Her footprints were the first mark on a pristine landscape. She had walked perhaps halfway to the school when she stopped and stood as still as any of the great old oaks, their dark limbs etched in dazzling white. With a deep prolonged breath she drank in the sweet coldness of the morning air and stretched toward the clear blue sky arched high above her. Looking back where she had been, she laughed at the meandering course of her tracks. Ahead of her lay an expanse with no mark on it. There was no movement anywhere. There was no sound. Fresh and frozen as if in a second creation, the old world had become new and magnificent overnight. With the taste of the air on her tongue, the beauty of vision in every sweep of meadow and hidden hedgerow, the bite of the cold on her tingling face—suddenly it was good just to be alive. For the present, nothing more was needed. Nothing more was possible. She was alive in every fiber of her being.

The exhilaration, the marvelous revelation of how complete, how good life could be, lasted only moments in time. Other girls began to pour out of the house and follow her across the snowy lawn. Laughing and shouting to the others a dare to overtake her, she plunged on across the white drifts.

At Christmas, the day after Frone and Ivy had returned home for the long holiday, a package came addressed to the whole family. It contained a book, bound in soft morocco leather with gold edges, and the title printed in gold was *Walden*. On the fly leaf there was an inscription: "To the Thurstons, who know how to suck the very marrowbone of life. With a stranger's sincere regards, Henry Hudson Cortland."

"That's the finest book I ever saw," Frone said, fingering the expensive leather binding, sniffing its good sharp smell.

"I'll bet that cost a pretty penny," Papa said. "I wonder, is it a true story or just a made-up tale?"

"It's true," Ivy said.

"Maybe Ivy would like to read it first," Mama said matter-of-factly. "Take it on, Ivy, and then the rest of us can have our turn."

Her tone closed off the possibility of any other remarks and Ivy tried to take the book casually, bear it off with large unconcern, walk slowly upstairs. She thought she had never loved Mama as much as she did at this moment.

But when she went back to school, she left *Walden* at home. She did not want to go through spring with this book, this memento of him, in her room. She already carried many of Thoreau's sentences in her memory.

Papa, with his new undertaking, made Ivy think of Thoreau's neighbor with the horse and his cycle of growing corn to feed the horse to work the land to grow the corn to feed the horse. . . . All her life it seemed that they had strained and worked and wrenched and never with any larger goal, any nobler purpose than daily bread. Was this what Mama and Preacher Grey were always trying to say, in another way, she wondered?

When the Institute closed in May, Frone and Ivy went home to a newly divided life. Papa, exuberantly pushing himself to work till the last minute in the day and the last ounce of strength in his muscles, spent most of his time at the new-house site. This valley he had chosen was smaller than Thickety Creek and he had bought the entire head of the cove—from the end of the dirt road which led from town to the topmost tree of the mountains enclosing the fully wooded cup of the valley. He had extended the wagon road perhaps half a mile and selected a place near the stream for their home. When he brought Martha over in the surrey to approve the location, she acquiesced with a minimum of interest in all his plans. She remarked only on the tall woods through which they made their jolty way, and on the thickness of the pines which covered one half of the upper mountainsides.

"That pine, that's what we're going to sell to the paper mill," Tom boasted, "and even if the lumber doesn't make us a fortune, that pulpwood should!"

As they stood at the new-house site, Martha said little except to remark on the nearby stream and to ask about the spring that would provide their drinking water.

"Oh, it's fine water, Martha-girl," Tom said. "This is civilized country we're coming to. We can build a show place here. And along the road on down the valley and into town live some of the oldest, the most solid citizens in all Nantahala County. I tell you, they're good livers. Over here you won't have any lack of church and school talk, either. The young ones can stay right here at home and go to that Institute or wherever they want. I tell you, Martha, it was barefaced luck brought me this chance to carry on my lumbering, the only living I know, and yet move my family closer in to town."

"But I never cared about being any closer to town, Tom," she said.

"We've got to care about it," he urged. "Town's going to be the life of this country before long. With these automobiles taking such a hold everywhere——"

She shuddered. "I wouldn't ride in one for a ten-dollar gold piece."

Tom Thurston laughed outright, his eyes wide with anticipation. "Oh, you'll be riding in one. Whenever I get all straightened out, I aim to get us a motor car."

She didn't smile. "Whenever," she said. "That's a pretty big 'whenever.' "

"We've got to look ahead, Martha. We've got to look up. Never gone to the poorhouse yet, have we?"

By the end of summer the new house was not quite completed, but the rooms were finished enough for them to move in. It was large, white with green shutters, and boasted a second-story balcony and iron grillwork above the long front porch also decorated with grillwork. There were four chimneys and Tom Thurston was especially pleased at their efficiency. "Draw? I reckon those chimneys do draw. Why, the other morning Old Blue wandered in there where I was kindling a blaze to test if the fireplace smoked or if it had a good draft, and first thing I knew the chimney sucked that hound right up out of sight!" He shouted with laughter.

Upon considering their new fireplaces, Frone was moved to wonder, "Who's planning to work up the wood for all those fires?"

"I'll help cut," Clay volunteered.

"I'll help carry in," Kin echoed.

"Big talk," their older sister said. "We'll see, when the new wears off if there are big piles of wood to match it."

They were all affected by the move, but Martha changed most and least of all. The only reconciliation she found for Cass Nelson's having bought her cherished farm lay in the fact that, a week before they left Thickety Creek, Tom Thurston went forward at Preacher Grey's Sunday service and shook hands to signify that he wanted to become a member of the church. Tacitly they had struck a bargain, Martha and Tom, and they each understood and their children understood it without a word spoken, a sign given.

"I'm glad you've finally trusted in the Lord, Tom," Martha said.

"I'm glad you're happy," her husband answered.

On the last day of August, Tom wakened in that dark early hour of morning just before the night gave way to daylight. He came suddenly and totally awake as he had when he was a boy on hunting trips. That had been a long time ago, before his folks ever moved to Thickety Creek, before he had ever set eyes on Martha McQueen or given thought to raising a family. He had been hunting not a single night since he married Martha. It was all right. Enough of his days were spent in the woods trying to wrench out an honest living for all those who depended on him. No regrets. A man couldn't live with regrets.

He listened to Martha's steady rhythmical breathing beside him. And he grinned to himself in the darkness. By thunder, he was still full of the old sap. A little beyond his prime maybe, but the sap still stirred in him. He would like to reach out right now and take Martha in the cool darkness, find her familiar flesh once more exciting and good to touch. But he did not reach out. He knew that her small body which seemed so helpless in its slumber would be transformed with wakefulness into a resentful stubbornness. The innocence which yet clung to her in sleep, even though she was a woman past middle age with full-grown children, that innocence which still attracted him, would be, he well knew, transformed at his intimate touch into reluctant knowledgeability. And the reluctance and the knowledge, like that in the Garden of Eden, would sully all the rest of their subsequent embrace. How, he wondered idly, waiting for the old stirring within him to subside, had she managed through all their years together to be at once submissive and unyielding, so fertile and so barren? Only once in all those nights of his impatient needs and strong hungers could he remember her responding totally, not sacrificially, to his yearning for her body, his thirst for her love. That was a night nine months before Clay was born. He was always sure that was the night the boy had been created. But Martha had seemed frightened of the self she discovered that night, and she had retreated into her old shell. Ah, Martha, Tom thought, if only you could have let go a little . . . But there were no regrets. A man couldn't live by regrets.

The blackness was giving way to greyness and he crawled carefully out of bed. His new sawmill had been set in place yesterday. He would go up to the clearing and fire up early, have a head of steam ready to rip out the boards by the time the first men came.

A luminous light edged the mountaintops. He paused on the porch and breathed deeply. The summer morning air was sweet as sourwood honey. He stretched and the pull of his muscles was good. And towering all around him were the mountains forested with the tall trees that would be livelihood for years to come. He was happy to be starting again, fresh and full of promise. Tom Thurston looked up. Then he went up the path toward the clearing.

Birds were making early morning noise in the open places and among the treetops. A grey fox disappeared into the woods just ahead of him. "Ah, boy, what you been up to this night?" Tom murmured. Just before he came to the sawmill he heard a whippoorwill call close by. He paused, stood listening. A whippoorwill's cry al-

ways reminded him of some vague loneliness, some half-human quality that haunted him. He remembered old Aunt Tildy's dark warnings about the omen of a night bird's voice. Grinning at such foolishness, affected by it too, he hurried on up the path. "Whippoorwill, whip—poor—will," the notes followed clear and quick and
then ceased altogether.

Daylight was reaching into the valley. Tom Thurston stopped
and looked at the new mill, the ground around it clear of even the
sawdust that would be there by tonight. He kindled a fire under the
boiler, then checked to make sure the men had filled the tank with
water. Eh law, as Aunt Tildy always said, he remembered one time
soon after he'd started his family, there wasn't enough water in the
boiler and the mill had blown up. A pure miracle that no one had
been killed. How had he ever managed to pay off on that failure?
And the next? He stoked the fire and went back to the house. It was
full morning.

After breakfast he returned to the sawmill. In the barn at the far
side of the pasture he heard a noise of hoofs. He hesitated. The roan
must be showing off this morning, kicking in his stall. A little wait
wouldn't hurt him and Nye would be along to feed the stock any
minute now, even though he hadn't come to his own breakfast yet
this morning. Tom had heard Martha wondering where he was. It
seemed to Tom that he could hear the old man's mumbling talk out
in the barn now. The racket of hoofs died down. Tom walked on.

Amos Knott was already in the clearing, his face flushed, breath
coming fast and hard, and Tom couldn't see any apparent reason
for his exertions. He nodded briefly, a heavy-set taciturn man Tom
found it difficult to like, but there was no denying he was an able
sawyer. A man could wish for freehearted folks around him in his
work, Tom thought, but it took every sort to make a lumber crew.
Knott strode over to the mill and started the engine. There was a
good head of steam. The shrill scream of the blade echoed through
the clearing as Knott laid a random log against its sharp new teeth.
It ripped through quickly.

"She's a beaut," Knott said, sawing a raw board easily out of the
heart of the small log.

Tom looked at the first length of lumber from his new sawmill.

Golden crumbs of sawdust sprinkled the ground. The smell of fresh pine was sharp and clean. He and Knott watched the blade whirl. "Does our crew ever get here, we'll be ready to roll," Tom said.

Suddenly from the direction of the barn, a whirlwind figure exploded. "You brute beast!" Nye Blankenship cried as he sighted Amos Knott. He ran faster, hobbled by his loose-fitting shoes.

The blood rose in Knott's face, purpling his heavy cheeks and nose. "Stay where you are and hold your tongue, you runty little——"

"To maim a poor dumb creature," Nye rushed on. "Your roan's up there this morning, Tom Thurston, plumb crazy with pain and fear. One eyeball's a-laying half out of its socket on his face."

"What's this about the roan?" Tom asked.

The sawyer shrugged, began an answer, but before he could shape words, Nye interrupted. "You took him out last night. Against my warnings I seen you tussling with him, blackhearted creatures the both of you——"

"Shut your lying mouth," Amos Knott said with deadly quiet. "I taught that feller a lesson."

"And you pleasured in it!" Nye shouted, close to Knott now. "That's the devilish part of you and your kind, Amos Knott: it didn't make you suffer to bring pain to other flesh——"

"And I'll teach you a lesson, too." Knott spoke to the smaller frenzied man as to a bothersome insect.

"Men," Tom Thurston said, "whatever this is about, it's got to wait. Our crew's here and it's our work to turn out lumber this day." But neither man heeded him or the other men—the cutters and the loggers and their teams who were gathering in the new lumberyard. Blankenship and Knott stood as though apart from everyone else and locked in mortal combat. "Amos Knott," Tom went on, "if you've injured my roan, I'll deal with you."

"Injured?" Nye Blankenship screamed hoarsely. "Why he's battered and blinded . . ."

But the hard-muscled sawyer moved toward him with two quick strides and only Nye's agile leap backward helped him escape the iron grasp at his throat. "You varmint, Amos Knott, one of the killers stalking this earth, you're lower than the beasts you bruise and maim. They kill clean and for food. But you——"

"Quiet down, Nye," Tom Thurston said. He tried to speak calmly, now that the moment he always dreaded between these two had finally arrived. But they were not looking at him or hearing him. Slowly he moved to come between them. Deliberately, decisively, as between two enraged animals, he stepped into the opening.

On his final stride, Amos Knott's powerful arm rammed out, clutching at Nye's threadbare shirt—at the same time knocking Tom off balance. Tom Thurston stumbled. He might have regained his footing, but the freshly sawed two-by-six lay just behind him. One foot landed on its edge, and his ankle turned. The loose piece of lumber shifted under him. He plunged toward the belt of the big saw and the path of the spinning blade. As it bit into his shoulder, he was conscious of the machine's high wailing scream. The fierce burning was that of a hundred suns. Merciful darkness folded over him.

"Lord God A'mighty," the logger, old man Gunter, cried and left his oxen standing in their yoke and trace chains as he ran to where Tom Thurston had fallen.

Blood like a rich red river spurted from the nearly severed arm and shoulder. "Go get *her*," Gunter said, "and tell her to bring something quick to stanch the bleeding."

Amos Knott switched off the engine on the mill. The silence was complete and terrible.

Nye Blankenship's eyes were glazed with terror and concern. He tore the ragged shirt from his back and handed it, wadded like a sponge, to Gunter who pressed it against the raw wound. "I wouldn't a-harmed Tom Thurston or his kin for the world," Nye moaned. Turning, he ran down the path toward the house. He repeated it over and over, "Not for all the world would I a-done him harm."

"Oughtn't we to carry him home?" Amos Knott asked.

"He's bleeding mighty hard," Gunter said.

"*She'll* know what to do, does she ever get here," one of the loggers said.

Ivy and Frone and Phoebe came first, younger and longer-legged than their mother. They stopped when they saw their father lying there. No one moved. The big sturdy men stood awkward and impotent in their work clothes, the patient oxen in the background. The smell of woods mingled with the brackish smell of new machinery and smoke from the fire under the boiler. And Papa lay there on the ground. A little distance away lay his old felt hat with the familiar holes burned in its crown by hot coals that had fallen from other sawmills, other fires.

Ivy ran to pick up the hat and lay it beside him and then she knelt on the ground and took the blood-soaked shirt from Gunter and held it against Papa's shoulder. She tried not to see the arm lying at a curious angle, like something discarded from this tall, athletic body, attached only by a shred of skin and thin strip of shirt.

Then Martha, followed by Nye, came to where her husband lay. From her pale face her woman's eyes looked out with wounded comprehension at all of them. Her breath came short and hard. Around her clustered the younger children, Clay and Kin, but she brushed them aside. She knelt beside her husband. Over her arm she carried a white linen tablecloth she had snatched up as she fled the house and now she thrust away the drenched old shirt with a strength that none of them would have believed she had and she tore two long strips from the cloth and bound the rest of the linen in a bulky pack against the open shoulder, all the while crooning as to a child.

"It's all right, Tom, we'll make it all right. Never fear, Tom, we'll do our best."

Then she looked around at the men. "Somebody go for the doctor. Hurry! We must get him to the house," she said. Her gaze searched the new lumberyard. "Nothing big enough. Gunter, you and Nye go down and take the widest leaf out of our dining table. It may not be long enough, but it'll have to serve to carry him on. Hurry!" Her chin quivered for a moment, but her voice held steady.

While the men were gone, Martha stroked Tom's face with her free hand, gently, studying his features as though memorizing them afresh. "Father in Heaven," she murmured over and over, "dear Father in Heaven, Thy will . . ."

The pallor spreading over his ruddy skin sharpened the square contours of Tom Thurston's face. Once, the eyelids fluttered and his blue eyes seemed to look straight up at her.

"Papa, Papa . . ." Frone standing to one side wept softly, over and over. "How could it have happened?"

Phoebe had taken the two barefooted boys by the hand, but Clay pulled away now and ran over to the saw, beating against it with his tough little fists. Frone rushed to him. "Stop it, Clay. That's no help now."

Ivy felt that time had never moved so slowly. A couple of the men crossed the lumberyard and led the ox teams back toward the barn. Others stood silent and staring. As she watched the patient heavy beasts plod off under their wooden yokes, it seemed to her that all the cruelty she had ever seen and hated had culminated in this moment. All the wounded flesh and bruised spirits, all the pain inflicted, sometimes casually, sometimes purposefully, became part of this moment and of her father's suffering. Why, in the briefness of life, couldn't they all live generously, kindly . . . ? She felt that she was suffocating in the terrible stillness.

"I'll go make the bed ready for him, Mama," she said, and turned to leave.

But her mother laid a hand on her arm. Ivy saw her mother's lips moving, but no sound came. Her hand ceased stroking her husband's face. His blood was a dark stain spreading over the white cloth that was to have eased its flow. Martha laid her head on his chest, as though listening for a heartbeat, but she clasped her arms about his neck, abandoning the wound, and Ivy knew that there was no longer any throb to hear from that stout heart.

"We've got to look up."

Papa's words flashed through Ivy's mind so clearly she almost thought he had spoken to her. Through her tears she could see that the sun, just breaking over the mountains into this deep valley, touched them all with sudden radiance.

"For nothing. It was all for nothing!" Frone cried out in anguished grief.

The sun fell on the bright blade of the sawmill and splintered into blinding beams of light. And the birds called more clearly than ever in the woods beyond.

CHAPTER 9
Today and Yesterday

R A I N locked them in the house. They ate midafternoon Sunday dinner, took naps and turns visiting with Mama. "Wouldn't you eat just a little more, Mama?" "Yes, Mama, some of us went to church. . . . Well, Ivy and Phoebe went." "I'll put the hot pad on your back, Mama, maybe that will ease the pain a little." And they came together again before Ivy's blazing wood fire.

Phil, working in his room, could hear them talking—slowly and briskly, harshly and softly, briefly or lengthily—in a sort of counterpoint to each other. He could not hear their words, but the alternating rhythms and patterns of their voices filled the house through the short grey afternoon before late autumn twilight closed in. He knew that they were indulging in the game they played best, the pastime of remembering what each one knew, of reminding each other of moments, people, experiences that were their common knowledge. Like misers who might haul out hidden currency from time to time and count it, fondle it, test its value, so they drew forth their past and spread it to the light and each recognized its old familiar shape afresh.

"She sold the sawmill the next week after Papa's funeral," Frone

was saying. The others were quiet a moment, following her thrust
far back into the years.

Kin nodded. "Mama couldn't bear the sound of the mill after
Papa died . . ."

"Well, what nearly killed old Kin and me," Clay said, "was working out that pulpwood and tanbark. We had to make up some way
for the lumber Papa was going to sell."

Kin grinned slowly. "Law, that was a sight, how Mama sold those
two big boundaries of timber to the tannery and Mr. Austin's pulp
mill and we got payments along to meet some of Papa's debts and
interest and taxes. Then you and I started work for them the next
spring after school let out, cutting and hauling some of the bark and
wood."

"I never stood so tall in my britches before or since as the day
Austin personally handed me my pay for the pulpwood I cut that
first week." Clay shook his head.

"You were just boys," Ivy said.

"Boys one day, men the next," Clay added. "No wonder I'm a
sucker about work today. It saved my life that year. I thought I'd
die, too, the autumn after Papa went. Lord, he'd made the tracks I
walked in ever since I was big enough to toddle."

They could all remember that autumn. Nye Blankenship, Amos
Knott, the loggers, the drifters who had come and worked a little
while and moved on, were all gone. Only Mama remained, gathering the children close around her and depending on the Lord to help
her through the transactions of lawyers and other men who came to
see her on business and left singing the praises of that "sensible
little lady." But Mama wasn't able to hold her children close. They
were going out, farther and farther out: Clay and Kin to school down
the road during fall and winter, to books and fights and Friday-
afternoon public recitations—and men's work at home.

"First thing I had to do that next spring," Kin said, "was gentle
Papa's big roan, the way old Nye had taught me how. Nearly killed
us both."

"A thousand wonders you didn't break your neck," Phoebe murmured.

"It made a man of him," Clay said.

"I reckon so. Between that school in the winters and working tanbark and pulpwood in the summers——"

"We jumped into manhood feet first," Clay supplied. "Maybe we came up clobbered now and then—but, by God, we always came up."

"That winter everything seemed to be going, changing," Frone said. She leaned an elbow on the arm of her chair and rested her chin on the palm of her hand as she looked out the window. "Papa's house burned just before Christmas, the big old white house on Thickety. I remember hearing someone say he guessed the insurance got hot, and I didn't know what it meant until I learned afterward that the Nelsons who bought the farm from us were famous for bad luck with fires. But for the white house Papa had built so grandly to be . . ." Her words trailed off.

"Sometimes"—Kin looked at Clay—"under the piles of tanbark, where it had been stacked for a long time, we'd find a copperhead——"

"And I'd pull out about five o'clock in the morning those days I was hauling bark, take my lunch with me," Clay said.

"I had nightmares about that fire," Frone went on. Each was contained in the counterpoint of his own memories. "I would dream that Papa was running to put the fire out and all he had in his hand was a dipper full of water. And along the way, as he ran, the water turned to blood."

Isn't it odd, Ivy thought, that I recall all these events they speak of, but they don't seem part of the reality of those years after Papa's death? Reality had only begun after Cort's letter came. She laughed out loud and the others looked at her. "Do you remember what a commotion was stirred up when I announced that Cort and I were going to be married?"

"Commotion?" Frone said. "Cyclone."

"It was the first completely happy thing that happened to me after Papa died," she said.

"The wedding dress came from Nelsons' big new store in town." Frone's voice was bitter. "Folks said their store was built with the insurance money from the house fire."

"The day his letter came," Ivy said, "I'd been out in the woods all day gathering greenery. Galax and ferns and mistletoe. I wanted to make it a special Christmas."

Frone nodded. "I was anxious to get home from my teaching that year, but I dreaded it, too."

"And when I came in off the mountain with my arms full of greens, you met me at the door, Phoebe, and announced all in a breath that I had a letter from New York."

"None of us even knew he'd been married," Frone said, "until you read Mama the part of the letter where he said his wife had been dead a little more than a year——"

"She died in Boston."

They could recall details of all these familiar moments, but Ivy knew she could never impart to them the confusion of sorrow and elation that tore her apart when she read that letter. But when Cort had come South that following summer and lived in town and spent much of his time with her—then, then it all turned to pure elation.

"Things never did seem the same again." Kin's voice was low and sad. "Not after you married and went up North to live awhile, and Frone got that teaching job in the other end of the state and met Jud."

They were silent. Clay jumped up impulsively from his chair and went out to the kitchen. There was no one around. He eased the new flat bottle out of his left hip pocket. It was full. He unscrewed the cap, tilted the bottle against his parched lips and took a long swallow. He felt the liquor hit his gut. Presently its fire began to spread through the rest of him. He wiped the top of the bottle on the palm of his hand and replaced the cap.

As he went back into the living room, he began to talk. "All the girls getting married, I guess everyone thought little old Clay would stay pinned here for life. That is, after Phoebe went off and found her Rutledge Harris the third, sixth, seventh—whatever the hell he is."

"Well, you may make fun of his name," Phoebe said primly, "but I can tell you one thing—sometimes I get down on my knees and thank God for bringing me Rutledge."

"Now, Pheeb, on your *knees?*"

"And when I think that the day Preacher Grey asked Mama to

let me go on that trip down to Charleston for a visit with some of his relatives, she almost didn't let me go!"

Ivy smiled at her sister's unaccustomed vehemence. "I guess Preacher Grey knew you had had little enough chance——"

"I hadn't been *anywhere!*" Phoebe said. "And then I landed down there among those folks with their old families and old houses and old money——"

"And old gossip," Clay murmured.

"Clay!" Ivy said softly. She rose to punch up the fire.

"I'll bring you another log," Kin volunteered, and went outside in the slow drizzling rain to the rick stacked higher than his head beside Ivy's garage. When he had built up the fire, he stood back and looked into it pensively. "Law, how those big oak and hickory logs used to burn."

"Well, I can tell you all one thing," Phoebe went on. "I kept my eyes open, and my ears, too. Before Rutledge's mother died, she told me I was more like her than any daughter she had."

Ivy nodded. No wonder Mrs. Harris had said that Phoebe was more like her than any daughter she had! She had only produced her other children; Phoebe she had created. Phoebe had gone like putty into her hands and been made into her image. But Ivy could remember her sister as Phoebe Thurston, quick with life and curiosity and an affectionate loving heart, not querulous about genealogies and false superiorities.

"Oh, the Harrises were what Papa always called good livers," Phoebe went on proudly. "They had a house in town, one of those old ones with its shoulder turned to the street—you came to visit us there, Ivy, when we were still living with Rutledge's mother."

"It was a show place," Ivy agreed.

"But I never liked the town house as well as the summer plantation," Phoebe said eagerly. "I knew that from the moment Rutledge and I first went out there and I saw the old home sprawling under the live oaks and Spanish moss. Out in the yard there was this enormous plantation bell. It rang at six and twelve and one and six every day. The Nigras came to work by it, ate dinner by it, chopped the cotton and hoed corn by it. I loved to hear the sound of that bell ringing over the fields." Phoebe straightened in her chair and looked

at all of them with the piercing eagerness they remembered from
her girlhood. "I tell you, down where I live Mrs. Rutledge Harris the
Third is *somebody*."

The others, embarrassed, glanced away from one another, but
Ivy looked straight at her. "Wasn't Phoebe Thurston somebody?
Oh, Phoebe, maybe we in the mountains didn't have tester beds
and French clocks and syllabub sets, but we had something
else. . . ."

"You know what I mean," Phoebe said hastily, flushing. But that
was the point. They knew exactly what she meant.

"Well by God!" Clay stood up again, walked across the room.
"There was none of them ever scared me." And they knew by the
belligerence of the words how often he had been scared. "I'm as
good as any man!"

"Of course, Clay," Frone soothed.

"That first crew I ever went to work with up North——"

Ivy nodded. "You were on your way up to visit Cort and me and
you met some fellow on the train——"

"Jim Perkins. Head of a New Jersey construction company. Old
Jim." Clay took a long draw on his cigarette and let the smoke out
slowly through his nostrils. "Seems like a century since I met Jim
Perkins on that train right at the beginning of the big boom. He had
a neat tight-knit crew opening up some of the country outside New
York and Newark and Jersey City, that whole big-city network.
At the end of our ride he offered me a tryout with his crew on a
brand-new lakeside suburb. It turned out the lake was really a
swamp when I first got there."

The others only half-listened, knowing it was partly the whisky
talking, but they were willing to let him have his turn in the confes-
sional, the upstage center.

"After the first week of work old Jim came to me and said, 'I
thought all Johnny Rebs were lazy, but you sure picked up the
dynamite somewhere. You're on the crew, Thurston.' And he offered
me fifty dollars a week. It looked like a fortune. 'Thanks for the job,'
I said to him. 'Leave that Johnny Reb stuff strictly out of it and
you've got yourself a worker, Jim. O.K.?' And old Jim never brought
the subject up again."

"Poor kid," Frone said. "I guess you learned——"

"You learned! You learned or you were out on your backside pronto." Clay slapped his leg. "There weren't any diplomas in that college. There was a pay check—or nothing. It was dog eat dog."

"Rough," Kin said.

"All but Jim Perkins. He was one of the smartest, finest fellows you'd ever want to meet. But even if he was a college graduate, I helped make his job for him there on that lakesite. He didn't ever forget it either. Jim knew all the surveying and construction in the books—but I knew it in the field."

"You'd watched houses being built all your life, hadn't you?" Ivy laughed.

"You're so damned right. And I'd seen some of the fool mistakes, too. But that summer we spent just laying off this development and helping sell it off, and that was the first suburb I ever saw. When I think about the ones that mushroom now . . . Well, I guess I helped start the ball rolling."

"Then you sure did a master job of it, as Papa would say," Frone laughed. "Why, Jud says that pretty soon Connecticut is going to be all suburbs, no cities, no country."

"Who bought all those first places you helped make?" Kin asked.

"Who bought them?" Clay threw back his head and laughed. "I'll tell you who. We got that swamp all dried out, built the lake and laid out these lots about big enough for a good-sized man to spit on. Then the development company advertised them in the New York papers. They charged ninety-eight dollars and fifty cents apiece for them. On May Day they opened the sale, and I tell you it was a catawampus. Folks swarmed out of New York, every nationality God ever thought of. I was fresh out of the hills of old Nantahala and I just stood and looked at them and wondered where they could all come from."

"No, we never had many foreigners down here," Phoebe said.

"And we missed a hell of a lot," Clay answered. "Lord, I got to know them all. Those Italians would come up there with a tub full of boiled corn and some jugs of red wine, anything you wanted, and you couldn't get past them without them offering some to you. They always wanted you to eat with them. Then there were the Ger-

mans and Swedes, the Jews and Spaniards, and, of course, the Irish-
men. Oh, they all came. From then on, I knew them all. I
knew which part of the old country they'd come from and I knew
the words to call them to get the different ones in a fight."

"I'm glad you weren't one of those foreign ones, had to fight it
out," Phoebe said.

"Oh, but I was, and I did," he grinned. "I was from the South. I
was 'Reb.' "

The others looked at each other and laughed.

"They could turn it nasty, the way they said it," Clay told them.
He sat down heavily in one of the chairs beside the fireplace. "The
time I remember settling *that* problem was several years later
when Jim Perkins and our crew were working out of New York City.
The depression had hit by then. There were plenty of rough characters around ready to grab your job if you made a fumble. We went
on this job up in Westchester and one of the men in the company
that hired us, he wanted to get his no-'count brother-in-law on the
payroll. He was eyeing my spot. One night right after we'd started
the work, Jim and me stopped in this little joint for a beer."

"That was one thing you'd learned," Frone said, "to drink."

"I'd learned that——" Clay paused. No one spoke. He glared at
Frone's interruption. Then: "Jim and I were in this little joint—it
was jungle hot—and the beer wasn't any good, but it was wet and it
was cold. Some other fellows were right alongside the bar and one
big bruiser, the one with the brother-in-law, was looking straight at
me. Jim Perkins muttered, 'Careful, Clay.' And then this son-of-a-
gun said, loud and ugly, 'Say, hillbilly, tell us, how do the whippoorwills sing down in Dixie?' "

He paused. Frone asked, her eyes twinkling, "And I suppose
you told him in a gentlemanly way?"

Clay was out of his chair with the excitement of just remembering. "I took one dive at him, right off that bar stool where I was sitting I made a flying leap, and I landed right on top of him.
I knocked him to the floor before he knew what hit him. I was boiling. I started hitting with my fists and I beat that character's head to
a poultice. All the time he was yelling, 'Get him off me. If there's a
man left in Westchester, pull him off. Help!' But those slobs stood

there and didn't move. When I was through, I stood back and said, 'That's the way the whippoorwills sing where I come from.'" And Clay roared with laughter at the satisfaction of victory.

"Well, he shouldn't have talked to you like that," Phoebe said tentatively.

But Clay stopped laughing. "Oh, hell, that wasn't anything. That wasn't a drop in the bucket. . . ." At a loss for words as he realized that she—perhaps none of them—could ever understand how it really was in that new, tough, vital world that he had met head on and determined to conquer, he slowly shook his head. (Had he conquered it, or had it conquered him? The thought was cold and persistent at the back of his mind.)

"You had some high old times, all right," Ivy agreed. She was smiling at the thought of some of the weekends during those years when Clay had come up to see Cort and her—a devil-may-care young man with the right clothes for his lithe muscular figure and dark good looks and always a different girl, a new car, a fresh adventure.

"They were good," he said. "Better than most."

"Cort always said you were the hardest-working man he'd ever known," Ivy said.

"That Cort," Clay nodded, "he always was two jumps ahead of everybody else."

"Except your sister," Ivy teased.

"Not excepting anybody," Clay said. "Smartest day's work you ever did was marry that man."

Kin spoke up. "He didn't do so bad getting Ivy, either."

"When you two got ready to move back to the mountains and build this place here, he had sense enough not to try to sell that big farm of his for a farm," Clay went on. "Cort came down to that development company I was working for and they turned it into 'estates' for some of the Broadway crowd that were beginning to buy 'country places' about that time. Oh, he knew the way the wind blew, that Henry Hudson Cortland."

"That was why he wanted to come back here," Ivy said. "He wanted real countryside, not something synthetic. And he thought this was the only place that might have true country after a while."

She remembered the joy she had felt in coming back to Nantahala County with her husband and her child and her very own
home. Not that she hadn't liked living for a while in the big old house
above the Hudson, knowing Cort's surroundings, his family and
friends, going into New York City sometimes and discovering a
whole new world of art galleries and museums and music and lec-
tures. But there had been moments when she remembered such little
things: the way a cowbell had tinkled years before in the Upper
Orchard and the sun was warm as liquid on her arms and face, and
the sound of the cowbell was the sound of all the peace and life
she had ever known.

"I reckon you've all been away but me," Kin suddenly said.

"Oh, you've traveled around, Kin——" someone began.

"I mean to live, to really know a place," he went on. "It doesn't
matter to me. I was lucky: I was born just where I want to be, and
the things around me—the living, growing things—they're what I
like to work with, and so there's nothing I need to go looking for."

"Boy, you've got it made for a fact," Clay muttered, and they
could not tell whether his tone was that of sarcasm or envy. "All I
need to have it made right now is a good woman." He frowned.
"They're all the same. Want to get a hold on you and then start re-
making you. Kathleen knew I drank when she married me."

"Maybe so, Clay, but——"

"No 'but' about it. Like that long slim drink of ice water from
Oyster Bay that I used to run around with. I'd have married her in
a minute—that was back in my heyday, too, when I had a pick of
the best—but after we'd gone together awhile she began to get positively—pro-pri-e-tary." He pronounced the word carefully, looked
at them and raised his eyebrows comically.

Ivy laughed. "Too bad you couldn't have put up with a little
proprietariness."

"Oh, she was a living doll, all right. And she might have looked
like a cool drink, but let me tell you that long blonde hair and those
big green eyes and her slim white hands hid a red hot mamma
underneath. Her father was president of some big textile company
with mills all over New England and half the South. They treated
me like a prince. They liked a Southern boy."

"Oh, Clay!" Phoebe sighed. "What a shame that you let such a golden chance slip by."

"A golden chance for what?" Clay asked. "A golden halter? I tell you, they're all pro-pri-e-tary!"

"Am I missing words of wisdom?" Phil asked as he appeared in the doorway.

Ivy looked at the well-cut grey flannel suit Phil had changed into. "Is it time for you to pick up Sherry Austin already?" she asked.

Phil glanced out the window where early darkness had already blotted out the view, leaving only the last light around the rim of distant mountains. The rain had finally stopped. He nodded.

"Dear, dear, I'd forgotten. You and the cousin-barrister are frolicking with the smart set tonight," Clay said.

"Any message you want carried in to them from the hinterlands?" Phil tried wearily to banter.

Clay shook his head, threw his cigarette butt into the fireplace. "Those would-be golfers and playboys and little country dwellers— oh, hell, they're the ones we drained the swamps and laid out the fields for. I sweated over half of New Jersey and New York so they could put up their little ranch houses with the picture windows, and a lamp on every table, looking into each other's back doors. You go find out what's on their minds, Senator."

"I'll have to know what's on their minds if I'm going to be their Senator," Phil said.

But just as he was going out of the door, Clay came up beside him. "Phil," he said, with studied carelessness, "you keep your ears open out there tonight and if you hear about any big new construction work beginning, you let me know."

"Sure, Clay. I'll keep it in mind."

"A man's got to work." He slapped his fist against the palm of his hand. "What the hell good is a man if he's not doing something, building something, taking his part? Almighty be! I've got to get this Hawk Williams mess cleared up tomorrow and stop burping around like a bee with a bellyache."

"You'll find something," Phil said.

"You're damned right I will, or be caught dead trying. Look at that muscle." He flexed his right arm. "You don't get that in a day, man. And I guess there's someplace they still need gristle like that."

"Sure, Clay."

As Phil drove into town and then turned west toward the hill on the outskirts of the city limits where the Miles Austin home stood in synthetic Norman grandeur, he shook his head again at Clay's dilemma. Then he put it out of his mind and fastened his attention on remembering, sentence by sentence, the conversation he had just completed by telephone with Senator Howard. Ann had told him to call her father before Monday and he had done so late this afternoon. The old man hadn't wasted time hesitating to admit that he and the other senator had gone ahead with a rough draft of the report and recommendations on their trip. He had spelled out some of them to Phil.

"Hold on," Phil interrupted him at one point, "that blanket item about tractors . . . you know they can't use tractors in at least three of those countries."

"The chairman of the party in our colleague's state also happens to be chairman of the board of a tractor manufacturing company."

"I should have guessed it. But while we were over there, he didn't seem so interested in machinery. He really seemed concerned about the people, about the little farmers who didn't even have a hoe or know how to use one——"

Senator Howard sighed audibly. "Of course he is. But our party has a hell of a time raising money in his state. Mr. Tractor is one of the few who can be counted on for support. And that's a fact of life, son."

"Which, slow as I may seem, I can grasp, Senator. I haven't worked in the Governor's campaigns all these years without learning something, but I had hoped this particular report could——"

"Be written in the rarefied air above politics? Now you knew that was impossible. Look, son, you got to the Senate by a sort of immaculate conception, by appointment instead of by blood, sweat and tears of campaigning. Now you'd better touch base with some of the realities before you come up against an opponent in the race that's ahead of you."

"Well, I'm going to fight that tractor deal, Senator Howard. That would siphon off a lot of the funds from——"

"And what if our colleague says he'll fight your proposal for more teachers and suggests you're offering it just because the teachers' association in your state supports you?"

"You know that's not the truth, Senator Howard." Even as Phil spoke, he realized the foolishness of his statement.

"It sounds like the truth. That's what counts. And he might well make that or some equal maneuver. You may have to let him have his tractors, son, but you can make him pay for them."

"*Quid pro quo?*" Phil said.

"That's the way the wheels roll," Senator Howard said. Phil did not answer, and when the old man spoke again there was a subtle change, a bristling, in his words as well as his tone. "Look, Cortland, what are you out to win by stirring up this kettle of fish?"

"I'm not trying to win anything, except maybe some understanding on the part of the public of how complex a problem it is to try to help a single individual, much less a whole country."

"That's a dangerous attitude. You're not in a position yet to begin an education program for the public. Look, Cortland, I'm going to let you in on a little secret. It may be one of the most important you'll learn for a long time. Anything you do up here, you win or lose. You've got an investment—your career. And you've got some working capital—the power you gained by becoming Senator. You can use that capital to make it work for your investment, or you can squander it. But every move you make, you dip into it one way or the other."

"You make it very simple, and very clear," Phil said. "Even to a beginner."

"It's better to win than to lose," Senator Howard went on. "In fact, around this city, you lose often enough and you're just not here. The ones who survive, the ones who lead—they've found out first how to win."

"By being quiet——"

"At first."

"By compromising—"

"Sometimes."

"Well, I may not have a second chance in the hallowed halls and cloakrooms of the Senate——"

"Oh, but I suspect you will." Senator Howard's voice was smoother now. "I suspect very strongly that you will. Some of your characteristics that may irritate me are quite likely the very qualities that would cause your people down there to vote for you. And I think you like being Senator Philip Cortland."

"Of course I do!"

"And"—the older man spoke more slowly and deliberately—"I think the Senate needs Phil Cortland."

Was this the carrot then? The big stick first, in the hard voice, the "realistic" words, the clipped surname, alternated suddenly with a soft flattering intimacy that suggested the world was yours for the taking. Phil thought about it as he drove up the hill to the Austin house. Had Governor Wentworth and the others counted on the carrot to keep him in line? Of course, he knew the primer of success on the Hill: that vow of silence during the first term; that unwritten pact which stipulated that differences should be negotiated away from the public glare. He just hadn't decided yet whether he wanted to succeed in this one important area which had opened up for him, perhaps unfortunately, during his freshman year of service —or whether he wanted to be a successful Senator for as long as he could stay elected to office.

Sherry herself greeted him at the door. "Phil, darling!"

He smiled at her success with the endearment, almost as throaty and casual as the actresses and jet-set girls made it. She stood on tiptoe and kissed him on the lips, lightly, so that her careful lipstick would not be disturbed. But he was disturbed.

"Down, girl." He held her at arm's length. She relaxed between his two hands with such suppleness, however, that he knew he should not have touched her.

Her knit cashmere dress, clinging and soft, was a rich black, the color of her heavily mascaraed eyelashes, the color of her high-coiled hair. He let go of her arms. She made a little pout. "That's not a very warm old Southern greeting. Well, shall we have a drink here or go on to the club for full festivities?"

"I had thought I'd say hello to your father."

"Mother and Dad went on hours ago," she said, going toward the wide stairway that curved up to the second landing from the foyer where they stood. "The new couple from Detroit—the man built the electronics plant here—they were having open house this afternoon. Mother and Dad are bringing them to the buffet later. I'll get my coat, Phil." She ran up the steps easily, reminding him of the few times, when they were teen-agers, that they had played tennis together, and how deftly she handled herself on the court.

On the way to the club she amused him with her adventures of the summer in Europe, entertained him with the minutiae of boredom which had made up her days since she came home: friends' wedding dates and babies' births and checking to see if the two events were a full nine months apart; learning whose husband made out with whose wife at the last New Year's Eve or July Fourth or Labor Day dance. She was brilliantly witty, like a diamond with a sharp cutting edge.

He let her out at the entrance to the dark stucco clubhouse and went to find a place to park. As he walked up the drive, he looked at the building, put up in the mid-1920's, at the height of the boom years, which he could barely remember, when all the city people in Nantahala County had believed they were destined to be rich by the end of the decade. On paper they already owned more than they ever had before. So they built a club to insure their new leisure against loneliness or originality.

Here those who worked together in the same businesses during the week and went together to the same churches on Sunday could also be assured of playing together on the same courts or courses or dance floors. The depression years had been bleak for the club, but no one recalled them now. And for the past couple of decades—with a new airport and new branch plants from companies in Massachusetts, Ohio, New York, Michigan; with their bright new executives—the club had flourished. Its careful membership and championship greens had meant, as those on its governing board often assured one another, "everything; the difference between progress and lag in a competitive growth situation."

Phil could hear the clatter of talk, the clink of glassware, as he entered the door. Sherry had already deposited her coat; she came up to him quickly and captured his hand.

"You were slumming last night, darling, after I left. Now come and see your silk-stocking district. Isn't that good political lingo, Senator?"

He nodded, stood still, refusing for a moment to follow her. "You do keep up with the news, don't you?"

"Not the news, darling. You."

"And where was I?"

"Agent 0-0-0-9-7 reporting." She made a mock salute, waved nonchalantly to someone coming in the door. "You and your uncle, Clay Thurston, were at Hawk Williams' to see if there was anything you could do for Lorna or the children."

"You're a pretty thorough agent. What's the purpose?"

"Nefarious purposes, dear Philip Cortland." She gazed up at him with eyes wide and blank. "Anyway, it wasn't very complicated. Lorna Williams has been our cook for years. Some neighbor came the last three or four days to take her place—and tote all the latest tidbits of news."

Phil sighed. "I've been trying to help Clay——"

"Don't fret, darling. Everyone knows we're not responsible for our kinfolks."

He raised his eyebrows, smiled at her easy dismissal of involvement. "Not everyone, Sherry."

"Well, I mean everyone here tonight. After all, most of them are just a generation out of the hills and hollows themselves, and there's some hillbilly back there now who would kill them with embarrassment if he claimed their kinship in public——"

"Wait a minute, Sherry, I'm not embarrassed that Clay is my relative. It's just the awkwardness of what's been done, or not done——"

"Forget it, darling. I mean, in this case, you were halfway across the world. How could something your uncle did on some crazy hunt possibly have anything to do with you and Washington and your staying there? Besides, Lorna says he didn't even do it."

"Let's hope Lorna knows something we don't."

"Forget it for tonight." She squeezed his hand. A couple were coming toward them. "These are the new people with the electronics company. She's a drag, but he could be right cute if he tried." And Sherry greeted them, introduced Phil.

It was her evening. Phil had been popular during the years he was growing up here and he found a few old friends. (Had he ever realized before, he wondered, how many of the brightest ones, the ones with original talent, had left?) He met a great many new people, some of whom he'd seen before, and most of them were eager to talk with a young senator. But Sherry dominated the cocktail party, the buffet supper, the conversation afterward.

Phil talked with them all, effortlessly using the attentive interest in other people which was his greatest political asset. There were the middle-aged young, the middle-aged old, natives and newcomers, the pleasantly wined and dined and the outright drunk, the ones on the way up, the ones on the way down and those who were holding on. The chief fact that struck him about them was how much alike they were. They talked about yesterday's football scores and compared their own golf scores for Thursday and Friday. They made a few political jabs, but Phil feinted with the unfriendly ones and took the flattering ones with grace. He watched Hugh Moore (who managed to transform an assortment of separate impeccable items of clothing into one total effect of cheap slovenliness) in his effort to win Miles Austin's acceptance. Flora May's efforts with Austin's wife were only slightly less vigorous—and successful—than her husband's. Austin paid them scant attention. During dessert there was discussion between a couple of the men who had recently returned from a trip to Europe where they had surveyed the possibility of opening plants in various countries there.

"The Dutch are easy to work with."

"Sure they are. But there wasn't a single place I visited in Holland where they could guarantee me two or three hundred women to work in a plant."

"A damned shame."

"You're right it is. Best people to work with anywhere, and short labor supply."

"I scouted out Italy——"

"Southern Italy's the only damned place on the whole continent where there's any labor supply today."

"I went down to Naples, found a dandy site not too far out of the city, asked those fellows there to give me a figure on the cost per square foot of building a plant. They fooled around a couple of weeks, three weeks, and finally I said what the hell and came on home. Never could get a cost estimate out of them."

"Phil——"

He turned abruptly. Miles Austin, standing just behind his chair nodded toward the door to the patio. "How about a cigar?"

Mrs. Austin, at the opposite end of the table, and Sherry, beside Phil, frowned. "Miles," his wife said, "no kidnaping tonight."

"Not at all, my dear." But he went his way imperturbably toward the French doors, and Phil went with him.

Outside the air was chilly. Summer's metal tables and chairs were stacked under an awning at one end of the patio. Everything was drenched from the long day's rain. The air had cleared, however, and the two men walked to the edge of the lawn which ran down to the clipped and manicured fairway in the darkness.

"Senator——"

" 'Phil' suits me just as well," he said.

"All right, Phil." The older man smiled. "I want you to know how proud we are here in the mountains to have a boy from Nantahala in the United States Senate."

"For a little while, thanks to Governor Wentworth," Phil said.

"For a long while, I think," Miles Austin replied, "thanks to your own abilities."

"That depends, I guess."

"Naturally. But keep it in mind, Phil." Looking down toward the fairway, he put his hands in his pockets. In the dim light, the heavy eyelids seemed to cover his eyes completely. "Yesterday morning at the airport I said that I wanted to mention the proposed industrial park to you——"

Phil nodded.

"The boys around here have been talking it up for quite a while now. Of course, it can't get far off the ground without some federal help for a new county water system. If I were you, I wouldn't spend too much of my time and energy in Washington running around securing that help, Phil."

Phil hesitated. "I thought you were president of the Greater Nantahala Development Association, Mr. Austin." It was a statement which could seem either naïve or unfriendly. But he knew why Miles Austin was opposed to any real surge of new industry in the area: the big reservoir of surplus mountain labor would be diminished. He wanted to test how close Austin would come to saying it outright.

"I am." There was no reaction at all in the older man's tone. It was a flat statement. "But first I am president of the Universal Paper Company."

Phil nodded.

"And to make paper we need pulpwood, water and people. We've taken steps to insure a steady supply of the first two. Gradually we're converting some of our machinery so that we'll need fewer people, Phil. But it's a long costly process with a paper mill, and until it's completed we don't want to see our labor supply dry up."

"There are a lot of our people here unemployed and underemployed, Mr. Austin. Can't we work out some way to bring in new industry without hurting the old?"

Austin looked at him. "Remember, Phil, you can't solve all the problems in your first year in office. Save a few for the second. Build up a good solid reputation among your old friends——"

The doors behind them swung open and Sherry came out on the terrace. "You two are charged with desertion," she said.

"We plead guilty," her father said amiably. "But I don't think it's my presence—or absence—you care about one whit, daughter. So I relinquish your guest" He stepped toward the door. "Good to have this little talk with you, Senator." He did not smile. His face was serious, composed and confident as he went in ahead of Phil and Sherry.

They refused an invitation to play bridge, a bid for gin rummy, and a challenge to join in a fling at the latest dance twist. Phil and Sherry moved from the dining room to the lounges, talking with everyone along the way. The noise of voices, laughter, had become a real din in the smoke-filled air. Several of the couples were quite drunk.

Phil felt that he might be in the state capital or in Washington or any other city—for these were not unique Nantahala people; they were as standardized as identical hair styles, clothes, jokes, food, newspapers and rebellious offspring could make them. But although they were not unique, neither were they universal. Paradoxically, just as Ivy and the family were unique—exasperatingly, humorously, sadly so—they were also touched by universality and Phil knew that his mother could have walked among the people in the foreign lands he had visited and won their friendship.

"Darling," Sherry asked him, "have you heard one word of this story Hugh Moore is telling? It's terribly cute." She leaned forward. "About your grandmother, or great-grandmother, or somebody, Lydia McQueen, and how she decided once to get rid of a bunch of moonshiners and troublemakers who lived up on the mountain above her—and she cleared them out herself! She must have been quite a gal."

Phil nodded. "She was that! But I don't think this story of Hugh's —well it doesn't sound accurate——"

"My grandma Dolly Moore told me all about it," Hugh was pleased at his prestigious knowledge, but disturbed by the bored expressions on the faces of most of those in his corner of the big lounge. "Say, did any of you hear the joke yet about the President and the first man on the moon?"

Phil admired Hugh Moore's ability to gauge his audience's interest level and switch his material accordingly. It was an aptitude helpful to entertainers, lawyers, cooks and the devil himself, Phil supposed.

"We could leave any time," Sherry whispered to him.

"I suspected as much."

They said as many good-bys as they had said hellos.

"Will you be out to lunch tomorrow, Sherry?"

"Call me in the morning, darling."

"Get back down this way soon, Phil."

"Good to see you, fellow."

"Next time I'm up in Washington, I'll call you. Maybe you can show me some of the big city sights . . ."

"Fix a parking ticket, make you a price on Rock Creek Park, anything you say," he answered.

"Do right by us up there, Senator."

"Sherry," another called, "you let me know about the dance Thursday, you hear?"

"Course I'll let you know. 'Night, darling."

As he went to get the car, Phil sighed in exasperation both with himself and with the evening. He had never seen a lonelier, more desperate, group of people. They held on to their little club to show how closely they were bound together, and essentially they were as uncommitted to one another as the lion and the impala of the jungle were uncomitted to each other. They made up for a lack of true community with the trappings of "community spirit." Words replaced actions. Symbols passed for realities.

He thought of Sherry and her figure as tempting as a rich ripe juicy pear. Her breasts were molded by some device to thrust themselves out to every glancing touch. As breasts grew less and less functional (could he, could anyone imagine her providing milk for infants from that perfect bust?), they grew more and more important in every lure of entertainment, commerce, psychology, fantasy.

He started the car, backed out of the narrow parking space. Wasn't religion, too, growing more formalized, more separated from daily life, even as lip service to its forms became more necessary for every public figure? What was the unfunny joke about the man who bombed his neighbor's house because the neighbor didn't join the movement to put "In God We Trust" above the Supreme Court building? When he had told that one to Senator Howard, the old man had nodded and said, "Yes. And there's the politician who smeared his opponent's reputation because the man didn't join a popular organization working for 'brotherhood.'"

"Curiouser and curiouser," Phil muttered, as Sherry got in the car.

"What is?" She didn't bother to rearrange the skirts that reached halfway up her thigh.

"People. Everything. You," he answered.

"And you," she answered back. "I gather from tonight's perform-ance, darling, that you've decided not to be a glad-hand senator. Well, that's all right. I guess a thoughtful, pipe-smoking, tweedy type is just as good an image to project."

"Thanks for including the 'thoughtful.'"

"All the more reason why you need a little effervescence in your life, Phil." She pulled her legs up close beside him on the seat. The fragrance of her perfume filled the car.

As they went around the circular drive in the semi-courtyard of the Austin house, she motioned for him to stop in front of one of the large oak side doors. As he brought the car to a halt, she reached over and turned the key, pulled it out of the switch and with one precise motion dropped the key on its chain ring down the neck of her dress. She looked up at him and smiled slowly. Without a word she opened the car door.

Inside the house she led the way upstairs to her own sitting room from which opened the spacious, extravagant bedroom. The bed dominated both rooms—set on a low dais, covered with a scarlet silk quilted spread on which her monogram had been appliquéd in white. Everything else in the two rooms was white—carpet, dra-peries, walls (partially covered with splashes of enormous abstract paintings), lamps, chairs—except for an occasional pillow or shade which repeated the scarlet or one of the intense colors from the oil paintings.

She threw her coat across a chair and ran one hand through her thick dark hair. It was a studied, sensuous gesture, revealing the in-ner curve of her arm, the perfect outline of her figure in the clinging cashmere. She gave a small thrust to each foot and kicked the black pumps she was wearing across the room. In her stocking feet she stood very close to him.

"Sit down, darling," she said. "I'll find you a drink." She put her finger tips on his chest to give him a gentle push into the big easy chair just behind him.

He braced against her gesture, however, then reached out and took both of her hands in his. His pulse throbbed at the touch of her warm flesh, soft and perfumed with years of creams and lotions and protection; her small bones were delicate as ivory. Slowly he loosed one hand and with great deliberateness reached it down the deep V of her dress. In the lace brassière between the tender fullness of her swelling breasts he felt the small metallic key. He drew it forth, dangling from its chain on his little finger.

"Not this time, darling," he said, half gently, half mockingly.

She did not seem to react. He admired her coolness. "What's the matter, Phil?"

"Nothing is the matter, Sherry. It's——"

"You seemed to find everything pretty much to your liking a few years ago."

"What was it you said last night about bygones being bygones and the past was a drag?"

She walked away, curled up on the white damask-covered sofa, one leg coiled beneath her. "Small talk. Chatter. Better sit down, Phil-baby. I've something to ask you." She reached inside her dress and rearranged the brassière that had been slipped askew by Phil's hand. When she had finished, she let her fingers rest lightly on her throat.

He sat down, not beside her but in a chair opposite. "Sherry," he began, "let's face it——"

"I already have," she said.

"Oh?" His glance was amused, quizzical, irritated.

"The summer after you left me. The summer I had our abortion."

The word exploded harshly in the cushioned, carpeted room and caught Phil by complete surprise. "Abortion?" As he repeated it, there was a chain reaction of astonishment, doubt, disgust, pity and slowly mounting guilt.

She watched him and waited.

"Was I supposed to know?" he asked. "Somewhere along the way I must have missed a couple of signals."

She shook her head. "No one knew."

"When—and where?"

"That August, in New York, in the dingy walk-up apartment of a gross little doctor who liked cash customers and let the credit go." Her voice had grown lower. "It was all secret and sordid—and it hurt like hell."

"But why, Sherry, why——" he began, then halted.

She smiled, not prettily but accusingly, sarcastically. "Because I didn't want to have your baby all by myself, darling."

That answered the question he had avoided asking: "Whose?"

"Or maybe I told you wrong at the very beginning: I should have said my abortion and our baby."

He could not help voicing his doubt. "Were you sure it was ours, Sherry?"

"I was sure, Phil." The way she said it he knew she was telling the truth, as she believed it.

"My God, Sherry"—he stood up—"how could you do it?"

She spread her flawlessly manicured white hands. "What else was there?"

"You could have told me."

"And what would you have done, darling?" she interrupted softly. "We'd talked through the marriage bit. I couldn't see us as a shotgun bride and groom."

"It had to be on your terms all the way, didn't it, Sherry?"

For the first time she looked away from him. She laid her head back against the sofa and closed her eyes. "My terms were pretty high, Phil. You know, a funny thing happened right in the middle of the operation, when I was so groggy I could hardly see that ogre of a nurse's face beside me or the stingy little light bulb dangling from the ceiling. I suddenly wanted to cry out, 'Leave it alone! Don't touch it! Don't take it—it's mine!'"

"Sherry!" He sat down beside her on the sofa and she flung herself into his arms. Tears stained by mascara rushed down her face. "If I'd listened to you, Phil . . ." she said, after a while. "Damn Dad's paper mill and my stubbornness and the mess I made of—of us."

"You were right last night, Sherry." He tried to talk easily, reasonably. "We can't let the past drag us back." But even as Phil spoke he knew such advice was futile. At the moment his legs felt weighted with lead and a knot was tightening in his stomach. (What had that specialist in Washington told him about tension and the ulcer that was beginning in his duodenum? The weird thought crossed his

mind that if he didn't have children at least he could have ulcers.)
"Why did you tell me now, Sherry?"

She looked up at him. "Because I hoped you might still care
about what becomes of me, about what I'd gone through for us,
about—about asking me again."

"Of course I care about what happens to you. I could only want
the best——"

"Don't talk about me as if I were one of your underdeveloped nations!"

"And I care about the rough time you had."

"But is that *all* about the future, Phil: good wishes and
good-by?"

"I didn't say good-by."

"But I don't want good wishes, either. I want you, Phil."

He released her from his arm gently as she sat up on the sofa.
"Is that why you told me about the abortion, Sherry—so that pity,
or guilt, or both, would convince me we need each other?"

She nodded. "Maybe, partly that."

He stood again. He felt tall and awkward and very old in this
bright, plush room. "Death is a strange base to build a life on," he
said softly.

"Death?" Her eyebrows arched, widening the blue eyes which
were clear of tears now.

"You killed the only living thing——"

"How can you say that, when it hadn't even been born, hadn't
even . . ." She paused.

"It was life," he said. He did not realize that the central belief
he had been taught as a child, the faith which infused his parents'
existence separately as individuals and together as makers of a family, was reasserting itself now through him—and this was a belief
and faith in the possibilities of life.

"Phil," she said, "I need you."

He walked the length of the room, and realizing how he once
dreamed of this moment as the pinnacle of happiness he wondered
at his total lack of pleasure now, even the pleasure of triumph or
revenge for the hurt Sherry Austin had dealt him in the past. How

could he answer her? What was his responsibility to her, to himself, to what had happened?

"I could help you in Washington——"

"I may not be there long," he said absently, seeking in his mind some solution to this moment. "When this Senate term expires, I may not run again."

"But you have to!" she cried. "You couldn't possibly give up being a senator to come back here——"

He looked at her, made attentive by the vehemence of her outburst. "Of course I could," he said slowly, deliberately, "if I didn't think I were useful, had some talent for the Senate. If I didn't think I'd win the race——"

"You'll win," she said. She was genuinely alarmed now and all at once Phil wondered if it were not the only genuine emotion she had shown all evening. "If you don't give up before you begin," she urged. "There's so much to be done in Washington, darling."

"There's a lot to be done here in Nantahala." Even as he stated the obvious, he could see that yesterday and today had made it obvious to him in a way he had not heretofore experienced. Now that he had stated aloud the idea of not returning to Washington—more as a gesture of modesty, a recognition of possibility, than as any clear-cut plan—he saw that it had certain advantages. He also saw that Sherry would not agree on their being advantages.

"Phil, you're teasing." She sat on the edge of the sofa now, watching his face intently. "Washington is the hub of the world. You couldn't bear to come back here——"

"You said it, I didn't."

"In Washington you help shape the world."

"I don't seem to be doing such a remarkable job running my own——"

"Phil!" She spoke impatiently. "We could have such a wonderful life in Washington."

He whirled and looked at her. "Is it Washington you want to marry, Sherry? Washington—or me?"

They looked at each other.

Somewhere in another part of the house a chime clock struck the hour and they could hear its faint echoes.

Phil sighed heavily and shook his head. He strode across the room and sat down beside her and took that beautifully preserved face which reflected her utter selfishness between his two large hands. "Sherry . . . Sherry . . ." As of this moment he could actually look at her with pity. "When will you ever find what you want? When will you know?"

"I want you."

He shook his head. "What can I do for you? Where can I take you? Another place, another time—it's what we don't have that's always best, isn't it?"

She was very pale. Phil wondered if she might not have looked like this when she came from the greedy doctor's office that August day several years ago. He took his hands away from her face, not having found an answer to his question, not expecting it, because no one knew the answer.

"Sherry," he said, "people are not to be used. They're not tools or weapons or gadgets or playthings, for you or anyone else."

"Spare me, Senator," she said. "Spare me your wisdom. Just tell me where we stand now, you and I."

"I don't know where we stand, Sherry——" he said.

"But not together?"

He did not have to answer.

Years ago she had told him that when she was a little girl, she had often had tantrums and then her father would try to punish whatever had provoked her and he would comfort her with gifts. Phil was reminded of this now because Sherry looked as if she might explode in a torrent of furious crying or hysterical laughter. "Sherry —don't," he said.

"Don't?" she repeated. Her voice trembled, but she kept it under control. She stood up and padded in soft stocking feet to the table beside her bed. From the lacquer box there she took a cigarette and lit it with the automatic lighter that matched the box. She drew a long deep pull of smoke into her lungs and released it in a blue haze. Then she thrust open the little drawer in her bedside table. An array of bottles and prescription boxes nestled there. She picked up one, then another. "This is to help you sleep. This is to keep you awake. This little friend tranquilizes. This one peps you up. It all comes in a bottle now, Phil-baby."

"Sherry, you have so much, everything. For God's sake, there's no need for you to——"

"You know, darling, you yourself don't come off Boy Scout clean on this charge of using people." She almost giggled, then caught herself with an effort. "Cool it, Sherry, cool it," she said to herself.

"I know," he replied. "But we can't set one wrong right by plunging into another mistake." Echoing what he had said earlier that day, in a quite different, yet similar, situation, he went on. "I don't like to be blackmailed."

"What are you talking about?"

"Blackmailed by fear or pride or ambition—or love. Or maybe sex would be a more accurate word."

She went back to the sofa and sat down and leaning her rich dark head against the white back blew a stream of smoke up toward the sparkling chandelier on the ceiling. "Good night, Phil," she said.

"Good night, Sherry."

His quick pickup of her dismissal seemed to alarm her. She said in a rush, "I'll never have any more children, you know."

He thought it an odd phrase—"Any more." "Of course you will," he said.

"I can't," she stated flatly. "Diagnosis by the best gynecologists in New York and Nantahala. My fat little friend in the city that August . . . he fixed me but good." Then, when he was silent, not knowing what possible words to say to her, she asked harshly, "How do you like them apples?"

"I don't, Sherry."

"O.K., Phil. Now you know the whole rotten bit. I wouldn't have told you this last, you know, if you'd asked me to marry you." Her eyes were glittering.

"You'd have waited till after we were married?"

"I'd have let you find out for yourself." Then, looking straight at him. "Do you have a girl now, Phil?"

"Sure, I guess so. You know how it is——"

"Don't put me on. I mean one. Is there One, Phil?"

Suddenly he knew there was, someone who would not even invite him in out of the snow. He nodded.

She took a last drag on her cigarette and mashed out the stub between her fingers. "Good night, Phil."

At the door he tried to find something coherent to say. "Believe me, Sherry, I want everything good for you. It's just that I don't have it in my power to give. For a few dollars you can buy an airplane ticket to Washington. It's a better bargain than I'd ever be— with all that's behind us, Sherry."

When she didn't answer, he pulled the door shut behind him.

Just as it closed he heard her say, low and brittle, "And damn you, chickadee."

He drove down the long winding road that led off the hilltop, and he thought: She'll get her wish. I feel damned already. At the gate he passed Miles Austin and his wife in their car. Miles Austin threw up his hand in a friendly salute. "And he'll never have a grandson," Phil muttered. "His blood line will stop right here, with this generation of hungry Austins. Virgin timber all gone. Virgins all gone." He didn't think the play on words was very clever. In fact, he didn't feel very clever, or very proud of himself in any way just now.

When he had put the car in Ivy's garage, he walked toward the house. The air hung heavy with dampness following the long day's rain. Against the increased roar of the stream in front of the house, he could hear the steady drip of moisture from rhododendron leaves along the path. He noticed Clay's sport car sitting out on the graveled parking space beside the garage. Inside the car the glow from a lighted cigarette was momentarily visible. Phil turned and went back.

"Clay?" He leaned in the open window.

"Who'd you think it was? Dracula?" Clay asked, but his tone was not as light as his words. "How's everything at the club tonight?"

"Clubby," Phil said. It seemed a long time since he'd come from the club. "What are you doing out here anyway?"

Clay pushed the wide felt hat back from his forehead. "Missy and me"—he patted the steering wheel heavily, fondly—"we're keeping each other company."

"It's pretty late."

"Don't you fret about me. I'm going across the creek and sleep at old Kin's tonight anyway. Just don't fret a minute about me, Senator."

"If that's the way you want it . . . but don't forget about tomorrow morning: bright and early and sober."

"Good night, Senator. . . . Phil."

CHAPTER 10
Today

THE ROOM was not even a courtroom. It was a shabby, dimly lit, crowded cave at the top of steep stairs. The treads of the stairs were worn and cupped in the middle and layers of dirt, city grime, country mud, had gathered in the corners. The office of the sessions judge who would hear Clay's case and determine its further disposition was permeated with the smell and color and feel of usage, years of usage—heavy feet trampling and shuffling, wetted forefingers turning the pages of dusty books, uneasy bodies tilting back and forth in the varnished chairs, spittle, sweat and dust.

Frone took one look around the room, at the massive black roll-top desk crammed to overflowing with papers, notes, yellowed clippings which spilled out of its rows of pigeonholes and half-open drawers, at the floor-to-ceiling glass-enclosed cabinets filled with row after row of fat law books, at the rickety chairs with cracks in their faded leather seats, and at the dingy single-bulb lamp brooding over the desk and the splattered spittoon beside the desk. She patted her felt sailor hat more firmly into place. "For this," her gesture implied, "for this sanctuary of justice we forsook the clean warmth of our beds, risked indigestion rushing through breakfast, we planned and prayed and agonized over the weekend."

The two with her, Ivy and Kin, stopped at the door. Phoebe had not come to face this Monday morning with them. "Somebody has to stay with Mama. Naomi isn't here yet. I'll volunteer." But no one was arguing with her. She stayed.

Phil and Clay had stopped by Hugh Moore's office on the lower floor of this old brick building next to the courthouse. "We'll see if that high and mighty gentleman is honoring us with his presence yet."

Clay had shaved very carefully this morning and dressed in a dark grey suit and a shirt with a button-down collar. Kin had grinned. "Clay, you don't favor yourself today, as Aunt Tildy used to say." They all knew what he meant.

At breakfast they had been careful with concern for one another: sober, thoughtful, trying to put one another at ease but passing the salt a little too quickly when one asked for it, pouring hot coffee a little too frequently when no one wanted it. They had made attempts at humor which died in mid-air, leaving them with averted eyes, not daring to look at one another. Drawn together in common bond against some outside threat, they tried feebly and unsuccessfully to find a gesture, a word, that would reveal the swell of inner affection and loyalty that each felt for the others. Phil, listening to their half-finished sentences, interrupting their faraway glances, was irritated by their unsophisticated solicitude for one another. They had been relieved when it was time to start in to town.

The smell of the office was stale to Ivy. She loosened her coat and longed for a fresh breath.

Kin waited, large and awkward, patient and hopeful, just inside the door, dangling a new hat in his great stubby fingers. The trim little secretary who had told them to come on into the inner office squeezed through the door past Kin before he saw her and jumped hastily to one side.

"Judge Anders," she said, as she approached the desk. Then she added a fresh pile of papers to those already waiting in a dozen mounds.

She went out and the elderly man at the desk swung his swivel chair around abruptly and placed the tips of his fingers together, tentlike, over his paunchy stomach. He wore antique steel-rimmed glasses and behind their tiny oblong lenses his eyes were keen, alert. "Come in, come in. Where's Clay Thurston?"

Ivy remembered the times she had seen Judge Anders through her life, at political rallies or school meetings or public forums where bonds for a new water system or sewage-treatment plant or plans to implement (or delay) school integration were being debated—and although she had not remembered any single statement he made on any of those occasions, she realized that his very presence had always lent them an air of stability and reasoned calm. "Ivy Cortland," she said, and introduced her sister and brother to him, too.

Judge Anders half-rose from his chair, as if making a gesture to the formalities of courtesy before reconsidering and sinking back to his seat and the more pressing formalities of law.

"Clay and my son Phil stopped downstairs to come with the lawyer."

"Hugh Moore?" the judge asked. His voice was high-pitched and he spoke rapidly.

Frone answered this time. "Yes. He's sort of a cousin of ours."

"I know. I know." The judge nodded, patting the tent of his fingers up and down on his stomach. Then, in an apparent attempt to relieve some of their tension, he said to Frone, "You're the one that married the Yankee, aren't you?"

She nodded. "Ivy and I. But I went all the way, moved to Connecticut to live."

"You're a long way from home." The old man seemed to take in at a glance her sensible flat shoes, plain brown coat, hair drawn into a tight knot beneath the sailor-style hat. "But your accent hasn't turned New England. Trace of mountain still around the edges."

"Still around my edges, too," Frone said, and the judge grinned briefly.

"I used to walk with Mr. Cortland"—he swung toward Ivy—"up in the Smokies, before you were married, before anyone had ever thought about there being a national park there. He was a great hand for exploring, Mr. Cortland was. Exploring where he was."

Ivy felt a catch in her throat. The judge had said it so well: an explorer where he was.

"I know you, too." The steel-rimmed glasses were focused on Kin, as Judge Anders continued his effort to relax their concern and uneasiness. "You set out some Catawba rhododendron around my house, eight, maybe ten years ago."

"Did it live?" Kin asked, his shyness giving way before his interest in the shrubs he had rerooted.

The judge nodded. "You did a dandy job, Thurston. The only Catawba rhododendron I know that's been transplanted to town and survived. Regular showpieces. You'll have to come by my place next June, see your handiwork in bloom."

"I'd like that."

There was a pause. Slowly Ivy and the others became aware of another presence in the room. Someone stood near the back, someone quiet, unassuming, watching them closely. Ivy almost jumped when she saw him.

"Well"—the judge leaned back in his chair until only the tips of his toes touched the floor—"your brother better be coming on. We've news for him."

Ivy felt her pulse pound and a lump filled her throat.

The old man looked past them into the shadowy depths of the room. He made an almost imperceptible gesture with his head.

The stranger came forward and they saw that he and the shadows were the same dusky shade. As he came nearer, Ivy and Frone scrutinized him more closely. There was something oddly familiar about him.

He was a slim man, tall, stripped to leanness by years of hard work and coarse food, and something else, too: a rigid inner discipline of self, holding under tight rein any outward betrayal of anger, fear, approval, hope. His hair was combed back dark and thick from a high forehead, and his light-colored eyes were clear and carefully expressionless as they gazed levelly out at the world. He wore spotless faded olive-green trousers and a brown wool jacket with patches sewed neatly on each elbow. High-top tennis shoes gave a certain spring to his steps, so that when he came up to where the others stood his body seemed at once taut and supple. Ivy, watching him, thought of a bowstring, tense and tight yet capable of bending under great pressure, giving and enduring. Ivy felt some recognition stir in her memory. Was it the backward thrust of those thin shoulders that seemed familiar?

Before the judge could continue, Clay's and Hugh Moore's voices resounded up the stairwell and through the open door.

"I can hold my liquor, at least," the lawyer was saying irritably, panting as he climbed.

"Show me a man who can hold his liquor and I'll show you a man with a serious bladder condition," Clay answered. His laugh was too loud, too quick.

Frone flushed, embarrassed and angry. There was no sound in the dim office until the two latecomers appeared at the door. Then Clay's flush matched Frone's. Hugh Moore began to talk.

"Good morning, Judge Anders. Frone, Ivy, Kin." He managed to ignore the stranger even while looking straight at him. "Cousin Phil will be along in a minute. Judge, I guess the sheriff has acquainted you with the facts. Is the sheriff here?"

"Sheriff Doggett had to go to the other end of the county just before daylight this morning," the judge said.

Hugh Moore glanced up from papers he was sorting in his brief case. "Anything serious?" he asked. Ivy could not help feeling that he seemed to sniff the air, pointing to trouble, and business, like an old retriever.

"Man stomped his wife to death along about midnight."

"That's serious." Hugh Moore glanced around to see whether anyone was smiling. No one was. He turned back to the steel-rimmed glasses. "My client here before you, Judge Anders, is Clay Thurston. We ask that the warrant against him be dismissed."

The judge leaned back even farther. He motioned for everyone to be seated. They sat abruptly in chairs nearest them, Clay and the lawyer directly before the judge. Only the stranger remained standing, dark and self-contained, stiff and yet relaxed.

"Who's he?" Clay asked.

Ivy smiled. Trust Clay not to ignore him, she thought. Hate him, curse him, help him, use him, yes—but never ignore him.

"I'm the man killed Hawk Williams," he said, softly yet distinctly.

Their surprise made a pool of silence like the pool of pale light that fell from the lamp onto the vast disorder of the desk below. They were not prepared for this calm assertion of violence, this proud assumption of guilt.

"You're the one did what?" Clay demanded.

"The man"—his voice shaded the word with all sorts of unstated dimensions—"the man who shot and killed Hawk Williams."

Ivy and Frone and Kin looked at one another and a tentative relief and thankfulness blended in their expressions.

"You couldn't have!" Clay blurted. "You weren't even there."

Frone bit her lip. Hugh Moore frowned in annoyance. "See here, Clay——"

"This is my hearing," the judge interrupted mildly. "I grant you that I am no stickler for formality, but perhaps we should go about this in somewhat orderly fashion." He straightened his chair. His feet were firmly on the floor. "Do you have counsel?" he asked the stranger.

"I can speak the truth for myself," he answered.

"Speak the truth for yourself, let your lawyer lie for you," Clay muttered. He glared at Hugh Moore.

Deftly the judge picked a paper off the desk without disturbing any of the rest of the accumulation. "The sheriff says you came in voluntarily Sunday morning and signed a confession of killing Hawk Williams."

"Yes, sir." He showed them nothing by his expression, told them with words only what he wanted them to know.

"And you"—the judge peered at Clay—"came in voluntarily four days before, and said you had killed Hawk Williams?"

Clay nodded. His face was angry, miserable, puzzled at memory of the experience. "I wasn't sure. I thought I could have. I guess I was pretty well liquored up, Judge."

Ivy recognized signs of the truculence that had occasionally flared up when he was younger, a truculence born of resentment at being questioned, at being treated as a child. Always at those times it had seemed he would rather be punished than be questioned about his actions. He could take physical pain for anything he had done, but he did not want to analyze it. Clay could be whipped, she thought, but he did not want to be condescended to or "understood." He would make physical atonement quickly, almost gladly, taking the pain gallantly for any real or imagined wrong he had committed. But he did not want to think about it, accept any intellectual or spiritual knowledge and anguish. "Let's get it over with," he had always said, as a boy, to Papa or a teacher whenever they had to chastise him; as a man, to an employer or a lover whenever they had to part with him. Over. Finished. Behind. Forgotten. Ivy knew this was what he was thinking now, how he was reacting.

"I knew how I felt about old Hawk," Clay told the judge. "I knew I *could* have done what they said. And once I knew *that* it wasn't hard to believe I might really have done it."

The stranger nodded. Ivy felt that he and Clay were bound together in a way none of the rest of them could understand. "But you didn't," he said softly.

"Who are you, anyway?" Clay barked at him, and his tone was equal parts irritation and admiration.

"My name is Homer Bludsoe."

Ivy leaned back in her chair. Her hands, in their soft kid gloves, were clasped tightly in her lap. So that was it! she thought. Memory of sun falling through beech leaves and the heat of a Saturday afternoon, the sound of a loaded wagon creaking down Thickety Creek road on a Sunday morning, flashed through her mind. The boy behind his father and mother on the wagon never looked to back or side, but he sat straight and tense—like a bowstring!

"You're Morg Bludsoe's boy," she said.

He looked at her, not quite concealing his surprise, and nodded. "Grandson of Big Matt Bludsoe," he added.

"You used to live at the head of Thickety Creek."

"When I was a boy. Before I started to school," he said.

Then Frone and Clay and Kin also understood who he was, remembering Preacher Grey and the Bludsoe wrestling match and Papa and things that had happened a long time back.

"Your father and mother and sister, you're the ones," Frone said, then finished lamely, "who moved to town."

"That's right."

"Was town better?" Ivy asked. Suddenly it seemed to her important that she should have an answer to this question. She had wanted to know for a long time.

"No," Homer Bludsoe said slowly. "Not better. Not worse either. Different."

"Were you sorry you moved?"

"Sorry—and glad." It seemed he would give them no final, clear-cut, definitive answer. "I got some schooling anyway. Not as good as lots of folks in town had, not as bad as the nothing I'd have gotten on Devil's Brow mountain. Betwixt and between. Just town. All our folks coming to it sooner or later. My family just come to it a little sooner."

Ivy was disappointed. She realized that all these years she had harbored in her mind the hope that Morg Bludsoe and his family had found some pot of gold at the end of their move from the wild hard-scrabble farm above Devil's Brow to the promises and progress of town. She had hoped that somehow the city would make up for all of those injustices and deprivations the valley had inflicted, wittingly or unwittingly, on the Bludsoes. And now she knew that instead of great strides of atonement, there had been, for the Bludsoes, only a small inching along on the road to fulfillment. "I'm sorry," she said, hating the inadequacy of the words.

When she looked up, Phil was standing at the door. They had not heard him come upstairs. His height, his shoulders, seemed to fill the doorway just as the outside freshness that swept in with him seemed to fill the room. The momentary interruption was welcome. Phil and the judge greeted each other, spoke of Governor Wentworth and a mutual friend in Washington, and Ivy realized that now her son knew more not only of other cities and the world but even more of Nantahala County and the state than she did.

"How's everything going here?" Phil asked, looking at Clay.

Clay had left his chair and was walking across the room nervously. "Well, if we can get through old-home week," he said, "maybe we can find out what the hell happened to poor old Hawk. This fellow here, Bludsoe, claims he killed him."

Judge Anders assumed authority again. "You want to tell us now or do you want to wait for your lawyer?" he asked Homer Bludsoe.

"I'll say now," the man replied. As he spoke, he looked at none of them directly but over their heads at shelf upon shelf of law books lining the walls of the room. "Easy to say, hard to understand. My wife and me, we raised up four children, all good, respectable folks. Nothing high and mighty, but respectable. We saw to it that every last one finished up high school, and when the oldest three couldn't get any jobs around here, we bought their tickets to Cleveland and Chicago and they found theirselves good paying jobs. A girl and two boys, all married now with nice houses painted up neat and trim, respectable. But that youngest girl, when her time come to finish up school, seems like we couldn't bring ourselves to part with her. We kept her home." He sighed.

They listened as attentively as if he told a story of high adventure. Ivy wondered at the intensity of feeling Homer Bludsoe could put into this little chronicle of everyday events.

"We oughtn't to a-held her," he went on, his tone changing as subtly as if he had shifted to some minor key. "We might a-known she was too pretty, too lively, to keep to ourselves. But we tried. And for our trying she took up with him. With Hawk Williams."

"The damn——" Clay exclaimed, then broke off.

"No matter all our pleading and threatening, she moved out from under our roof, away from our board, and I figure he paid for the little old room she went to live in. A room in a trashy night-time place, a cheap honky-tonk, it was. How could a girl like that, our little girl, with schooling in her head and love at home, go off and live in a hole, a hellhole like that?"

Since the question was not addressed to them but to the pounds of silent books beyond him, they did not try to answer his painful plea.

"She was there three months. Sometimes he beat her up. And her mother and me sat there at home looking at one another, going crazy. Crazy grief. Crazy fear. Crazy." He shook his head lightly, as if to break out of a nightmare. "Once when he whipped her, she called the police, but when they got there he'd gone. And the police looked at one another and laughed. Told her she better forget 'that one.' To them it was just 'nigger fighting.' No police take that serious." After a moment Bludsoe said, "Nobody to protect my girl. I had to."

He paused. The judge was not looking at Homer Bludsoe but at the Thurstons. And Phil was looking at all of them, his mind leaping ahead to the conclusion of this grim and ugly episode, wondering how he could help bring it to some useful conclusion.

"A feller like Hawk"—the low, clear voice spoke on—"there's no words, no threat, no begging, no human talk, can reach him. Only locked up, or dead: they the only ways to take hold of his mind. I hadn't no way of putting him under lock and key."

"Surely the sheriff, somebody——" Frone began. Ivy wondered if she had been in Connecticut so long that she had forgotten how it could be here.

But Homer Bludsoe was reminding her. "No white law to do much about a black man hurting a black girl. And Hawk, he had strings he could pull in this town."

"You mean Hawk had more influence than you?" Frone demanded.

For the first time Homer Bludsoe looked directly at them, at each of them, and a cry burst from his throat. "Don't none of you know? Don't none of you know anything? All that's tearing apart this world today between black and white, and you still don't see? You still don't hear? You still don't know?"

There was a brief silence. The word "know" seemed to reverberate softly from the corners of the room. Then Judge Anders said easily, naturally, "All right. They're trying to know now. We all are. Now suppose you finish up telling us about you and Hawk."

Homer Bludsoe looked away, as if regretting his brief lapse of control. "Not much more to tell. Last Tuesday evening just before sundown I found my girl on the steps of our house. Her arm— her right arm, too—it was broken. And when I seen her there, like a little dove or mocker with a broken wing, I knew what I had to do. It wasn't hard to find out where old Hawk was. He'd bragged it up all around town how he was going to take a hunting party of white men out for drinking and feasting up on the mountain that night. I got my gun and found where they were. By the time I got there they was mostly all high as a rocket. All but Hawk. He was passing out his white lightning, mouthing his dirty tales, fixing some kind of meat over the fire. I was right in front of him in the bushes, and when he was all alone by the fire I shot him. He jerked up kind of surprised-like, and then he fell down, splattered with blood. He never even seen who done it."

They sat looking at him, waiting.

"I come on home."

No one spoke.

"I wasn't running," Homer Bludsoe said to the judge. "I just come home. I come on home and told my wife to make up our girl's bed again. She'd be living home again now. I put away my gun. The next morning I went on to work."

"You weren't scared or sorry about what you'd done?" Hugh Moore asked, with his professional lawyer's tone.

"There wasn't no good way out of a mess like that," Homer Bludsoe answered patiently. "But then later I heard that Mr. Clay Thurston was under arrest for the killing I'd done."

"Why didn't you just lay low and see what happened?" Hugh Moore suggested.

The slim taut stranger was looking back at the books again, as though there were some secret he could bury there, or find there. "My Bludsoe folks, nobody rightly knows who they were, back when the generations was starting. But my pappy and my grandpappy, they wouldn't say they were Negro because they were ashamed of that. And they wouldn't say they were white because they were afraid of that. When they first brought me to town, I didn't know whether I was country or city. I turned it all over in my mind a lot, this way of separating people, and I determined one thing: A man's got to be whatever he is without shame or fear."

Ivy noticed that Phil, too, was listening intently to this dark man who possessed his measure of dignity in this world. In the background of her memory she could still hear those wagon wheels jolting down the Thickety road and hear Papa calling, "Good luck!"

"So just like I was taking medicine to heal me of sickness, I purged myself of shame and of fear," he went on, stating it as sim-

ply as if he had emptied an old pocket of burdensome trifles. "The
only place I could begin was inside myself. I can't be ashamed or
afraid of myself. I'm a good brick mason. I make my own way. And
that's why I had to step out and say I killed Hawk Williams."

"Just like that?" Hugh Moore asked, and the overtone of sarcasm and disbelief in his voice made Ivy ashamed for him, for all
of them. As Homer Bludsoe had demanded only a moment ago,
couldn't he hear what was being said?

Bludsoe was looking straight at the lawyer now, however, and
he said in a hard, clear voice, "I know that a black man and a white
man are equal, Mr. Moore. And being equal, I can't let no other
man pay my debts."

The office was very quiet. A large green fly buzzed on one of the
window sills. Ivy thought: They had said to themselves that Bludsoe was a Negro like Hawk Williams. He was a Negro—like himself. The casual cruelty and unintentional callousness of even their
(hers, her family's, all white people's) best intentions was apparent
to her once more. To allow each man his own personality: this was
the only equality, the irreducible minimum—and maximum—of
dignity. This was what Homer Bludsoe demanded. Perhaps it was
even what poor Hawk Williams fought for in his cruel, perverted
way. All at once she felt a surge of gratitude to this slight, iron-
willed, quiet man—Homer Bludsoe—who would not be less than a
man, or permit those around him to be less.

"Well, we've let the trail go cold somewhere," Hugh Moore said
sourly. "I don't reckon we're here to argue what's equal and what's
unequal. A warrant for——"

"Shut up, Hugh." Phil stood up and, although he spoke to the
lawyer, he was still looking at the brown man. "You get a lawyer,
Homer Bludsoe," he said. "And tell him to send me his bill." He
held out his hand.

The other man took it tentatively. "I'm much obliged, Senator,
but seems like I couldn't accept——"

"Equals have to accept from one another, as well as give," Phil
said. But to himself he was wondering if this might not be essentially the same gesture that he and Clay had made at the home of
Hawk Williams' widow a couple of nights ago, when they had dis-

tributed coins and offers of welfare. Bludsoe had committed the murder all right, but wasn't he, the Senator, trying to buy off his own guilt for a larger, older crime that had helped perhaps to make this immediate one possible? He had had his eyes opened abroad. Why had he found it so difficult to open them here at home?

As if answering his very thought, Bludsoe said, "We all have to pick up our own load."

"I never heard so much talk," Clay burst forth, as if from a trance, "so many dam-busting words in all my life. It just leaves me blinking worse than a billy goat in a hailstorm. Take the big senator's help, you poor bastard . . ." Clay suddenly threw his arm around Homer Bludsoe's shoulder. The shoulders that had stiffened at the white man's words relaxed again under this impulsive comradeship.

"I'll see about it," Homer Bludsoe conceded.

Clay's leathery, well-manicured hand slapped him easily, twice, on the shoulder blade. "You do that."

Hugh Moore's lower lip jutted in surly petulance. "If you don't mind, I'd like to get this 'hearing' cleared up and be about my business. May we assume, your Honor, that the warrant against Clay Thurston is dismissed?"

"You may," Judge Anders replied.

"Then I take it my presence here is no longer needed."

"You take right," Clay answered. Now that his own danger had passed, he was like a schoolboy dismissed early from class. "And you better take your presence out of reach of this old cannonball." He flexed his muscle.

"Clay!" Phil spoke sharply.

The judge leaned back in his old chair again and suppressed a smile. He motioned for Clay to put down his arm. The judge's vest had wrinkled up above the swell of his stomach and an expanse of shirt was visible in the gap between vest and trousers. "I think we'd better let Mr. Moore go under his own power," he said to Clay.

Clay went to the window at the far end of the room. "Send me a bill, Hugh, for your trouble," he said.

He stood there while Hugh Moore finished his transactions with the judge and stalked out, taking leave of no one. Clay still stood there as the judge gave Homer Bludsoe a summary of the procedures that lay ahead of him.

When the judge had finished speaking, Ivy said, "I'll have the bail bond I signed for my brother transferred to Homer Bludsoe."

"All right," Judge Anders said.

"Then you can go home till the grand jury hearing," she said to Bludsoe. "I'll come by to see your wife and daughter."

For the first time they saw a reaction from Homer Bludsoe. "We'd be much obliged for that. She's really a good girl. Her grades in school, they was always the best of any of our kids. This—this trouble, it was like a sickness. Talking with somebody like you might help her get over it."

"I'll come," Ivy said.

She and the others shook hands with Judge Anders. Phil felt their relief and relaxation matching his own. He regarded the slim, proud stranger who had assumed the burden of guilt and he hoped that he himself could carry his own burdens as well.

"I wonder if you know," Judge Anders was saying to them, "this office here, it used to belong to an ancestor of yours."

"No," Frone said. "We didn't know."

"This used to be Robert Moore's law office. Wasn't he kin to your mother?"

"He was her uncle," Ivy said. She looked around the room again. "Frone and I remember Great-uncle Robert well."

"I'm glad," the judge said.

"I never knew before where his office was," Ivy said.

"This was where he kept his books and papers," the judge went on. "I suspect his real law office was in his head. And his spirit."

Ivy nodded.

"Well, Senator"—Judge Anders held out his hand to Phil—"you could do worse than take some of Robert Moore's spirit up to Washington. And whenever you get ready to run for that Senate seat for a full term, come to see me."

"I will," Phil said, meeting old Judge Anders' incorruptible gaze.

"Well, Judge," Clay said, making ready to leave the ancient grimy office, "we were right up to the lick-log that time, weren't we?"

"I'm glad the facts came clear," Judge Anders said tersely. Phil noticed that he said the facts, not the truth.

Outside the office building they stepped into the chilly grey October day. Monday morning, the day and hour they had dreaded so long, was behind them, and neither the chill nor the greyness could reach them. They looked at one another and smiled, and tears filled Frone's and Ivy's eyes. Yesterday's rain had stopped, but Saturday's high autumnal brilliance had disappeared, too. Winter's bite edged the air.

Phil was waylaid on the sidewalk by the reporter who had been out to see him yesterday. "I was afraid I might be too late," the young fellow panted. "They sent me out to cover an accident——"

"Take it easy." Phil smiled at him. He drew a long envelope out of the inner pocket of his coat. "You're too late for the hearing. No news there anyway." (He spoke casually, stalling this eager beaver from getting to Homer Bludsoe, at least for the moment.) "But I told you I'd try to give you something for the paper today. Here are some notes I made before breakfast."

"That's swell, Senator." He took the envelope.

"You can find a headline there if you look," Phil said. "And good luck, fellow." With the old rush act, he began to steer his mother toward their car parked before a nearby meter.

As they drove home, Phil told her of his plans, plans he had worked out during the sleepless night.

"I want you to come to Washington for a visit right away, get to know Ann Howard better. I'm going to marry her."

Ivy tried quickly to adjust her thoughts from the crisis they had just weathered, tried to recall every detail of Ann Howard's appearance. Light shining hair, a skin almost translucent in its clear coloring, handsome features except for cheekbones a trifle too high, a bony structure too pronounced. But these were all trivia, beauty or plainness that would change with time and alter with circumstance. Of the inner stuff of Ann Howard she knew little, but she sensed a great deal.

"That is, if she'll have me," Phil was finishing.

"She will," Ivy said. She wondered if this were only a mother's confidence speaking. Then she added calmly, "She's no Sherry Austin. She'll give once—and for good. And take once and for all."

Phil flushed, surprised, and glanced at her. But his mother was looking straight ahead and said nothing more.

"As for that damned report"—he shifted to less tricky ground—"I'd hoped to build my fame and name on it, but looks like I'll have to settle for some good infighting that nobody will ever hear about, that may help some little fellow halfway across the world."

Ivy nodded. "That's all right."

"I think the other two have already agreed on the big points. But I can question till perhaps they'll all remember next time what I was trying to say about those damned countries and our possibilities there—not as cold-war contenders but as concerned human citizens."

"That's the way we'll win, Phil," Ivy said. "By forgetting our image and our score on some popularity poll, and never selling the future short."

"It's immoral," Phil said slowly, "to use people for our own purposes. I found that out. Yet we do it all the time—as individuals, nations, ideologies, and we destroy the reason for life."

"Which is . . . ?" she asked.

"The fulfillment of life. Each to its highest potential." His eyes felt strained, they burned from lack of rest last night. But he peered through the windshield as he drove carefully and he seemed to see everything with unusual clarity.

Lightly she laid her hand—ungloved now, large and veined and tough-fibered—on his arm. "I only wish your father could have lived longer. So much pride, so much joy. I'd like to share it with someone."

By the time Phil and Ivy reached home, Clay was already there with Kin and Frone. His car was stopped at the narrowest part of the drive, and one door was standing open.

"He must have been in a hurry to let them out," Ivy said.

As they went in the front door, Phil and Ivy could hear Phoebe crying. "Poor old Mama," she was saying, the words lurching out between sobs, "poor old Mama."

Ivy looked up the stairway. Naomi stood at the top. She shook her head, indicating that there was no need for Ivy up there. She made a motion for her to go on in to the others.

They were standing awkwardly around the room. Phoebe, in front of the fireplace, was crying into her rose-colored handkerchief, and the others wore expressions ranging from gravity to guilt.

"Mama had a bad spell while we were gone," Frone said. "It scared Phoebe."

"Of course it scared me," Phoebe flared. "It might not worry any of the rest of you, but it hurts me to see Mama suffer. She was gasping, she could hardly breathe or speak to me, Ivy, and she was as white as death——"

Ivy was pulling off her hat and coat and gloves. "Go check your plane reservation," she said to Phil.

He was glad to leave the room. "I'll finish getting my things together . . ."

Ivy hurried out, too. "I'll go up and see Mama . . ."

"Oh, I phoned the doctor," Phoebe called after her. "I did exactly what he said. She's had the emergency medicine, and a sedative . . ."

But Ivy was already upstairs.

There was silence for a moment until Kin said, helpfully, hopefully, "Well, there's no more to worry about for Clay, Phoebe. He didn't have anything to do with that Hawk fellow's death after all." No one answered. Phoebe was wiping her eyes. "It was one of the Bludsoes used to live up above us on Thickety. That was kind of a funny thing, wasn't it?"

"So funny we're all splitting with laughter," Clay said. He took the last cigarette out of a package and crumpled the paper savagely.

"Well, as far as I'm concerned," Phoebe said, "we've all worried over Clay long enough. This whole weekend, the only visit we've had together in years, we've spent all our time and thought on Clay and his troubles. And poor old Mama lying up there dying!"

"No, Phoebe," Kin said, his weathered face growing pale and

stricken at the possibility, "Mama won't die just yet. I've got to tell her about my wild-flower garden when I finish it for Mr. Austin——"

"Well, she almost died this morning! And nobody here but me, and Naomi. I was scared half out of my mind."

"Not far to go," Clay muttered, letting a long stream of cigarette smoke flow from each nostril.

"Now look here"—Phoebe turned toward him, her neat little corseted body trembling with leftover fear and anger—"I've had about all of your wit and meanness I intend to take. You can drag yourself down in the gutter, it doesn't matter to you. You don't have any wife to be disgraced!"

"That's right, Phoebe. Kathleen got out while the getting was good."

"You don't even have a job to lose!"

"Looks like I don't have much of anything," he said.

"Well, you've still got the Thurston name," Phoebe said, "and you're doing all you can to disgrace that."

Clay did not rise to her anger. Each point she jabbed at him seemed to make him only more pensive. "Don't even have Old Blue, or Lightning. Or Count Basie. None of them any more. Not a single dog I can call and have it come running to me. Lord, Kin, you remember how we used to name everything that set foot on our place? You and me and the sawmill men. We knew every mule and ox, stray cat and hound, even some of the roosters and one or two of the foxes that got to stealing Mama's chickens—we had a name for everything."

Kin nodded. "Sure I remember, Clay."

"Names made everything personal, especially the nicknames," Clay went on. "Like everything belonged, had a place somewhere." He took a long pull on his cigarette and sat down suddenly on the sofa, staring out the window.

As if it were a signal, the others sat down, too. Frone reached down and massaged her ankles slowly. "When the rest of you get my age," she said, "maybe you'll——"

"Some of us will never be your age, Frone," Clay teased.

"Don't be too sure, Mister," Frone answered sharply. "Or maybe it's just as well to get old when you're supposed to as try to stay a boy when you're damn well past the age."

For three days past they had sought, in their trouble, all that united them. Now, in their relief, they discovered all that divided them.

"It wasn't to be a boy that I wanted to go on one last hunt," Clay said. "Damn it all, can't any of you understand just one little glimmer? Those last months up North there I got so I couldn't bear the sight or sound or thought of all those little lots I'd helped lay out, none of them big enough to cuss a cat on without getting fur in your mouth. Or those little houses I had helped build, throwing them together out of a pattern like Mama used to cut quilt pieces, all alike, out of a bolt of cloth. Those houses coming up everywhere, spreading like maggots over the countryside, and the people in them living like locusts, swarming over the country and never seeing it, never breathing the air or tasting the water, never feeling the ground beneath them—but devouring it. Crawling out, covering it, chewing it up. I couldn't bear it!"

"Well, you made a good living from it," Phoebe said.

"If you'd had sense enough to save any of your money . . ." Frone nodded.

"We didn't save anything," Clay cried. "Money nor anything else. They nor me, none of us. Not a damned thing. And that's why I got to thinking about going on one more hunt. I wanted to see wildness again, the beginning and the end of the world, get out in it, be part of it. I wanted everything sorted out clear and uncomplicated one more time: who was the 'we' and who was the 'they,' who was the hunter and what the hunted."

He didn't seem to notice Ivy come into the room, but the others looked at her questioningly.

"Mama's all right," she said. "She's under the sedative now. I think she'll be better when she wakes up."

Phoebe sighed. "She scared me so."

"Poor old Mama," Clay said. "I don't even have the nerve to go up and see her."

"Clay's telling us why he wanted to go on that fool hunt," Frone explained. She started to stand up. "Should we fix some lunch, Ivy?"

Ivy motioned her to sit back down. "Naomi will have it ready in a little while. She doesn't like anyone with her in the kitchen."

"The hunters used to be the kings of the mountain," Clay went on. "Big-hearted, hard-drinking, stout-fisted men, lords of the universe. I thought there were still some left."

Frone and Ivy looked at each other and Frone shrugged, still rubbing her ankles.

"And then I got home and found out there wasn't anybody left but riffraff with gizzards instead of hearts. They'd sprawled around cutting every bush bigger than a toothpick, dumping their slop jars into every creek and river, shooting at every bit of game bigger than a blue jay till, by God, it's about all gone! And you know why they'd go on my hunt with me?" Clay did not wait for an answer. "I promised them some of Hawk Williams' rotgut liquor."

"Fine bunch of friends you had," Phoebe said.

"That's what I'm telling you," Clay shouted. "They were nothing. They were dead. Zombies. Even old Hawk, mean and full of the devil's own wickedness, at least he could do *something* and do it right: he could make rotgut and he could bust a steer in the head or stick a pig in the throat and kill it. He had hate and anger gnawing at him. These others—little itches and twitches, that's all they know. Itches and twitches: by God, I'm a poet," he winked at them.

"You're crazy," Phoebe said.

"And selfish," Frone added. "How do you know what kinds of hunger blaze in other people, Clay? You think you're the only one——"

"Do I? Well, take my brother here. My good, kind, steady brother who's never caused anybody a minute of bother and worry, who's so good to Mama and to everybody. Do you hate, brother? Do you have any wrestling bouts with hate, love, pride, greed——" He broke off.

Kin was getting up slowly from his chair. He stood, in the neatly brushed, double-breasted suit he had worn to town, and he glared at Clay. "Whatever I have is my own," he said. "You've never known about it, and you never will." He turned deliberately and walked toward the door. Out in the hall, as he opened the outside door, out of their sight, he called back, "What gave you the right to feel so special, Clay? Like Phoebe says, why is it you that we always have to fret about?" And he shut the door behind him.

They were stunned. "You sure touched a raw nerve." Frone shook her head. She unpinned the sailor hat which she had forgotten until now. "I've got a splitting headache."

Phoebe was following Kin toward the door. "Poor Kin, you've hurt him. I'm going to go and talk to him. I'll try to bring him back for lunch, Ivy."

"Yes," Ivy said. "Tell him Phil's leaving this afternoon. It may be our last time all together for a while."

"And see if you can't *behave*," Phoebe flung back at Clay as she went out the door.

"What the hell's the matter with everybody?" Clay asked. He fumbled for another cigarette, remembered that he had finished the pack, and swore.

"You're a fine one to ask," Frone said. "You throw the harpoon and then wonder why we fight back."

"I didn't mean to hurt anybody. Honest to God, I came back here meaning never to hurt anybody again in my whole ever-loving life." He stood up and loosened his necktie with such a wrench that one of the buttons at his collar flew off. "Let it go," he waved his hand so grandly and tragically that Ivy felt a sudden hysterical impulse to laugh. She could not seem to find anything to say to any of them just now. The morning had been too full already.

"Clay, why don't you get on back to New Jersey or New York or wherever your last job was and get back to work again?" Frone spoke to him patiently, as to a child. "You work like a demon, Clay. Nobody can beat you at that. Why, Jud says——"

"Jud?" Her tone had galled him, and he turned to her furiously. "Who gives a good damn what Jud says? Who's he to be passing judgment on me or how I work, or don't work if I choose?"

"I'm just trying to pay you a compliment."

"Forget it. You pay me something with your right hand, I wind up owing something with my left. Forget the advice, and Jud's compliments, and all of it!"

"Well, I will," his older sister said. "And while I'm about it I'll

forget the next predicament you land in, and I'll forget to answer
one of those big rush telegrams asking for two, three hundred dollars to get you out of some jam, and I'll——"

"You do that," Clay answered. "You keep your little old shriveled-up dollars with your little old shriveled-up heart and soul. Why,
you're so drained and parched I'll bet a dollar to a doughnut you
haven't slept with Jud for so long he can't remember the last time."

When he hushed, there was a shocked silence. Ivy could not
bear to look at Frone's face.

"Poor bastard!" Clay uttered his last growl with the waning fury
of a baited bear. "If he wasn't such a frost-fried persimmon of a
man, I'd say he was one character had every right to go out and buy
himself a good lot of loving."

The silence seemed frozen. Then Frone spoke. "At least your
sister and Judson Mather have managed to have four sons. With
all your big he-man juice, where are your children, Mr. Thurston?"

Clay looked at her. Their gazes locked in inseparable suffering
and hate and love. He said wearily, "Where the rest of my life is,
down the drain."

Frone choked a cry back in her throat and plunged toward the
door. "How could you talk to me like that? Or make me hurt you
so?" She sobbed. "I always loved you best. Of all the family, you
and——" She rushed up the stairs.

The room was very still with only Clay and Ivy left.

"And then there were two," Clay said.

She did not know what to say to him. She moved about the
room, arranging, tidying, setting a book straight on the shelf here,
balancing a lampshade there, as unconscious of her movements as
of breathing.

Clay walked to the mantel. He picked up a delicate Dresden
figurine which stood at one end and quite deliberately he loosed it
from his fingers. It smashed to the hearth and shattered into a dozen
fragments.

Ivy looked at the broken Dresden and at Clay, and she was
frightened. She was frightened at her own anger boiling up in her,
and of something in Clay she could not comprehend.

"Put it back together, Ivy," he said. "You're so smart and neat. You think the world is all so well arranged. You live here in your pretty little room, and you make everything tidy. Well, deep down in the gut of it all, it's nothing but chaos." He said it triumphantly, as if in victory rather than defeat. He went on talking.

But Ivy was listening to what he was not saying as well as to what he was putting into words. And even as Clay spoke, as he seemed so positive, the question was in his eyes. His face was framed in doubt. "This is the way it is!" he shouted in words, and his whole being asked, "Isn't it? Is it? Am I right, Ivy? Tell me I'm wrong." Only someone who ached to believe in purpose, design, could disbelieve so fiercely.

But she was weary with the long ordeal of waiting and worry just past, and she could not fit her mood now to his. "Clay," she said finally, "you may be right. The beginning and end of it all may be just chaos. But I can hold out against it. I can impose my own little order wherever possible. I can look up . . ."

The words caught them like a trap. Old familiar words.

"Papa," Clay said. "Papa always said that. And he looked up, Ivy. And what happened, Ivy? The greenness is gone. The woods aren't there, the water's ugly. What happened to it all?"

"*We* happened to it, Clay," she said. "Papa cut it, sold it. We used it, lived on it. You did your share of hunting it clean. And Papa thought he was doing the right thing. We didn't think about it one way or the other. *We* happened to it, Clay."

"You're lying. We all loved this land. Where did it all go, Ivy? Up there in Jersey, down here in Nantahala——"

"Why, it went with you, Clay. Down the roads you helped survey. Down the streets you helped lay out. And down your gullet with a thousand drinks. Through your pockets like a sieve. That's where it went."

He shook his head, as if in pain. Then he said, "I was just looking for something bigger, better, all along the way." Suddenly he gave a dry laugh. "Say, maybe I found it right there at little old Oak Ridge. Maybe the secret and the joke was all there, wrapped in one."

Ivy shook her head.

Out in the kitchen Naomi dropped a pan lid. The noise brought Clay's and Ivy's eyes to the broken figurine on the hearth.

"I'm sorry, Ivy," he blurted.

And while she was telling him it was all right, half truly meaning it, half lying, he left the room.

The front door slammed.

She heard the roar of his racing car as he gunned the motor . . . .

Ivy had been alone only a moment when Phil came to the door. She looked at him and thought of Ann Howard. Phil would be going to Washington this afternoon. She hoped that he and Ann would be married. They would be the beginning of another family. She began to laugh. Tears ran down her face. She laughed and cried. Phil stepped forward and put his hands on her shoulders. She wondered if she might not appear to him like the double masks of drama: tragedy and comedy joined inseparably. She tried to stop, but she did not know which to stop first, the laughing or the crying.

Then she heard Mama's bell ringing upstairs.

CHAPTER 11
Today

(And All Our Yesterdays . . .)

THE HIDDEN power of the motor throbbed under Clay's finger tips. He could feel it flow up his arms and tingle along his
nerves. It made him feel alive and purposeful and full of authority.

He had always been able to handle a car. Maybe that was because he had handled horses, too, and learned the light touch that
was never loose, the steadiness that was never slack, driving them
to the limit but always with control and care. Sometimes he thought
that the only times in his life when he had any definite sense of
control were when he was holding a pair of reins or a steering
wheel.

Today all other control was almost gone. At this moment he
felt gripped by a curious exaltation and terror. It was a queer, con-
tradictory feeling and he had known it only once before in his
life. A half-dozen years ago he had had one of those rare once-in-a-
lifetime nights of gambling. He had started out with five hundred
dollars and he had vowed to Kathleen and himself not to lose a
penny more. No checks, no I.O.U.'s. Just ten new fifty-dollar bills.
Then adios, good-by, fare thee well. But he need not have worried,
for that was his night. He won a few, lost a few, and then gradually,

steadily, the dice began to roll for him. He won and won; again, again. Some of the boys stayed in, some began to drop out. It made no difference. He was hot.

Others came in and filled the gap. He rolled and rolled, and something about the way the dice fell away from him told him every time they'd come up right. And mostly they did. Again and again. It was as though all the flowers of springtime bloomed at once, or all the birds in the world sang at the same moment. It was stars and stripes and hallelujah all the way! Men looked at each other and shook their heads and by midmorning—three or four o'clock— there wasn't another game going. Everybody was watching Clay Thurston hit the big run. He was alive in every nerve and tissue, alive and aloof in a way he had never imagined possible, for even as he felt the tension and excitement gripping him like iron, he felt himself standing aside, watching, participating as a spectator at his own triumph. The triumph grew and grew. He could not seem to lose. He did not know or care what amount of money grew before him. He rolled the dice.

The money did not matter now. What mattered was this exultation rising like a gorge within him. Clay Thurston bestrode the world. Whatever he might have undertaken in that moment—conquest of a queen, a country, a continent—he could not have been denied. Or deflected. Or defeated. For he was a conqueror. Alexander the Great and Hannibal over the Alps, Napoleon and a whole covey of Caesars. He knew what they had felt. He, too, was invincible.

Of course, in the end, sometime around noon, the dice had begun to grow cold. They rolled erratically. He won—and lost. And then he lost more steadily. Once you were on the skids, the action picked up speed. He was back to twelve hundred, to the five hundred—to nothing. And when Clay left, he walked home because he had let Kathleen use the car the night before and he didn't have fare enough for a taxi. All the way home he had experienced this exultation—he had stood on Everest—and terror—he was deep, deep in a valley, a gutter, with no toe holds by which to climb out.

He felt that way now.

He made a slight motion with one finger and the car's sensitive power steering responded. He was enthralled by the horsepower at his command, yet he guessed he would always miss the horseflesh that had once been just as sensitive to his touch. The warm breath, the beating pulse, the flared nostrils, the head tossed back with mane flowing, the healthy sweat. Horses might be creatures to admire, but he could never love them as he did this car. For a car had given him his first escape toward freedom.

Driving down this valley now, in flight once more from the nagging, confining demands of his family, he could remember that year when he had begun to drive. Behind him lay the months and years of dreary Saturdays and endless Sundays, when time seemed to doze over the cattle and barnyards and the fields beyond and was droned away with the steady bees during long afternoons. That was in the summertime. But in the winter, on days like today, when the cold wind was a dead hand stretched over the mountains and every tree was stripped to its skeleton of trunk and limb, every path and trail cutting the hillsides stood out in bare relief, and the ground below was brown turf, leaves and stones, and the sky above was a leaden-colored blotter, on those days the hills closed in like walls and Clay's restlessness grew into a mighty longing. He was homesick for places he had never seen. He was nostalgic for times he had never known. He knew only that he must go.

When he dribbled together a little money by borrowing from everyone he knew and bought the broken-down old Model-T his boss on the building job in town was getting rid of, Clay knew that the Saturdays and Sundays would be bearable for a little while longer. He had found a way to annihilate them. He could use them up with the speed of wind in his face, scenes flickering by like snapshots flipped through the album on Mama's parlor table. Suddenly he was mobile, and free.

He laughed aloud to himself now, and leaned his head out of the window to feel again the raw wind as he had felt it years ago in the seat of that prehistoric car chugging along this road which had been as rocky as the surface of the moon seemed to be today. The wind was no good. It sobered him abruptly, damp and cold. He drew his head in and touched the automatic button that slid the window shut.

Between that Model-T and little Missy here, how many cars had there been? He could almost hear the shrieks and laughter, the horn blowing and the tires screaming, up North, down South, wherever he was over the years. Down the long straight roads and around the curves, using up the gas and the rubber and the years. He could hear all those sweet words whispered beside him. The first girl he had ever had . . . they were parked in a car . . . He grinned and shook his head.

The parade of cars, the parade of girls. The astringent costly smell of shaving lotion, hair tonic, the good cloth of his new suits. When Kathleen had come along, she had made it seem as if the party would never end. She could cook a roast rare and tender, and dance slow and drive fast, and she could type better than any other dozen secretaries put together. So they had come through depressions and war. He had been building some of the long anonymous buildings at Oak Ridge during World War II and Kathleen had typed in an office there. But they could not come through the battle of the bottle.

"Damn it to hell," he muttered, reminded of his sisters' faces, and his brother's, and even poor old Mama's on her deathbed even now. The way everyone looked at him these days! ("Is he drinking? Did he get hold of a bottle this morning?")

He hadn't realized he had already come to the city limits. He skidded to a halt. That red light had changed before he could snap his finger. Dangerous for authorities to fix a light like that. He'd mention it to Sheriff Doggett if he ever saw him. To hell with Sheriff Doggett and that big old Judge Anders and Hugh Moore, especially to hell with Hugh Moore. All of them.

He opened the glove compartment and took out a pint bottle. Half full. He laid it on the bucket seat beside him and patted it gently.

At the next traffic signal he swung the car right toward the mountains and took a highway that would lead him eventually up toward Thickety Creek and the Devil's Brow pinnacle beyond. It was a new highway, and it obliterated all the landmarks which might have told Clay he was on familiar territory. Nevertheless, it led to the woods, to the mountains.

Oh, he had been eager enough to get out of them once upon a time. That first trip north! He had just wrecked the little Model-T, and he decided to go where the pay was bigger and his next car could be better. Never, since that very first time, had he ever gone back to the city—Jersey City, Newark, New York, the whole swarming mass huddled there together along the brink of the seaboard—without feeling a challenge and a swell of excitement. Each time he went there was the lure that something special might be about to happen. And he had always fortified himself with a few drinks under his belt. He couldn't permit a doubt in his mind that he was meant for something special. Other clods might labor with dutiful patience and apathetic spirit throughout their days, but not Clay Thurston. And someday, sometime, somewhere, there would come a moment, a revelation to define the purpose and reward of all his work.

Then, just after he divorced Kathleen (or Kathleen divorced him, if he was going to be strictly honest with himself), he had realized that the moment and the revelation were not going to come. He had been certain of it one rainy day the week before he came back to Nantahala County. Remembering that day, he pulled Missy to one side of the highway, took the bottle off the seat and had himself a long scalding drink of bourbon. When he laid the bottle back down, he patted it again, as if in reward for its ready comfort. The whisky spread through him warmly, but memory of that afternoon in New York spread through him icily. He sat in his low sleek car, fire and ice, and looked out the window.

He had gone to the metropolitan offices of the construction firm. They perched up in the sky in one of those new glass and steel towers in midtown Manhattan, and he tried to tell himself over and over that they could be there only because he and thousands of others were down below grubbing in the mud, out in the provinces and suburbs putting up playlike houses to be sold wholesale to playpeople, and keep the money flowing in to this sleek home office. But it did not matter what he told himself, for they had told him—with the politest, clearest, most impersonal efficiency—that they would not need him in any future construction, in any capacity. He did not bother to listen to the explanations—construction syndicate, no individual hiring on their part any more, no more personalized craftsmanship in the interiors of their houses, competition, mass production—because he knew that he was out of work. And all of a sudden he felt quite old to be out looking for work.

When he came out of the bright, busy lobby of the skyscraper, it was already late afternoon. The air was misty, grey, hard and damp and chilly as steel. The streets glistened dully, buildings loomed up into the fog. He turned down Madison Avenue. People flowed toward him, opened like a wave of the sea around him, and passed on. He looked into their faces but not their eyes. Occasionally, when he caught someone's glance, he and the stranger looked away quickly, passed on.

Shop windows beside him were full of expensive beautiful things, things that filled him with longing for quantities of money. Loneliness was bitter in his mouth, tight in his chest, squeezing the breath from him. He wanted to cry out to all these gay, clever, useful people, "I am here." He wanted some affirmation that he was here and now, that his identity was unique and of value. One of the plate-glass windows he passed reflected his image, and he was startled to see that his hat still sat at a jaunty angle above the lined, experienced hardness of his face and the flash of his eyes. The glass might have been reflecting the image of a stranger.

He walked on, looking at the sidewalk. Millions of steps would be necessary before this concrete surface bore one visible indentation, was scarred by any real mark of human wear. His own footsteps were no more than the mist which melted away. He thought of times at home, behind the plow, when he had been turning new ground. Every step then had left its print. There behind him, at the end of every row, were the clearly defined shapes of his shoes, following behind him in the soft earth.

He started the engine of his car again. It lurched slightly as he swung it back onto the highway and he cautioned himself to drive carefully. Then he threw back his head and laughed. He was out in the country now, heading toward the mountains. He could already feel the road climbing at an easy grade as he tried to drown that loneliness he had tasted there in the city that afternoon.

It was the loneliness which brought the terror mingling with his exultation now. He felt poised at the edge of some great new throw of the dice, some gamble more immense, with higher stakes, than he had ever dreamed of before. The pulse was throbbing in his temples.

Why, what did that family of his know of living? They clucked and fluttered like chickens in a chicken-pen, never tasting the wine or the dregs, never grappling in the mud or throwing out a lariat to the stars, never gambling at all.

"It's been the best, Missy," he said out loud, feeling the little car leap ahead as he fed her an extra spurt of gasoline. "I wouldn't take a million for all that's been. Or give a dime for what's to come." He tried to grin.

But the terror was larger than the exultation now. It was grim and persistent. "What if your gamble is really through—and you've lost . . . ?"

They all said he'd "won" the case of old Hawk Williams. Phoebe and Kin and that jackleg, stuffed-shirt lawyer, they thought he'd won. He'd found out that he could have killed a man, carelessly, pointlessly, brutally. Was that winning? "I hope," he muttered, "I hope there's a hell for the good somewhere."

He was winding up into the mountains now. Missy was climbing smoothly, powerfully. This little old car had always reminded him of that Oyster Bay blonde, years ago. Fire and quality and suggestions of a luxury he would never taste. He clutched the steering wheel and poured the gas to her. She held the first curve with a steady hug. "That's right, baby," Clay whispered.

The next curve was not banked right, and he felt the rear wheels slide in one big half-circle as he came around. He held steady and the car pulled out of it. He laughed, and the exultation and the terror were balanced in him now, as they had been that night when he had won all the money in the world and he was risking it on the last rolls of the dice, even when he knew they had turned against him.

An outthrust spur of the mountain created a sharp turn, and it caught him and the car unaware. With a twist of the wrist, a quick flick of his fingers, Clay tried to bring the wheel around. But it was too late. The machine left the highway, arced out beyond the roadside weeds and laurel bushes, then plunged down the steep bank into the valley below.

CHAPTER 12

Today and Tomorrow

THE CEMETERY was on a hill high above Thickety Creek. Its view swept a full three-hundred-and-sixty-degree horizon. The near mountains encircled the valley below with a scarred greenness, but beyond rose distant ranges one after another in frozen blue waves. The sky seemed close and gentle.

As they came to bury Clay, not one of them but knew why Mama had insisted he should be here. It was an ill-kept inaccessible little country graveyard, but it held the remains of those Martha McQueen Thurston had loved best in life, and its view was majestic. There would be wide sky and free winds and tangled trees and wild vines here for a long time.

While the minister intoned the words of the Bible Mama had chosen, they looked out at the mountains where they had grown up.

" 'Whither shall I go from Thy spirit?' " the solemn young pastor read in a fine deep baritone, never revealing for an instant any hint of the awe and anguish and eventual wonder of the passage. " 'Or whither shall I flee from Thy presence? If I ascend up into heaven, Thou art there: If I make my bed in hell, behold Thou art there. If

I take the wings of the morning and dwell in the uttermost parts of the sea; even there shall Thy hand lead me, and Thy right hand shall hold me.' "

Frone did not see any of the other people with her in the cemetery. She stood tall and stiff in her heavy black suit and low-heeled black calf shoes that seemed appropriate to this tough damp turf. Her hands (long and white as Papa's had been) clutched her handbag with tense ferocity. Staring at the vault locking Clay's casket in tight and pointless security, she felt locked in, too. All the warmth and fluidness of tears or blood or grief seemed to have been used up during Monday evening's nightmare and yesterday's long comprehension of Clay's death and their fruitless efforts to understand it. Now she was drained, sealed in the tight husk of her body.

Her body had always meant so little to her. She never yearned for clothes of any special quantity or quality, and little of her time or attention had been spent improving or preserving the skin, the features, the figure that were hers by nature. What had mattered was another world, within, of the mind and imagination. On Thickety Creek, long ago, she had created romantic kingdoms none of the rest of her family dreamed of, and when the abrasions of time and a so-called maturity had dimmed those kingdoms, she had turned to teaching and the creation of another world in her mind. She had succeeded because she had been able to communicate dimensions of that world to her pupils and therefore she could arouse and sustain them. During all the years since she had given up teaching, the years in Connecticut with Jud and her pragmatic, successful sons, she had dwelt in secret in this world. Her body she had given to them in the necessary and usual ways—love and the labor of birth and daily tasks—but it was still her books, her thoughts, her occasional and very private dreams that she nurtured and mourned over the way other women nurtured and mourned the complexions of their girlhood, the suppleness of their youth. Her body had meant so little to her; and to Clay his body had been all. Yet, different as they were, she had cherished him as she had none of her other brothers or sisters.

The first thing she had seen, night before last when the rescue crew brought him up from the fractured wreckage of the car, was his shoulder. Where his shirt and suede jacket were torn away, there gleamed the old scars of a burn he had had as a child from a tub of scalding wash water. And Frone, recalling with pain the long days of that burn's healing, felt her sharpest stab of grief. Grief not only for Clay but for all of them as they once were, back in that distant golden moment when everything seemed possible and failure was only an abstract word.

"He's broken to pieces," Phoebe, standing beside her, watching the rescuers labor up the steep embankment, had said in a small bewildered voice.

Kin, covered with dirt, leaves, sweat, left the men and came over to stand with his sisters. He breathed heavily from fatigue and shock. It had been he who came to Clay and his car first, before anyone else. Trying to reply to Phoebe, Kin said, "He always set so much store by his clothes, by what he wore, what he ate, everything fine, nothing but the best——"

"And it was nothing," Ivy murmured. "Nothing."

"Don't say that, Ivy!" Phoebe had cried, shocked, as they stood to one side and watched the ambulance drive away from the sharp curve of the mountain.

"I didn't mean that *he* was nothing," Ivy said, walking alone as Kin helped Frone and Phoebe back to the car. "I just wondered if he ever knew how much more he was than steaks in his stomach and silk on his back and gasoline in that high-powered engine——" She broke off.

Frone knew what Ivy had been trying to say. Gazing now at Clay's casket and vault and grave, because she did not want to see anything or anyone else, Frone knew that none of them had yet realized he was there, forever quiet, his hungers forever satisfied. He could rile me to such anger, she thought. But it was so easy to forgive Clay, to like him. I suppose, contrary to what we say, we dislike people more for their virtues than for their vices. The vices, if they do not happen to be the same as our own, or even if they do, make us feel superior. Others' virtues make us humble. We can all forgive Clay's faults in death more easily than we can forgive each other our feeble living attempts at excellence.

And then she did turn her frozen face slightly to look at Kin and

her sister Ivy, with tall alert Phil just a step behind, and Phoebe and
Phoebe's daughter, Lucy Kate, who had come to comfort her
mother. (Could that brittle girl comfort anyone?) These were
Frone's family here. These and some of the others who had come
out this raw autumn day, whose names she did not even know,
related in a network of kinship she could not untangle if she wanted
to. Frone shivered.

The minister's words and his prayer and a hymn were finished.
"Lead, Kindly Light," Mama had wanted them to sing.

As they left the cemetery, Lucy Kate walked with her cousin
Phil. He was the only one with whom she could feel the slightest
bit at ease. After all, he was a senator, not one of the mountain characters. . . . Her high narrow heel caught in a vine and she stumbled, clutching at a straight square gravestone beside her. Phil
held her arm. She laughed up at him prettily, then stood on one
foot and slipped her other foot more firmly in her shoe. "Guess I
didn't wear my hillbilly clothes," she whispered to him.

Phoebe, who had come up to them, heard her daughter's
words, and her pale, drawn face colored slightly, then grew white
again.

But Lucy Kate did not notice. She was glancing at the stone she
had clutched for support. "Lydia Moore McQueen. 1846–1896. Precious above rubies," she read.

"That was your great-grandmother," Phoebe said.

"I know, I know." The glance she gave her cousin Phil seemed
to say, "Let's don't get them started on this."

Phoebe did not miss the glance either. Strangers paused to speak
to her, offer sympathy, some who had known Clay years ago when
he was a young man and had made many friends in town, but she
did not hear what they said. She was hurt at her daughter's rejection of the past, this past that she, Phoebe, had seemed to reject, yet
carried within herself as intimately as bone and blood, even as she
had once carried Lucy Kate.

She recalled the few minutes that she and Ivy had had alone together late last night. Lucy Kate, tired after her long drive up from
South Carolina, worried about returning late to college from her
long weekend that had turned into a week, had just gone to bed.

Phoebe had sat downstairs alone, with only one small lamp on in the darkness, and she had sobbed uncontrollably until Ivy found her and put comforting arms around her. They had not spoken for a long time.

Then Ivy said, "We were all so worried that he might have killed a stranger. We never thought of him killing himself."

"You believe he did?" Phoebe asked, her breath still coming in little gasps. "He did kill himself?"

Ivy nodded. "We know that. Whether he intended to or not . . ." She looked away, out of the window, leaving the question dangling between them.

Phoebe twisted the wet handkerchief in her hand. "It wasn't Clay I was crying for just now, Ivy."

Her sister had looked at her again and nodded. "I know. I know."

"But you don't know," she cried. "None of you knows. Clay, you, me, everyone was worried that he might be sent to prison . . ." The handkerchief twisted into a tight little knot. "There are lots of prisons, Ivy. We all live in prison from the minute we're born. I thought when I married that I was getting a kind of freedom, away from the mountains where it was so harsh to make a living, away from drudgery and commonplaceness. So I escaped to the worst prison of all."

"Don't, Phoebe. Sh-h," Ivy comforted.

"Oh, it's an awful thing to try to live someone else's life," she had rushed on, "to smother out your own tastes and ideas and habits and the little things you've come to love in life, all so that you can fit into the image someone else has set up for you. I know, oh I know, because all my grown-up years I've tried to be a Harris and not a Thurston. I've tried to deny my blood for something that seemed better. But it was a killing thing to do. It buried part of me. Do you understand, Ivy? Can you understand at all? Am I Phoebe Thurston any more? I'm not even Phoebe. I'm Mrs. Rutledge Harris, and she's not a real person at all. She's something made of watered blood and secondhand ideas and other people's wishes." Her tears were scalding.

"Dear, dear little Phoebe," Ivy had said tenderly. "Oh, you're not as far from Thickety Creek as you think you are."

And although she went on talking, nothing else she said or could have said eased Phoebe's sense of loss as much as that one sentence. Phoebe thought about it now, and wondered. For what she had really cried about last night was not only her own separation from the past but her daughter's complete alienation from it. Her pretty, saucy, irreverent Lucy Kate had suddenly been shown up to her as a shallow callous clothes hanger. Why had she, Phoebe, been so determined all these years that her daughter should not grow up as she had? Had it been so bad?

She looked now, all at once, at the tombstones clustered in this family plot, at the tallest, which was Papa's, and she could hear once more his swelling gusts of laughter which had filled the big white house on Thickety Creek or the woods where he worked with the timber men or the carriage when they rode to town or church or sociables. Why had she been so anxious for her precious daughter to miss this?

Phoebe went with the others toward the row of cars waiting to go back down the steep hill from the cemetery. She shook some stranger's hand, acknowledged someone else's brief words of comfort. At the car door she glanced back to the grave where Clay's coffin stood waiting under a blanket of red roses for the earth that would cover it as soon as everyone had gone. It would have pleased Clay to know they buried him next to Papa. She supposed they would be returning before long to place Mama there in the empty space on the other side of Papa.

Lucy Kate and Phil and Ivy were already in the car when she got in. Frone and Kin rode in the car ahead. Phil started the motor and they followed slowly. "I suppose Kin is the only other one of us who'll be buried here," Phoebe said.

"Mother!" Lucy Kate turned her chic blonde head. "Don't be morbid."

Her mother did not seem to hear. "Mama and Kin," she went on. "The rest of us will be buried with our husbands, scattered from South Carolina to Connecticut——"

"You positively embarrass me, Mother." The girl spoke with an irritation that seemed familiar to her.

Limbs of trees and untrimmed bushes brushed against the car as it moved down the narrow little road. Phil swerved to avoid a deep rut and almost struck a man who was walking along the wrong side of the road. Phil saw that it was Leck Gunter, who had been to talk with him last Sunday morning (it seemed a year ago), and he tried to wave to him.

"Watch out, Phil," Lucy Kate giggled. "That might be one of our bearded cousins."

"Lucy Kate," Phoebe said slowly, as if from a distance, "will you be quiet?"

The startled girl turned to answer, but made no sound.

"I hate to say this about my own child," Phoebe went on, her voice barely audible, "but you're a silly person, Lucy Kate. All at once I have to admit it. You're proud for the wrong reasons and ashamed for the wrong reasons. I'm through explaining or apologizing to you and your delicate feelings. Maybe it's all my fault, or maybe only partly my fault, but you should have learned a long time ago that you don't have some silly sentimental legend for a heritage. You have real flesh-and-blood people who ought to make anyone stand tall."

The others in the car listened to Phoebe in hushed surprise. As if all the years of her deferment to others, the years of conforming, of accepting and seeking acceptance, had dammed up within her, the floodgates now burst and she rushed on.

"You had a great-grandmother who was as strong as these hills, and you ought to thank God that she milked and worked in the fields and drudged for her family and her community instead of sitting around protecting her lily-white flesh, asking to be waited on. She wasn't served. She served."

Lucy Kate made an effort at a reticent smile, but it disappeared.

"And your grandpa, and your grandma Thurston who is lying back home,"—she choked a moment, then went on—"they were mortal human beings with a lot of living to be done and they did it without whining or being ashamed or being worried too much about what other people thought. They had a place in this world. They carved it for themselves, and although you and some of your

friends might not think it very important or valuable, it was both
to them. They knew who they were. They knew that all right. Mama
lying up there in bed this minute—she knows!"

Ivy covered Phoebe's hand with her own. In the front seat both
Phil and Lucy Kate looked straight head. Ivy made no comforting
remark, but the warmth of her sturdy hand brought Phoebe a certain steadiness. She wondered at her own outburst, but she knew
that for once she had spoken as truthfully as one ever can.

Just before they reached the house, Ivy said, "It's been a long
weekend. I wonder, have we simply remembered everything and
learned nothing?"

No one answered until Phil said, "I think we've all learned a little. Your mother was talking to all of us, Lucy Kate."

Ivy looked at him, and for the first time in thirty-six hours she
felt something like reconciliation stir within her.

Martha Thurston told two of her daughters and two of her
grandchildren good-by. She had heard details of the funeral with
grief and dignity. Now she said good-by in the same way.

First, Frone, who had to leave after an early lunch where no one
had eaten Naomi's food but only pretended to.

There were eighty-four pounds of Martha Thurston's flesh left,
yet she lay in the white expanse of bed and pillows with mind acute,
memory intact. When her children had come yesterday morning
to tell her of Clay's death the afternoon before, her spirit had
reeled under the impact of this sledgehammer blow. She had looked
at them from the depths of her wide stunned eyes and repeated his
name over and over, "Clay. Clay. My Clay . . ." Then she had
said, " 'Though He slay me, yet will I trust in Him.' " The sharp
moaning cry that wrenched from her then was the only sound they
heard her make before she turned toward the wall and began to
speak silently, in prayer. Only her lips moved.

Now she took Frone's hand and held it against her face. Her
oldest child had always found it difficult to express affection. They
exchanged words, but it was the grip of Frone's hand, the awkward
embrace she attempted, that told Martha Thurston what she
needed to know.

"I'll come back down soon," Frone offered, in a tight, strained voice.

"It's all right. I know Jud and the boys need you," she said. What she really knew was that Frone would not come back until she had to.

"If there's anything you need, Mama, I'm leaving some extra money with Ivy . . ."

Martha Thurston smiled and shook her head and patted Frone's hand again.

And when Phoebe and Lucy Kate came up, before they left in Lucy Kate's convertible for the long drive back to the lowlands, her youngest daughter used almost the same words. "Mama, I've written a check for Ivy to get you anything extra you want or need . . ."

The old lady shook her head again.

"Oh, Mama!" Phoebe cried, and buried her plump cheek against Martha Thurston's wasted, bony face.

Tears were in Lucy Kate's eyes, too. How easily the young cried, Martha thought.

"Tell Rutledge to bring you and young Rutledge and Lucy Kate back up for a visit soon," she said.

"Mama, I'm so sorry—about everything . . ."

"I know, Phoebe." This woman with the fur stole around her shoulders and wide streaks of blue-grey in her dark hair, had she once been little Phoebe? "You were a good little girl, Phoebe," she murmured. Then, with seeming irrelevance, "We have to learn—if you live on the land long you do learn—to last, to survive. Folks in the cities may find short cuts, tricks, easy ways to bypass or soften calamity. I don't know. But the only way I know is what Aunt Tildy used to tell me: Tough it out. Endure."

Her body was weak and tired. So many words exhausted her. She tried to smile with all the brightness she could muster when Phoebe turned at the bedroom door and waved good-by again. Lucy Kate had her arm around her mother's shoulders as they left the room.

Phil came much later, after Martha had had a nap. "Here's your big fine grandson-senator to see you," Naomi was saying. He made no demands on her and laid his finger across her lips when she started to speak. She felt relief at being permitted to hoard the little store of breath within her lungs.

"You be right here next time I come back from Washington," he instructed her, and she tried to decipher how much he was teasing and how much he was serious. "Somehow I can't imagine a trip back to Nantahala County without seeing you."

His words pleased her. She tried to show him this pleasure with her eyes and with the skeleton-thin hand she lifted toward him.

"Next time I come," he went on, taking her hand and laying it carefully back on the soft blanket, "I'll have another member of the family for you to meet."

She could see that even with all their grief—the memory of Clay aching in her like the agony from some raw nerve—this grandson could not quell or conceal his season of happiness.

"A wife?" she whispered.

He nodded. "Named Ann. Smart and pretty, too, like you, Grandma Thurston."

She shook her head in slow modesty. "That girl's getting the handsomest——"

But he would not let her go on. "I'll bring her to meet you. That is, if I don't miss this plane and lose my girl and my job all at the same time." He looked back at her from the door. "*I* go, but *we* shall return."

"Soon," she told him.

In a little while she heard the car leave the driveway. Naomi gave her her midafternoon medicine. "Mrs. Cortland's gone to carry him to the airport. Some of his friends phoned and offered, and then he was wanting to call a taxi." The slim dark woman shook her head and smiled sadly, knowingly. "I already knew she was saving those last few minutes so they could go alone together."

Martha Thurston did not have to make a reply this time. She and Naomi understood each other without talking.

After Naomi left her, in a few minutes she heard Kin's patient, steady steps come up the stairs and turn into her room. They stopped, as she had known they would, when he saw that she seemed to be asleep. Then she opened her eyes.

"Mama?" he asked softly.

"Yes, Kin." It was an answer and a question and a reassurance. She pointed to the low walnut chair beside her bed.

He sat down. They did not speak. The house was still. The little old lady seemed to melt away into an even smaller heap under the bedclothes. Her white hair spread around her face as light as foam. When her eyes closed, all evidence of life in her body disappeared. The large muscular man seemed oversize for the chair he sat in, but he remained perfectly quiet, leaning forward slightly as his elbows rested on his knees and his hands hung loosely clasped between his legs. The rhythm of his deep breathing moved his massive chest and shoulders. They sat thus for a long time.

When she finally opened her eyes and looked at him, it was as though she had given a signal for him to speak.

"I found a heart-leaf plant for Mr. Austin's garden," he said, softly, easily.

She barely nodded. "Today?"

"Yes. Along that road up to the cemetery," he said. "I sighted it as we drove back." After a moment he added, "I couldn't help but think Clay would have been glad to know I found it."

She closed her eyes again and there was another lengthy quiet.

Kin loosened the necktie at his throat. He wasn't accustomed to wearing a tie and it made him self-conscious. The gesture reminded him of the expensive necktie Clay had given him a few nights ago. Yesterday morning Kin had taken it up to the undertaker's. "I'd like for my brother to be buried with this," he had said, clumsily unwrapping the length of rich heavy silk from tissue paper. Its box had been misplaced somewhere, but he didn't think he had wrinkled it. As the sober-faced young man looked at the tie, Kin told him, "It cost a lot. My brother liked good things."

"I can see that." The undertaker's assistant nodded formally. "I shall make sure that your wishes are carried out."

Now Kin was more pleased than ever that he had thought of this small secret gesture. He would never have been comfortable wearing a tie that probably cost a third as much as his suit. And somehow he felt that he had spoken to Clay in returning his generosity.

Mama stirred slightly on the bed. "Kin?" She looked at him anxiously. "You'll keep our last home place, across the creek there, and the woods that are left with it, won't you, Kin?"

He was surprised by her sudden question. "Yes, Mama."

He found no hardship in making this promise. He intended to live there for the rest of his life. "I'm finishing up Mr. Austin's garden in the next week or so," Kin went on, in a low, gentle voice. "Then I'm going to make one over at the old place. It will be my best."

Martha Thurston smiled. Her bony fingers reached out and intertwined with the thick strong fingers of her son. She lay very still, holding his hand thus, aware of the roughness and calluses. He and Ivy were the only ones of her children who could begin to comprehend how she felt about land; about the earth, ground, plain old dirt. All of her life she had wanted it tended, cared for, made rich and productive. And every plan she had made, every hope she had ever cherished along this line, had been cruelly aborted. None of Tom's efforts at farming, stock raising, tending land, had succeeded. And they had ended by cutting, stripping, using it all. . . . She sighed wearily.

"Kin," his mother whispered, and he could feel her fingers moving like the claws of the little pet bluebird he had once cherished.

"Yes, Mama."

"Kin, I reckon I'm like this old earth itself. I keep living on, being killed a little bit at a time."

"Mama, don't try to talk." The suffering and hope in her eyes hurt him a great deal more than had Clay's sudden death.

But she was speaking to herself as well as to him. "The Lord made heaven and earth. I've loved them both with all my heart and with all my might . . ." Her might was waning. She raised her eyebrows and made the slightest motion of a shrug.

Kin sat very still while she rested again. Tomorrow when he went to dig that big green heart-leaf plant, he would break off two or three of the tenderest leaves and bring them to Mama. Crushed, they would fill her corner of the room with their rich, spicy fragrance. He remembered the first time she had ever shown him a heart-leaf. It was a midsummer afternoon, the day that Preacher

Grey and Morg Bludsoe met in a wrestling match Papa had arranged, while Mama guided his steps up on the mountain to find plants. He shook his head, wonder and satisfaction combined in the hint of his smile. And it was Morg's boy who had stepped out on Monday morning and saved Clay . . . Saved him? . . . The puzzle was too intricate for Kin. He thought once more how fresh and old-timey the heart-leaf would smell to Mama.

Before Ivy and Phil left for the airport, she told him that she wanted to show him something. Hurriedly, they went to the old house across the stream and there, in the big square bedroom where Clay had been staying, Phil saw Clay's tools of surveying and carpentry and all manner of construction, ranged along two walls. Some of them were old, all well-worn, but they were absolutely clean of rust or dirt or breaks. A workman who respected his tools had hung these carefully for future use.

That neat obsolete workroom suddenly appeared to Phil as a summary of his whole foreign journey and much of this week he had been at home; it was symbol of a world precariously balanced between old and new, yesterday and tomorrow. He looked at his mother's pale, lined face and at the tears flowing freely down her cheeks.

"You just cannot make yourself ill mourning for his death, Mother," Phil said. "I know there's nothing I can say now——"

"I'm not mourning because Clay died," Ivy said. "We all die. But it seemed so purposeless, so lacking in grandeur"—she made a small helpless gesture—"and in the midst of such grandeur. That bug of a car dashed against those craggy mountains . . ."

Phil nodded. "I know."

She pulled the door shut behind them.

As they drove to the airport, he was aware of how straight she sat beside him, overcoming her human fragility with her human strength. He searched for some words that she could keep after he was gone. At last he spoke. "A year or so ago I remember reading that Sophocles said one must wait until the evening to see how splendid the day has been."

She did not respond at once. Then she agreed. "Yes. I can remember little moments of our life together, when we were growing up, and I see how—how insignificant, perhaps, and yet how splendid, too, it all was."

Phil went on. "I stopped off last Saturday to see you overnight, a sort of sidetrack from my larger trip. Well, I've stayed nearly a week, and I want you to know I've discovered this was just an extension of the trip."

"Oh, Phil!"

"Maybe that's what your old friend, Leck Gunter, was hinting to me: If I can know my family, my folks here well enough, maybe I can understand people on the other side of the world, too."

"There are so many ways of looking at people," she said. "At Clay, at faraway strangers, at friends. But basic to all the ways: we can see the differences separating us, or we can see the likenesses binding us."

He glanced at his wrist watch, and stepped a bit harder on the accelerator. "The trick is to give each its due regard, I suppose. Uniqueness and universality."

Turning toward him on the seat so that she could look directly at her son as he drove, she asked, "I've wondered, the past few days, with all our differences and upheavals and quarrels and reconciliations, was I foolish to try to bring the family together, to hold us together?"

Phil started to answer promptly, reassure her, but she went on.

"I wanted us to realize our interdependence, learn forgiveness, practice a little love." She looked at him. "Was it a foolish whim?"

"No," he said thoughtfully. "It was an affirmation, a parable. I hope some of us can appreciate it."

She made an impatient gesture with her hand. "I'm not talking about appreciation."

Abruptly Phil remembered that Sherry Austin had assured him, long ago on Sunday night, that a senator, a person, he, was not responsible for his kinfolks. Now he knew what answer Ivy—and Ann Howard—would make to her: Maybe not, but he must be responsible *to* them.

As if his mother knew that he had thought of Ann, she said, "I suppose we won't be talking in quite this way ever again. . . . Oh, don't mistake me, I'm not sorry. I'm just trying to recognize change. Thought of you and Ann has given me something to hold onto these two dark days. But I want to tell you something I might find difficult—corny as the young ones call it—to say before Ann."

"You tell me," he said, smiling at her.

"You made a speech once, Phil, in which you said that atomic power had given us a new dimension for death."

"Yes. I remember. Pretty big ideas——"

"The ideas can't be big enough for what we're dealing with to-day, Phil," she said sharply. Her face was no longer stamped with grief but with a high seriousness.

"You're right," he said, swinging into the airport drive. "And I was right: a new dimension for death."

"Then the only way to counteract that is to find a new dimension for life."

He nodded. That would be a damn good phrase for him to use in that block-busting minority report he and Ann would write on his foreign travel, and in his follow-up request to be transferred to a committee on regional and national human resources.

"I'm not talking about professional optimism, and blind confidence," Ivy was saying. "I've known enough of that. Papa was always certain his plans would work out right, whether or not he had any reason for certainty. What I'm talking about is the hardcore optimism, the tough faith that life itself is worth preserving. Is it a belief, Phil, or just hope, that we can find a new totality of living just as we've found a totality of death?"

"It's belief," he said, and switched off the engine.

They sat a moment in the narrow parking space.

"Then take it back to Washington with you, Phil." She tightened the scarf around her throat and began to open the door. "That trite phrase, Phil, about the tough minds and tender hearts—take it with you. Remember, we've had about all we can take of the tough wizened little hearts of men and big, lazy tender minds."

She reached for his hand suddenly, not looking at him, and squeezed it with such strength that he almost winced. She had developed that grip long ago by milking cows and hoeing corn and wringing out heavy washes, and recently by digging gardens and lifting her own luggage in distant places and caring for her mother's aged body.

"You're quite a woman, Mrs. Cortland," he said.

"I bet you tell that to all the girls." She tried to speak lightly, climbing out quickly and waiting while he got his bags. "I bet you'll be saying that to Ann Howard in"—she consulted her watch—"approximately two hours and forty-seven minutes."

"How did you guess?" He was relieved that they could maintain this casual note at the moment of departure. "But lucky me! I'd be right in both cases."

"Lucky everyone," she said.

She stood outside and watched the plane taxi down the runway, take off, and disappear into the late October sky. Phil into the air. Clay into the earth. The poles of her life. Yet she could see and hear each one of them so clearly they seemed to be with her still. She loved them, and so she suffered now.

Walking back alone across the concrete drive, Ivy thought of how they had spent so many hours since Monday night and Tuesday morning, asking, "Why did Clay do it?" "Was it an accident?" "It had to be an accident!" "Why?" And she knew, as clearly as if Clay had spoken to her, the part of his death which was not accidental.

Clay felt that no one cared. The point is, she thought, he didn't care enough himself. "Like me! Love me!" Clay had always demanded of the world, even when he was defying it most belligerently, fighting it most savagely. Perhaps especially then. But all the ripping and tearing and rebellion had been a casing, a skin for the raw, quivering protoplasm of him which begged, "Like me! Love me! Let me know that I am here and that I matter—that I matter to you because you wanted me, because without me your life would have been less gay, less real . . . it would have been less. Let me believe that without my life all life would have been somehow smaller, less important."

Ivy sighed. "But the secret—ah, Clay, the secret, was to say, 'I like! I love!' And then you possessed the world."

ABOUT THE AUTHOR

WILMA DYKEMAN lives with her husband and two children in Newport, Tennessee. She is the author of THE TALL WOMAN and THE FRENCH BROAD and co-author, with her husband, James Stokely, of NEITHER BLACK NOR WHITE and SEEDS OF SOUTHERN CHANGE. Miss Dykeman was born in the South and has lived there nearly all her life. She has her own column on the editorial page of the Knoxville, Tennessee *News-Sentinel*. In addition to her writing, she finds time to lecture, travel, and care for her home and family.